Past Praise for Ja

"Once again, Wright outdoes herse[...] impactful eeriness. This tale takes on fresh frights with dizzying skill in its parallel 1915 and present-day timelines in small-town Wisconsin."

Booklist starred review of *The Lost Boys of Barlowe Theater*

"Jaime Jo Wright takes readers on a journey that leaves them with a renewed sense of hope. Jaime masterfully weaves a narrative that demonstrates the resilience of the human spirit in the face of adversity. *The Lost Boys of Barlowe Theater* is a story that stays with you long after you close the book."

Lynette Eason, bestselling, award-winning author of the EXTREME MEASURES series

"In *The Vanishing at Castle Moreau*, Wright pens an imaginative and mysterious tale that is both haunting and heartwarming."

Rachel Hauck, *New York Times* bestselling author

"A hair-raising thriller. . . . Wright excels at wringing the eeriness out of her premise and elegantly weaving the thoughtful meditations on what happens after death into the fast-paced murder mystery. This will delight Wright's fans and earn her some new ones."

Publishers Weekly on *The Premonition at Withers Farm*

"Wright pens another delightfully creepy tale where nothing is quite as it seems, and characters seek freedom from nightmares both real and imagined."

Library Journal on *The Vanishing at Castle Moreau*

"It's rare when a book carries me so deep inside its world that I forget I'm reading. Buy this book. Now. You'll absolutely love it."

James L. Rubart, Christy Hall of Fame author on *The Premonition at Withers Farm*

"Dark, suspenseful, and decadently atmospheric, *The Premonition at Withers Farm* is an exceptionally satisfying read that weaves together past and present, light and dark, love and death."

Hester Fox, author of *A Lullaby for Witches*

NIGHT FALLS

PREDICAMENT
AVENUE

Books by Jaime Jo Wright

The House on Foster Hill
The Reckoning at Gossamer Pond
The Curse of Misty Wayfair
Echoes among the Stones
The Haunting at Bonaventure Circus
On the Cliffs of Foxglove Manor
The Souls of Lost Lake
The Premonition at Withers Farm
The Vanishing at Castle Moreau
The Lost Boys of Barlowe Theater
Night Falls on Predicament Avenue

NIGHT FALLS

PREDICAMENT

AVENUE

JAIME JO WRIGHT

BETHANYHOUSE

a division of Baker Publishing Group
Minneapolis, Minnesota

Published by Bethany House Publishers
Minneapolis, Minnesota
BethanyHouse.com

Bethany House Publishers is a division of
Baker Publishing Group, Grand Rapids, Michigan

Printed in the United States of America

Library of Congress Cataloging-in-Publication Data
Names: Wright, Jaime Jo, author.
Title: Night falls on Predicament Avenue / Jaime Jo Wright.
Description: Minneapolis, Minnesota : Bethany House Publishers, a division of
    Baker Publishing Group, 2024.
Identifiers: LCCN 2023046612 | ISBN 9780764241451 (paperback) | ISBN
    9780764242915 (casebound) | ISBN 9781493445349 (ebook)
Subjects: LCGFT: Christian fiction. | Detective and mystery fiction. | Novels.
Classification: LCC PS3623.R5388 N64 2024 | DDC 813/.6—dc23/eng/20231010
LC record available at https://lccn.loc.gov/2023046612

Unless otherwise indicated, Scripture quotations are from the King James Version
of the Bible.

Scripture quotations labeled NIV are from THE HOLY BIBLE, NEW INTERNA-
TIONAL VERSION®, NIV® Copyright © 1973, 1978, 1984, 2011 by Biblica, Inc.®
Used by permission. All rights reserved worldwide.

This is a work of fiction. Names, characters, incidents, and dialogues are products
of the author's imagination and are not to be construed as real. Any resemblance
to actual events or persons, living or dead, is entirely coincidental.

Cover design by Jennifer Parker
Cover images from Adobe Stock and Shutterstock

Author is represented by Books & Such Literary Agency.

Baker Publishing Group publications use paper produced from sustainable forestry
practices and postconsumer waste whenever possible.

24 25 26 27 28 29 30   7 6 5 4 3 2 1

To the women who have taught me that
to fear is to die slowly, but to hope is to glimpse
into eternity and find everlasting Life.

Momma (Joann Wright)
Mom (Joanne Sundsmo)
Gramma (Lola Greenwood)
Natalie Walters

And to Christen Krumm,
who first dreamed up Anderson and Effie,
sketched them out, and then gave them to me
to do with whatever I willed.
You're pretty trusting, my friend, pretty trusting.
Hope I did you proud! Much love.

HER

Sometime in the Past

I CAN HEAR THE DARKNESS. It is like a breeze on a frigid winter's night that rattles the leafless branches. It is like the cold that travels through your open mouth and down your throat, a frozen kiss stealing your breath. It is like a blizzard that swallows you in its swiftness, blinding behind and before, and side to side. Darkness is winter. It is the end. It is death.

I can hear death.

I can hear it whispering like a phantom swooping through the forest. My name is ever so soft and yet violent as the storm it implies. Death is cloaked in mystery. It is ghoulish in its tasteless form. It is an unspoken secret, perhaps the most well-kept secret of time itself.

Death.

Still, I run my fingers across the granites, the marbles, the pillars of names etched with dates and epitaphs. Someday they will topple and crumble. Children will run over the mound flattened by time and never know they trample upon someone's lost memories.

Beneath their feet lie the bones of the one who once ran just as they do now. Who once loved. Who once hoped. Who once was sure death was merely a wraith that flittered through their consciousness, but who couldn't possibly grab ahold of their future.

Now this place is my home. It is where I lay my head to rest. My memories. My dreams. My beating heart. They all cease here, are encased here, and here they will be forgotten.

I hear time.

Tick. Tick. Tick. Tick . . .

Time is not a friend of hope.

Hope is not found in the grave.

1

EFFIE JAMES

May 1901
Shepherd, Iowa

IT WAS TERRIBLE, truly, that moment when you stared at a behemoth in the dark and knew you'd beheld a monster.

Effie hadn't an ounce of resistance left within her. Terror had evolved into a ghastly stillness. The kind that choked her, like bony fingers wrapped around her throat, squeezing with a methodical joy as it watched the life drain from her eyes.

"Effie."

It was an awful feeling when you realized the dirt mounded beside the cavern in the ground was meant to cover you after you were dead, like a cold blanket.

"Effie."

There would be nothing left to fellowship with but the creatures that burrowed through the ground and eventually through her remains. A terrible—

"Effie!"

Effie James jerked from her thoughts, her shoulder bumping into the tree against which she huddled in the darkness. The whites of her sister's eyes were bright in the moonlight. The house rose ahead of them, silhouetted in the midnight moon's stare.

"What's *wrong* with you?" Polly persisted. Her form was more petite than Effie's, and it was swallowed by the man's shirt she had buttoned to the collar and stuffed into the trousers they'd stolen from their brother's dresser drawer.

Effie shook her head to clear away her wandering thoughts. Unwieldy and disobedient thoughts that rambled and raced into blocks of words and images that weren't happening anywhere else but in her own mind.

It didn't help that only a few yards from the house's back porch rose gravestones that inspired a myriad of imaginative musings, lonely sentinels of memories. It was an ancient graveyard, the oldest stone dating back to Thomas Jefferson and George Washington.

"Effie!"

The skin on her arm was pinched—quite persistently. She startled again and stared through the night at Polly.

Her sister released a sigh of loving annoyance and shook her head. "Effie James, you're doing it again. Where did you go this time?"

"I've been here all along." Effie tilted her chin up a bit.

"Mm-hmm." The disbelief in Polly's response was evident. But there was humor in her voice when she added, "Do try to stay attentive."

Effie sucked in a stabilizing breath. "I'm always attentive."

"Of course you are."

An affirming pat over the pinched skin ended the small tiff, and the James sisters stared ahead into the night. Graveyard on one side, two-story house on the other, with a backyard between them boasting a gazebo roof with a pulley and a bucket.

The sisters knew this because they'd passed 322 Predicament Avenue countless times. Everyone in Shepherd had. It was, after all, the strangest and most mysterious place in the entire small Iowa town. A place of transients that came and went. Or died. People in Shepherd weren't certain what happened to the people who stayed in the house at 322 Predicament Avenue, just that they would come and then would disappear.

Occasionally, dirt in the cemetery seemed to have been trifled with, giving way to rumors that perhaps the unknown occupants of 322 Predicament Avenue arrived but never really left. They'd just moved to a different permanent location on the property.

Effie and Polly weren't the first ones to sneak onto 322 Predicament Avenue in the dead of night. It was a rite of passage for many young people. Except Effie and Polly were *supposed* to be obedient, proper daughters of Carlton James, the town's bank president. The James children—specifically the daughters— didn't do daring and dreadful things.

Until tonight.

At twenty, Effie should have been the voice of reason for her sister, who was two years her junior. But trying to cage Polly was like trying to keep dandelion fluff from blowing in the breeze. Polly was a free spirit, and while Effie was the cautious, bookish one, her fierce sense of loyalty meant she would follow precocious Polly anywhere—even to Predicament Avenue at midnight.

"Now," Polly whispered in Effie's ear, "tradition states we must plant both feet on the back porch and kiss the iron door knocker's lion head before we leave."

Effie stared at her sister. This wasn't the first time she had heard the rules of the Shepherd miscreant tradition. She'd just never fathomed she'd be partaking in it—especially at her age. But what Polly wanted . . . well, she couldn't say no.

Polly's eyes sparkled with moonlight dust and eagerness. She was thrilled. She was passionately excited.

Effie, on the other hand, shifted her attention back to the run-down, hopefully empty house. It was a monster. A monster of stories that swirled with rumors of murder and death. If they survived tonight and returned home safely to their beds, why, it would be a miracle.

"Are you ready?" Polly whispered.

"For what?" Effie couldn't help but ask another question to avoid the inevitable.

Polly gave a small, stifled giggle. "To kiss the iron lion."

"Hardly." Effie shifted, the maple tree she hid behind offering a minuscule amount of cover. "Polly, you *do* realize how juvenile this is?"

"Of course!" Polly chirped. A flash of her teeth meant her pretty face beamed in a smile. "Charles has done it, and so has Ezekiel." The mention of their younger brothers only solidified Effie's argument.

"Yes, and they're fourteen and sixteen. Not of marriageable age with reputations to protect."

"Now you sound like Mother. Let's go!" Polly tugged on Effie's shirtsleeve—well, the borrowed shirtsleeve from her brother. Polly had insisted they dress like young men and avoid being hindered by skirts and underskirts and corsets.

The next few seconds were a flurry of their feet pounding on the grass as they ran across the patchy yard toward the house.

Shutters tilted from the windows, leaving the dark voids in the house's side to seem like ghouls glaring at them. The back porch tilted to the west due to its foundation having settled there. Some of the fieldstones that held it up had sunken into the ground.

Polly gripped Effie's hand, and Effie felt little reassurance at being half dragged toward the house.

One never knew when someone was living at 322 Predicament Avenue. Tonight would be the night they'd come face-to-face with a nameless occupant. A homeless hobo. A weary, shamed woman of the night. A criminal needing a place to hide. Goodness knew *who* lived there! It changed. Always. There were petitions to knock the place down to eliminate such issues. All petitions had failed so far. This was, after all, private property. Owned by the Oppermans.

Effie's toe caught a divot in the lawn, and she stumbled, her hair slipping from the loose topknot.

Polly hauled her to her feet. "We're here," she whispered in a conspiratorial hiss. "The bottom step. Look!" With a gleeful toss of her head, Polly hopped onto the bottom step. "Two feet!"

"You have two feet on the step," Effie pointed out, her uneasiness growing. "But we're supposed to be on the porch."

"Yes." Polly nodded with anticipation. She dropped Effie's hand, and even the night's faint light made it possible for Effie to see the delight in Polly's eyes. "And here I go."

Polly hurried up the final two steps, landing with a quiet thud onto the porch. She shifted quickly so her foot didn't go through the gaping hole of a missing floorboard.

"Polly!" Effie's nothing-good-is-going-to-come-from-this feeling was growing thicker by the moment. She couldn't muster the courage to lift her foot to the bottom step, let alone follow Polly onto the porch.

Polly ignored her, tugging on the dilapidated screen door whose hinges squeaked.

"Shhh!" Effie hissed.

Polly waved her off and ran her fingers over the ornate lion's head. Its fangs formed the portion that would knock solidly against its base.

"Hurry up!" Effie said. She shifted, looking nervously over her shoulder. Only graves. Only stones. Only possible spirits to rise from the dead, their bony arms extended, flying toward them in wraith-like glee to suck the life from the living and carry them into the afterlife.

A scream ripped through the night.

Polly froze, her lips pressed against the lion's head.

Effie felt a chilling sensation run from her head to her toes. The breeze stilled. The trees didn't dare to rustle a leaf.

Another scream from inside 322 Predicament Avenue, this time with a gargled, strangled, "Noooo! Please—"

Effie waved wildly at her sister. Polly stepped to the side and pressed her nose to the windowpane. An ethereal silence followed. Effie heard her own breath escaping her nose with nervous energy. Her breathing was louder than she wished and was certain to give them away.

"Polly!" Effie whispered frantically.

Polly's body was stiff, poised at the window of the darkened house like a soldier at attention.

"Polly?" Effie became more insistent as she saw Polly begin to sway. Her sister's knees gave way, and she slumped to the porch with a thud that maximized every nighttime echo and bounced off the gravestones in the cemetery behind them.

Effie launched forward to help her younger sister but stopped short as Polly hauled herself up and with a disoriented wobble hurtled down the steps toward Effie. Horror rippled across every shadow and crevice on Polly's face. Her skin turned white as though someone had drained the blood from her insides until what remained was the shell of a woman who had seen the worst of evils.

"Let's go," Effie urged, gripping Polly's arm.

Unresponsive, Polly stared at the graves and their stones lit by the moon and by the premonition that one day, a stone would be all that remained of any of them.

"We'll go get help." Effie tugged on Polly.

"Help," Polly muttered.

Effie nodded in affirmation, urging Polly to follow by yanking on her clammy hand. Her mind was already compiling scenes of terror inside 322 Predicament Avenue. Inside would be found the lifeless body of a woman whose screams they were the last to hear. Her killer would have fled, leaving behind footprints in a puddle of blood. Perhaps a clue on the kitchen table. A sudden cold realization curdled within Effie: Polly had *seen* what had happened!

Polly stumbled to a halt, and the movement jolted Effie backward as Polly held her fingers in a viselike grip.

"What is it?" Effie gasped, looking at her sister with both dread and resentment that they were here in this very moment.

Polly's eyes were wide. Her hand trembled on Effie's arm. "Do you hear it?"

"Hear what?" Effie replied.

"Silence," Polly breathed. "There's nothing. Just . . . silence."

The horror on Polly's face must have mirrored her own.

They had heard the last sounds of a life being stolen from this earth. Was this what death sounded like once it had visited?

Death seemed far too victorious in its silence.

Norah Richman

Present Day
Shepherd, Iowa

A SCREAM THAT RIVALED every horror movie's soundtrack sliced through the night, piercing every crack and uninsulated crevice of 322 Predicament Avenue.

Norah bolted upright in bed, the sheets damp from her restless dream-filled sleep. Her T-shirt stuck to her chest and strands of hair to her cheek.

She'd dreamed the horrible scream. Those screams visited her many nights, riddled with the echoes of her sister's voice.

Another scream shattered the now very real stillness, dispelling the idea that she was dreaming.

Norah scrambled from her bed, ignoring the way the slanted wood floor beneath her feet groaned and creaked. Those were the familiar sounds. The omens of an old house with many memories lost to time that tried to escape every day.

She snatched a hoodie from a nearby chair and tugged it on over her sweaty T-shirt. Flinging her door open, Norah looked both ways down the hall. She boasted occupancy in the back bedroom, which had always been Aunt Eleanor's bedroom when Norah was a kid. Now it was hers. Hers and this godforsaken house that meant her past would never stop nipping at her heels, and that people—*humanity*—would always be mere steps away.

That was what she got for inheriting Aunt Eleanor's old farm-house on Predicament Avenue and for not being able to shake off everything she owed to her dead sister. A bed-and-breakfast had been Naomi's dream, not hers.

The recurring screams were shape-shifting into a mix of hysterical sobs and wails. Norah ignored the anxiety crawling up her throat, creating an instant quiver in her hands. She recognized the screams. She understood them all too well.

They were the screams of death.

Her bare feet took the wooden stairs to the second floor that consisted of four bedrooms in the perfectly square house. She flicked a light switch, and the futile comfort of LED bulbs flooded the darkness.

The doors of the third and fourth bedrooms stood open. Norah heard the rumble of a male voice coming from room three. She hurried toward the doorway, skidding to a halt when she reached it.

Mrs. Miller huddled against the far wall, her rounded heavy-set frame shuddering with her uncontrolled wailing. Her pink velvet pajamas were a brilliant backdrop to the man lying in the bed. He lay still, his balding head on the pillow, his eyes staring straight up at the ceiling, his mouth agape.

Norah knew with one glance that Mr. Miller was dead.

The occupant of the neighboring room had rounded the Millers' four-poster bed and was reaching for Mrs. Miller. He was shirtless, wore flannel pajama bottoms, had a mass of tousled dark hair, and his thick black glasses were jammed crooked on his face.

Sebastian Blaine's accented voice filled the room as he crooned calmly toward Mrs. Miller. The English-born guest was also an enigmatic and increasingly popular true-crime podcaster. That he was staying at her bed-and-breakfast already had her nerves taut and ready to snap. Norah distrusted the man, and not even the sight of Sebastian's shirtless, muscular form could change that.

True crime was not meant for entertainment. Not in a podcast, not in a documentary, not ever. So it was sheer irony that he was here at the deathbed of her most recent guest.

"Water?"

Norah snapped out of her intentional effort to find the negative about the man in front of her—and not the dead one.

Fingers snapped with urgency. "Miss Richman! *Norah!* Can you get Mrs. Miller a glass of water?" Sebastian's insistence, along with the pooling brown of his eyes, jolted Norah back to the grave moment.

She pushed hair from her face, her fingers trembling against her cheek as she did so. She wasn't good with emergencies. They immobilized her. They triggered every barely healed wound and sent her spiraling.

"Norah!"

Sebastian's command caused her to rush to the en suite. She twisted the knob for the cold water, and it gushed out of the spout. Snatching a paper cup from the too-modern paper cup dispenser she'd had installed on the wall, Norah held it under the water. The cup's thin sides buckled as it filled with water. Glasses were so much better, but people were careful about germs these days, and most weren't keen on the old-fashioned glasses Aunt Eleanor had supplied for her guests in their bathrooms.

With the cup full, Norah hurried back into the bedroom,

averting her eyes from the dead man on the bed. She handed the cup to Sebastian, whose fingertips brushed hers as he gripped it.

He offered the cup to Mrs. Miller. "There, there," he crooned in that sultry, deep accent of his. "Steady now. We must settle down, Mrs. Miller. Deep breaths an' all that."

"My husband . . ." the older woman whimpered in reply, her hand shaking so violently that water from the paper cup spilled onto the wood floor.

Sebastian ignored Norah's attempt to find something with which to wipe up the water. Instead, he ran his sock-covered foot over the floor to soak up the drips. "Can you find Mrs. Miller a chair?" His question was directed at Norah, who stared at him for a moment before Sebastian cocked his head and raised an eyebrow. "Aye?"

She was helpless. Hopeless. Helpless and hopeless. Norah spun and made quick work of pulling an antique wing-back chair from beneath the window. Its clawed feet scraped on the floor, pushing up one corner of a faded antique rug.

"Aye, that's right," Sebastian said as he assisted Mrs. Miller onto the chair. Her well-rounded backside made a spring in the seat groan. He patted her shoulder. "I've already called 911, even though we know they'll be of little help to your husband now." He crouched in front of Mrs. Miller.

Norah had to give the man props for being so calm and gentle. She held on to the bedpost for dear life, her body on the verge of uncontrollable shaking. This was going to be a setback. It was everything she'd tried her entire life to avoid. But death was inevitable. And Norah detested it.

"Norah?" Sebastian was looking up at her from his crouch in front of the pale and eerily silent widow. "The medics will be arriving any minute now. Will you go an' let them in?"

She nodded and took the opportunity he'd just handed her to get out of the death room, away from the bald man with his unblinking stare into the otherworld. She might be the owner of 322 Predicament Avenue's bed-and-breakfast, but no one in her family, and definitely not Norah herself, believed she'd be any good at running such a business.

She was here only for Naomi's sake.

The only thing worse than death itself was the way a soul passed. At least Mr. Miller had died in his sleep. Unlike Naomi whose decomposing body had been discovered weeks after she'd gone missing. Unlike Naomi whose murder had rocked the community of Shepherd, Iowa. The town's first murder in over a century. This safe, quaint, historic place.

It was a macabre fact that the murder of 1901 had also been committed on the grounds of 322 Predicament Avenue. It too had been violent, with repercussions that reached well into the future.

Death had been a guest here at Predicament Avenue for decades, and it was clear that Death wasn't ready to check out quite yet.

Dawn was breaking on the horizon. The pink streaks of sunlight matched the pink blossoms on the crabapple trees in the front yard. Norah had given Mr. Nielson the side-eye as he'd entered the house with his assistant. Nielson Funeral Home, with himself as the mortician, had been the same ones to care for Naomi's remains—after the county coroner was finished with them, and after they'd been mutilated further by an autopsy.

"Norah." Mr. Nielson hiked back up the porch steps once the body had been loaded to be transported to the funeral home. The expression on Mr. Nielson's face was one of sympathy.

Though this recent death wasn't Norah's personal loss, Mr. Nielson knew she was returning to the scene twelve years ago when she was nineteen. Naomi had frozen there in time and had left Norah behind to age alone. And she hadn't aged well. At least Norah didn't think so. She'd become a shell of what she'd intended to be. Worst of all, she was half terrified of people. Even ones she knew well. Who knew what secrets they were hiding? Who could she trust really? Shepherd was a small town, its population the kind where everyone knew everyone else, and it had been the same way when Naomi was alive. For the last twelve years, Norah had looked into every face of every person she met and asked the internal question: *Did you murder my sister?*

It was the not knowing that made trusting others almost an impossibility.

"Norah?" Mr. Nielson's raised voice encouraged Norah to lift her eyes and meet the mortician's. He had wrinkles. He was balding, not unlike dead Mr. Miller. He was wiry. Why were morticians always skinny? "We'll need to consult with your guest, Mrs. Miller, on the specifics of what she wants done with her husband's remains."

"What do you mean?" Norah frowned. She knew she should understand what he was talking about and yet she was unable to put her thoughts in order.

"Well, I understand the Millers are from Washington State. She will need to determine if she wants the body returned to their home, or perhaps cremation would be a possibility. It would make for easier transport, and I—"

Norah held up her hand. "You'll have to take that up with her."

"I realize that, but someone will need to be her go-between for the time being." Mr. Nielson's expression had a look of expectation.

Her go-between? Norah bit back a whimper. Her nerves were frayed to the point she wanted to retreat to her room and scream into her pillow. "I-I'll see if I can help her contact their children," Norah offered reluctantly.

"They have children?" Mr. Nielson's brows rose.

"I don't know. I assumed that . . ." Norah drew in a shuddering breath to collect herself. "I'll look into it."

"Good." Mr. Nielson eyed her. "Will you be all right, Norah?"

She offered him a pitiful sniff and a nod. That he didn't believe her was obvious.

"If you called your parents, you would—"

"No." Norah pinched her lips together and shook her head. Her parents had taken their first vacation since Naomi's murder. They were somewhere in Sweden, and she wasn't going to interrupt their time in Europe with news of a death unrelated to them. They had gone reluctantly as it was. She might be thirty-one, but her parents knew Norah's anxieties in the not-so-distant past had kept her locked away in their house, terrified of life and of people. Therapy and counseling and medical assistance had finally helped her back onto her feet and onto a good path, and Norah wasn't about to give them a reason to think she might be backsliding.

Even if she was.

A shrill cry from the newly widowed Mrs. Miller echoed through the thin walls of the house. "It was there! The apparition! At the end of the bed . . . just *staring* at us with those gaping holes for eyes!" Her wail clipped off. There were murmurs as someone apparently tried to calm her.

Norah and Mr. Nielson exchanged a look.

"Is she talking about . . . ?" Mr. Nielson let his sentence hang.

Norah shuddered. Apparitions. Spirits. Ghosts. Call them what you will, but it was no secret that 322 Predicament Avenue had long been rumored to be haunted.

Norah bit her lip and shook her head at the mortician, refusing to engage in further conversation about the ghost of Shepherd, Iowa's first murder victim back in 1901: Isabelle Addington.

It was why Sebastian Blaine was here. And God help him if he tried to link Isabelle's vintage murder to Naomi's current unsolved case. Others had tried to build a narrative and a mystery around 322 Predicament Avenue's bad luck with violent death.

Norah refused to entertain such an idea. The fascination

with cold cases, both historical and recent past, was something she would never understand. Every murder left behind silent victims. Families that would never be what they had once been.

A police detective made his way down the flight of stairs behind where Norah and Mr. Nielson stood in the front entryway of the house. Mr. Nielson gave Norah a reassuring grimace and took his leave.

She mustered the willpower to pivot where she stood and face the detective.

"Detective Dover." He flashed his identification out of habit, even though Norah had known him since high school. Back then they'd just called him Dover. "Sorry," he added sheepishly, "Habit."

Norah gave a silent nod.

"It was nice of you to step in for Mrs. Miller and assist Mr. Nielson."

She hadn't been assisting the mortician. His assistant had assisted. Norah had hidden in the corner, cowering. But she wasn't about to admit that to Dover. Nor was she going to admit it in front of Sebastian Blaine, who approached them from the side drawing room as if he owned the place. He gripped a mug of steaming coffee in his hand—had he helped himself to brewing it in the kitchen? His glasses were now straight on his face, unlike earlier during the havoc. His jaw was covered in a midnight shadow. He was remarkably, annoyingly calm.

"You discovered Mr. Miller?" Dover questioned Sebastian, who took a sip of coffee and nodded.

"Actually," he corrected, "Mrs. Miller discovered her husband. I came to help since my room is directly across the hall."

"Right." Dover nodded, then directed his attention to Norah. "And you were in the room as well?"

"Yes," Norah replied, wrapping her arms tightly around herself and praying for this all to be over soon.

Dover glanced up the stairs as Mrs. Miller wailed again. He winced and cleared his throat uncomfortably before continuing. "Well, the good news is Mr. Miller's death seems to be from natural causes. There should be no reason for an autopsy. He had a history of heart issues."

Norah blanched at the word *autopsy*. She noticed Sebastian had caught her expression. His eyes narrowed. She looked away.

"Unfortunately," the detective went on, "Mrs. Miller insists there was a woman in the bedroom right before her husband's heart attack." He gave Norah a meaningful grimace. "We know what that means."

"A woman?" Sebastian took a loud slurp of his coffee.

Dover turned to Sebastian. "You've heard the stories . . ." His words trailed off.

Sebastian nodded, ignoring Norah's shifting of her feet. "The ghost of Isabelle Addington? Aye. That's why I'm here. Investigatin' the historical cold case for my podcast *Cold, Dead, But Never Buried*."

"Oh, that's *you!*" Dover broke into a grin, and the two men exchanged handshakes. "I've heard your podcast. You do a thorough and unbiased investigation. I appreciate that you don't cater to conspiracy theories and the like."

Norah wondered if she slipped away whether she would go unnoticed.

"Conspiracy theories can sometimes contain elements of truth," Sebastian was claiming. "You need to know how to tell the difference between fact and fiction."

"No kidding." Dover hefted a deep breath. "Even with eyewitness testimony! Mrs. Miller *insists* Isabelle Addington's apparition was what instigated her husband's heart attack. I've no evidence of that—there's certainly no way to prove death by paranormal."

"She's not claimin' the spirit *killed* him, is she?" Sebastian raised an eyebrow, slurping his coffee again.

"No. Just that the appearance of the *ghost* made him go into cardiac arrest. Actually frightened him to death."

"I've heard worse." Sebastian's words and Dover's nod of agreement did nothing to make Norah feel better. "I interviewed a man once who said he would wake up in bed to find razor blades in the sheets and cuts on his flesh."

"How is that worse than cardiac arrest?" Norah inserted out of curiosity and then bit her tongue as her voice drew the attention of both men. She hugged herself tighter, regretting her question.

"Maybe it isn't," Sebastian acquiesced. "I believe the idea of razors an' blood simply sounds more violent."

"Yeah," Dover agreed. "So, Norah?" He studied her for a second and then continued, "You don't have to worry about our investigating Mr. Miller's death any further. I'm not concerned about chasing a ghost—literally. Mr. Nielson said that all signs support there was no foul play, paranormal or otherwise. But . . ."

Norah didn't like the way Dover dragged out his words.

". . . I would advise you to seek counsel," he concluded.

"Counsel?" Norah's voice squeaked. Her mouth was dry. She needed a drink of water.

Detective Dover gave a cynical roll of his eyes toward the upstairs. "Mrs. Miller doesn't impress me as the kind to let something go. She is adamant her husband was murdered by a ghost."

"That's . . . no." Norah shook her head. "Why would I need counsel for that? *Legal* counsel?"

Detective Dover shrugged. "These days you can be sued for just about anything. And you own this place, which means that technically, you're responsible for the actions of its permanent residents."

"A ghost is hardly a permanent resident." Sebastian stated what Norah was thinking.

Dover laughed. "It probably won't go anywhere, and I might be exaggerating my concern. But remember several years ago, that kid and his family sued the sandwich shop for advertising a half-foot thick steak sandwich, which he'd measured to be five inches? They settled with the restaurant, but I mean—"

"At least the kid had math in his favor." Sebastian raised his mug, and a drip of coffee sloshed out onto the wood floor.

Norah eyed it.

Sebastian ignored it.

Dover chuckled. "Math, hauntings, sandwiches—point is, people find ways to try to get justice, founded or not. Again, to be on the safe side, I'd get a lawyer's counsel on this one. If Mrs. Miller even *suggests* a lawsuit, you might have to revisit the place's history to prove her ghost claims have no validity. And let's be honest, such a lawsuit has a slim chance of going anywhere, but the bad publicity it might bring about this place? You can't run a successful B and B if you don't have any guests."

Or if you go bankrupt paying a lawyer in defense of a woman claiming death by ghost! The idiocy of the situation swept away any empathy that was gnawing at her on behalf of Mrs. Miller.

The last thing she wanted to do was revisit the history of 322 Predicament Avenue. From the turn of the century or from twelve years ago! But now a third death had marked its place in the house.

Norah felt the skeletal claws of history snatching at her ankles, stealing her breath away. No, she couldn't revisit history here, not at Predicament Avenue. She had buried it, and it needed to stay buried. Along with tales of Isabelle Addington, Shepherd's first murder victim, and Naomi Richman, Shepherd's last.

3

EFFIE

May 1901

HER FINGERNAILS had been bitten to the quick, but that didn't stop Effie from gnawing at them when no one was looking. There were some things a person must do to manage their nervousness, and for Effie this was one of them. Her father had all but dragged her back to 322 Predicament Avenue. The hubbub was fast growing as curiosity seekers noted the doors of the abandoned house open, men coming in and out, and now a plethora of onlookers had gathered. *Murder.* The word spread quickly once spoken, and there was no stopping it. Regardless of the creepy tales that hovered around the property, there had never been a proven homicide in Shepherd, Iowa. It was a peaceful small town where everyone knew everyone, where churches were central to daily life, and evildoing was thwarted.

Effie stood just outside the front of the house on Predicament

Avenue, staring up at its two-story frame that seemed to tilt toward the east as if it were tired of standing. It wasn't a very old house; it had been built maybe thirty years prior. But it was a tired house. A dying house.

"Are you all right?" A woman sidled up to Effie, who stepped away from the unwanted attention.

"Yes, of course." Effie nodded quickly, avoiding the searching gaze that was filled more with curiosity and inquiry than concern. Word had spread—by whom and how, Effie wished she knew. Yet immediately after she'd reported the incident early this morning, somehow it had leaked. Polly had collapsed into a catatonic state of shock on arriving back home. Effie's shouts for help had awakened the James household and turned their world upside down. "This is why there are *standards* of decorum and etiquette!" Mother had wailed before collapsing onto a velvet settee with a handkerchief clasped in her hand. In spite her theatrics, however, Mother was a strong woman and had summoned the tenacity to tend to Polly and send one of their brothers for a doctor.

Father had been less than understanding—not that Effie could blame him. She had behaved like a hooligan, not a young woman of marriageable age, and not at all with the standards expected of a lady of society, such as she was. The daughter of the bank president. Others would be more forgiving toward Polly. And that was another troublesome burden altogether.

"Was there blood?"

"Hmm?" Effie swung her head around to look at the insatiably curious woman. She frowned, registering the question. "No. I mean . . . gracious!" Effie leveled a look of sheer censure on the woman, who had the decency to offer a sheepish smile and leave Effie alone.

Effie watched as the woman joined a few other townsfolk. The small group began poking around the perimeter of the house. One of them pressed her face against a window, not unlike Polly had done only hours before. A shudder ran up Effie's spine. Polly had not shared what it was she'd seen, but Effie could imagine. The woman's screams, followed by silence? It all bespoke of violence and outright death.

"Why did I have to return here?" Effie muttered under her breath. A willow tree in the front yard waved its branches like a ghoul hovering over it as a silent witness. Her father stood on the front porch, his coattails pushed back and his hands at his waist. He was in an animated conversation with the constable.

A man exited the front door, his trousers tailored to his cut figure. He glanced at Effie, then said something to her father and the constable.

"Effie." Father's commanding baritone jolted her into obedience, and Effie moved through the growing crowd of gawkers.

Father extended his hand to Effie as she went up the stairs. She recognized the third male as Rand Fletcher, a local businessman who lived down the street from 322 Predicament Avenue. He was handsome in an angular sort of way, and Effie had been only a few years behind him in school. He shifted his eyes away from her as she looked up to meet his gaze.

That didn't bode well. Effie tried not to squirm. Mr. Fletcher had always been friendly, if not warm, and confident. He had a habit of meeting women with a direct expression as if they were his equal. Now Effie felt diminished beneath the aversion of his attention. As though she were indeed beneath him—or was foolish or had done something horribly wrong.

Carlton James, Effie's father, glowered at her from beneath his bushy gray brows. "Be honest now."

"I'm nothing if not honest," Effie responded, biting her tongue at her father's darkening expression. She *had* acted immaturely, caught up in her sister's mission to be adventurous and take risks before . . . well, Effie had never been an adventurer, nor was she a risk-taker. She was a good Christian woman with ideals and hopes of having her own home one day, and it certainly wouldn't be anything like this dreadful house on Predicament Avenue that—

"Euphemia!" Carlton James's bark was worse than his bite, Effie knew, but when her father used her full name, she not only listened but felt thoroughly chastised.

The constable, whom Effie recognized as Constable Talbot, cleared his throat. "Miss James, you have raised quite the alarm in our community."

Effie exchanged a glance with Rand Fletcher. Once again, he averted his eyes.

"I merely reported what I . . . what my sister witnessed." Effie felt her throat tighten with a growing desperation she couldn't explain. "We heard screaming, and then there was just . . . nothing. Pure silence. But Polly had looked through the window and—"

Rand cleared his throat, pointing over his shoulder with his thumb toward the innards of the house. "There is nothing inside, Miss James." He skimmed his gaze across Effie's face. "No body. No woman injured or dead."

"Which matches what I saw when I first arrived here," Constable Talbot concluded.

"Me too!" Gerald Ambrose piped up, a member of the town council and owner of the local drugstore. He stomped his feet on the porch as if to clear mud from his already clean shoes. "Except I did step in some moldy food on the floor in the kitchen."

"That has no bearing on this." Constable Talbot dismissed the comment. Two ladies approached the bottom of the stairs, stealing Constable Talbot's attention for a moment. "Mrs. Jarvis, Mrs. Clements."

"We're here to offer our assistance with cleaning up after the body." The older women exchanged glances, but Effie could see the curiosity etched into the fine lines of their powdered faces. Murder did that to a town. Everyone and their mothers' brothers would turn out to tour the murder house, to see the bloodstains and speculate on what had happened.

Effie recalled reading in the paper about a town not much different from Shepherd, where over three hundred people gathered and made their way through the home where a family had been axed to death in their beds. Of course, the victims had been removed, but only after twenty or so had already viewed them, attempting to help the police.

It was what people did when a serious crime had been committed in their small town—offer their help while pretending not to be curious. In the end, though, it was mostly a fascination with the macabre. And it sickened Effie.

"Constable," Effie broke in, desperate to end this growing carnival before it became newsworthy. "My sister and I may have acted foolishly, but my sister has taken to her bed and—"

"Enough." Her father's hand on Effie's arm stilled her. She shot her father a questioning look. What was to be secretive about Polly's condition? Everyone knew the truth about Polly, and now? The events of last night had been too much for her. They had paralyzed Polly, stolen her words, shocked her into a weakened stupor . . .

Effie's eyes burned with tears. No one, not even her own father, could comprehend why she'd followed Polly last night, and why now she was growing desperate for the others to understand the terror they had been through.

"Mr. Fletcher, are you certain you saw nothing—?" Effie's words broke off as Rand Fletcher stifled a cough.

"Really, I've no more to do with this." Mr. Fletcher's expression toward Effie was a mixture of apology and concern. "I will leave you to it," he said to the constable. "Pardon me." Mr. Fletcher pushed past Effie, nodding at the two women who still waited with eagerness to clean up the bloody mess left behind by the alleged murder.

Constable Talbot held up a hand toward them. "Ladies, I appreciate the offer, but I won't be needing your services today."

Disappointment creased their faces. Mrs. Jarvis tried once

more. "Might we not come inside and help make sure you didn't miss anything?"

"Nothing to see, ladies. Please move along now." Mr. Ambrose waved them off, also dismissing another five onlookers who'd gathered beside them. "There's no murder. Nothing inside to see that you probably haven't seen already."

Murmurs rippled among the folks as they withdrew. Effie cast urgent looks between the men before her. Her brow furrowed with growing horror. "We *did* hear a woman scream." Effie ignored the squeeze of her father's hand on her arm. She stiffened, insisting that she be heard. "My sister saw something. Something awful right there in the kitchen." Effie waved her arm at the house.

"Did *you* see it?" the constable asked. "The assumption of murder is quite a leap."

Effie was brought up short. "Well, no, but I—"

"And your sister isn't in any condition to speak of what she saw?" The constable's eyes shifted to Effie's father.

"My daughter is not well."

Not well? Effie reared back to stare at her father. Not well was an understatement to say the least. Polly was so terrified that she'd been whimpering while curled up like an infant in her bed! Any expression of energy and strength had been drained from Polly, like someone had opened a valve and released her spirit, leaving only her soul to remain.

This was far sooner than Effie had wanted. Far sooner than she thought it would happen. The horror of what Polly had witnessed had snatched from Polly the last remnants of her will to continue marking off the dreams of her wish list. The things she wanted to do before . . . well, 322 Predicament Avenue had been one of Polly's wishes. Effie had accompanied her because it was what a loyal sister did when the other one was dying.

The men stared at Effie. Father cleared his throat. Mr. Ambrose crossed his arms over his chest.

Constable Talbot chose to dismiss Effie's insistence and instead address her father. "There's no evidence of anything out of the ordinary here. I appreciate your willingness to help us by coming here." He turned to address Effie. "And I appreciate that you brought it to our attention. While I can't say what exactly your sister saw or you heard, Miss James"—he managed a thin smile, likely meant to appease her—"it's apparent it wasn't a murder. Thank the Lord for that."

"Yes," Mr. Ambrose agreed.

Effie and her father bid the men goodbye and slipped through the thinning crowd back toward their carriage. The driver assisted them inside and closed the door. With a jerk, the carriage started moving forward, the horse's shoes clopping along the cobblestone street.

Effie eyed her father, who stared out the side window, tapping his finger against his bearded chin. He was agitated, that much was certain. His gaze seemed to linger on the graveyard behind the house on Predicament Avenue, and then it shifted to his gloved hands.

"I'm sorry, Father." Effie said what she knew her father expected and preferred she'd say.

Her father turned his dark eyes on her, the seriousness in them spearing her. An uninterpretable expression passed over his face, and then his jaw clenched. He ran his hand over his peppery-gray beard. "I didn't expect this from you, Euphemia." Carlton James's direct conclusion landed squarely on Effie's shoulders. "You are supposed to look after your sister, not follow her in her shenanigans."

He had a point, but then how did one tell Polly no? Polly, who was the pride and joy of the James family. The effervescent and delightful Polly who was the thread that wove the entire family together into a cohesive unit.

Carlton cleared his throat. "She wasn't well to begin with."

"I know." Effie's admission sounded small to her own ears.

"And this—whatever this was—only toppled the last of her strength and reasoning."

Effie didn't answer. Her father wasn't wrong, but he didn't understand either. He didn't grasp how Polly had pleaded with Effie to go to Predicament Avenue, just like they had whispered and conspired to do when they were younger. Yet they'd never been brave enough, most assuredly not Effie. Effie had always told Polly it was foolhardy and inappropriate. But last night? The sunken paleness in Polly's expression spoke louder than her pleas. Time was oh so limited.

"And to report a *murder*?" Carlton's disapproval was clear. "With no evidence of—"

"There *was* evidence!" Effie interrupted, shifting in her seat in the carriage. "Polly saw—"

"What?" Carlton frowned. A father's censure. "She cannot tell us now, can she? Did she tell you? Did she detail for you what she saw?"

"I heard the woman scream, Father." Effie's insistence didn't carry with it the conviction she felt. The fact was, no matter what Polly had seen, and no matter what she had heard, as of now the house on Predicament Avenue was empty. There was no corpse whose blood had soaked into the floorboards. There was no mangled woman lying exposed to confirm Effie's story. There was no crime, no murder, nothing but the empty shell of 322 Predicament Avenue. "A woman was murdered, I know this." Effie's statement hung in the air between them.

Drawing in a breath, her father finished the conversation in a tone rich with disbelief. "So you say, Euphemia. So you say."

Mother preferred to take her tea inside, read a book inside, and recline inside. It was the ladylike thing to do. Effie smiled as she reached for the book on the top of her pile. Perhaps this was a rebellion of her own making, not influenced by Polly's mischief. The out-of-doors was a haven, the sky a canopy of light, and the breeze God's whisper.

After two days, the debacle had decreased in its drama as far as the town was concerned. But inside the James manor, nothing was as it should be. Mother held a vigil by Polly's bedside. Effie's brothers came and went in silent solemnity. Father proceeded to treat life as normally as possible while attempting to dispel any lingering wagging tongues and discrimination against his daughters' untoward behaviors. Effie believed it all to be a continuing nightmare.

The terror of that evening had been overshadowed by Polly's condition now. She had yet to respond to anyone. Her eyes remained closed, her skin grew paler, she writhed and whimpered—either in pain or from being haunted by the visions of what she'd seen—and Effie could hardly bear it. Polly hadn't been healthy, but Effie had contributed to pushing Polly over the edge. Were they now waiting for her to die? Plagued by the last visions of her life being the taking of another life?

It *had* happened, Effie knew. With all of her heart she knew. Yet she lacked Polly's ability to convince others to believe her. Effie was straightforward, reserved, cautious, and bookish. In the shadow of her younger sister, she had no talent for persuading others to believe an outlandish story of murder. Especially with no evidence to support her claims.

Effie was thankful to be alone now with her thoughts, where she could be completely honest with herself and with God. She opened her book, smoothing the first page with a tender caress. *Ben-Hur*. She had already read it once, but the adventure, the devotion, the *faith* . . . it spoke to her very soul. Such a story should be heralded. Effie could imagine the chariots, the Romans, the leprous sister, and the mother. She could fathom the agony and the tragedy and the—

"Miss James?"

Startled, Effie slammed the book shut as if she were reading one of Polly's romance novels Mother so disapproved of.

She noted a carriage had stopped beneath the arched canopy of the drive that curved around and offered shelter at the entrance of the James manor. Before her stood a stooped elderly man dressed in a well-tailored suit, his hat in his hands, wisps of white hair rising from the age-dotted skin of his mostly bald head. He had a round nose, a white beard, and a mustache so full she could hardly see his mouth.

"I apologize for being so forward." The old man's tone was confident in spite of his breaking of etiquette. "Do allow me to introduce myself." His voice was accented and polished. British.

Curiosity piqued, but with her reservedness arousing caution, Effie stiffened, clutching *Ben-Hur* in her hands. "May I help you? My mother is inside, and my father is not at home."

The older gentleman smiled, and it warmed his expression.

Effie rather liked him immediately, regardless of her suspicion of the stranger. She looked beyond him to the carriage, noting the form of another man waiting inside it.

"Miss James," the man began, drawing her attention back to him. "My name is Gus Cropper. I'm the assistant to Mr. Lewis Anderson of New York."

She perked up at hearing the name Lewis and rubbed her thumb absently over the matching name of *Ben-Hur*'s author. It was a name she'd long admired. She nodded politely. "A pleasure to meet you."

Mr. Cropper cleared his throat. "Mr. Anderson was inquiring as to whether he could have a moment of your time?"

"*My* time?" Effie heard the surprised squeak in her voice. Never had a stranger—and a man at that—requested any time of hers. "Are you certain he's not looking for my father?" Having a prominent bank president as a father could leave her at a disadvantage at times due to the fact that businessmen might seek to approach her by means of persuading her father concerning a financial investment. It was a ploy sometimes used, but never so direct as to approach her prior to a proper introduction—at her private home, no less.

"Yes. You, Miss James," Mr. Cropper clarified. "He has some questions for you regarding your experience the other evening."

A pall settled over her. The book slipped from her grip onto the blanketed ground. "I'm afraid not," Effie replied. She had so hoped the fiasco had blown over.

"It's of grave importance," Mr. Cropper added.

"Be that as it may, I see no need to revisit the experience with a complete stranger." Effie lifted her chin a bit in hopes of appearing firm in her response.

Mr. Cropper locked eyes with her. "Lives hang in the balance, Miss James."

"They do?" Effie couldn't help but ask, then bit her tongue at the audacity she'd shown to challenge him.

Instead of being offended, Mr. Cropper tipped his head toward the carriage. "Perhaps my employer could best answer your question?"

Mr. Cropper turned and started back toward the carriage. Effie followed, though warily. This was unorthodox to be sure, and she was in no position to make any more errors in judgment.

The door of the carriage opened, and a lean form stepped outside. The man was wearing a tailored suit with a silk kerchief of azure blue in his chest pocket. He removed his hat and brushed back sandy-brown hair from a broad forehead. His deep-set eyes were piercing, and Effie couldn't determine whether they were shrewd or something else entirely. Either way, intelligence was etched into every crevice of his face, his chin, his jawline.

After Mr. Cropper made the introductions, Effie found her voice—and the etiquette her mother had drilled into her from an early age. "Mr. Anderson, welcome to the manor. Would you like to come inside? I can have tea and cookies served."

There was no change in his expression. He dipped his head

in acknowledgment. "Thank you, but no, Miss James. If I could have but a moment of your time?" His words were also distinctly British.

"Very well." It was all so affected and stilted, Effie sensed every warning rising within her. She didn't know this man, and he refused her proper invitation into their home where his visit would be overseen by house staff as well as by her mother. Not to mention, what business was any of the recent events to him?

Still, Effie extended her arm toward a black iron table and chairs that sat just off the brick driveway amid what would be rose gardens come summer. If Mr. Anderson wished to ask questions, Effie owed it to Polly to try to understand. She noticed Mr. Cropper hung back at the carriage.

Taking their seats, Effie swallowed back nervous energy caused by the unorthodox meeting and the equally mystifying reason why this stranger thought she could offer him anything about the other night.

As Mr. Anderson folded his body into the chair beside her with both ease and confidence, she noticed he was taller than she'd thought when first approaching him. "You've just recently arrived in Shepherd, have you?" Effie struggled for polite conversation.

Mr. Anderson's hazel eyes seemed to summarize her with one look, draw a conclusion, and tuck it away in his mind for later. Though it was disconcerting to have someone form an opinion about her with no foreknowledge, somehow Effie had the distinct impression that whatever conclusions Mr. Anderson drew, they would be correct. And that was more unsettling than she wished to admit.

"I've been in America for a few months now. Mr. Cropper and I arrived in Shepherd yesterday. It was then I heard about your *experience* of a few nights ago. I'd like to ask you a few questions about it—that is, if you're willing."

Effie nodded stiffly. "I'm not sure what you want to know that I could provide."

"Anything you think insignificant might be of interest to me. I would like to hear of the events you witnessed."

"You believe I witnessed something?" Effie asked. He seemed to have expectations that she might regale him with some sordid tale of crime and gore, neither of which was available to offer.

"Did you?" he asked in return.

Effie folded her hands in her lap to avoid the urge to begin gnawing at her fingernail. "My sister did. I did not."

"You saw nothing?" Mr. Anderson looked at her with narrowed eyes.

Effie swallowed uncomfortably. "I . . . no. I *heard* something, but the authorities have confirmed there is no evidence of harm coming to anyone in spite of what I heard."

Mr. Anderson shifted in his chair. She caught a whiff of tobacco mixed with nutmeg. "What did she sound like, this woman?"

Effie stared at him for a moment. He didn't even pause at her declaration that the police believed nothing had happened. Instead, he assumed her story was accurate. Effie hesitated. The man was drilling her with his intense stare, apparently weighing not only her words but also her movements, her expressions. Effie squirmed and gave in to the need to bite her fingernail.

Mr. Anderson's eyes dropped to her finger.

Effie dropped her hand back in her lap. "Sound like? Well . . ." How should she answer that? She fumbled for words. "She . . . she cried out *no* a few times."

A shadow passed over his face.

Effie hurried to continue. "But perhaps I imagined it? I'm not certain now. It was the middle of the night. There were screams, and then my sister and I ran away." Like any proper-minded woman would. No. A proper-minded woman would never have been there to begin with.

Mr. Anderson leaned forward, resting his elbows on his knees, folding his hands in front of him as if going to prayer. Instead, he burrowed his gaze into hers. Effie noticed blue flecks in the hazel that were more predominant than green or yellow. "Did you see anything out of the ordinary?"

Effie attempted to recall because the intensity of his stare was so interrogative that she felt she had no choice. "Not really. Everything seemed normal until we heard . . . until Polly saw—" Effie bit her tongue. The flicker of interest in his eyes was obvious.

"Saw?" Mr. Anderson inquired.

Effie chose her words carefully. "My sister saw something, but she is very ill and hasn't been able to elaborate on it."

"Is there any way I could perhaps speak with your sister?"

Effie pictured Polly in the upper level of their home, curled beneath her bedsheets, unresponsive and in a weakened state. The image made Effie stiffen and look down her nose at the stranger whose questions were obtuse and vague. "Absolutely no way," Effie stated through pursed lips.

But Mr. Anderson was not intimidated by Effie's attempt to appear severe. He almost looked as if he found humor in it. "Well then." He pushed off his knees with his hands and stood.

Effie quickly followed suit.

"Thank you for your time, Miss James."

"You're welcome."

Mr. Anderson turned back toward the carriage. He took a few steps, but Effie stopped him, unable to squelch the question she felt she had every right to ask.

"Why do you want to know these things, Mr. Anderson? You're not even from Shepherd."

He looked over his shoulder at her. "My wife has been missing for ten months, Miss James. I have reason to believe she was last here in Shepherd. My fear is that the cries you heard were hers."

Effie's hand flew to her mouth. She regretted being so blunt.

Mr. Anderson's lips pressed together with what appeared to be suppressed grief, also a hint of anger. "Have you ever heard the name Isabelle Addington?"

Effie shook her head, wordless.

He gave a quick nod. "Had you heard of her, you would remember. As it is, perhaps you did *hear* her. That is why I'm in Shepherd, Miss James. When one's family disappears without a trace, only the brutally detached let them go. I am the opposite. I am fiercely devoted, and I *will* find Isabelle. I *will* bring her home." He heaved a sigh. "Even if she is dead."

With that, Mr. Anderson strode toward his carriage.

4

Norah

Present Day
Shepherd, Iowa

HER HANDS SHOOK as she attempted to pour coffee into a mug. Norah bit back a curse as it sloshed on the counter. She snatched a cloth from the sink and mopped it up, then opted to take the half-full mug rather than fill it any further. With her trembling hands, she'd be lucky to make it to the kitchen table without spilling the entire mug onto the tile floor.

The kitchen was located in the back of the house at 322 Predicament Ave. Its tile flooring was white, discolored from time, and the walls were white, also tinged with yellow from smoke and steam and hours of cooking and baking since it was last painted in the late nineties. Dish towels of sunny yellow hung off a towel bar over the sink. Aunt Eleanor's choosing. She had loved yellow and sunshine and happiness.

Happiness didn't exist at 322 Predicament Avenue.

"Am I your only guest now?"

Norah yelped, and more coffee sloshed onto the wood table where she'd just taken a seat.

Sebastian Blaine. He positioned himself in the doorway of the kitchen with that self-confident side smile, his square black-framed glasses, dark eyes, and broad shoulders.

Norah wiped up the coffee using the sleeve of her sweatshirt. The very presence of the man in the kitchen reminded her that he was indeed the only guest now at Predicament Avenue's B and B. She was home alone with a strange man, no longer under the tenuous protection that Mr. and Mrs. Miller had brought with them.

Ignoring that Norah hadn't responded, Sebastian approached the table, pulling out a chair and making himself at home. He crossed his ankle over his knee, studying her. "Are you a'right?"

Was she all right? There was no way to answer that. Norah cupped the coffee mug between her hands and stared into the black brew as if the abyss could drown her and send her into eternal peace.

Sebastian eyed her. "It was a rather frightenin' night. It's understandable if you're shaken."

Norah avoided his direct stare. He had no idea what traumatizing was. Traumatizing wasn't a dead man in a bed from a heart attack. Traumatizing wasn't a rumored ghost that haunted the old house. Traumatizing was—

"Do you want to talk about it?"

Norah sucked in a violently anxious breath, clenching her teeth. She was either going to scream at him to go away or curl up into a ball in the corner of the room and rock back and forth. Retreating into herself, into her mind, into the dark places where no one else could follow. Instead, she focused on her five senses in an effort to avoid the latter. Hearing. She could hear birdsong outside. The refrigerator humming. The soft breathing of Sebastian Blaine as he watched her.

No, this wasn't helping.

Smell. She could smell her coffee, dusky undertones with a hint of chestnut. She could smell the dish soap on the sink—garden apple—a sickeningly sweet scent. Norah preferred lemon. She could smell—

"It's not workin', is it?" Sebastian broke into her self-induced therapy session.

Norah slid her eyes up to meet his. She saw kindness there and knew in that moment he wasn't someone she needed to fear. He was well-known, a trustworthy guest based on references provided, and he was . . .

"Groundin' yourself is difficult." Sebastian offered an encouraging smile. His eyes were far too knowing as they peered at her through his glasses. "I know. My sister has horrid anxiety. She's battled with it for two decades now, and it never truly goes away."

Norah swallowed. She tried lifting the coffee mug to her mouth, but her shaking hands made doing so impossible. She put the mug back on the table with a thud.

"It's a'right to admit you're not a'right."

"And it's *all right* if you leave me alone, please." Norah's voice sounded small even to her own ears. The plea in her tone erased any authority she might have included with the request.

Sebastian didn't move. "I could, but I prefer not to leave a lass alone when she's in a hard spot."

The man had no idea. None. Being here was only *adding* to the curdling of her stomach, the black shutters at the corners of her eyes, the shortness of her breath, the clawing panic in her throat . . .

A hand brushed hair away from her face. Norah felt a cold washcloth pressed to her forehead, her head resting on a rolled-up dish towel doubling as a pillow that was lodged in the man's lap. He sat cross-legged on the kitchen floor, concern etched into the crevices on his face as he looked down on her.

"Hello." A smile. A repositioning of the cold cloth. "You took a fall off your chair when you passed out."

Norah whimpered, wriggling to sit up and leave the odd comfort of his pillowed lap.

"Shh, shh, shh," Sebastian crooned, his hand pressing just enough on her shoulder to indicate she shouldn't move, but not enough to make Norah assume she was trapped. "Give yourself time."

"I need to . . . I need to get up." Norah struggled to sit, and this time Sebastian didn't resist. He aided her until she was leaning back against the kitchen cabinets. The tile floor was cool beneath her. She drew her knees up to her chest. The wet washcloth had fallen from its place on her forehead.

Sebastian swiped the cloth up from the floor and tossed it above her head into the sink. "You blacked out so quickly, I failed at catchin' you." His crooked grin seemed to communicate that she needn't feel ashamed. "I guess I'm gettin' old."

"You're not old," Norah mumbled around a thick tongue. The room was spinning. She was already feeling the anxiousness digging at her gut again.

"I'm almost forty." Sebastian's smile made lines and dimples appear in his cheeks. "My nieces tell me they'll gift me with black roses an' a black balloon bouquet when my birthday comes round. I advised them that if they're goin' all black, they should throw in a devil's food chocolate cake too."

"How old are your nieces?" Norah asked. She knew what he was doing. He was attempting to redirect her mind from the horror, the panic, the dread of . . . everything.

Sebastian stretched his arms toward the ceiling before clasping fingers behind his head. "Emmy is eight. Elizabeth is twelve. I've a nephew also, but he's only three and seems to side with his uncle—he was quite energetic about the chocolate cake."

"And they live in—"

"Lancashire. Where I was born. I'm the rebel who came to the States about twelve years ago now."

"For your podcast?" Norah hadn't listened to Sebastian Blaine's podcast. His fascination with crime was in direct juxtaposition with hers.

He shrugged. "Among other things." Pushing off the floor, Sebastian reached over Norah and filled a glass with water, then handed it to her. "Sup it up now."

She obeyed for no other reason than that she was thirsty.

Sebastian, who wasn't remarkably tall, slid down to sit shoulder to shoulder with her. He smelled like a chocolate chip cookie. She didn't know why he did, but it was comforting.

"My sister is older'n me by five years. I was the lad of the family. Still am." He grinned sheepishly.

"Your parents live in England?" Norah took another sip of water, thankful her nerves were steadying. Although she had the new conundrum of Sebastian's cozy way of sitting next to her that made her stomach do a flip. She wasn't sure how to interpret this.

"Lancashire County too. They're all there. I go back from time to time whenever I can. I travel a lot for research, which is why I'm here."

Norah nodded, staring at her water glass. A silent camaraderie settled between them.

Sebastian broke the silence by clearing his throat. "There's no need for you to feel alone here, Norah. I'm available and willin' to pitch in for whatever you need. I'm here for at least a few weeks."

"Because of Isabelle Addington's ghost?" Norah dared to eye him directly. She searched his face. "Or . . . other stories?"

Sebastian gave her knee a friendly, reassuring pat. "Let's just keep it to Isabelle for now, yeah?"

Norah agreed, although she didn't completely trust him. He was after all an investigator of old crimes and mysteries. Truth be told, her sister's murder was as much a mystery as the legends that swirled around Predicament Avenue and Isabelle Addington. It was her worst fear. She'd already lived through Naomi's murder once—she didn't want to do it all over again.

"Norah?" a man's voice called, his tone gravelly from age, along with the inevitable wobble.

"She'll be in the kitchen," another voice said, sounding not much different from the first.

Two stooped-shouldered men rounded the corner from the hallway. Norah couldn't help but feel relief at the sight of them. Brothers and neighbors to 322 Predicament Avenue for as long as she could remember, Otto and Ralph Middleford were the epitome of crusty old bachelors who'd given their time and devotion to labor but who now enjoyed a more leisurely life that included a greater number of coffee breaks. They were the neighborhood handymen and gossips, the lovable types Norah knew she'd be hard-pressed to live without.

"Come here, ya little scamp!" Otto's arms were spread wide, his knobby fingers waggling in her direction.

Norah hurried into the safety net of his hold, smelling deep of his vinegary cologne that clung to his shirt. A familiar scent since the first day she'd crawled onto his grandfatherly lap when she was three.

"Where's the body?" Ralph, the younger of the two brothers and the no-nonsense type, leaned heavily on his shepherd's crook cane. He'd been diagnosed with multiple sclerosis a decade before, and it was taking its toll the older he grew. "That dead man better not be lounging around on the bed upstairs." Ralph's bushy eyebrows rose in defense of Norah.

She pulled back from Otto's hug and gave Ralph a shaky smile. "He's not. Mr. Nielson came and removed his body. Mrs. Miller— the man's wife—will be staying at a hotel for the time being."

"Good," Ralph groused. He shuffled toward the coffeepot. With a side glance at Sebastian, he harrumphed and said, "You a guest here?"

"That I am," Sebastian answered.

"Well, leave our girl alone." Ralph's direct order made Sebastian smile.

Norah drew in a long breath and let it out. Otto, the more sensitive of the two men, gripped her hand and led her like a gentleman back to the chair. Like his brother, he eyed Sebastian with a similar protective glint. "You're that podcast fella? Old crimes and all? Norah here, she's been through the wringer. No need for anyone to take her back there ever again."

"I've no intention to do such a thing." Sebastian looked a tad confused, and for a moment Norah dared to hope he didn't even know about Naomi. It was wishful thinking. "I'm respectful of people's trauma," he finished.

Norah wished Otto hadn't brought Naomi into the conversation. Why propose the idea if Sebastian hadn't posed a threat? She needed folks to just avoid it. Avoid the tragedy that was Naomi. Pretend it hadn't happened. Move on. All the unhealthy things she'd been doing for twelve years in order to get to the place she was today. A place where she could interact with other human beings without losing her composure.

"Good." Ralph handed Otto a mug of fresh coffee, who in turn set the mug in front of Norah. "We spoil our girl. 'Specially when her parents go off globe-trottin'. Her aunt Eleanor was a peach of a woman, and Norah here, she's no different in our eyes."

"She's family," Otto added.

"Family," Ralph echoed.

"Thank you, boys." Norah gave them both a warm, bittersweet smile. Aunt Eleanor had always referred to them as "the boys next door," and Norah had adopted the moniker. "I'll be fine."

"What, after all you been through? I heard they're blaming Isabelle for killin' the man." Otto slumped onto a chair next to Norah.

While she'd rather not revisit what she'd just successfully come out of, she knew the brothers. They were highly curious. As curious as they were protective. It would go better to just answer their questions, and then they would let it go.

Norah answered quickly. "Mrs. Miller said there was a woman standing by their bed, and it frightened Mr. Miller so bad that he suffered a heart attack."

"Could happen," Ralph said, nodding.

Otto slapped the tabletop. "'Course it could. Seen Isabelle's ghost with my own eyes at least six times."

"You have?" Sebastian's expression shifted from caring and considerate to intrigued. He pulled out a chair and sat down across from Otto and Norah. Ralph did the same at the head of the table, hooking his cane on the arm of his chair.

"Sure have." Otto nodded with vigor. "Once when I was in my fifties—Norah here was just a wee little thing—I was in the back fixin' a door for Eleanor. Looked up at the attic window and there she was, her face just staring down at me. If I'd've had a camera, I could've taken a picture of her. She was that clear."

"Was she young? Old?" Sebastian prompted.

Ralph snorted. "She'd been dead more'n a hundred years! What do you think?"

"She was neither," Otto said. "Just a face and two big holes in her head where her eyes should've been."

"Delightful." Sebastian raised his brows. "And what do you know about the story of Isabelle Addington? Is it true she was murdered in this house?"

Norah shoved back from the table, her chair scraping against the floor. The three men were startled out of their conversation.

"Good grief." Otto reached for her. "We're insensitive old coots."

"No, no." Norah waved him off nonchalantly. "I . . . go ahead. I just need to check on a few things."

She hurried from the room, sensing the eyes of the three men boring into her back. How quickly Sebastian had forgotten that she'd just recovered from a severe panic attack. How fast the boys had forgotten about Naomi—about Norah's sensitivities. And could she blame them? It had been how many years now? Twelve, almost thirteen. Like a true sign of bad luck.

Norah avoided the security of her bedroom, forcing herself to climb the flight of polished wood stairs as she had the night before when Mrs. Miller's screams had jolted her from her sleep. She was going to need to clean the Millers' bedroom. She couldn't afford to turn down any reservations that came in from guests, and if the room wasn't ready . . .

She let her thoughts hang and disregarded the fact that no one would be making a reservation and arriving today. That she could give herself a chance to rest and collect herself before going to that room. But it would keep her busy. She needed to be busy. Needed to focus on other tasks and activities.

Entering the Millers' room, Norah paused just inside the doorway. Thankfully the bed had been stripped of its linens. She had enough in the linen closet to put clean ones on the bed, as well as a replacement mattress pad. The plastic cover she had every guest mattress encased in was also missing, the mattress clean underneath. Should she replace the entire mattress? Who would want to sleep in a bed a man had just died in?

Norah moved to the window and pushed back the flimsy white curtains. The street below was empty save a single car that drove by. The yard was patchy brown with green grass poking up through last year's remains of a lawn. The windowpane fogged from her breath. Norah rubbed her sleeve across the glass to clear it, then checked the hinged lock on the bottom half of the window. Locked. No one had snuck into the room through the window and terrified Mr. Miller.

Norah knew what had happened. She didn't want to admit it, but she knew. It had happened to her before too. It was the place between dreaming and wakefulness when a person was apt to see things that weren't really there, and yet they seemed so real that they became instant memories.

Norah had seen Isabelle Addington before.

She had seen her for the first time shortly after Aunt Eleanor had died a year ago.

Mrs. Miller wasn't wrong. There was a ghostly apparition that would stand beside your bed and stare down at you. You could feel its presence there even before you opened your eyes. And when you finally did, the shadow woman would vanish almost as soon as you spotted her.

Norah understood the terror of that moment. She understood how someone with a weak heart might have a physical reaction to the shock and fright.

What she didn't understand was why anyone would want to know more about Isabelle Addington or about the history of 322 Predicament Avenue. She didn't understand her houseguest's fascination with the first murder of Shepherd, Iowa, and she didn't understand why, nearly thirteen years later, Isabelle Addington could return to haunt her, but Naomi couldn't.

5

EFFIE

May 1901
Shepherd, Iowa

THE DINNER PARTY was long and drawn out. Effie found it secretly amusing, watching those around her parade about as if they were royalty. Royalty in Shepherd? A small Midwestern town where, if they were to travel to another town a hundred miles away, no one would know them. They would have little influence over the world at large, only here in this small patch of earth where nothing interesting or extraordinary ever happened anyway—except for a bit of haughty gossip perhaps.

Effie hid behind a potted fern that brushed her shoulder. Her dress was green with lace at the elbows and at her neckline. She'd worn her rather plain brown hair swept up with a silk flower on one side. Her gloves were white. Her feet hurt in the "delightful little shoes," as Mother called them. She longed for

Ben-Hur, a cup of tea, a blanket, and the peaceful crackling of a small late-spring fire in the fireplace. Instead, she was here at the Charlemagnes' dinner party, pretending everything was as it should be and ignoring the glaring fact that Polly was home convalescing in bed, with Mother beside her anxiously praying that somehow Polly would regain her sense of reason.

But the Charlemagnes were important people, and so were the James family. With Mother preoccupied with Polly's care, it was Effie's duty to accompany her father, to carry on the façade that everything was fine. To raise her chin and defy any chatter that she and Polly had caused a stir over nothing and had clamored for attention by crying "murder."

It was more than for her own amusement that Effie hid in the corner by the plant. It didn't matter that the incident at 322 Predicament Avenue had supposedly blown over. She could still see some of the women tittering behind gloved hands.

Oh, what that Euphemia and Polly James wouldn't do for attention!

How indiscreet to be out at night, alone, as young women!

The audacity of Euphemia James! We didn't think she had it in her. Poor Polly, though it is completely understandable. The poor, wretched dying girl.

Effie squelched a scream. She would keep up pretenses for Father's sake. She would be everything she needed to be for Polly's sake. And right now, that meant drawing attention from Polly and taking any blame on her own shoulders. Even if that ruined her hopes of meeting a fine young man, being courted, marrying, building a home—everything honorable and yet so far from being attainable at the moment.

She shifted her attention back to the hosts of tonight's event. Mr. Charlemagne, owner of Charlemagne Steel and Wire Company, a manufacturer of telegraph wires, boasted that the nation was connected by message because of the Charlemagnes of the world. It was a silly boast, but one that Effie's mother took to heart, especially since Patrick Charlemagne—son and eligible bachelor—was home from the university and his travels.

"He would be a suitable match," Mother had told Effie as Effie prepared to leave the James manor that evening with her father. She'd fluffed the lace around Effie's elbow, untucking it from where it had snagged and hidden itself under the silk sleeve. "He's the eldest, a fine Christian young man, and the family is of good standing, known for their integrity."

Effie could argue with none of that, and now she watched Patrick carefully. He was of average height and build, with kind blue eyes, carefully styled dark brown hair, his trim mustache making up for a thin upper lip. Mother was right. He would make a good match, for his wife would enjoy stability, kindness, and most likely affluence. And they were already familiar with each other. Friends even. It was good to see Patrick again.

She adjusted her gloves. Hiding behind a potted plant would do nothing to increase her chances of securing a marriage with Patrick Charlemagne.

"So we meet again." The distinct baritone rumbled in Effie's ear. She yelped and twisted to look up into the cavernous eyes of Mr. Lewis Anderson.

At a loss for words, Effie cleared her throat instead.

Mr. Anderson didn't seem to notice her discomfort. "Stuffy things, dinner parties. Don't you agree?"

"No." Effie shook her head. "I rather enjoy them." Perhaps not the whole truth, but she felt irked at Mr. Anderson's sudden appearance.

"Hmm. Never mind then."

Was he goading her? Effie tilted her chin up a tad. "May I help you, Mr. Anderson?" Best to deal with the man now. Was he a journalist? He must be. His story of a missing wife hadn't set well with her. It pulled at her empathy, and Effie didn't appreciate that—especially if it were a falsehood so as to garner a story.

"I've already told you—anything you remember from the other night would be of help."

Effie eyed the man. "Are you a journalist?"

"Are you telling the truth?" He raised an eyebrow.

"You question my honesty?"

"I question why there was no sign of what you claimed happened at the house on Predicament Avenue and yet you insist you heard a woman screaming."

Effie pursed her lips.

Mr. Anderson ignored her lips and kept his eyes boring into hers. "If you were caught in a lie, you would gracefully, if possible, back away from it. The shame and embarrassment of having this sad little town turn out to gawk at a bloody scene only to find nothing? Pure poppycock, and you at the helm! Completely and reprehensibly misguided of you and your sister to claim such untruths. And you, the daughters of a respected banker?"

He'd definitely done his research. Effie fiddled with her gloved fingers.

Mr. Anderson continued. "You continue to claim you *did* hear something that night and your sister is in ill health because of it? A strange falsehood to cling to in light of your position in Shepherd. Therefore, I must pose the question again, Miss James. What did you see and hear? And please leave no detail unaccounted for."

"You're a detective then?" Effie asked, feeling every ounce of confidence seep away under the Englishman's intense stare.

"Hardly. I told you the truth, just as I believe you have told me the truth. So, with the truth established, shall we move forward?"

"Move forward?" Effie frowned.

Mr. Anderson issued a small sigh that either meant he was becoming exasperated or more likely indicated he couldn't catch a decent breath due to the clouds of perfume emanating from the ladies in the room. "Yes. Explore what you know to be true,

what I believe to be true, and what evidence will prove is true."
The dark spears of his eyes rattled Effie, leaving her shaken.

"I-I . . ." She was flustered now. "There was no evidence."

"So we've been told." Mr. Anderson leaned in closer, his breath brushing her ear. "But do you wish to let the entire town believe your sister is capable of such dramatics and lies?"

Effie drew away from him, incredulous as confusion sliced through her. "What do you mean?"

"There are those here tonight expressing sympathy for your ill sister. Others, though, claim this is all theatrics. That your sister has always loved attention, grappled for it, and now she convalesces in order to have the condolences and empathy of the people of Shepherd."

"My sister is doing no such thing!" Effie cried.

Mr. Anderson lifted his finger to his mouth to shush her. "Then you must prove it."

Effie stared at him. Had he really just taunted her by questioning her sister's honesty? Polly, whom everyone loved and adored, who was facing the last months or year of her life, curled up in her bed, unresponsive and traumatized? How dare he! How dare *anyone* accuse Polly of manipulating events for attention! Claiming a woman was murdered? It was appalling and horrible and—

"I see you're coming to understand why I have approached you once more." Mr. Anderson broke into Effie's swirling thoughts. "Only you and I believe something actually *did* happen, and if it did, then two people's welfare are at stake. That of my wife's, Isabelle Addington, and that of your sister, along with her good reputation."

"Sir . . ." Shocked, Effie struggled to find her voice again. "Whatever I did or did not hear is of no matter. Nothing was found in the house. Absolutely nothing. There is no way to prove my experience."

"I don't believe it." He turned his gaze onto the mingling

guests. "I don't believe you to be the type of woman to allow her sister to be spoken ill of."

"Excuse me?" Effie wasn't sure if his statement was a compliment or pure insult.

Mr. Anderson's expression did nothing to imply his intent. His face was one of stony seriousness that both frightened and intrigued Effie. More frightened, she confirmed to herself, and less intrigued.

"You may be my only hope, Miss James." Mr. Anderson was still perusing the guests, eyeing them with unspoken censure.

"How?" Effie noticed the lines beside his eyes, his hair that tapered over his ears as though he was two weeks beyond when he should have last had it cut. The shadow of his whiskers made his long face appear stronger, more mysterious.

"Will you accompany me there?" He turned abruptly to face her. "My man Gus will go as well. I would like to walk through the house and see if anything strikes you as different, or suspicious, or perhaps inspires a clearer memory of the night's events."

Effie frowned. "I never went in the house that night. I barely made it to the bottom stair of the back porch." She noticed Patrick Charlemagne across the room. He was engaged in a lively conversation with Bethany Todd, and Effie knew instantly that her hopes of becoming part of the Charlemagne family were dashed. Bethany was the epitome of beauty, grace, and kindness. She was also—aside from Polly—Effie's dearest friend.

Bethany deserved a pleasant, strong man such as Patrick. Effie wished the same for herself, but no. Apparently her behavior with Polly the other night had doomed her to doing penance with a strange Englishman who could easily be mistaken for an undertaker while at the same time be oddly and almost seductively handsome.

"Will you?" he asked again, his voice dripping with a mesmerizing quality that seemed to hypnotize her. And being hypnotized was never a safe position in which to find oneself.

"You told him what?" Bethany Todd stared incredulously at Effie, her eyes as big as Mother's salad plates. She had approached Effie no more than an hour after Effie had found herself agreeing to an appointment tomorrow with Mr. Anderson and his assistant Gus.

Effie wrung the gloves she'd nervously pulled from her hands with not a little desperation. "I don't know what I was thinking. I just—"

"You were enamored by a striking and foreign stranger." Bethany searched the room for Mr. Anderson, who had suspiciously vanished. She sighed dramatically. "Oh, to be wooed by a mysterious man who has no boundaries but those of his own making!"

Effie gave a small laugh, then quickly composed herself. "Bethany, you're being ridiculous. He's married—he's searching for his wife!"

"Did she run away?" Bethany tilted her head forward again, her face alight with curiosity. "Was it a torrid affair, and now he wants to find her and her lover and do away with them both? Oh, Effie! What if he's the killer and you're walking right into his trap?"

Bethany made a reasonable point. Effie mustered courage. "Really, I highly doubt that."

Bethany scowled. "Well, if you are murdered, I will tell everyone who was responsible."

Effie choked and then cleared her throat. "I appreciate your tenacity to rise to my defense."

Bethany smiled, and Effie noticed her watching Patrick Charlemagne as he chatted with another man in their spot across the room. She didn't respond to Effie but seemed to realize Effie was waiting and so turned toward her. Her blue eyes shimmered with concern. "But really, Effie, you going to that place unattended and with a stranger—it's foolhardy. Even if none of the events from a few nights ago had happened. At worst you'll be found viciously murdered in the graveyard behind the house, and at best, if anyone finds out about it, your credibility—already on delicate ground—will be shattered."

"I think that's a tad extreme." Effie stated what she wanted to believe was true, while inside she felt the nagging realization that Bethany wasn't necessarily wrong.

"Why go, Effie? Truly, why? Stay home. Let the man poke around the old house without you. Why in heaven's name did you say you would go?"

"For Polly." Effie breathed her sister's name without bothering to disguise the tremble in her voice. She met her friend's worried eyes. "Polly needs me to defend her. She cannot prove what she saw. She can't even *say* what she saw, and now she's—" Effie's hand flew to her mouth as tears choked her words.

Bethany hooked her elbow in Effie's and drew her closer. Effie fought back tears, breathing in a whiff of Bethany's perfume.

"Listen to me," Bethany pleaded. "Do you remember what happened last year with that strange man who was reported as having been seen loafing about the property? And then, just like that, he disappeared?"

Effie knew Bethany was still trying to talk her out of tomorrow's appointment with the Englishman. Effie came to her own defense by making a reasonable deduction. "But that man was some kind of peddler or wanderer. A homeless man. It's common that people are seen coming and going from there. The Oppermans have done nothing to lock the place up tight. It's merely a piece of land and an old graveyard to them. They're miserly and refuse to sell the place, so it becomes an eyesore and a draw for transients."

"Or," Bethany continued, "people have discredited what is really happening there. A fresh grave was dug a few years ago. Your own brother, Ezekiel, saw it with his own eyes."

"Yes, but it was empty. Just a hole in the ground. The Opper-mans had it filled in, and nothing came of it."

"Still, are you sure you should go with that man, Effie?" Beth-any lowered her voice and squeezed her arm around Effie's.

Effie wanted to be. "Well, no, but—"

"But?" Bethany urged.

Effie met her friend's eyes. "Polly."

Bethany sighed as she allowed her gaze to sweep the room. "I know, Effie. I know."

Effie knew she understood, but that didn't change Bethany's concern. Even so, Polly could not shield herself, and if what Mr. Anderson's observations of what others were saying were in fact true, Effie couldn't abide that. She would do anything for Polly . . . while she was still alive to love and defend.

6

GUILT MARRED an otherwise sunshine-filled afternoon. Effie had snuck like a child once again from the James manor to avoid questions from Mother, who would have something to say about her escapade with Mr. Anderson—a married man, no less. No one in Shepherd knew Mr. Anderson, so suspicions would arise were she seen alone with him. One could hardly count the elderly assistant as a proper chaperone since he too was a stranger. And foreigners, which would only add to the mystery and be fuel to the flames of wagging tongues.

Effie made sure to pull away from the window of Mr. Anderson's carriage so she could not be seen from the outside. He had met her at the corner of her street, and she had climbed into the carriage so quickly to stay hidden that she had tripped and almost landed in the man's lap.

"We're almost there, sir," Mr. Cropper—or Gus, as he'd insisted Effie call him—announced.

Mr. Anderson sat in stony silence across from Effie. His face was unreadable, no expression of friendliness or kindness, but neither did he appear cruel or wicked. He was simply impassive, and Effie gave up trying to interpret what he might be thinking.

"Ah, here we are." Gus was quite the opposite, she was finding. Congenial. Proper. Hospitable. Effie felt somewhat at ease, but it was only because of Gus, who now extended an arthritic hand to assist her from the carriage.

Mr. Anderson hopped down and offered Effie his arm. She took it, but only after a surreptitious look in both directions up and down Predicament Avenue. It wasn't a busy street, for that she was thankful. Effie caught a whiff of tobacco on Mr. Anderson's coat sleeve. A pungent, sweet, and warm scent that didn't match his aloof demeanor.

The house at 322 Predicament Avenue tilted farther toward the east, as if the recent kerfuffle there had burdened it even more. The old willow tree in the front yard waved its feathery branches like a specter in the daylight. A rickety-looking swing hung from one branch, its ropes frayed and threatening to snap if anyone attempted to sit on it. Effie stared at the peeling paint on the white-turned-gray side of the house with its two large windows. They were fogged and stained with dirt and time, like a brittle old man with rheumy eyes and horrible secrets.

"Shall we go in?" Mr. Anderson rubbed his gloved hands together, more in impatience than anticipation. "Are you afraid?" His voice cut through her hesitation.

"Of course not," she said and gathered her skirts. She wasn't afraid of the house—well, that wasn't entirely true. But he needn't know that she was also leery of him. Leery of all of it. But if she could find *anything* to corroborate Polly's claim that she'd seen a woman murdered, then Effie would grit her teeth and go forward.

Mr. Anderson's eyebrow rose as he extended his arm toward the front door. "Well then?"

Effie gave him a narrow-eyed look. He might as well realize she was here only for her sister and not for him. She climbed the few steps of the porch, watching her footing. Mr. Anderson followed with Gus trailing.

Pulling the wobbly screen door open, Effie reached for the doorknob, then hesitated, her hand hovering over the tarnished brass knob that was loose in its bore hole. "Why must I go first?" she inquired.

"Because I was being gentlemanly." Mr. Anderson dipped his head toward the door. "If you prefer that I be heroic, I am more than willing to go first."

Effie glared at him and then wavered as she saw the twinkle in his eye. He was teasing her! In the middle of searching for his wife, he was practically *flirting*! Effie sucked in a nervous breath and coughed. His mouth quirked in a grin.

This was highly inappropriate—as was the rush of attraction that flooded her for this mysterious and *married* stranger!

Effie beseeched God for stamina and wisdom as she twisted the knob, the door giving way easily. It was silent as it drifted inward, a methodical swing that made Effie wonder if there were a ghost on the other side assisting its movement.

She paused in the doorway. With daylight and sunshine, there should be nothing at all terribly frightening here, but somehow the moment the door stopped opening, Effie was the recipient of a strange brush of air that smelled of must, of time, and of something tangy and inexplicably unpleasant. Effie dared to look over her shoulder at Mr. Anderson. "Perhaps you should go first."

"Are you asking me, or will I offend you if I acquiesce?"

Englishmen were so pompous!

"This was what my great-great-grandfather fought against in 1776," Effie muttered rebelliously under her breath."

"Pardon?" Gus piped up from behind.

"It's nothing," Effie responded quickly, but she saw the spark of something in Mr. Anderson's eyes. He'd heard her remark against the Crown.

"You're quite the colonist, Miss James." This time, Mr. Anderson's mouth didn't quirk even the hint of a smile. "Now that we've established it is best that an ocean separates you from me most days, shall we proceed?"

Effie hovered a leather shoe-clad foot over the threshold.

"I've no qualms about going first, Miss James."

At the sound of a distant carriage, Effie recalled the need to remain out of sight from prying eyes. She surged ahead into an empty entryway. A hallway to the left led to an equally vacant sitting room, while a hall to the right led to the kitchen.

Her footsteps echoed on the marred hardwood floor. Cobwebs hung from the corners of the doorway to the kitchen. She scanned the room to get her bearings. Like the farmhouse itself, the kitchen was square. It consisted of a sink, a cast-iron stove, a window with a broken bottom-right pane, and a simple oak table with no decorative embellishments. On the table were two plates with gray-and-brown mounds of moldy food. A cloth napkin lay wadded on the floor beneath the table. More food was scattered across the floor, with a tin plate upside down nearby as if it had been thrown there.

Mr. Anderson moved past her, being careful with his steps. He crouched and dipped his fingertip in the food mess on the floor, then lifted it to his nose. Sniffing, he brushed his hands together to rid himself of the filth. He rose to his feet. "Did you smell any food?" he asked Effie.

"Excuse me?" She looked around for Gus and noted the old man was still at the front door. Apparently, he had no intention of coming in any farther.

"Food. Do you recall the scent of a cooked meal the night you were here?"

"No." Effie shook her head. "But I was outside, and I—"

"No matter." Mr. Anderson waved her off. "If someone had been here and had prepared a meal, I'm sure your mind would have registered it." He eyed the two plates on the table. The food was so moldy as to be unidentifiable. "That food has been there for some time. Did you hear anything else besides the woman screaming?" He turned toward the stove, running his fingers across its cold top.

"No," Effie replied, "I heard nothing else."

"Hmm." Mr. Anderson opened the oven door. He withdrew a cast-iron pot and lifted its lid. "Ah. There were potatoes for dinner." The lid clanged back onto the pot. "That would explain it."

"Explain what?" Effie had no idea what Mr. Anderson was looking for.

He didn't answer. Instead, he brushed past Effie and moved back into the entryway and the hall beyond. "The upstairs. Will you come with me?" He waited, a patient expression on his face.

Gus exchanged looks with her and motioned for her to follow.

Mr. Anderson's footsteps were heavy on the stairs. The wooden stairwell was narrow, the floral wallpaper on either side faded and peeling. Effie tried not to touch anything as she climbed behind him. Everything was coated in a layer of grime and dust. Spiderwebs hung from the ceiling, and the sunlight that met them through the window at the top of the stairs only illuminated more webs that had trapped flies and an assortment of other insects, all of them dead. The spiders were also long dead, their food stores having dried up.

Reaching the landing, Mr. Anderson surveyed the upper level of 322 Predicament Avenue: two rooms on the east side, two on the west. A short hallway split the upper level, along with the stairwell.

Effie chose to remain at the window, in the sunlight. Mr. Anderson ducked his tall frame and entered the first room. From where she stood, Effie could see it was empty. No furniture, nothing to hint at life or family or past residents. The same was true with bedroom number two. Both rooms looked out over the front of the house and the street beyond.

Mr. Anderson, after investigating the two front rooms, moved on to the third and fourth.

The third room was, to her surprise, an altogether different story from the first two. This one was furnished. The wood floor creaked loudly under Mr. Anderson's weight. A small dresser stood along the far wall. Next to it were a bed frame, void of any mattress, and a full-length mirror—a luxury for a farmhouse— tilted on its stand and reflecting their images back to them.

Mr. Anderson reached out and touched the mirror. His brow furrowed as he stepped closer to study a seam in the mirror's walnut frame. He thumbed the edge of it, then moved to look around at its back. There was the briefest intake of breath, quick and sudden-like. Then he lifted his face to Effie with no evidence to convey that anything was out of the ordinary. "Please come," he said.

Effie walked toward Mr. Anderson and the mirror, her footsteps across the floor sounding hollow to her ears. For the first time since coming upstairs, Effie heard nothing. No clock ticking. No birds singing. No noise from the street or voices of passersby.

A spirit could whisper, and she would hear it. The skin on her arms and legs grew cold beneath her dress. She wrapped her arms around herself, feeling her hands start to tremble.

"Look at this," Mr. Anderson said, pointing.

Effie came closer, aware of his tall frame near hers. He didn't move aside for her, so she was forced to press into his arm and shoulder to see what he was showing her.

On the back of the framed mirror was brown paper backing, put there to protect it from getting scratched or marred. The paper was stained with a spatter of dark brown spots.

"What is it?" Effie breathed.

"You can't tell?" Mr. Anderson moved toward the dresser positioned against the wall, off-center from where most would have placed it. There was a loud scraping sound, and Effie jumped, twisting where she stood by the mirror to see Mr. Anderson shoving the dresser away from the wall into the center of the room.

It was now obvious to Effie, and so awful in its reality, that she wanted nothing to do with it. Behind where the dresser had stood, the wall was stained with the same dark spatter as the back of the mirror. It appeared that whatever had stained the wall had run like trails of water down it. A dried, sticky mess covered the wood floor where the dresser had been. A trail of it ran across the floor where Mr. Anderson had pushed the dresser away.

Mr. Anderson towered over the ugly stain, hands at his waist. His jaw clenched and unclenched before he spoke again. "You see, Miss James? I believe you *did* hear a woman screaming the other night."

"No. No, it's not . . ." Effie couldn't disregard the awful sight of the blood that cursed this room with it stains. Stains that someone had taken the time to hide by rearranging the furniture. "Polly and I wouldn't have seen inside this room. It's upstairs. Polly looked only in the window on the back porch, the one with the view into the kitchen."

Mr. Anderson seemed to weigh Effie's words. With his shoulders set, he strode from the room and took the stairs down two at a time. Effie hurried after him, hiking up her dress so she didn't trip. The pounding of their feet echoed in the empty house. The walls were like a coffin that hid the secrets of the body it entombed. And yet there wasn't a body. Only blood. Only the remnants of something awful and terrible.

Effie rounded the corner into the kitchen, grasping at her throat as she watched Mr. Anderson push the table from its position. The floor beneath it was clean with the exception of the scraps of old food, crumbs, mouse droppings, and dust. He kicked over a chair and growled.

Gus hobbled into the kitchen behind Effie, worry etched into every wrinkle on his face. "Mr. Anderson?"

Effie hugged the wall as Mr. Anderson ignored them both and grabbed hold of the cast-iron cookstove, yanking it back and forth. Its metal chimney groaned and protested, as did the stove itself. Too heavy to move aside completely, Mr. Anderson managed only to haul it a few inches from where it had sat, enough to bend the stovepipe. Effie startled as it popped free from the stove with a clamor.

"Mr. Anderson!" Gus attempted to hurry to his employer's side, but Mr. Anderson had already ducked behind the stove, and in a swift motion he grunted and then stood. A butcher knife was clutched in his hand, blood clotted along its wooden handle and the blade.

He held up the knife, his face an array of expressions that made Effie take a step backward. Not that she feared *him*, but the blade in his hand was further proof of Polly's claims. It was the reason why her sister was curled into a state in her bed, traumatized, her life wasting away in silence.

"This knife." Mr. Anderson flung the weapon onto the stovetop with a clang. "That's what your sister saw! Whoever killed Isabelle finished her off here in the kitchen. She must have escaped and attempted to flee. That was the scream you heard."

Effie sucked in a sob. If that were true, then—

"But where is she?" Gus's question sliced through the kitchen. A kitchen that pretended to know nothing but had witnessed everything. A room and floor and walls that had been saturated with murderous truth and were now silent.

Mr. Anderson stilled as he noted a cupboard against the wall beneath the window beside the back door. He hauled it aside and stared at the floor beneath.

The stains beneath where the cupboard had stood told the story. A testament to the violence Polly and Effie had innocently stumbled upon, a violence Polly had witnessed the last throes of.

"But . . ." Gus choked, his voice weakened by age and shock. "Where is Isabelle?"

Was Isabelle Addington the woman Polly had seen? Effie clapped her palm over her mouth and stumbled from the room, through the entryway, and out the front door. She gulped for fresh air, ignoring the open carriage that wheeled by and the curious looks from its occupants. She held on to the doorframe to steady herself. Was it Isabelle Addington—Mr. Anderson's wife—or not? This was the evidence that had been hidden. Sloppily hidden and sloppily overlooked.

It validated Polly's spiral into petrified silence.

It vindicated Effie's need to prove her sister right.

And it only worsened the truth.

Death had indeed come to 322 Predicament Avenue.

Cold, Dead, But Never Buried
Podcast hosted by Sebastian Blaine

*I*S A SOUL seduced into murder? Does it crave death like a child after sweets? Does it come upon a soul like a demon taking over the body and senses? Or perhaps man is just that innately evil, just as Cain was toward his brother, Abel, and we are all but a footstep away from committing the dastardly deed ourselves.

This month we'll be exploring the 1901 unsolved mystery of the death of Isabelle Addington at 322 Predicament Avenue. We'll investigate who she was, or who she is thought to have been. We'll take the listener with us as we journey to her place of death. We'll question if Isabelle still remains there, crying out for resolution. We'll also investigate the origins of Shepherd, Iowa, a little town nestled in the Midwest. A town of peace, shattered by the brutal stealing of life—twice—with no resolution, neither then nor now.

7

NORAH

Present Day

NORAH THUMBED the pause button on her phone, ceasing the accented voice of Sebastian Blaine and his podcast. Her hand trembled as she gripped the device. The man of the hour was loafing on the back porch overlooking the old gravestones, coffee mug in hand, bare feet propped on another porch chair. His dark curls were askew, his glasses framing his rugged features, and for a brief moment Norah reconsidered. Then she remembered Naomi.

Norah shoved the screen door open, stepping onto the porch. Sebastian looked up at her lazily with a sideways grin that both attracted and irritated her further.

"Good mornin'."

"What's this?" Norah held out her phone for Sebastian to see. On the screen was the podcast's episode art.

An eyebrow lifted. "My podcast?"

Norah sucked in an anxious breath. "My sister's murder." It was an accusation without question.

Sebastian dropped his feet from their perch on the chair and leaned forward. "I never mentioned your sister."

"You said 'twice.'" Norah waved her phone in the air.

"Twice?"

Was he really that obtuse? "The brutal stealing of life—*twice*." Norah parroted the podcast episode that had been posted earlier that morning.

"Aye, so there's been murders here in Shepherd. But I didn't mention your sister's name."

"It won't take a rocket scientist to figure it out." Norah could hear the bite in her words. Like a cornered and wounded animal snapping at someone whose intentions they couldn't predict. That was Sebastian Blaine. His friendly nature, his warm expressions—they were all a cover to be the perfect patron of her B and B so he could weasel his way in and create a sensational series of crime podcasts. Norah continued, trying to temper her words but not succeeding. Her voice quavered with frustration and not a little anxiety. "The stories of Isabelle Addington are one thing, but my sister's murder is *my* life too. My story."

"It's public information." Sebastian's answer was far from comforting.

Norah jammed her phone into the pocket of her jeans, trying to calm the shaking of her hands. He didn't know—he couldn't know—what it was like to have a sister brutally taken from you. To not know who was safe and who wasn't. To have a killer never identified. To never be able to fully grieve the tragic loss of her twin, let alone find closure in a case that had grown so cold, there was a good chance it would never get solved.

"Listen . . ." Sebastian patted the empty chair in invitation for Norah to be seated.

She ignored it. She didn't want to be nearer to him.

Sebastian accepted her refusal, palmed his coffee mug, and

cleared his throat. "I promise, I'm not plannin' on investigatin' your sister's murder. I'm here to focus on the story of Isabelle Addington, her history an' what happened to her."

"Then why allude to more than one murder in Shepherd?"

Sebastian expelled a sigh. "Because it's interestin'! Most towns these days can't say their crime rate is so low that there's only been two killin's in a hundred years. It was a statement of fact, not an outin' of your sister's circumstances."

"You don't owe me my privacy." Norah stated the thought that raced through her mind, as much as she hated it. "But slander—"

"There's no slander in a fact, Norah." Sebastian stood, probably sensing the urgency in Norah and maybe catching on to her veiled threat. Not that she would have the guts to do anything about it, but Sebastian had run away with Naomi's story on his podcast, which was what frightened Norah the most. Naomi's story wasn't just her story. It was part of the public record. If done properly, Sebastian could cover it with little threat of recourse from Norah. And it was a story that oddly paralleled Isabelle Addington's murder from 1901 . . .

"Norah?" Sebastian's deep voice soothed her nerves, though she didn't exactly want it to. That was probably why his podcast was such a hit. A sultry male voice with a Lancashire accent?

"What?" She eyed him, guarded.

"Sit down, would ya? Let's chat for a bit. Get it out in the open before this becomes a problem."

Instead of sitting down, Norah moved to the porch rail that Otto had repainted white just last summer. She looked out at the backyard, to the edge of the woods beyond and the gravestones that tipped and sank into the earth, burdened by time. One grave stood out among the rest. A new stone with roses carved in each corner. It was front and center in the small cemetery, its date boasting a new century compared to the graves behind it. Old graves. Old ghosts. Forgotten people.

And then there was Naomi.

Norah sensed Sebastian's presence beside her as he joined her at the rail. He followed her gaze.

"Your sister?"

Norah nodded.

"It's nice to have her so close." Sebastian's words were rife with understanding that took Norah aback for a second.

She gave him a sideways glance. "I can't have people coming here to fawn over her grave because she's some true-crime celebrity victim."

"I've no intention of doin' that to your sister," Sebastian promised. He shifted, and Norah caught a whiff of his cologne. Pine mixed with something fresh. Maybe it was just his deodorant. Either way, he smelled good. He smelled safe. Which was not at all what Norah wanted him to smell like.

"It's been almost thirteen years, and we have no answers," Norah stated, her vision caressing her sister's name etched into the gravestone: *Naomi Elizabeth Richman.* "She had so many dreams. This place, it was her dream."

"The house?" Sebastian clarified.

Norah nodded. "Naomi loved the lore and the whispers in the night. The ghost stories of Isabelle Addington. The tales of her murder, the disappearance of Isabelle's body, and all the unanswered questions about what actually happened at 322 Predicament Avenue in 1901."

Sebastian gave a small laugh. "I think your sister and I would've gotten along quite well."

Norah sighed. "Probably." She turned to Sebastian. "Please don't hurt Naomi by making her story popular."

Sebastian looked down at her, his eyes soft behind the lenses of his chic glasses. "You mean don't hurt you?"

Norah didn't answer. It felt too selfish to admit that he was right. That it was herself she was trying to protect. She'd come this far, and to have Naomi's murder revisited now and be aired publicly?

"I won't hurt you."

Norah heard the man's promise. She just didn't believe him.

Norah didn't trust anyone who just showed up on her doorstep without a reservation. She was instantly suspicious of such people. Not to mention she was still shaken from her interaction an hour ago with Sebastian Blaine. So much so that she'd considered the idea of putting the house on Predicament Avenue up for sale and finding a small nondescript apartment somewhere where she could hide for the rest of her life.

A young woman wearing a green chunky stocking cap, long dark hair hanging over her shoulders, perched on the porch. A smile wreathed her friendly face and was eerily familiar, though Norah couldn't place it. She wore ripped blue jeans, a cropped vintage T-shirt, and an oversized cardigan to ward off the chill of the morning spring air.

"Hey! I just arrived in the area, and someone recommended staying here. You wouldn't happen to have a room available, would you?" The perky girl's voice was equally cheerful.

Norah assessed the girl warily, even as she realized she really was becoming a suspicious, prematurely old lady of Predicament Avenue. She did have a spare room. Three, in fact. She needn't put the young woman in the *death room*, as Norah had begun to think of Mr. Miller's room. Instead, her new guest could stay in bedroom number two. A room with no history of sightings of Isabelle Addington . . .

Norah couldn't afford another death-by-ghost situation.

"Come inside." She stepped aside, feeling utterly inept at greeting guests with warmth and hospitality. It was everything Norah could do not to ask for a full criminal background check, references, and a search on the dark web to make certain her guests were who they said they were. It was an extreme reaction—exaggerated and ridiculous—but that was what happened when your sister was abducted, assaulted, murdered, and left to decay in the woods.

Norah fought back the hovering familiarity of her PTSD. People didn't help. The new guest wouldn't help.

She had picked the wrong career.

She had picked it for Naomi's sake.

"Harper?" The incredulous male voice echoed down the stairs, along with the thudding footsteps of Sebastian Blaine.

Norah shrank into the wall as the young woman took a quick step forward and launched herself into Sebastian's embrace.

"Dad!"

Dad?

"Why are you here?" Sebastian held his daughter out from him, his hands on her upper arms. "I thought you were in South America with your mother?"

Harper screwed her face into a *yeah-right* expression. "Mom's lost her mind. I swear. She's somewhere in Patagonia now, exploring the natural world with her boyfriend."

Sebastian shot a look toward Norah, who was frozen in place. He cleared his throat and lowered his voice. "How 'bout we chat on that later? How did you know where I was?"

Harper waggled her phone in the air. "Find-a-friend, bruh."

"Okay, okay." Sebastian looked uncomfortable. He kept glancing at Norah, who frankly had no desire or reason to move. She could escape, but then she'd have to come back and check Harper into a room. Best to get it done so it was out of the way.

"Can I get you checked in?" Norah forced herself to offer a wobbly smile.

Harper met her eyes. "Sure! That'd be great."

"Wait." Sebastian held up his palms. "You're *stayin'*?"

"Is that a problem?" Harper hefted a sigh and craned her neck from left to right as if prepping for a fight.

"We talked about this." Sebastian's tone shifted into a fatherly sternness Norah recognized from her youth.

"*You* talked about this." Harper gave her dad a flippant pat on his shoulder. "I just listened. I didn't agree to anything. Besides, you know your podcast is better when I'm involved."

"I don't need my nineteen-year-old daughter investin' her life into crime-solvin'."

Norah could tell there was more to Sebastian's words. The way his countenance darkened made it clear something else was troubling him.

Harper turned her shoulder to Sebastian and graced Naomi with a grin. "So, about this room . . ."

Norah winced in remembrance, her gaze settling on a framed picture across her bedroom resting on her dresser. She went to the picture and picked it up, the silver frame cool beneath her fingers. Her thumb rubbed over Naomi's face, her smile frozen in time at nineteen. Nineteen years of age and then she was no more, leaving behind a tsunami of memories that never lessened with time. The notion that time healed and lessened pain was a myth. Time merely mocked the absence, taunting, heralding the missing pieces that could never be replaced again by anyone. Ever. Naomi was gone, and every eternal hope or promise or effort of faith felt more like pouring alcohol on an open wound. God was on His throne, yes, but His promise that He'd walk alongside her in grief was as elusive to Norah as a fairy tale.

Naomi's blue eyes twinkled up at her. The graduation photograph had captured her playful and adventurous spirit. Even then, at nineteen, they were as different as night and day. Naomi was blond as corn silk, lithe and athletic, outgoing, vivacious, extroverted. Norah was the dark twin, and in more ways than one. She was olive-skinned like their father, with wavy brown hair, thoughtful and cautious, friendly yet less likely to attract a crowd with her demure personality. Their mother had always teased that although they looked and acted nothing alike, they shared the same soul. Norah believed that to be true because half of hers was missing now.

She set the picture frame back on the dresser, facedown. Looking at Naomi tonight dredged up more than just the pain of grief and the stark awareness of death. It revived the nightmares, replayed scenes from that fateful day. The lights of squad cars flashing outside the front window of 322 Predicament Avenue. Her mother's wail, Aunt Eleanor's strained voice, and her father's horrified shouts. It had taken place right here in this very bedroom on the first floor, when Norah had leaped from the bed and barreled toward the door. Two police officers had caught her, grabbing her around the waist as she screamed and beat their arms. Her urge to race out into the night, to chase after Naomi's ghost had compelled Norah.

"She's gone, miss." The officer's grip was painful around her waist.

Norah screamed, kicked, clawed at his hands. "Let me go!" She was half his size, and he was determined. She could smell his aftershave, coffee on his breath. This was what she would remember of this night. The night her sister's body had been discovered. The night they'd confirmed that Naomi was truly and forever dead.

Norah gave her memories a stern and forceful beating into submission. She had spent almost thirteen years learning how to leave her house again. Learning how to breathe without her oxygen competing with panic. Learning how to grieve . . . no. No. She had not learned that. She had barely learned to survive. Grieving was an entirely different mountain, and one she would die on.

Annoyed that she was allowing her thoughts to take her back to the dark places she had spent so many years trying to escape from, Norah reached for a sweatshirt and pulled it on over her head. Coffee and alcohol were out of the question—they did nothing to help assuage her anxiety. She needed decaffeinated tea with a splash of milk, no sugar. Her nutritionist had told her sugar was the devil when it came to a nervous system's proper functioning. Sugar had a negative effect on her mental health and emotional well-being. It was like pouring gasoline on a glowing ember.

Norah trudged down the hallway that was lit only by small light fixtures mounted on the wall, milk-glass sconces from the 1920s. She glanced at the grandfather clock in the entryway as she passed it. One o'clock in the morning. Sleep was elusive as usual, and Naomi felt close. So close. Norah paused in the doorway, her vision drifting to the darkness of the sitting room to her right. Once she'd thought she'd seen a shadow there, the form of a woman. Now her eyes searched the darkness in a desperate hope that a spirit would linger there. It wouldn't be Isabelle Addington's either. That legend was of little interest to Norah. No, she wished to be haunted by her sister. To be followed by her spirit. To feel Naomi's breath on her neck, and the chill of the air as Naomi entered the room. She ached for the comfort of knowing Naomi was wandering beside her.

Yet there was nothing but darkness. Stillness. The ticktock of the grandfather clock. Norah forfeited her irrational hopes and padded into the darkened kitchen. A nightlight over the porcelain farm sink cast a yellow glow across the stove. She eyed the teapot but opted to fill her mug with water and pop it into the microwave. Two minutes later, she dropped a peppermint tea bag into the hot water and added a splash of milk. Making her way back toward the hallway, Norah stilled at the bottom of the stairs. She looked up toward the second floor.

Murmuring voices drifted down from the upper level— insistent, argumentative. Concerned, Norah clutched her mug of tea with both hands and climbed the first few stairs only to hesitate once more when she made out the voices of Sebastian and Harper.

"Dad!" Harper's plea was watery with tears.

Sebastian's tone was void of any of his typical pleasantry and calmness. Instead, it was sharp, stifled only by the obvious attempt to keep his voice down. "You need to leave. You shouldn't be here."

"And go where? Grandma and Grandpa's? Dad, I'm not going back there."

"Why not? They're chuffed about you."

"I don't care how proud they are, they're not *you*."

Silence. Norah's grip tightened on her mug. She really should go back to her room and leave the father and daughter alone. Eavesdropping was poor form. It was evident Sebastian wasn't happy his daughter had followed him here, but the why of it confused Norah.

Sebastian cleared his throat. The old floorboards groaned beneath his weight. "I don' know why you've come here, Harper. I've nothin' to offer you, an' you know that."

There was desperation in Sebastian's tone but also a firmness that brooked no further argument. She couldn't imagine what Harper must be feeling as her father sliced through her hopes with his words.

Nothing to offer? He was a successful podcaster, well established in the world of true-crime entertainment. Despite the fact that true crime was considered *entertainment*, Norah wanted to hurry up the remaining steps and argue on Harper's behalf. Nothing to offer? How about being a father? How about love? How about stability?

Harper's next words were resigned. "I've had nineteen birthdays, with most of them being celebrated by you with a gift card. But maybe—" Harper's voice broke—"maybe I need more. Maybe you just need to *be* more."

Wow. Norah held her breath.

"Go to bed, Harper. We're both tired." Now Sebastian's tone was one of defeat. Then came the firm closing of a door.

Harper sniffed, drawing in a shuddering breath. There were footsteps, the house giving up Harper's whereabouts with its creaking as she traversed the hardwood floor in the hallway. And then her bedroom door—bedroom number two—closed.

All was silent.

Norah was more certain than ever that this house was a tomb that sucked hope from the hearts of anyone who occupied it. It was as if the sun had gone down at 322 Predicament Avenue the night Naomi's murdered body had been found, and it had never risen again.

8

I GOT THE BUSHES all trimmed." Otto's announcement came on the heels of Norah's phone ringing. She waved at him with a smile of thanks. He plodded over to the coffeepot, making himself at home like the boys had done all her life. She drew comfort from the familiarity of Otto's presence and the way he puttered about the place as though it were his own home.

"Do you have a few minutes to talk?"

Norah turned her back to Otto and shrank onto a kitchen chair. The voice of her attorney, Rebecca Kline, in her ear did nothing to bring her inner peace.

"I don't want you to become overconcerned," Rebecca stated. "I know what happened there two days ago with the death of one of your guests. I half expected you to reach out to me, so now I'm calling you."

Norah pressed the phone to her ear harder than needed. "I didn't think there was anything to be worried about legally." Which wasn't completely true, considering Dover had advised her to seek counsel.

Rebecca cleared her throat. "Well, theoretically, you're right.

Nothing at your business was the cause of Mr. Miller's sudden death, but we can't ignore the fact that he did die at your house. This means, if Mrs. Miller is motivated, she and her attorneys may seek retribution."

"But I didn't do anything," Norah argued.

"Still, if she claims something in the house was responsible for Mr. Miller's heart attack, and if she can get any medical documentation to back that up, you could have a lawsuit on your hands. It's unlikely, but possible."

"Because of a ghost?" Norah looked up as Sebastian entered the kitchen. Did the man never leave the B and B? Never go anywhere else? He hovered around the place like someone with no purpose in life.

Otto pulled out a chair, his wrinkled face drawn in question as he listened to Norah's one-sided conversation.

Rebecca laughed nervously. "Well, I've done a bit of research on this type of thing. Thankfully, the legal world hasn't gone so off the wall as to litigate successful lawsuits against ghosts. However, if Mrs. Miller and her attorneys can make the claim that you run a haunted house essentially—meaning you capitalize on its notorious history, either directly or indirectly, as a draw for your clientele—then an argument could be made that your place of business contributed to literally scaring someone to death. It's why the owners of some promoted haunted houses hand out waivers for people to sign before they're allowed inside."

"I don't run a *haunted house*. I run a bed-and-breakfast." Norah hated the way her voice sounded defensive.

Otto reached out and patted her knee in a grandfatherly gesture of comfort.

Sebastian was pouring himself a cup of coffee, but Norah could tell he was listening intently too. The privacy in this house was nonexistent.

Rebecca continued, carefully measuring her words. "You're right, Norah. You don't advertise the place as a haunted-house attraction like at Halloween. You do, however, have a page on your website devoted entirely to the story of Isabelle Addington, as well as guest testimonies that they've seen and/or interacted with her spirit. It's set up as a draw to bring in future clients."

"I do?" Norah frowned.

"Haven't you looked at your site?" Rebecca sounded surprised.

Norah looked to Otto, trying to draw strength from his sympathetic eyes. "Yes . . . I mean, sort of, but when I inherited this place from Aunt Eleanor last year, along with the website, I just assumed you'd looked over everything connected with the business." Wasn't that what attorneys were for? She didn't want to add that she'd made it a habit to avoid the internet—including her own website. It was all too overwhelming. Apparently, she was a pathetic excuse for a business owner.

Rebecca was silent for a moment, and then Norah heard her carefully controlled intake of breath. "Norah, I'm just cautioning you that we should be ready. There are loopholes should this become a lawsuit, though I can't imagine any lawyer in their right mind would take on a case like this. But your website *does* claim the house is haunted, and you *do* have an ancient graveyard at the back of your lot that adds to the allure. Add that together, and without a waiver releasing you from any responsibility, they could make it their contention that the ghost itself is a fabrication made to entertain and scare your guests. In this scenario, that fabrication took things too far and the apparition or actor—take your pick—again, literally scared Mr. Miller to death by way of a heart attack."

Norah's mind was spinning now. This was all based on possibilities and wild theories. "Can't we just talk to Mrs. Miller and work something out, avoid a lawsuit?"

"Her husband just died—she's upset, grieving." Rebecca's voice was grave. "Which means what you propose isn't likely to happen. Not to mention, if she *hasn't* thought of pursuing any of this, then we don't want to inadvertently provide her with the idea."

Norah didn't care for Rebecca's cut-and-dried way of dealing with the issue. "Well, maybe we can . . ." Her words trailed as Sebastian sat down across from her at the table. With Otto and Sebastian there, Norah should have felt reassured, like everything was going to be all right. Instead, a feeling of claustrophobia was spiraling toward severe anxiety. She didn't have the money to lay out to protect herself against the implausible what-ifs of a grieving widow's claim, one that threatened to put Norah out of business.

Rebecca, unaware of how Norah was churning inside, wasn't finished yet. "So here's what we do. Let's prepare a response so that, in the event this does go south, we're not caught with our proverbial pants down."

"What should our response be?" Norah put the phone on speaker and set it on the table. There was no use hiding anything now. Sebastian had been there the moment Mr. Miller died, and Otto was just—well, Norah needed him.

"There are some basic things we can say and do. I can run through those with you, but first we need to get our story straight about Isabelle Addington and any influence she has had or still has on your property."

"She's dead." Norah's blanket statement made Sebastian's eyebrows shoot upward.

"Yes, but if she haunts—"

"She's *dead*, Rebecca. She's not roaming the halls in the night or—" Norah stopped. Could she honestly say that? Hadn't she just last night searched the darkness for Isabelle's ghost, wishing to see her spirit but hoping it was Naomi's instead?

"Okay. Here's what we need. Compile what you know about Isabelle Addington's murder back in, what, 1901? And look into the property records of the place. See if there's any other history anyone could dig up and say influences the *haunting* atmosphere. Have you used the old cemetery to attract guests? Tours of it?"

"There are only seventeen graves there. Hardly worth charging people for tours." Norah was irritated by the thought. She had no intention of bringing curiosity seekers to Naomi's peaceful place of rest.

"Good. So, you're not collecting money for haunted tours?"

"Of course not." She glared at the phone.

Rebecca was unfazed on the other end. "I'm not saying we need to panic, but just be prepared. I realize Mr. Miller died of natural causes, but your property has already been linked to Isabelle Addington and . . ." Rebecca broke off, hesitating.

Norah could feel the blood drain from her face.

Otto moaned quietly.

Sebastian Blaine had the decency to wince.

Rebecca cleared her throat. Her voice gentled. "Norah, you run a business out of the only house in Shepherd ever to be associated with murder. And the fact that you and your sister were *living* in the house with your aunt when Naomi went missing . . . well, it ups the sensational factor. Someone looking to take advantage of your property's history associated with the only two killings in Sheperd—to make some connection to Mr. Miller's heart attack—well, it could get ugly, not to mention expensive, even if it's not something I see as a legitimate threat. You're also the only family in town who's had a family member murdered. That isn't something we can just ignore. Coincidental? Maybe. Something a bunch of overambitious lawyers think they can build a lawsuit on for a poor elderly widow whose husband was frightened to death? I doubt it, but there's always the media, and now you have a popular true-crime podcaster as your guest!"

Norah shot a glance at Sebastian, who kept his eyes focused on the phone in the middle of the table. He didn't seem all that perturbed, and Rebecca had no idea that he was listening in on the conversation.

Norah exchanged looks with Otto, whose eyes expressed

concern. "I don't think Sebastian intends to cover Naomi's story—just the historical one."

Rebecca gave a small laugh over the phone. "Okay. But let's be prepared anyway. For now, and for anything in the future that could come up."

Norah didn't respond. She couldn't. She stared at the phone until Rebecca issued a hesitant farewell with a promise to touch base in a day or two.

"I can't do this," Norah whimpered into her palms.

Otto mumbled a crotchety oath under his breath. "I always said humanity is devolving instead of getting smarter."

"There isn't any action or claims yet, and there's no press to speak of." Sebastian's words made Norah feel a tiny bit better. But then considering who'd said them . . .

Sebastian shifted his eyes to Norah. She lifted her gaze to meet his and was surprised by how she was drawn to the understanding she saw there. After his rude rebuttal to his daughter last night, she hadn't felt particularly warm toward him this morning.

"I think I can help you," Sebastian added. "This is what I do anyway. It's why I'm here. I came to this place to research the cold case of Isabelle Addington, so why don't we work together? It will help me, and it will help you. We'll collect the facts, explore the history, and—"

"And sensationalize Naomi's murder while you're at it?" Otto's gruff voice interrupted.

Sebastian appeared to be offended by Otto's harsh words, who was only trying to protect Norah. "No. I've already told Norah that has never been my intent. Norah's family's story is not—"

"But you can't just ignore it either." Norah stated the brutal reality of it. Even Rebecca had been less than subtle when she'd brought it up. "My sister and Isabelle Addington are the only two known murders in Shepherd, Iowa. They were both attached to this place, and both murders remain unsolved."

"Then let's solve them." Sebastian turned his coffee mug between his hands, the mug making a scraping sound on the table.

Norah noticed him glance at Otto. Sebastian's smile was cautiously kind. "I'll be careful with Norah, Otto. Don't worry."

Otto's bushy brows drew into a protective v. "You'd better," he groused. "She's our girl—the only one we got left."

Norah's heart ached at the thought. Aunt Eleanor had died, Naomi killed. Otto was right. Norah was the last to take care of 322 Predicament Avenue. She was living out her murdered sister's dream. Part of her wished she could have switched places with Naomi. Naomi would have risen to this occasion with energy. Norah merely prayed and wished it all to go away. It was a never-ending nightmare.

Norah tugged on her cardigan, the spring air nippy. She slipped her feet into clogs and stepped out onto the back porch of the farmhouse Aunt Eleanor had purchased over fifty years ago. Her aunt then turned her attention to bringing the historic building back from what would have been an inevitable death. Eleanor had poured her whole self into restoring the dilapidated house. And now? Now Norah owned perhaps one of the most beautiful old farmhouses in Shepherd, if not the most shrouded in lore. And, for better or for worse, having a cemetery in the backyard only added to the mystery and aura of the place.

She tugged the door shut. The knocker against the antique lion head pounded its iron-on-iron announcement. A brooding maple tree extending its branches overhead was budding with the promise of green leaves. A squirrel hopped from branch to branch, chattering at being disturbed. Beyond the maple, the patchy spring lawn was dotted with gravestones, some tilting east, some broken at their ornate granite tops, others sunken into the earth. It wasn't a large cemetery. It boasted seventeen graves of seventeen forgotten people, with three of the markers marking nine of the souls who'd died. Father, mother, child. Father, mother, child. A pattern that was repetitive not only here but in small family graveyards throughout the Midwest.

Movement among the forgotten graves snagged Norah's attention, and she stiffened . . . only to relax when she noticed it was Harper. Her dark hair was pulled back into a ponytail, her arms wrapped around herself as she stood, back to Norah, staring down at a flat-topped marker.

Something about Harper's dejected young form tugged Norah toward her. So different from herself at nineteen, her interaction with Harper yesterday had reminded her of Naomi. Maybe that was what had compelled her, a memory.

Harper looked up as Norah approached. She sniffed and, with her sleeve, wiped her eyes. They were red-rimmed. That she'd been crying was something the young woman couldn't hide. The feeling of offense toward Sebastian resurfaced in Norah.

"Are you all right?" Norah asked.

Harper hugged herself tighter. Her brilliant pink hoodie hung over her petite frame like a blanket of emotional protection. She nodded. "I'm fine."

"I-I heard you and your father last night," Norah ventured.

Harper gave a little sigh. "Sorry."

"No, no. I was awake. I just didn't want you to think I'd been spying." Norah stuffed her hands into the deep pockets of her chunky cardigan.

Harper sniffed again. "Dad means well, I guess. My parents are free spirits, and I was never part of their plan. They never married or anything, and a kid sort of messes up the plans of dreamers."

Norah didn't press Harper for anything more. She knew what it was like to have people poke and prod at your private emotions.

Harper shifted her feet, nodding at the marker in the ground. Its granite top was so worn, the words that had been etched into it were illegible. "I wonder who this was. If they feel forgotten today or if they don't even care where they're buried."

Norah looked down at the stone. She'd seen it many times since she was a girl. "There aren't any records that I know of for this graveyard."

"It's so sad," Harper concluded, still staring at it. "Being forgotten. A whole life was lived, and now . . . it doesn't even matter. The world just goes on without you after you die."

Norah gave Harper a sideways study. She wasn't a therapist, but she'd done enough therapy herself to hear the undertones of loneliness and the burden of something deeper.

Harper dug the toe of her shoe into the grass. "Dad and I, we're a bit too similar, to be honest. We both like to get into things and figure them out. I just wish—" she hesitated—"I wish sometimes he'd figure *me* out."

"If you need to talk to someone—" Norah started.

"I'm pregnant," Harper blurted out.

Well, she *had* been going to recommend the name of her therapist. Norah fidgeted with a button on her sweater. She was *not* someone who was emotionally capable of helping Harper with something like this.

Harper turned to face Norah. "Dad doesn't know."

Norah prayed for some sort of supernatural grace to know what to say. She had no words. She wasn't upset, she wasn't judgmental, she was just . . . what did a person say to a young woman who was carrying a child and whose parents didn't know? The world today was more understanding of such things, so she assumed parents would be too. This stuff happened. It was a matter of figuring it out. But the experience had to be traumatic all the same. Having a baby was life-changing—no, life-*altering*.

Harper swiped at another tear. "I was dating this guy, and then we broke up two months ago. I just figured it out—I don't think I'm more than ten weeks along. I came here 'cause Mom, frankly, won't give . . . well, and I can't tell Grandma and Grandpa. They're old-fashioned, churchgoing and all that." Harper sucked in a wobbly breath. "I am too. Not old-fashioned, but I have faith and grew up going to church 'cause of Grandma and Grandpa, and I vowed I'd not do anything until I was married . . ."

Norah really had nothing to say now. Not that faith and church were foreign to her. She'd grown up much the same way. But when Naomi had died, the idea of faith seemed so distant, so much like a fairy tale.

"I figure Dad will be the most understanding—which sounds weird, I know. But I have to get up the guts to tell him." Harper jammed her hands into the front pocket of her hoodie. "But he flies solo. He always has. Mom said he didn't stick around much after I was born, and . . . I don't know. A girl needs her dad, right? Is that too much to ask?"

Harper leveled large expectant eyes on Norah, as if she had some sort of monumental wisdom to offer from her thirty-two years of life. But her life hadn't been like most. Her dad had always been there, sure, but after Naomi's death, Norah became an additional burden because of her own emotional terrors. And now that she was over thirty and finally standing on her own? Mom and Dad had hightailed it out of Shepherd for a much-needed time of restoration in a place that didn't scream of Naomi's memory.

Norah realized Harper was still waiting, watching for a response. She cleared her throat. "I-I don't know what to say."

Harper smiled. "Thanks."

Norah gave her a confused look.

"For listening." Harper nodded. "You're the first person I've told, and I didn't really want advice so much as someone to listen and not look like they were going to pass out at the news." She laughed nervously, then nudged the flat-top grave marker with her shoe. "Why is it easier to tell strangers things?"

Norah squeezed her eyes closed for a long moment and then opened them to reflect back the question Harper had just asked.

"I'm not sure I'm the best person to ask if you want to feel better about things. I can barely leave my own house."

Harper reached out to squeeze Norah's elbow in a gentle show of camaraderie. "Sometimes life is scary, isn't it?"

Norah grimaced but nodded. "Sometimes I envy the people buried here. The stillness. The peace."

"But death is scary too," Harper said.

Norah nodded in agreement.

"So, how do we not be afraid?"

It was a question Norah had been trying to answer for thirteen years.

9

EFFIE

1901
Shepherd, Iowa

THE NEWSPAPER SCREAMED the headline *Murder at 322 Predicament Avenue* the following morning, even though by then it wasn't news to anyone. The rumors of death and mayhem at the abandoned house had revitalized within hours of Mr. Anderson's reporting of their findings to the local magistrate. Of course, the lure of his own story became fodder for gossip as well. An Englishman, his missing wife—Isabelle Addington—and now this discovery? A lurid and macabre ending to his search perhaps? Or was it a secret and torrid affair that had ended in murder? A missing body? Perhaps Mr. Anderson wasn't as innocent as he made himself out to be. Tongues wagged behind closed doors and gloved hands.

Effie shrank into the settee in the sitting room of the manor and wished it all to go away. Her mother snapped the newspaper in her hands and whimpered as she read it. Effie exchanged looks with her friend Bethany, who sat opposite her, the most apologetic look on her pretty face that Effie had ever seen.

"I'm so sorry," Bethany said, rushing to amend the snap of the newspaper. "I saw it this morning and felt you should see it as soon as possible."

"Of course we should!" The paper rustled as their mother folded it and tossed it with a dramatic flair onto a side table. Katherine James smoothed back the grays of her otherwise dark hair, then made an absentminded gesture to pick off imaginary lint from her sleeve—all while eyeing Effie with a motherly censure that left Effie unsure if she should feel more chastised than she actually did.

"You accompanied *that man* unchaperoned to investigate the murder of his *wife*?" Katherine was unable to modulate the trembling in her voice.

Yes, she had, and her intention was that no one would ever know. Only Bethany, who of course could not be held responsible for leaking it to the gossipy newspaper that masqueraded as local news. No. Effie was certain it was the moment she'd rushed from 322 Predicament Avenue after Mr. Anderson had brandished the blood-coated butcher knife and she in turn had lost her breakfast in the bushes. Passersby had seen her, the police knew she had been in attendance, and it was a small town. Such exciting news!

Effie bit back her cynicism and reminded herself that she'd done it for Polly. For Polly! Now no one dared claim Polly was manipulating circumstances for attention or brazenly crying wolf. Nor was Polly acting, as she lay in a wretchedly afflicted position of shock and whimpers in her bed upstairs.

Effie glanced at Bethany. She had dreaded this confrontation, prayed that it wouldn't be necessary. But now the paper had splashed her name beside Mr. Lewis Anderson's for the entire town of Shepherd and surrounding communities to see.

Mr. L. Anderson, accompanied solely by Miss Euphemia James of Shepherd, Iowa, daughter of the president of the First National Bank of Shepherd, were the first two to uncover evidence that supports Miss Polly James's claim of witnessing a gruesome and most horrific slaying last week at 322 Predicament Avenue. What they were doing at the address, aside from investigating prior suspicions, is unclear. However, a source states there may be some unknown relations between the couple, and we are certain that will also be investigated.

The implications the paper was making was pure gossip fodder, a way of taking stunning news and making it even more extraordinary by crafting rumors and scandal. Married man, bank president's unmarried daughter, and the alleged murder victim was the married man's wife?

Effie had practically memorized the report. "They left out that Mr. Anderson's assistant was with us." She offered the peace offering in hopes it would be sufficient but knowing full well it wouldn't be.

Katherine James pinched her lips together before responding with the bite of sarcasm. "Oh, that improves the situation tenfold. You were accompanied by *two* men—one supposedly married, and now what? Widowed? And the other one is unmarried. A much better circumstance, for certain."

"Mr. Anderson's assistant has to be over sixty years of age—"

"Euphemia." Katherine sucked in a steadying breath and eyed her daughter. "Unchaperoned is *unchaperoned*—especially when the paper states it in ink for the entire community to ruminate on!"

"Mrs. James, I'm certain that once people understand the circumstances, they'll be more than forgiving." Bethany sighed wistfully.

Both Katherine and Effie turned their attention to Bethany, and it was Katherine who responded, "You and I know better, Bethany, but thank you for your good intentions."

"Well, I had no intention of gossips spoiling Polly's name and calling her a liar." Effie defended her actions while understanding her mother's concerns were well founded.

Katherine had the grace to grimace and soften her expression even as she stated the truth of the matter. "Polly is in no condition to defend her claims, that is true. But, Euphemia!" Katherine's voice broke as she leveled a pained wince on her daughter. "Patrick Charlemagne—as well as other young men of upstanding quality—this changes *everything* for your future circumstances."

Effie didn't dare look at Bethany now, knowing of her friend's social interactions with Patrick Charlemagne. Effie was certain her chances with him were already out of the question, yet her mother wasn't wrong when it came to the others. She tried not to think about the cost to herself as she attempted to protect Polly. "It's 1901, Mother. This isn't the days of Queen Elizabeth, along with the nonsense of falling into a man's arms by accident, requiring marriage to salvage a woman's good name." Effie's words fell flat even as she spoke them.

Katherine's dark eyebrows lifted. "Perhaps not, but now you have attached a probable *murder* to this outing, the questionable activity of this . . . this *foreigner*, and no one knows if his wife was the victim or not. He can't assist in repairing the situation by offering marriage to you because we don't know if he is still married, or if he's widowed, or if he ever was married! Do you not see the awful rumors coming from this, Euphemia? You were sneaking around with a man at least ten years your senior, uncovering violence and *blood*, and now your name has been printed beside his for the community at large to gossip about. Whether this is the days of old or a new era with more freedoms for women, it is of no matter. You will be the center of every dinner table conversation for weeks until the murder is solved. My church ladies' group will be tittering behind their hands!"

"I wasn't sneaking around with him." It was all Effie could

think to say. Other than that, her mother was correct. She would indeed be the center of conversation, a nightmare in and of itself.

"It is probably best that we send you away for a time. If we can allow this brouhaha to fade, then perhaps it will be all right."

"No!" A desperate look at Bethany assured Effie her outburst was founded. Bethany's stricken expression mirrored her own. "I can't leave Polly."

Pain fluttered across Katherine's face. She nodded. "I understand, but if you go to live with my sister in Chicago just until—"

"Then the rumors will be that Effie is with child!" Bethany interrupted, then covered her mouth with her hand in shame for stating it aloud.

"Oh, heavens." Katherine's fingertips pressed against her mouth. "You're absolutely right."

"Do my intentions and motivations mean nothing?" Frustrated, Effie found her throat tightening. "For the good of whoever was the victim of bloodshed? For Polly who doesn't deserve to be talked about—not now, not when she—"

"It is the way of things." Her father's voice echoed as he pushed one of the pocket doors open and entered the sitting room. Carlton James was buttoned up in his tailored suit, his hat tucked under one arm. "I wish you had spoken to me first, Euphemia, before this situation exploded beyond my control."

"There is nothing I did that . . ." Effie bit her tongue as another man strode into the room behind her father.

Mr. Lewis Anderson. The corners of his eyes were lined, and the deep-set eyes told her nothing at all about what he thought of the situation at hand. His hat was absent from his head, but his hair was neatly combed. He wore a gold pin on his silk tie, his suit coat also boasting a square of silk kerchief. But what made the man most striking was the aura that exuded from him. An aloof sort of confidence mingling with an unspoken emotion Effie could not decipher.

His eyes met hers, and Effie thought she saw an apology in them and perhaps something else as well. She averted her eyes. He was part of her problem, after all. A *married* part of her problem, which had made matters so much worse, more complicated.

Mr. Anderson cleared his throat. "I sincerely apologize for putting your daughter in a spot. I was unthoughtful, driven by my desire to uncover what had happened to my . . . to Isabelle."

"Your wife?" Katherine inserted, eyeing him with the shrewdness of a mother.

Mr. Anderson gave her an indecipherable look but said nothing further.

Carlton James tossed his hat onto a nearby chair and strode across the room to stare out the front window. Their yard stretched quite a distance before meeting up with the cobblestone street. A wrought-iron fence bordered the property. Yet it didn't feel high enough now or secure at all. Effie could sense her father's concern in the way he stood, his back to them, his coat shoved back with his hands resting at his hips.

"I am happy to give an interview to the press," Mr. Anderson offered. "I will explain the circumstances that brought me to the old house and why I'd requested Miss James's company."

Carlton turned to face the Englishman. "And you truly think that will silence the tongues of a Midwestern Christian community? Have you ever attended an assembly of the Ladies' Society of Benevolent Morality?"

"I didn't realize such a group existed," Mr. Anderson said.

"Oh, it certainly does!" Carlton James shot a look at Effie as though she should have foreseen her future.

Had the victim been lying in the house and still alive and in need of assistance, would she be under scrutiny for rushing inside with Mr. Anderson and Mr. Cropper simply for attempting to help?

"Does no one care about Mr. Anderson's feelings?" Effie startled them all with her audacity. The room fell silent as Mr. Anderson's gaze dropped to her. She wasn't one to be flippant and impulsive, but somehow the gravity of what they faced superseded propriety. "Considering his wife has potentially been—I apologize, Mr. Anderson—*murdered*, there is so much more here to contend with."

Katherine eased slowly into her chair.

Carlton James cleared his throat.

Effie met the cavernous stare of Mr. Anderson, and for several long seconds neither of them blinked.

At last, Mr. Anderson broke eye contact.

"There is no doubt," Carlton acknowledged, "that the situation in which we find ourselves is both reprehensible and tragic. There is no pleasant outcome to be had in any of it."

"I-I have a possible solution," Bethany inserted hesitantly. "It's quite ridiculous perhaps, and I know I'm not a part of this family and so I really should excuse myself."

Katherine waved off Bethany's attempt to be polite. "You have been a dear friend to Effie her entire life. Even today in bringing us the newspaper."

Bethany smiled gently, and Effie noticed that even in the clamor and tension, Bethany maintained a genteel delicacy. Effie wished she were half as beautiful and half as sweet. Instead, she was average in appearance and personality, and when pushed, she was more forthcoming than she was discreet. Bethany would never have gotten herself in such a dilemma, and yet somehow she still would have figured out how best to help Polly.

"Please tell us, what is your solution?" Carlton addressed Bethany, who folded a kerchief in her lap, probably for something to do besides give either of the men in the room her direct attention. It was intimidating, Effie was sure, to be proposing anything to Effie's father and to a complete stranger.

Bethany issued a delicate cough. "I'm thinking that this outlandish problem requires an equally outlandish solution. At least a temporary one."

The look of apology Bethany cast Effie made Effie straighten in her seat. She braced herself. Bethany would wish her no ill will, but . . .

"What if you were to announce your intentions toward each other?" Bethany asked. "If you were to do so, then it wouldn't seem such a scandalous thing, your . . . uh, proximity of yesterday."

"Absolutely not!" Effie said.

Their father held up his hand to silence her.

Bethany continued, even as her voice lost confidence in the idea, as though hearing it aloud revealed its ludicrous elements. Her voice dropped to almost a whisper. "You announce your engagement to the papers, stating belatedly that circumstances regarding Predicament Avenue had gotten ahead of the announcement. It may not completely assuage the rumormongers, but at least it gives some backbone as to why you were together."

"It will not rectify things." Thankfully, Mr. Anderson looked none too enticed by Bethany's bold proposition. "It would imply that Miss James had dalliances with a married man *prior* to the *possibility* of his wife's passing."

"So true." Effie's father quickly shot down the notion, and the glance Bethany gave Effie was tinged with relief.

"Perhaps it sounded better in my head," Bethany mumbled.

"I appreciate your desire to help," Mr. Anderson offered Bethany the small comfort of his nod. She seemed to take respite in it, even as her cheeks warmed from embarrassment.

Effie gave her friend a wobbly smile. Bethany had meant well.

"The fact remains, what's happened has happened," Mr. Anderson stated. "Unfortunately, we shall have to deal with the repercussions. An investigation will be forthcoming into what occurred at Predicament Avenue. With no body, there is no confirmed victim and—"

"For your sake, I do hope it wasn't your wife, Isabelle," Katherine interjected. Mr. Anderson dipped his head. "Still, it does nothing to help with respect to my daughter—my *daughters*—and their involvement in this horrible set of events."

Carlton leveled a dark look at Mr. Anderson.

"No. And I'm afraid, Mr. James, that the honest truth is that nothing can be done." Mr. Anderson's words began to take on an ominous, dark quality. "I'm sorry for the inconvenience this has caused, and I have no desire to sully your daughter's reputation, but we've had a crime committed and, if the evidence is correct, a murder. A murder *your* daughter Polly witnessed, which has been reported in the papers." He paused, letting his words—and the implications of them—sink in.

"What are you saying?" Carlton shot a look at Effie. She met her father's eyes. They were both realizing the truth of Mr. Anderson's statement.

"It appears there's a killer loose in Shepherd, Mr. James, and Miss James here and her sister have been aligned with the heinous crime as witnesses. And *that* poses a far greater threat than a tarnished reputation."

The clock on the mantel ticked away.

Effie could see the worry making its way into the fine lines of her mother's face. Bethany sat looking very uncomfortable. Effie's father was staring at the ceiling as though he could peer straight through the floorboards and into the room where Polly lay unresponsive, tended now by one of her brothers.

After his warning, Mr. Anderson had politely excused himself, and no one had the wherewithal to stop him from exiting.

Now Effie heard his footsteps fading in the entryway of their home. She shot to her feet and, ignoring her mother's cry of her name, hurried after Mr. Anderson. His broad form had already exited the front door. Effie chased after him. The flurry of her footsteps behind him made the man stop and turn on the walkway, bordered by bushes turning green in the springtime promise of beauty.

"Are you saying my sister is in danger?" Effie blurted out without regret.

Mr. Anderson swiped his hat from his head, holding it before him in his fists. "I'm saying it is a possibility, yes."

Effie descended the steps of the veranda, her hand poised for balance along the railing. "I don't understand. Why would—?"

"Give it a moment of thought, Miss James, and it will all make sense." Mr. Anderson's words weren't delivered callously. Just a straightforwardness that, for the moment, Effie appreciated. The dramatics of the morning had her nerves feeling taut and exposed.

"But Polly is no threat to whoever is responsible for what happened. She hasn't spoken a word since that night."

"True, but if she regains her faculties, that could change the ending to the perpetrator's story—an ending they will not want. Anonymity is their primary goal at this point."

"If there's no body, then there isn't a crime, right?" Effie was desperate to find justification that would release Polly—and herself—from the danger of retribution.

"Miss James," Mr. Anderson said matter-of-factly, "with what we found at the house on Predicament Avenue, and with the knife, it's not a question of whether a crime was committed. It is a question of *to whom* and *by whom*."

Effie studied Mr. Anderson, who seemed patient enough under her perusal. The breeze lifted his hair from his forehead, but it didn't soften the angular lines of his face or the mystery she saw in his eyes. "And your wife? You truly believe she was the one attacked?"

"For more reasons than I can count, I pray not." The gravity in his tone was perhaps the first sign that he cared for the situation emotionally, beyond the logic and the reasoning of solving the questions that hung over the house on Predicament Avenue.

"And you love her?" Effie let the question slip out before she could stop it.

"My wife?" Mr. Anderson gave a solemn nod. "More than the breath in my body," he answered.

Effie's heart sank for reasons she couldn't explain. She felt empathy for him—a wife who had gone missing who he presumed might have been murdered. And for herself because she found him an egregious interruption to her sensibilities. The way his eyes were like hooded pools of secrets that belied not the secrecy of ill intent but some unspoken pain—some hidden burden that he had buried so deep within that he appeared cold and distant and even rude.

"I am sorry, Mr. Anderson," Effie breathed. "Truly."

"Stay well, Miss James." He dipped his head and repositioned his hat.

Effie nodded in response. "And you."

But their eyes stayed latched on to each other, gauging and searching. For the first time, Effie felt as if Mr. Anderson was letting her in just a little bit. It was a place she was shocked to find she wanted to go, and it was a place she knew was not hers to venture into.

It was Isabelle's place. Isabelle Addington. His wife.

Her

Sometime in the Past

HAVE YOU EVER opened your eyes in the night and stared upward into the black? Have you ever crossed your arms over your chest, pretending your bed pillow to be the last you lay your head on as you are laid to rest in your coffin? Have you wondered, as you stare into the dark abyss, what it will be like when your casket is lowered into your grave and the first thuds of dirt land atop you, sealing your fate?

I have. It will be where I am sooner rather than later. This nighttime darkness will be my forever vision. Eventually I will smell only the musk of the earth, the decay of my flesh, the lingering of my perfume on the buttons of my dress. I will hear nothing, for there will be nothing to hear. I will be alone with voices only in my head, memories replaying in circular fashion, over and over again.

But I will not beat on the roof of my coffin, nor will I gasp for air. I will not be buried alive, for I am dying. Even now. In death, someone else will make certain my arms cross over my breast. Someone else will place a bouquet of roses or wildflowers in my grasp to mask the scent of death. There will be dried petals, spiced candles, and a filmy gauze of white decorating me in my eternal sleep. At least that is my hope.

They say that your soul leaves your body when you die. That you float toward heaven and God's outstretched palm. Or you plummet below into an eternal flame of torment and mockery for your sins. But does your soul leave you so quickly, and do you hear those grieving around you? Do you hover over them, observant and thoughtful? Do you hear the words they speak of you after you are no longer there as a witness?

"She was a lovely person."

"Not to speak ill of the dead, but . . ."

"God rest her soul."

"Oh, her poor family . . ."

Or do you merely sleep in your tomb until soon the voices fade, the earth suffocates, and all is as it should be? Still. Alone. Silent.

Have you ever opened your eyes in the middle of the night and sensed that soon this world would not be powerful enough to hold your soul?

Have you ever wondered what happens to you after you die?

10

EFFIE

May 1901
Shepherd, Iowa

THE RESIDENCE of 322 Predicament Avenue had become a carnival of sorts. It seemed nearly all of Shepherd had traversed through the house, touring the
crime scene either in utter awe or complete horror.

"They may as well sell tickets." Bethany tucked a wayward
strand of hair behind her ear.

Effie held Bethany's arm, looped through her elbow, close
to her side. The stares from those who passed them made her
shiver in a way that had nothing to do with the murder but
rather with their curiosity about what Euphemia James's relationship was to the enigmatic Englishman, who had yet to leave
town on the claim that the blood of his wife stained the floor of
the house on Predicament Avenue. That had been made clear as

recently as this morning, with the newspaper monopolizing on the continued saga by making it a front-page story:

> *Mr. Lewis Anderson from London, England, announces his intention to work alongside Shepherd's constable in the investigation of the recent findings at 322 Predicament Avenue. If anyone has any information regarding the presumed victim, one Isabelle Addington, it is requested that they be forthcoming in contacting the Shepherd police. Efforts have been made to reach out to the Opperman Trust, deed holder of the Predicament Avenue property. Meanwhile, Miss Euphemia James, linked to the initial declaration of misdeeds at the house, has not been seen in the company of Mr. Anderson. It is believed that her sister, Miss Polly James, is still suffering from a severe state of shock and therefore has been unable to answer any questions.*

The two friends' stroll downtown was their attempt at bringing a bit of calm and normality to a volatile situation, one that had the potential not only to ruin Effie's future but also to tarnish the reputations of her siblings.

"It will all pass in time," Bethany assured Effie with a bright smile. Her skin was porcelain pale, her lips a bright pink, and her effervescence was enough to almost make Effie believe her. "Just think of the adventure you can share with your children someday."

"I hardly think someone's murder should be considered 'adventure.'" Effie's gentle chiding went unnoticed by Bethany.

"Has Mr. Anderson been to visit you?" Bethany inquired, likely in an attempt to make conversation. Yet it only exacerbated the issue.

Effie flushed. She had begun to think of him as merely *Anderson*. The direction of her unseemly thoughts made conquering the current circumstances all the more difficult. "He has no reason to, Bethany, you know this."

"Do we know why Isabelle Addington was even here in Shepherd? It's so far from England, and with no connection whatsoever? And why does she have a different last name than Mr. Anderson?" Bethany stopped to admire a display of hats in the millinery window, her sudden halt causing Effie to pause as well, their arms still linked. Bethany continued, "She must mean so much to Mr. Anderson for him to be so faithful to search for her. And why did she go missing in the first place?" Bethany sucked in a gasp. "What if she *ran away* from him? What if she didn't want to be with—?"

"Please stop," Effie interrupted. She hadn't the heart nor the stomach for such things. It would be ages before she would forget the blood congealing on the floor beneath the dresser. Months before she could look at a full-length mirror and not think of blood spattering its back as though someone had whipped a knife up through the air, only to bring it down in a vicious thrust, over and over again.

"I'm sorry, Effie." Bethany turned, concern on her face. "It's just all so confusing. There are so many questions that remain unanswered. And here you are wrapped up in the middle of it—you and Polly."

Effie stared through the millinery window at the hats with their laces and ribbons and feathers, all of it holding little interest for her. She couldn't blame Bethany for asking the questions she did. Effie had the same questions and more! But just this morning the gravity of what had happened replayed in her mind as she sat beside Polly. Her sister's eyes were sunken, her cheeks growing hollow. Every now and then, a whimper would release from her dry lips. A frightened whimper as if in her unconscious state she, too, was replaying what she'd seen. Her frail body had refused to bear the shock of it, instead taking to her bed and finding safety in the recesses of her mind.

Bethany straightened as she studied Effie, and Effie could sense the well-meaning worry in her friend's gaze.

"All will be well," Bethany encouraged, yet her words sounded hollow to Effie's ears.

It seemed as if a nightmare, and it acted like one too. Effie lay in her bed, sleep as elusive as the feeling of security. What her family—what Anderson—didn't comprehend was the way the woman's screams were as fresh in her mind as the night she'd heard them. The woman's cries of "no" and the pleading for her life—it was nauseating. It was petrifying. One did not simply go about her normal life after hearing such a thing, let alone having it followed up with the discovery of the evidence that almost guaranteed there'd been a killing.

What had happened to the peaceful days she'd spent reading beneath the weeping willow? Or the sweet and tender anticipation of dinners and conversing with potential matches for a future of quiet wifely duties? She remembered the dinner party at the Charlemagnes' just a few nights before. The stark difference between Patrick Charlemagne—whom she hadn't even had the opportunity to speak with—and the darkness of Anderson was blatant. Effie longed for the predictability of a good Methodist man like Patrick, not Anderson and the way he had swooped in and brooded like a vampire from the novel *Dracula* that her mother swore Effie should never read, but she had anyway.

The floor outside Effie's door creaked, bringing her wandering thoughts into the present with a jolt. She rose up on her elbows, staring at the crack beneath the door. If it was Father, there would be the flickering light from his lantern as he made his way to the lavatory. Only Father moved about the house at night, with the exception of her sixteen-year-old brother Ezekiel, whose penchant for sneaking out at night was somehow unquestioned and not concerning since he was a young man.

She held her breath to listen. Father often cleared his throat as if it were dry from sleeping. Effie heard nothing. There was no light.

The floor creaked again.

Ezekiel. That rascal brother of hers.

Effie swept off her blankets and swung her legs over the side of her bed, her nightdress falling around her ankles. This was not the time to add more trouble to the James household. She had no idea what Ezekiel did at night with his pals, but if he were caught—especially now—the James family might not recover from more scandal.

Tugging her door open, Effie looked both ways down the hall. Her parents' doorway was a short jaunt from her own. The door was firmly closed, and while there wasn't much light except that which came in through the window at the end of the passage, Effie could tell there was no movement from within. There were no shadows. Only stillness.

She took a few hurried steps to the top of the winding stairwell that traversed downward to the main floor. If Ezekiel were sneaking out, chances were he'd go the main route. The furniture pieces below were dark masses in the night, reminding Effie of monsters, crouching, ready to pounce. Teeth poised to sink into her neck, to drain the blood from . . . Oh, she should have listened to her mother and never read that awful book *Dracula*. She guessed that if she were married to Patrick Charlemagne, that would be a confession he'd find unseemly for a good Christian wife. If she were married to someone like Anderson, then maybe he'd merely be inspiration for the darkness.

Effie spun around. Another creak came from behind her. She squinted, making out the framed pictures on the walls, the corner table with the potted fern, and the narrow carpet runner. Darkness swallowed everything else.

Her breathing had become shallow, faster. A sense of foreboding entered Effie's being, and she questioned the reality of the supposed innocence of the night. The James manor was safe. It wasn't Predicament Avenue with its stories of transients and its graveyard. The manor was the home of a stable family, a strong father, security, and . . .

No. She was not alone. Effie could feel it as strongly as she could feel the banister at the top of the stairs beneath her palm.

"Ezekiel?" she whispered. A quick glance toward her bedroom told her nothing had altered. Effie shifted her attention to the far end of the landing, past the mauve velvet settee nestled into a corner surrounded by more potted greenery. Her brothers' rooms were near there. Both doors were closed. Just around the corner was Polly's room.

Effie tiptoed in that direction. She would check on Polly. Though her sister was eighteen and a woman, Effie had not lost her sense of duty to her younger sister. Besides, tonight someone would be with Polly, keeping vigil by her side.

As she passed her brothers' rooms, Effie stopped. If it was Ezekiel or even fourteen-year-old Charles . . . She twisted the knob on Charles's door, opened it a crack, and peeked inside. The boy lay still beneath his bedding, his chest rising and falling slowly. She quietly closed the door and turned to the door opposite.

Ezekiel the troublemaker. A thick fear gripped her throat with no good explanation as she took note of Ezekiel in his bed, soft snores proving it was really him and not a pile of pillows.

The floor creaked again. This time it was distinct and in the direction of Polly's room. The hired nurse perhaps? Effie shut Ezekiel's door. She knew the floors creaked only due to the weight of someone traversing them. What bothered her was the fact that each creak she'd heard had long pauses between them. As if some person were sneaking through the house and stopping after each noise, hoping not to be detected.

Effie continued tiptoeing toward Polly's room. She held her breath as she rounded the corner and saw the door partly open. She hugged the wall as she neared Polly's room. Another creak alerted her senses further, and Effie stilled. It had to be the nurse moving about the room.

Effie peeked around the doorframe. Surely she would find her sister curled in her bed, and she would once again be assured of how ridiculous her imagination could be. She would not witness someone pressing a pillow against her sister's face, smothering her cries. Nor would there be anyone wielding a knife, stabbing the prone body of her sister as she pled for her life like the woman at 322 Predicament Avenue had. There wouldn't be—

Hands clawed at Effie's neck, shoving her back into the door. The knob ground into the small of her back as thumbs squeezed into the hollow of her throat. The moon was wicked on this side of the house and lent very little light to the room. Effie gargled, straining for breath, her fingers raking at the hands that clutched her neck. She could smell peppermint. A whiff of peppermint and then even her ability to smell dissipated as oxygen was withheld from her lungs. The man's thumbs dug into her throat with an insistence that intended her death.

"Miss James!" The night nurse's scream ripped through the eerie silence of her struggle against a man whose features remained hidden by a hat pulled low and his face covered with a kerchief.

Effie's assailant dropped his hands at the nurse's horrified scream as she approached from the hallway carrying a pitcher of water. In an instant, Effie's assailant ran back into Polly's room toward her window, which was open allowing in the cool May night air. The man slipped through the window, wrestling with the trellis outside until the thump of his feet and the sound of his fleeing across the gravel drive persuaded Effie that he was gone.

She sank to the floor, grabbing at her throat, gasping for air that refused to make its way into her lungs. The nurse was beside her, her cries for help echoing in Effie's ears.

A door slammed.

Footsteps thundered toward them.

Her father's bellows filled the hallway.

Her mother's cries soon followed.

Ezekiel and Charles entered the room and hauled her up from the floor to lie beside Polly per their father's command. Effie grappled for Ezekiel's hand only because the feel of his familiarity brought comfort amid the terror that had wrapped itself around her.

The nurse hovered over her.

"Call for the doctor!" Effie heard her father shouting.

And then came the dreadful realization that although it had been she who had been strangled, it was Polly's room the intruder had entered.

Effie struggled to grab on to her sister. No one was connecting these important pieces. In her semi-aware state, Effie desperately tried to speak, to choke out that they needed to protect Polly.

But no one was listening.

11

NORAH

TELL ME WHAT YOU KNOW," Sebastian said, his voice thick with the accent of an Englishman.

Startled, Norah stared at him from across the table in their corner booth at the small diner in downtown Shepherd. He couldn't know that she knew that he didn't know that Harper had told her she was pregnant! Could he?

Norah's thoughts flew into a panic. It wasn't her place to out Harper's news. Why had she come here tonight anyway? She could barely leave Predicament Avenue, let alone be expected to dine in public. She understood Sebastian's offer to take her to dinner wasn't a date; it was to discuss all things Predicament Avenue and the crimes committed there. Yet that wasn't why Norah had agreed to come. It was for Harper. Maybe she could somehow stand in the gap for Harper. Convince Sebastian to look at his daughter and see her desperate need for a father. For input. For a safe place to fall.

But she hadn't expected him to ask her outright!

"Norah?" Sebastian prodded with that sexy deep voice and those chocolate eyes. "Well? What do you know?"

"I . . ." she stammered. It was Murphy's Law that Norah had just gotten her feet under her after years of processing Naomi's murder only to have a nineteen-year-old woman with Naomi's personality show up at the door of 322 Predicament Avenue. It was as if Naomi had returned. Only she hadn't. Instead, it was Harper Blaine. And it wasn't fair—nor was it healthy—to transfer her feelings about Naomi onto Harper.

"What do you know about the history of Isabelle Addington's murder?" Sebastian clarified.

He looked at her through his rectangular black glasses. Dark brown curls flopped over his forehead, his jawline needed a shave, and he had a Spanish look about him even though he was English.

Norah grounded her emotions by studying the way Sebastian's eyes blinked as he watched her. One. Two. Three. Four. He wasn't asking about Harper. He didn't know. She didn't have to tell him. She—

"Norah?" His tone was softer now. "Are you goin' to be a'right talkin' about this?"

Norah nodded and reached for her ice water. The glass was cold against her palm, damp from condensation. There had been condensation on the grass the night the police had come to the door to inform them that they'd found Naomi.

"Isabelle Addington?" Sebastian's voice brought Norah's eyes up to meet his again.

Oh. Isabelle Addington. They were here to talk about the age-old ghost story—not about Naomi, not about Harper. Norah took a gulp of water, then set the glass down on a napkin. "Um . . . as the story goes, a woman named Isabelle Addington was murdered at the house in 1901. Apparently, there was an investigation after some locals found a crime scene but not a body."

"How did they know who the victim was?"

Norah picked up her fork and fiddled with its tongs, wishing the food would come so they could quickly eat and then leave. She dropped the fork back down on the table. "I don't know many of the details except that she was murdered there. Some say she was buried in the graveyard behind the house, but that was never confirmed."

"That's suspicious." Sebastian leaned back in the booth as the server arrived with his plate of deep-fried walleye with coleslaw on the side.

Norah smiled at the server as her plate of chicken carbonara was set in front of her. She should have opted for a salad or bowl of soup. No way would she get the chicken past the lump of anxiety in her throat.

Sebastian speared a piece of fish with his fork and waved it in the air. "I mean, think about it. I found an article online from the *Shepherd Chronicle* around the time of the alleged murder. In it is a request for anyone to come forward who had information about Isabelle Addington. There was an Englishman in town claimin' she was his wife. So, from what I've found so far, there was evidence of a murder, no body, a stranger claimin' his wife was missin', and an assumption that the blood spilled at Predicament Avenue was from this Isabelle Addington—the supposed missin' wife."

Norah poked at a piece of pasta. He already knew more than she did. Or more than she wanted to try to remember. Naomi had always been the one fascinated by the story of Isabelle Addington from the moment they were old enough to be regaled with ghost stories. "Aunt Eleanor said that the way the story was handed down to her, Isabelle Addington was something of a mystery to everyone."

"No one from Shepherd truly *knew* Isabelle?"

Norah shook her head. "Not that's been preserved anyway."

"You're not curious to learn more?" Sebastian chewed and swallowed.

"I've never been fond of ghost stories or . . . those kinds of stories. That was Naomi's thing." Norah pushed her chicken to the far side of her plate.

Sebastian's chest rose and fell. He leaned his elbows on the table and looked earnestly at her, attempting to make eye contact. Norah looked at her food instead.

"I know this isn't goin' to be easy, but I'm willin' to walk through it with you if that's what you want."

Norah glanced up at him. "That's kind of you." It was a mumbled appreciation with no commitment. She got the feeling she needed to offer Sebastian something more or he'd nose his way deeper into her life, into her struggles. That wasn't a place she was willing to share with anyone—except Naomi. And that wasn't possible. "Part of the challenge with finding out more information about what happened back in 1901 at the house is that the records office was demolished when a tornado went through Shepherd in the late 1930s."

"It's not unusual for a natural disaster or other circumstances like fire to do that. It's unfortunate, though. It leaves a lot to question." Sebastian nodded, wiping his mouth with a napkin. "I do find it interestin' that an Englishman was in town claimin' Isabelle Addington to be his wife."

"Why?" Norah took a sip of her water.

"What would bring a Londoner to a small town like Shepherd? An' if the answer is that he traced his missin' wife here, then why would his English wife be in Shepherd?"

Norah frowned. "What's wrong with Shepherd?"

Sebastian raised his eyebrows. "Nothin', but back in those days, people didn't usually cross the ocean to go to a small farm town in the middle of the States. It'd require quite a bit of travel to come all the way to Shepherd, Iowa."

Norah stabbed at some pasta as she considered his words. "I guess that makes sense."

"So then," Sebastian concluded, "I wonder what else was goin' on that isn't in the records we do have?"

"Such as?"

He shrugged. "What was it that motivated an Englishwoman to leave her husband and come all the way to Iowa from London? An' then her husband followed her here, claiming she'd been missin'? If her body was never found, how do we know it was Isabelle Addington?"

"You sound like Naomi." The words slipped from Norah's mouth before she could stop them, then hung there between them. She poked at her pasta and chicken but didn't lift any of it to her mouth.

Sebastian filled the awkward silence. "It sounds to me like your sister asked good questions. Questions that deserve answers."

Norah lifted her eyes. "It's all in the past, though. Isabelle Addington has nothing to do with Naomi's death. They both just happened to be associated with my house. With my aunt Eleanor's house."

"Coincidence?" Sebastian prodded gently.

Norah gave him an affirmative nod. "Yes. That's all."

"An' you don't suppose Naomi was researchin' and came upon somethin' she shouldn't have?"

Norah couldn't help but scowl at the idea. "After a century, I doubt anyone would care if she had."

At Sebastian's skeptical look, Norah set her fork on her plate. "It's happenstance. It sucks, but that's the truth of it. Naomi was fascinated by the story of 322 Predicament Avenue, and when she and I moved in to help Aunt Eleanor after we graduated, Naomi always wanted to see Isabelle's ghost—like Otto claims he has. But we never saw anything. Not even a shadow. Whatever happened to Naomi has nothing to do with that old story."

"You've never seen anythin'?" Sebastian's eyes were leveled on Norah in a way that made her shift in her seat. He was kind but nosy too. She sure wasn't going to acknowledge that since Aunt Eleanor's death, yes, she *had* seen something or someone.

The vision of the woman standing over Norah in the night, strands of hair falling over thin shoulders. But then Norah would blink, and the vision was gone. A nightmare? Sleep-induced? And why after Aunt Eleanor died and not before? All the years of sleeping in this supposed haunted house had garnered Norah nothing but a lackluster interest in Isabelle Addington's nonexistent ghost.

Until now.

Until Sebastian Blaine.

Until Mr. Miller's heart attack.

Until ghosts were rising unwanted from the dead like unfinished stories. Naomi's. Isabelle's. Two cold cases. One location. And one dead bed-and-breakfast guest.

"You've seen somethin', haven't you?" Sebastian's recognition broke into Norah's jittery thoughts.

"What?" She startled. "No. No."

Sebastian stared at her, and Norah dropped her gaze. She frantically searched for a change of conversation, away from all these triggering questions and to a safer place. "Why did *you* come to Shepherd, Iowa?" Norah blurted out the question and then realized it was more than obvious. He'd come for his podcast. She knew that. And for the story of Isabelle Addington.

Sebastian was quick with his response. "I first came to the States about twenty years ago—not too long before I met Harper's mum. An' then when Harper was born, I felt like a cad returnin' home to Lancashire."

"I see. And you live in Nashville?"

Sebastian nodded. "I try an' get home every so often to see my mum and dad. My family."

"With Harper?" Norah asked, then bit her tongue. Harper wasn't a particularly safe subject either.

Sebastian eyed her for a second as though unsure of her motivation for asking. Then he nodded. "Aye. I took her home with me a time or two. But Harper's mum wasn't keen on my takin' her out of the country. Fact is"—it was Sebastian's turn to drop his gaze—"Harper's mum wasn't keen on *me*. She's controllin'. Wanted Harper to herself an' nothin' to do with me. So, Harper believes I'm just an uninvested father."

Norah's heart squeezed at the reflection of hurt in Sebastian's admission. "Why do you let Harper believe that?"

Sebastian pondered for a moment before drawing in a deep breath. "She loves her grandparents, an' I don't want to cause tension for her. It's not fair to a kid to be caught between parents who frankly don't like each other. Even worse, if they find a place of security like Harper has with her grandparents an' then they're tossed about from place to place. So I've just let her be."

Norah ran her fingertip around the rim of her water glass. "But if you don't explain that to Harper, won't she think you don't care?"

"I don't want to burden her." Sebastian locked eyes with Norah. She saw honesty in them and felt perhaps he was giving her a part of himself in exchange for the pieces of Naomi she'd shared with him.

"Maybe she wants to be burdened with it," Norah suggested hesitantly.

Sebastian's brows drew together. "What do you mean?"

"Maybe now that she's an adult, she needs you to be her father—not protecting her from the truth but trusting her with it instead."

Sebastian chuckled. "Sometimes findin' out the truth is too painful. It's easier to figure out how to get by an' pretend the past doesn't haunt you."

Norah didn't answer. She couldn't. She understood Sebastian's point all too well.

Feeling chilled, Norah rolled over, tugging her blanket higher around her neck, unwilling to open her eyes to the night that enveloped her bedroom.

After a quiet drive back to Predicament Avenue, she had parted ways with Sebastian and retreated to her room on the first floor. For the next hour, she could hear him pacing the floor of his bedroom on the upper level. Murmurs through the vents told her he'd chatted with Harper for a bit.

By early evening the sky had grown dark, and the sounds from her upstairs guests stilled. The entryway clock chimed nine and then ten, at which time she must have drifted off to sleep. Now she'd been awakened by the cold pinpricks on her skin as though it were winter, and she'd failed to turn on the heat.

Norah's head felt weighted down, and she allowed it to sink deeper into her pillow. She drew a shaky breath, pulling in her knees and curling into a ball beneath her down comforter. Her mind raced to unravel the confusion that swirled like a fog. She'd been dreaming. Hadn't she? Of a dark opening in a forest. A dirt path that wound its way into the bowels of the woods. Clods of mud were kicked up along the trail, and there was a tree that had fallen during a storm and crashed across the pathway, leaving a trunk that had rotted with age, its leafless branches like scraggly arms reaching out to capture anyone who tried to cross over it. She had been hiking along the trail, squinting into the blue-black depths of the woods. Listening. Always listening.

Norah.

The whisper was a chilling reminder that she wasn't alone. Was never alone. In her dream she had stopped, her shoes sinking into the earth, the trail turning mucky and wet. Like swampland rising to drown the earth, and yet it wasn't sticky and humid, but cold. So cold. Like the winter when raindrops became icicles, and the air suffocated a person with the chill of its breath.

Norah squeezed her eyes shut against the memory of the nightmare. The dirt path. The woods. She'd seen them before. The muddy pools of slimy clay earth, the chilling sensations that hugged with a violence she wrestled against, even now as she was gaining awareness.

She could hear the song of a lone bird. A high-pitched musical string of chirps. It broke through the silence of her iridescent thoughts. Insistent. Pleasant and yet out of place. The woods pulled away from Norah, growing black, the opening in the forest narrowing.

The bird continued to chirp and then there was a clinking sound, like a lid snapping shut. The bird was silenced, as if someone had reached out and snapped its feathered neck.

Norah's eyes fluttered open. Her bedroom was completely silent, shrouded in vampire black, the space a dark cave of isolating outlines. The walls, the wardrobe—she could barely make out its form. Norah lay in her bed, shivering, unable to move. Stiff like a corpse, her breathing was the only sound that drifted to her ears.

In.

Out.

In.

Out.

And yet she wasn't alone. Norah could sense it. *Feel* it.

A click.

And then . . . the bird began to chirrup once more. A lone shrill whistling breaking through the night.

Norah's body tensed, her calves so tight that she felt the onslaught of a leg cramp.

Whistling. A bird flitting among the trees on a summer day.

Only it had to be past midnight. She was in bed at 322 Predicament Avenue. The only bird in her room was the—

The birdsong was shuttered, once again by a metal clap.

"Shhh." The whisper dissipated as the shadow of a woman drifted past Norah's bed and disappeared through the open crack in her bedroom door. A door that had been firmly shut when Norah had gone to bed.

And then, in the gutting silence, a single chirp, like a bird gargling for its last note before death made sure the poor bird lost its song forever.

12

SHE HADN'T MEANT TO SCREAM, hadn't meant to awaken the house. But now Harper wrapped arms around Norah as she sat on the mattress next to Norah. Harper's oversized red hoodie fell to her knees, which were clad in black leggings. She sat cross-legged while Norah sat on the edge of the bed, her feet pressing against the bed frame. She was too afraid to put her feet on the wood floor. Like a child, Norah was terrified that skeletal hands with decomposing skin and black fingernails would slide from beneath the bed and grab on to her ankles.

No. Her feet would stay wedged against the bed frame.

A shiver rattled through her, and she felt Harper's arms tighten. Harper looked up at Sebastian, who strode across the room to peer out the window.

"Dad, she's trembling." Harper's observation met Norah's ears.

"I-I'm all right." Norah tried to reassure Harper, who ignored her.

"Dad, seriously."

Sebastian left the window and moved to crouch in front of Norah. She had the irrational thought that he should hop onto

the bed with them before the skeletal corpse dragged him beneath it to the depths of hell.

"It'll be all right." Sebastian's hands settled on Norah's knees.
She felt the warmth, the strength of them. "You had a scare, but
you'll be fine."

Held by Harper, comforted by Sebastian, Norah felt oxygen
flowing more smoothly through her. Instead of cold, her skin
grew hot as she grew more aware of Sebastian's touch. She
pulled away from Harper, which caused Sebastian to remove
his hands from her knees.

"Tell me what you saw." Sebastian stayed balanced in his
crouch before her.

Harper stuffed her hands into the front pocket of her hoodie,
her dark straight hair feathering on the sides of her pretty face.
Her eyes were earnest, concerned.

Norah drew strength from them while at the same time feeling guilty for seeking support from a young pregnant woman
who had more than enough stress in her life.

"Norah . . ." Sebastian urged.

Norah hefted a steadying breath. "I-I didn't really see anything. It was . . ." The bird. She remembered the bird now. Taking
courage that Sebastian hadn't already been sucked under her
bed, Norah put her bare feet on the floor and stood. She pointed
to her dresser, to the gilded box atop it. Reaching for the box,
she said, "This is a music box. It was playing."

Norah tipped the box over, then righted it. Its lid was closed,
the hinges keeping the box shut on a spring and gear timer. "But
there's no way it could have played on its own." Norah brought it
over to show Sebastian. "The bottom opens here, and you have
to wind it with the key." The key lay on a starched doily next to
where the music box had been. "This latch has to be pushed to
the right to initiate the bird." Norah demonstrated by taking
her thumb and moving a lever. At the motion, a small oval lid
popped up and with it a bird with colorful feathers of Indigo

blue and emerald green, with flecks of red in its tail. The bird's wings fluttered, its chirping filling the room. "It will only play for a certain amount of time—" the lid snapped shut and silenced the bird—"before that happens."

Norah held the box in her hands and looked expectantly at Sebastian.

He took it from her and studied it for a moment. "You said it was playin' while you were in bed?"

Norah nodded. "There's no way that music box could have played on its own. And it played twice."

"Twice?" Harper adjusted her position on the bed, the mattress springs protesting beneath her.

"Yes. I was dreaming," Norah explained, "and then I heard the bird. It stilled. Then it sang again. Someone had to have handled it. It's the only way." Her voice quavered. "I saw her." She glanced at Sebastian, remembering their conversation over dinner and how she'd withheld this from him. The other times the woman had hovered over her bed, just like she had the night Mr. Miller had died of a heart attack.

"Who?" Sebastian's frown was dark, protective.

"A woman." Norah pointed at the door, avoiding looking at Sebastian. "My door was open, and she slipped through it and disappeared."

Sebastian handed her the music box and hurried from the room. She could hear him marching down the hallway, his footsteps making the floorboards groan and creak. The house was old and tired and didn't want to be disturbed at night any more than she did.

"You won't find anyone," Norah called after him.

Harper scrunched her brows together. "Why not?"

"Because she wasn't *real*. She wasn't alive."

Harper drew back, eyeing Norah with suspicion. "You think it was a ghost?"

"No!" Norah bit back her exclamation. "I mean . . ." Her eyes rested on another item on her dresser. Frowning, she reached for the yellow plastic card next to her hairbrush.

"What is it?" Harper's question mimicked Norah's own.

It was the size of a credit card. *Shepherd County Library* was printed on it, along with an address and cutesy little logo.

"This isn't mine," Norah said. She flipped the card over. On the back was a worn white strip, the expiration date of June 2013 printed there. And then—

Norah's watery cry of disbelief had Harper hopping off the bed and hurrying to her side to look down at the library card.

"Who's Naomi?" Harper asked, flipping the card over. "Naomi Richman? Is she related to you?"

Still in shock, Norah stared at her dead sister's library card, now in Harper's hand. "She's . . . my sister."

Perplexity warped the area between Harper's well-shaped brows. "Is it not supposed to be here? In your bedroom?"

Harper didn't understand. How could she know that not only was the library card not on her dresser before she'd fallen asleep, but the card was always kept in Naomi's wallet? A Coach wallet that she'd prized, and the library card was treasured by Naomi just as much as the luxury-brand wallet. A card and wallet that, among other items, had been in Naomi's purse along with her current read in 2011, *A Discovery of Witches* by Deborah Harkness. A purse filled with belongings that, while Naomi's body had been found, had remained missing for nearly thirteen years.

"Norah?" Harper's hand on Norah's arm pulled her back to reality.

Norah took the library card back from Harper, then shifted her gaze to the door and Sebastian, who reentered with a shake of his head.

"There's no one out there, not a soul. The door is locked. I don't see how . . ." He bit off his words as he took in Norah. Her face was void of color, and her hands were beginning to shake again, the library card vibrating up and down with her tremors.

"What is it?" A worried look at Harper, then Sebastian moved to take the card from Norah. As he did, she almost followed the movement, wanting nothing more than to press her face into the man's broad chest and ask him to hide her from the world. From the present awful world and the *otherworld* that seemed to collide in her bedroom tonight. Reality and spirits. Communications from those who had died.

For the first time since Naomi's murder, Norah was able to hold a piece of her that had gone missing the day Naomi was killed. Only it wasn't supposed to be here, in her room, without explanation. Murder victims didn't return their lost items thirteen years after their death. Murder victims didn't return from the dead, period.

Unless they did.

Norah combed her fingers through her hair, leaving her hands tangled above her ears and her elbows poised on the table. She held her head, weighing whether she was dealing with an anxiety attack or a migraine. Both were probably inevitable before all this was over. "How did my sister's library card get in my bedroom?" She lifted her face to look between the father-daughter duo. Norah reminded herself that Harper had yet to spill the beans to her dad about her being pregnant.

Sebastian's dark brows were pulled together in concentration. He'd shifted from his extroverted and lighthearted self to a more focused, investigative mode. Norah appreciated this, except it also meant he would probably start digging in places he'd said he wouldn't. "You've two options," he began. "One, a ghost somehow left the card on your dresser, or two, you did see a lass in your room last night, who's more real than you're givin' her credit for."

"I'd take living human over ghost any day," Harper concluded.

"Really?" Norah got lost in the debate for a second. "That'd mean someone could actually hurt you. But a ghost . . . not so much."

Harper considered that. "Well, I've watched those ghost-hunting shows, and some people have kitchen knives thrown at them by spirits."

"That's just fishin' line and camera tricks," Sebastian inserted.

"And yet you're here chasing after Isabelle Addington—a dead woman's spirit," Harper said.

"Correction." Sebastian held up his index finger. "I'm here to find out what happened to Shepherd's first recorded murder victim and"—he swept his arm around the room—"uncover the mystery that is 322 Predicament Avenue."

"But back to my sister's library card . . ." Norah interjected, even though at this point she'd prefer to engulf herself in the story of Isabelle Addington and forget her own life's story that was fast coming back to haunt her.

Sebastian nodded. "As I said, gettin' the police involved would be your first step. What will they do? Not sure. Maybe run prints on the library card. Prob'ly question you an' make you think you're wrong and the card never was in Naomi's bag to begin with. Thirteen years is a long time to remember what your sister kept in her purse."

"I *know* what she kept in her purse." Norah couldn't help but be a little annoyed by Sebastian's veiled challenge.

He tilted his head in acquiescence. "Sure you do. But will they believe you? It's not a big thing, a library card. Won't say much, do much, or tell much to affect a cold case."

"I like the fingerprinting idea." Harper pulled her feet from the chair, and they landed with a thud on the kitchen floor. "If it was a real intruder, and they did leave prints, maybe the person could be identified."

"There's no sign of a break-in," Sebastian went on to argue. "I'm not sayin' you don't call the police; I'm just cautionin' you that it's likely not much will come of it."

Harper leaned forward. "They never identified Naomi's killer?"

Norah swallowed back a sourness that rose in her throat. She shook her head, unable to find words.

"And no one ever found it weird that with only two murders in the history of Shepherd, both were related to this property?" Harper probably didn't mean to be insensitive, but Norah didn't miss the quick, stern shake of his head that Sebastian directed at his daughter.

"So, other than what happened to Isabelle and Naomi, Shepherd's been peaceful?" Harper held up her hands. "There's never been any more violence in this town? I mean, is that even possible?" She looked to her dad.

Sebastian turned his coffee mug, its bottom scraping on the table. "Sure, it's possible. That's the appeal of living in a small town. Where things like murder rarely happen."

"The appeal of living in a small town?" A spurt of anger rushed through Norah, and she slapped her hands on the table, shoving away from it and marching to the door off the kitchen that led to the backyard. She waved her hand toward the old graveyard. "I'm surrounded by death. Always. Since I was a little girl. And this place—I hate it." Norah spun around to meet the startled gazes of Sebastian and his daughter. "I really do," she added, her voice starting to tremble. "This place was Aunt Eleanor's dream—*Naomi's* dream. I've been sucked into it like one of those graves out back. It's going to eat me alive." She wrapped her arms around herself, feeling the anxiety rippling through her nerves.

Sebastian was looking beyond her, captivated by something outside the screen door. He rose from the table and approached, Norah moving aside to create distance between them. Staring out over the cemetery, he seemed to ponder for a moment before asking, "Was she buried out there?"

"Naomi?" Norah's voice squeaked because tears were so close to the surface.

"Isabelle Addington," Sebastian answered.

"No one knows." Norah twisted to look out the screen door. "There's no headstone or marker with her name on it. No record of her burial in the town's other cemeteries either."

"Let's go look anyway." Sebastian extended his hand toward her. His eyes were gentle, pools of chocolate-brown, and Norah wished she could trust them. Trust that he was the sort of person who could harbor her, quench her fears, provide answers. Right now, he was simply diverting her attention away from Naomi. She knew that. Knew that he was reading the shivering in her body, the nervous wobble in her voice.

Yes. Isabelle Addington. A diversion.

Anything to get her mind off Naomi's neon-yellow library card and the vivid memory of the woman's ethereal form slipping out her bedroom door and whisking away into the night as though beckoning Norah from beyond the grave.

Find us. Find us both.

It was Isabelle who had beseeched Norah. Two unsolved murders of two innocent women. If she couldn't help Naomi, perhaps she could help Isabelle and then finally the woman could rest in peace.

And leave 322 Predicament Avenue alone.

13

EFFIE

May 1901

THE DOOR OPENED, and Effie all but pushed past a stunned Gus. "Please. Is Anderson here? *Mr.* Anderson, I mean." Effie was quick to formalize his name, for it was only in her mind that she'd been casual toward him.

Gus opened his mouth to answer, but the elderly man was interrupted by his employer ducking into the entryway. Concern creased his face. "Effie?"

The use of her first name surprised her. Perhaps murder and shock were enough to put aside such formalities.

Effie had first gone to the boardinghouse to find Anderson. He hadn't been there. She'd been redirected by a far too inquisitive boardinghouse owner that Mr. Anderson and his assistant had checked out of the boardinghouse and rented a small house on 10th Street—the one owned by the Charlemagnes. Of course. The Charlemagnes owned a lot of property, some rentals, some for sale, some industrial. They made their money that way. But for Anderson to rent a house meant he intended to stay for a length of time

"Please, I need your assistance." Effie looked between the two men.

"I'll put the tea on," Gus stated in a no-nonsense fashion, then shuffled away.

"Are you all right?" Anderson's brows drew together as he eyed Effie. She knew he was taking in the marks on her neck that were impossible to hide. Bruises that extended the width of fingers.

"No. I am not all right. I need your help." Effie went ahead of him into a small sitting room. When she took a chair, and Anderson the chair opposite her, she made efficient work of informing him what had happened the night before.

"And you're here? Alone? Have you gone mad?" The concern in the man's voice thickened his accent and deepened the creases beside his eyes. "No escort? Where is your father? Should you even be up from your bed?"

Effie had not anticipated the barrage of questions, nor the worry that laced the man's features. She toyed with the strings of her purse that rested in her lap. "My father is at the police station insisting that they grant us a security guard. But it wasn't me the intruder was after—it was Polly!" Effie's voice was scratchy, her throat sore, her body aching from the attack, but she had no intention of admitting that to anyone. "My mother will not leave Polly's side and rightfully so. The night nurse has agreed to stay on to assist, but Polly is still unresponsive. I can no longer sit back and do nothing. My sister has been targeted for what she saw. The paper has done nothing to provide any help in protecting her. Please. I need your assistance."

"To accomplish what?" Anderson was guarded, and yet he swept his gaze over her again as if to convince himself she was indeed all right.

"Go with me to Predicament Avenue. To see if anything's been missed. More clues. Who is behind all this? I must know. I *must* protect Polly!" Her words ended in a whimper, and for a moment Effie thought Anderson was going to move to sit beside her. He started forward and then, as was proper and necessary, leaned away from her.

His eyes darkened. "Miss James—"

"Effie."

"Effie," he continued, "my wife is dead. This is only the beginning, and until the culprit is caught, danger abounds. I made an error taking you there the first time. An error of judgment as to your reputation, and an error of judgment regarding your safety. Forgive my bluntness, but you added little to what we discovered. Had you not been there, I still would have found the remains of the violence."

Effie's head snapped up to frown at him. "I was the one who indicated we must look in the kitchen, which is where the knife was found. If not for me, the weapon that inflicted all the violence would still be behind the stove and out of sight. And if he comes after Polly, she can't . . ." Effie's voice caught as tears threatened to surface. "*Please*, I dare not go back there alone. I know that doing so would be foolish. But with you—"

"No." Anderson shook his head.

"But—"

"There are other ways to find answers." He shifted in his chair. "Ways I'm already exploring on my own, no thanks to the police who seem to find it an embarrassment that we discovered what they did not at Predicament Avenue." Anderson paused, then added, "However, you are welcome to accompany me to the Opperman home."

"The Oppermans?" Effie's startled exclamation took him aback.

"I'm told they own the property at 322 Predicament Avenue."

Effie nodded. "Well, yes, but no one really associates with the Opperman family. They're not very friendly."

"How is it then they own 322 Predicament Avenue and, I understand, quite a few other properties around town? At some point in time, they must have had some influence here in Shepherd. And I assume they know what is going on at their own property."

Effie shook her head, reaching up to tuck a wayward wisp of hair behind her ear. She noticed Anderson's eyes followed her movement. "Mr. Opperman was influential years ago. Before I was born even. But after he died, all his assets were left to his wife, and she's . . . not in good health. In her mind, that is. No one knows why she's neglected Predicament Avenue or left her other properties to be abandoned. Father says the Charlemagnes have tried to purchase them from her, but she refused. Foolish pride, he says." It was the only explanation she could give Anderson.

"Be that as it may, someone must be tending to the house and the cemetery behind it. If you want to find out who is hunting your sister in the middle of the night, and if I'm to have any hope of finding . . . well, we must interview them."

"They won't speak to you," Effie insisted. Most everyone in Shepherd knew this to be true. The Oppermans were known more by the legalities of the Opperman Trust that owned various properties than by any congenial relationships to the remaining living Oppermans.

"Not to me, no, but they will speak to the man affianced to the daughter of the man whose bank manages their land trusts and holdings."

"Pardon me?" Effie drew back. Certainly she hadn't heard him correctly.

Anderson looked over his shoulder as if checking to be sure Gus had not entered with tea and would overhear. "If we use the influence of your name, and Mrs. Opperman believes I am your betrothed, it wouldn't be untoward of us to approach her with questions. Especially in light of recent events . . . that is, your attack." His mouth was set in a grim line. "They owe us any assistance that can be given."

Effie struggled for words. His reasoning made sense, but posing as her affianced? It may give him credibility if aligned with the James surname, but . . . "But you're married! And if they've read the paper—"

"Let us not fool ourselves, Effie. My wife is dead." A look of sadness flickered in Anderson's eyes.

"There's no body, though."

"Nevertheless, my wife is dead." He emphasized each word, his unblinking eyes boring into hers. Anderson slid forward to the edge of his chair and reached for her hand. It was the first expression of kindness she'd seen from him, the first physical touch that sent a pulse through her, and the first moment she dared to look at him. Truly look at him. She allowed herself to peer into his eyes, to glimpse behind the polished English façade. And for a brief moment, Anderson allowed her.

She saw grief there. Loneliness. And, lurking in the depths, fear. The sort of fear she couldn't understand or place. It was not for her. It was darker than that. More urgent. And Effie knew then that Anderson had more secrets than he was prepared to expose.

"One thing you must learn, Miss James—*Effie*—and that is to trust me." Anderson squeezed her hand. "I've been searching for Isabelle for months. I've crossed the ocean to find her. I'm well acquainted with having to obtain information creatively. And to be frank"—he released her hand—"nothing will stand between me and Isabelle."

"I know," Effie acknowledged. "We need to find her. Or—" she hesitated—"her body." Effie searched the man's face, the crevices on his forehead, the depths of his eyes, the angular cut of his unshaven jawline.

"Will you trust me?" Anderson's voice dropped an entire octave.

It sent ripples through Effie as her eyes locked with his. In that moment, her own plans and intentions to try to find whoever had broken into Polly's room faded away. She noted the determination in Anderson's eyes. Determination plus something else she couldn't quite put her finger on. "Yes," she breathed, "I will trust you."

Her gloved hand rested lightly in the crook of Anderson's elbow. She could feel the warmth of his arm through the material of his suit coat. He shot her a look that was neither reassuring nor was it a warning. Instead, it was almost as if he was making certain Effie wasn't going to run away. He must have felt the way her body tensed as she descended from their rented carriage after arriving to the Opperman homestead.

It seemed Anderson was ignorant about the Oppermans and how intimidating they could be. He also didn't know how reclusive they were, the numerous times the family had refused to mix with the community of Shepherd. That they had money was obvious given the property on which she and Anderson now stood. Anyone who lived in Shepherd knew that the Oppermans were not churchgoing folk, nor were they—dare she say it?—normal. Effie wasn't certain how else to describe them.

Anderson was soon to find out.

The front door opened, and a rush of musty air flooded them, smelling like old laundry that had been wet for days. The great room behind the woman who stood in the doorway was cloaked in darkness, and Effie could tell that all the curtains had been drawn, the windows shut. No interior lights glowed as well, whether by flame or electricity.

Mrs. Opperman eyed them through squinted eyes. Her features were narrow, lined, with thin lips and a slender neck. She wore a black silk dress, buttoned to the throat. Though Mr.

Opperman had passed on five years prior, it seemed Mrs. Opperman had no intention of leaving her mourning behind. "Yes?" She spoke to them through the screen door.

Effie looked at Anderson, her eyes pleading for him to take the lead.

"Mrs. Opperman, I presume?" he responded.

Mrs. Opperman's eyes narrowed even more. "Yes." Her voice was high and matched the sallowness of her complexion.

"My name is Lewis Anderson, and this is Miss Euphemia James, my fiancée and the daughter of Mr. Carlton James of—"

"I know who they are," Mrs. Opperman snapped.

Effie looked down at her shoes. Anderson's attempt to deceive in hopes of gaining Mrs. Opperman's trust and goodwill would not be as easy as he might have expected.

"Let me get straight to the point," Anderson continued.

"Please do." Mrs. Opperman pinched her lips together.

"I've been told you own the property at 322 Predicament Avenue, yes?"

"This nonsense again?" Mrs. Opperman pushed open the door and stepped onto the porch, letting it slam shut behind her.

Effie tried not to wince as she caught a whiff of cat urine drifting from the house.

"We've already spoken with the police about it, and we know nothing."

"I understand that. I was hoping to get the names of the individuals who have recently stayed there." Anderson was infusing a disingenuous politeness into his tone, and Effie was afraid if Mrs. Opperman snapped too much at him, he might well lose patience and bark at her.

Mrs. Opperman frowned. "How am I to know who has stayed there? Hobos and transients come and go, and they can have it. I merely keep it because it is part of my late husband's trust, and I'd be wretchedly upset if one of those Charlemagnes were to get it. They want to own the whole town—them and people like your father." Mrs. Opperman leveled a glare on Effie. She was surprised at the animosity in the woman's expression. She'd not known anyone to dislike her father. He was a good man. Ethical. Fair. Wealthy? Perhaps, but then so was Mrs. Opperman.

Anderson drew a careful breath. "You've no idea then who may have been—?"

Mrs. Opperman held up a hand to stop him. "As I said before, I've no concern over that property as long as it stays in the trust. So no, I've no idea who may or may not have been staying there."

"And the cemetery behind the house?"

"What about it?" Mrs. Opperman eyed them suspiciously.

Effie couldn't help but hold on to Anderson's arm a bit tighter.

"Do you have any family buried there?" he asked.

Mrs. Opperman sniffed. "Family? Absolutely not. Those graves have been there since my husband's great-uncle first settled in Shepherd."

"Why then don't you sell the property if it is such an annoyance and there are no familial attachments to it? Would it be that much of a disappointment if it were sold to someone such as Miss James's father?"

Effie looked between Anderson and Mrs. Opperman. She was unclear as to what Anderson was attempting to accomplish. At first, she'd thought he hoped to gain some names or insights as to who may have been in the house the night Effie and Polly heard the screams. But now his line of questioning had Effie herself questioning.

Mrs. Opperman hesitated only a moment, but it was enough for even Effie to notice the hitch. The woman's chest rose and fell. Her voice lowered and became a thin thread of irritation that threatened to snap at any further questions.

"We are Oppermans. We don't sell." She spun, whipping open the screen door and marching inside. Again the door slammed shut behind her, followed by the resounding slam of the main door.

Anderson looked down at Effie. "Well, that settles that." Turning, he guided her back down the steps toward the carriage.

"What do you mean?" Effie's confusion was palpable.

"Mrs. Opperman was remarkably defensive, and she cut short the conversation. The question is *why*? Why care so much about a property you don't keep maintained, a property where you allow strangers to drift in and out of? What is it about 322 Predicament Avenue that is so important to the Oppermans? And is it important enough for someone to kill for it?"

Effie was astounded by Anderson's insight. She hadn't gathered that at all. She'd merely ascertained that Mrs. Opperman was peeved and verging on infuriated. "Maybe the two are unrelated?" she offered as Anderson helped her up into the carriage. "Perhaps the Oppermans have a vested interest in the property beyond just ownership, and the violence there the other night has nothing to do with them."

Anderson rounded the carriage, running his hand along the black horse hitched to it, and swung up onto the seat beside her. "The deeper question is, what business did Isabelle have at 322 Predicament Avenue that would bring her such harm?"

Effie stiffened at the thought. "I've put faith in you, that the woman Polly saw was Isabelle. But what if the woman Polly and I heard wasn't your Isabelle? What if it were someone else entirely?"

Anderson stilled, not flicking the reins in his hands that would urge the horse forward. He stared down at them instead, his fingers toying with the straps of leather. Finally, he took both reins in one hand and reached into his inside coat pocket. Pulling out a folded piece of paper, he handed it to Effie.

She gave Anderson a hesitant look, suddenly feeling as if she'd pushed too far with her question. Yet he didn't appear angry or annoyed. He merely waited.

Effie unfolded the paper, noting a feminine penmanship to the letter inside.

I am sorry. Please forgive me. Your songbird is here. You will find me in Shepherd, Iowa.

Isabelle

Effie pulled her gaze up to meet Anderson's. "It's all right there. In the message!"

He offered a grim smile.

"She sent this to you in London?" She stared at him, ignoring the way the breeze lifted his hair from his forehead.

Anderson took the letter back and tucked it into his coat pocket. "She did. On receiving it, I immediately booked passage to come retrieve her."

Effie nodded. "Is 'your songbird' Isabelle? Is she referring to herself?"

Anderson's expression instantly darkened. His body tensed, and a muscle in his jaw twitched. Adjusting his grip on the reins, he flicked them against the horse's back. The carriage jolted forward. "You know enough," he stated.

Effie sensed Anderson pulling away—perhaps not in body, but in spirit. What little warmth and comradeship that had evolved between them today had been withdrawn under his protection.

Isabelle Addington was dead. She had to be. Effie knew this to be true. Knew the letter in his pocket was his last missive from her. But why had Isabelle left him? And why was he coldly willing to assume her death without demanding proof of her body? Instead, what echoed in Effie's memory were his words *"My wife is dead."*

But was Isabelle Addington the woman Effie and Polly had heard that night? Assumptions had been made, yes, but they were based on reasoning and circumstances.

That Isabelle was dead? Yes. One couldn't fathom the bloodstains left behind wouldn't have almost drained a corpse empty.

Effie jolted as the carriage hit a rut in the Oppermans' drive-way. She looked toward the Opperman farmhouse. As she did, a curtain quickly fell back into place, but not before Effie saw the beady stare of Mrs. Opperman, her expression thick with accusation and malice.

14

EZEKIEL SPRINTED down the steps as Anderson guided their carriage around the circular brick drive of the manor. His hair was mussed, and urgency marked every motion of his body. Effie stiffened in concern. Her hand went absently to her throat, caressing the bruises there. The nightmare of the evening before was fresh as she grabbed for the carriage door before it stopped moving.

"Whoaaaa!" Anderson crooned to the horse, sensing the emergency also.

Ezekiel fell against the carriage, gripping the door. "Polly. It's Polly. Effie, you need to come quick."

Without waiting for assistance, Effie flung herself out, tripping on the carriage step and steadying herself on Ezekiel's outstretched arm. She gave no thought to Anderson as she hiked up her skirts and ran toward the house. Charles met her at the door, his face filled with worry.

"Is she . . . ?" Effie couldn't say it. Not those words. The words she'd dreaded hearing since Polly had been taken to her bed.

Charles shook his head.

"Oh, Effie darling, you're here. Where have you been?" Her mother hurried Effie toward Polly's room.

Effie flew into the bedroom that only the night before had been a place of terror but was now more like an oasis. Afternoon sunlight sparkled across the floor through the open window. The delicate pink roses covering the wallpaper print looked almost real as they stretched their vines around the room. The four-poster bed was piled with white linens and pillows, with Polly supported by what looked like a cloud of soft cotton.

Dr. Reginald stood at the bedside, his stethoscope hanging from his neck, spectacles perched on the end of his nose. The nurse was busy squeezing water from a cloth into the basin.

Polly's eyes were closed, her skin pale with two pink splotches on her cheeks rivaling the roses on the wall for vividness. Her nightgown was fresh and clean, her hair lying in waves around her shoulders.

"Polly?" Effie's watery cry of her sister's name was met with the slow fluttering motion of Polly's eyelids.

A flood of relief washed over Effie. Her sister hadn't died! She had regained her senses! Effie's knees gave way, and she sank onto the bed next to her sister.

Polly smiled weakly. Her light laugh was a ghost of what it had been only weeks before. She reached out and laid her hand on Effie's. Polly's skin was cool.

"Oh, Effie, I've had a spell." Her voice was faint and trembled with exhaustion. She coughed, then coughed again. She lifted her handkerchief to her mouth and dabbed. As she pulled it away, Effie saw the spots of red, even though Polly wadded up the cloth in an effort to keep it hidden.

"Doctor?" Effie lifted her worried gaze to Dr. Reginald, who was conversing quietly with their mother now. They both glanced in Effie's direction.

The exchange of looks between the doctor and her mother dampened Effie's relief. She grappled for Polly's hand, holding her cold fingers as gently as she could, though she wanted to cling tightly.

Dr. Reginald dipped his head in apology. "Miss James, your sister has come around for now, but as we've discussed, I'm afraid these episodes—ushered in by shock and trauma—will only increase. Still, there are things we can do to help make your sister comfortable—"

"B-but there are asylums." Effie cast a desperate look at her mother, whose watery eyes met hers. "Such places have been helpful in treating tuberculosis cases."

"Euphemia—" her mother struggled to speak—"we've been through this already."

Dr. Reginald held up a hand to stop Effie's mother from having to explain it again. He chose his words carefully, aware that Polly could hear him. "While there are similarities with tuberculosis, after my examinations, I am confident we're dealing with encephaloid cancer of the lungs."

Effie's chest convulsed at the diagnosis.

The doctor continued, "Her symptoms support my research and my correspondence with other experts in the field. There are other factors at play with her symptoms that rule out tuberculosis and support my diagnosis. I did read of a case where this happened with another gentleman who had moments of increased ability. However, Polly is experiencing considerable dyspnea now. That difficulty to breathe is enhanced by pain in specific regions, which again leads me to believe the diagnosis is correct."

"But—"

"Effie . . ." Polly's voice was strained. Her fingers squeezed Effie's weakly. "We cannot fight this." Her eyes slipped shut as she struggled to inhale a deep enough breath to satisfy her lungs. "You need to be safe."

Polly was concerned for Effie's safety even as she lay there preparing to meet her death. Polly opened her eyes and peered into Effie's. Effie saw concern reflected there, an understanding of what she'd witnessed and what might yet come. "Effie, don't go back . . ."

"Young lady," Dr. Reginald inserted, leaning over them, "do you remember what you saw?"

Effie looked sharply at the doctor. Now was not the time! The shock of remembering could send Polly back into a catatonic state.

Polly paled more than Effie thought was possible. She looked past the doctor, past her mother and Effie. She shook her head. "No. I don't." She coughed, then sucked in another breath. "I-I just know that Effie needs to be safe."

"*You* need to be safe!" Effie pulled Polly gently into her embrace. She gave the doctor a glare over her shoulder. "No more questions."

"Euphemia." Her mother's voice reminded Effie that she wasn't in charge. And yet she had to say something to protect Polly from further trauma. Effie leveled another look on the doctor, who had probably been coached by the constable to question Polly should she regain consciousness.

"My sister need never revisit that night again." Effie was firm, though every part of her was shaking on the inside. She felt Polly relax into her, and Effie glanced down quickly. Her sister had fallen asleep. Effie looked between Dr. Reginald and her mother. "Don't ask her any more questions. Let my sister live her remaining days in peace."

Effie plunged into the depths of her soul to find the courage Polly had shown, the bravado that had taken them on their midnight jaunt to 322 Predicament Avenue. She tried to summon hope, some sort of faith that all could be made right. But Effie could not find it. Any of it. All she could find was the feeling of desperation. Desperation to avoid the truth that Polly was dying from her disease, or because of whoever had decided she'd witnessed their crime and so must be silenced. Effie wanted to rewrite that night at Predicament Avenue, to turn today into a dream of beauty and not a dreaded nightmare.

Yet that was what fear was after all. When a person lived afraid of death, when they could feel death's cold breath on their neck every moment of the day, there was no courage left to be had. No anticipation. No hope. Only the force of one's own will to try to outrun the fear before they were eaten alive by it. Before their greatest fear became their worst reality.

Effie slipped from her sister's room, leaving the doctor and her mother behind. As she made her way to her favorite spot beneath the willow tree in the backyard—so much like the one in the front yard at Predicament Avenue—Effie prayed for a miracle. She prayed that God in His mercy would reach down and with a slight touch of His hand spread healing through Polly's body. She wanted to believe it was possible. Didn't the Bible say "ask and you shall receive"? She had asked, begged, pleaded, even mustered the faith that God would answer her prayers.

But He hadn't answered her prayers, which had left her faith shaken. The unfairness of having her best friend ripped from her life was an agony Effie couldn't bear. She was terrified of the day when Polly's eyes would close and never open again. What hope was there when God remained still and refused healing?

"Effie?"

She issued a garbled cry as she spun. The touch to her shoulder was light but unwelcome. Her face was wet with tears, her soul tearing in two, and she didn't desire anyone's company or comfort. There was no comfort that could be given. None.

Anderson stood beside her. Effie wiped at her tears with the heels of her hands, ducking her face away from this stranger who had entered her life as unwelcome as Polly's imminent death.

"Please, leave me be." She tried to be polite despite her tears.

Anderson didn't move, nor did he say anything.

Effie lifted her face and beseeched him more urgently. "Please, Anderson. I want to be left alone."

He remained silent, but there was gentle understanding in his eyes she didn't expect. Concern, yes, but there was more. There was solidarity in grief. In loss. In the awfulness of death's march on life.

Effie turned away, bracing her palm against the trunk of the willow tree, her back to Anderson. She spoke to him over her shoulder. Not because she wanted to, and not because he deserved to know, but because something inside of her compelled her. A magnetic pull toward Anderson with no explanation other than that she knew he grieved the absence of his wife.

"My sister, she is . . . dying." Effie said the words aloud for the first time. "Nothing can be done to save her." The finality of the statement sent Effie collapsing against the tree. She wrapped her arms around the trunk, though she could not reach around its circumference. The bark felt rough against her cheek. "I've prayed. I've pled. Why won't God answer?"

She didn't expect a reply from Anderson. He wasn't part of this struggle.

"I know," he said quietly.

Effie turned to gaze at him in disbelief and with mutual understanding. "But your wife—"

"Is dead," Anderson finished, a placid expression on his face.

His matter-of-fact tone bothered Effie. "We don't know that yet." She shook her head, somehow wanting more than ever to find holes in their suppositions and conclusions. To find some reason to believe Isabelle Addington might still be alive or that maybe it hadn't been her at all. "No one has found a body. We don't know for certain it was *her*."

Anderson offered her a glimmer of a smile. But it was a sad one. "I know what it's like to fear death."

Effie shifted her attention to the new grass beneath her feet.

There was a tiny white alfalfa flower growing there. Its delicacy reminded her of the love between family, the fragility of life, and the finality of death. She lifted her eyes to his.

Anderson shifted his stance, tilting his head to study Effie closer. "Do you know why we are afraid of death?"

Effie waited. Unable to respond or tears would surely flow again.

Anderson seemed to comprehend that. He continued, "We're afraid of death in part because we're afraid of the grief that follows. Death is momentary, but grief is what's left behind. The remnants of every memory, every moment, every emotion. Grief is all the unspoken words that will never be said, the lost I-love-you's, and the emptiness of the shadows they leave behind. Grief is a demon that stalks us."

"How do we escape the demon?" she whispered. She could feel the tears begin to shove past her restraints, their hot paths trailing down her face and leaving invisible scars she would never be able to wipe away no matter how much she tried.

"We don't. We embrace it." Anderson's response wasn't what Effie wished to hear.

"As you have done?" she ventured hesitantly.

Anderson's mouth pulled in a worn smile. "No. I haven't embraced grief."

"But you admit so easily that your wife has died." Effie tried to understand.

"The truth of reality isn't always what's known." Anderson laid a hand over his heart. "Grief is a beast we wrestle with only when we're ready to face it." His hand moved to her face, his fingers brushing away the tears. "You're afraid of death that's yet to come, while I'm terrified of grief that still waits to be recognized."

Cold, Dead, But Never Buried
Hosted by Sebastian Blaine

WHAT CAN THE HOUSE at 322 Predicament Avenue tell us that no one else can? Are there clues in its walls, evidence under its floorboards? Does the spirit of Isabelle Addington roam the hallways at night, waiting to be discovered and listened to?

If she's here, can she tell us of her death? Can she explain why she was at 322 Predicament Avenue in the first place? Can she whisper the identity of her killer in our ear?

I'm stationed here in a room on the very property where Isabelle Addington was murdered. Today I'll be exploring the graves in the backyard cemetery. Some of their headstones are worn to the point of being illegible. But I feel they're not there by chance, nor are they unconnected. No crime was ever condemned in a court of law by an argument made from intuition and acting on one's gut. But sometimes crimes have been solved that way, with the evidence to be swept up once the pieces fall together.

My gut is telling me to investigate these graves. Are Isabelle's bones lying in the earth here, or is there more to her story than a single grave?

15

NORAH

Present Day
Shepherd, Iowa

A STICK BROKE beneath Norah's feet as they crossed the yard toward the graves that dotted the back lot before merging with the woods that stretched at least ten acres before running into the property of the neighbors to the north of Predicament Avenue.

The small neighborhood was both private and pleasant. And with the historical cemetery keeping the property larger than most and respected by all, 322 Predicament Avenue had an aura of stepping back into time. Into an era when life was slower. It was why Otto and Ralph had spent years here, gardening and trimming. It gave them something to do that their own personal half-acre plots down the street didn't offer. Aunt Eleanor had been grateful to have the boys managing her yard work, and over the years this place had almost become as much theirs as Eleanor's.

But today, Norah observed Sebastian as he strode ahead of her, intent on the stones that marked each grave. Harper had opted to stay inside, and Norah couldn't blame her. Last night had grown long after Norah awakened them with her screams. The discovery of Naomi's library card was still eating at Norah's insides, but for now she would welcome Sebastian's attempt to distract her. Besides, it had to be a coincidence. There was no way Naomi's ghost—or Isabelle Addington's—had been in her room last night. She'd been half awake. The library card must have fallen from wherever it had been tucked behind all these years. Or maybe when Norah had used that old handbag yesterday, it had fallen out of it? Norah was probably wrong in believing Naomi had kept the card in her missing wallet. She tried to recall thirteen years back as to whether she had borrowed the library card. The purse she'd used yesterday was certainly from that era. It was possible that—

"That's an old grave." Sebastian pointed to the grave that dated back to the eighteenth century. Its crudely carved epitaph had withstood the weather and time's passing better than some of the graves that were dated a hundred years later.

"A lot of folks don't believe it's for real," Norah said. "They don't believe a man of European descent would have been buried in Iowa Territory back in that time period."

"Europeans hadn't come this far west yet?" Sebastian asked, his hands jammed into the pockets of his jeans, his stare fixed on the headstone.

"They had, but only a few here and there. There weren't any settlers as yet. This land still belonged to the Indigenous peoples, and any Europeans around these parts were mostly French explorers, trappers, and traders."

"So then who is this bloke?" Sebastian asked.

"No one knows," Norah answered. "His story has been lost to time."

Sebastian nodded. "Like so many." He moved down the row, eyeing each stone, reaching down to right one that was leaning badly to the side. "She's not goin' to move."

"No. Aunt Eleanor once talked about having a grave restoration service come and work on preserving the graves, but that never happened."

"Do most believe Isabelle Addington was buried here?" Sebastian shifted an expectant look on Norah.

She pointed to the back of the graveyard near the edge of the woods. "Some think she's buried back there along the tree line. Others say no one ever found her body, that it's all just a hoax."

"So there is a gravestone?" Sebastian asked.

Norah grimaced and stepped respectfully around the grave of a child who had passed away in 1863. "There's a marker, yes. Whether it's hers or not depends on which version of the tale you believe."

"Are you saying some think her marker was put there just to make the story more intriguing?"

"Let me show you." Norah approached Isabelle Addington's grave marker, Sebastian coming to a halt near her. Too near her. His arm brushed hers, and while he didn't seem to notice, Norah did. She stepped to the side a bit to put some distance between them. Pointing at the stone, she read it aloud: "I. A.— died May 3, 1901."

"That's different." Sebastian studied the flat-topped stone that had lichen growing in the etchings and around the edges, with little pillows of soft green moss at its corners. "Only initials."

"Right." Norah bent down and chipped away at the lichen with her thumbnail. "That's part of the debate as to whether it's really Isabelle's grave."

"The date is correct." Sebastian had pulled out his phone and was thumbing its screen. "Your town has a decent online archive of citizen records. It lists an Isabelle Addington as having died here May 3, 1901."

"No one contests she died here." Norah was successful in removing a piece of lichen in the *A* on the stone marker. "Just whether or not this is her grave."

"When did the sightin's of Isabelle begin?"

Norah shook her head. "They've always been." She shot Sebastian a pointed look. "Isn't that how ghost stories work? But who's to know who's telling the truth? Otto claims he's seen her, and I've never known him or Ralph to lie."

"An' your aunt? Did she ever see an apparition?"

Norah returned her attention to the lichen more for something to do to avoid Sebastian's inquisitive stare. She wasn't sure which side of him she preferred more. His easygoing side or this investigative side where he asked way too many questions.

"Aunt Eleanor didn't *believe* in ghosts. If she saw or heard anything she couldn't explain, she always chalked it up to being a shadow or a reflection or just her imagination—something like that."

"You said you an' your sister stayed here as children?"

"As children and after we graduated high school." Norah shifted uncomfortably, losing her balancing in her crouch by the grave and planting her knee in the damp grass to steady herself. "My dad traveled a lot. Mom liked to go with him. But we loved Aunt Eleanor, and we loved Otto and Ralph. They spoiled us." Norah couldn't help the fond smile those days evoked for her . . . before violence and horror stained everything.

"Did *you* see signs of Isabelle?" Sebastian asked.

They'd been through this round of questioning before. Norah countered his question with one of her own. "What does it matter if we did or didn't? You're trying to solve Isabelle's cold case, aren't you? Not sensationalize a ghost story."

Sebastian was unfazed. "True. Call it curiosity then."

Norah rolled her eyes. "No. I didn't see any apparitions as a kid or I'd have never stayed here. Naomi didn't either."

"But you do now?"

Norah stilled. She looked at Isabelle's supposed grave. The date stared up at her like a bad omen. She ran her fingers over Isabelle's initials. "She comes now. Every so often." Norah allowed herself to be vulnerable from her position beside the grave. She looked up at Sebastian. "I feel for her. It's as if she can't rest . . . and neither can I."

Harper's phone chimed that she'd received the text. Norah avoided looking at her in the sun visor's mirror so as not to call attention to Sebastian—who was behind the steering wheel—of her texting his daughter.

> Did you tell your dad yet?

Norah waited, covertly checking her phone, which she'd silenced. Soon a text came through from the back seat of the car.

> Heck no.

Norah waited a few seconds and then responded.

> Are you going to?

> Yeah. Just need to figure out the best timing.
> He gets cranky with me.

Norah hadn't seen the crankier side of Sebastian, but she'd heard its potential in the overtones. And "cranky" was probably an understatement for what his reaction would be when he learned his baby girl was to have her own baby.

> Are you feeling okay?

Norah had to ask. She'd always taken care of Naomi, and now it seemed only natural to offer the same to Harper.

Nauseated, but so far nothing too bad. Just don't
offer to make bacon tomorrow morning, please.
I almost puked this morning from the smell.

Norah bit back a smile.

Sebastian flicked on his turn signal, but he'd caught her smile from the corner of his eye. "Somethin' funny?"

Norah looked out the window at the homes passing by, which were fewer and farther between as they neared the outskirts of Shepherd. "No," she answered. "I just saw a funny meme on my social media."

"What's it say?" he pressed.

"Umm . . ."

"Dad, is that a cow?" Harper pointed out the window as if a cow grazing in a pasture, surrounded by at least ten others, was a rare sighting.

He gave her a suspicious glance in the rearview mirror. "Moo. It is. An' that's excitin'?"

"I-I guess it's just been a while since I've seen cows," Harper fumbled.

Norah kept staring out the window.

Silence.

"Why do I get the feelin' you both are hidin' somethin'? Should I be frettin'?"

"No!" Both Norah and Harper responded simultaneously.

Sebastian pressed his lips together as he steered the vehicle into the Opperman driveway. "You both think I'm doolally, but I'm not. I'll get it out of you."

"Dad, we aren't hiding anything that you need to worry about."

"Why don't I believe you?" He shifted the SUV into park and killed the engine. "Never mind now. We're here an' we need to get inside."

"How did you connect up with these people?" Norah asked, already regretting agreeing to come along. It wasn't just the awkward interlude she and Harper had barely escaped, but it was the fact that she was outside of her comfort zone. Way outside.

"A bit of research goes a long way, lass." Sebastian shut his door with the toe of his shoe. "The town records from back in 1901 might've been destroyed, but there's still the locals. And these people are often willin' to help."

"Just say you called the county land office," Harper said with a toss of her hair over her shoulder. "Dad, you make it sound loftier than it is. People don't realize how much of your info you get online and from a few simple phone calls. They just subscribe to your podcast 'cause you have an accent and it sounds sexy."

"Oof! Right in the heart!" Sebastian melodramatically clutched at his shirt as they hiked up the sidewalk to the front wrap-around porch. "Not to mention smarmy. Callin' me *sexy* with me bein' your father."

"Hey, I'm just quoting your reviewers."

Norah smiled to herself. The playful banter was refreshing after the scare of two nights ago and the tension she'd felt yesterday at the grave of Isabelle Addington.

Sebastian knocked on the door, and it swung open. A middle-aged couple greeted them with smiles. The man was shorter than Sebastian, balding, with glasses, sporting a green polo shirt and khakis. The woman had permed hair with speckles of gray through it, her dress very 1950s in style. She even wore a ruffled apron at her waist.

"Come in, come in!" she cried, beaming. "You must be Sebastian Blaine!"

"Yes, ma'am. An' this is my daughter, Harper, an' my . . . friend Norah."

Norah noticed the pause in his introduction and wondered why the hitch in his voice. Had he wanted to introduce her as the owner of 322 Predicament Avenue but then thought better of it? Or was it something else?

"Do come in." The woman waved them inside as her husband led the way through the entryway of the old but remodeled farmhouse.

"I know we met Mr. Blaine on the phone earlier," he explained to Norah, "but in case he didn't bother to tell you, I'm Ron Daily, and this is my wife, Betty. She's who you're probably most interested in talking to, seeing as it's her family line that owned this place and the property on Predicament Avenue."

"You're an Opperman?" Harper interjected as Betty motioned for them to take seats around their dining room table. She had definitely prepared for their visit. A plate of cookies sat in the middle of the table, a pitcher of iced tea and lemon slices, along with a sugar bowl in case they wanted it sweetened. Each place had an empty glass.

"I am!" Betty smiled again. Her face was pretty but lined. Norah assumed she was probably in her early sixties. "My father was Chuck Opperman, and my grandpa was Aaron Opperman."

"An' they owned this farm that you live on now?" Sebastian took a cookie offered to him by Ron.

"Yes." Betty poured tea in all their glasses without asking if they wanted any. Norah hoped she didn't notice her not drinking it. She wasn't a fan, plus iced tea didn't seem like a good pairing with chocolate chip cookies. Betty was pouring tea into Harper's glass. "They owned this farm back in the 1900s. My grandpa's mother owned it. Mabel. She lived here along with my great-uncle Floyd, who . . . what are the right words to use these days?" She looked at Ron.

"He suffered a brain injury," Ron said. "We were told he was kicked by a cow as a child. It happened on farms, you know. A tragedy."

"Ah." Sebastian looked to Betty as she set the pitcher back in the center of the table and picked up the sugar bowl. She offered it to Harper, who took it and then sent Norah a lost look as though she'd never put sugar in her iced tea before.

Betty swept her dress around her hips as she sat down. "Yes. My grandpa had gone off to college around the time of the events you're inquiring after." She broke a cookie in half on her plate. "When Mabel Opperman, my great-grandmother, passed away in 1923, that's when Grandpa inherited this property."

"And that's when most of their properties were sold off," Ron added, "including the place on Predicament Avenue."

"What happened to Floyd?" Norah asked.

"Well," Betty answered, "unfortunately back in those days, if family wasn't up to the task, then there were places for them."

"Institutions." Harper's tone was flat.

Norah became very interested in her cookie, picking at a chocolate chip. Every part of her wanted to scream in repulsion on behalf of this Floyd Opperman she had never met and who was now long deceased.

"Yes. My grandpa didn't know how best to care for him, and at the time they trusted those places to be fair and kind."

"Some were." Ron tried to make it better.

It didn't work. Norah set her cookie down. She'd lost her appetite.

"Anyway . . ." Betty brushed off conversation about Floyd and continued, "My grandpa said his mother refused to sell off the Predicament Avenue property even though she also refused to invest a penny into it. The place became run-down and abused. People came and went. It was like a shelter for the homeless, only there wasn't any supervision. People just did as they pleased there. My grandpa said he was glad to be rid of it after his mother passed."

Sebastian nodded. "An' he sold it to . . . ?"

"Oh, I'm not sure he even bothered to sell it. Just let the bank take it in payment for a defunct loan." Betty took a sip of her tea. "It stayed in the hands of the James family then—they were the bank owners and president—until it finally got sold in the seventies to Eleanor."

"You knew my aunt Eleanor?" Norah straightened, looking directly at Betty.

"Of course I did! We went to church together. She was about twelve years my senior, but the sweetest lady. You're a blessed girl if she was your aunt."

Ron nudged his wife with his elbow. "Remember how Eleanor would bring flowers to put on the altar for Sunday morning and that one service we all ended up swatting bees?"

"Oh, heavens!" Betty's laughter filled the room. "I *do* recall that! A big bouquet and poor Eleanor had no idea how many honeybees were hiding in it. Poor pastor had to cut the service short so the ushers could rush off and get bug spray."

Norah bit her bottom lip and smiled. She vaguely remembered something about "Eleanor's bees." She'd never understood it, but now it all made sense.

"What can you tell us about Predicament Avenue?" Sebastian palmed his glass of iced tea. He'd already drank half of it sans sugar.

Betty nodded. "Well, aside from the obvious story of the murder that took place, my family was always tight-lipped about it. But I was able to find some photographs for you."

Ron handed his wife a manila envelope. She opened it and pulled out a set of old black-and-white photos, some with stained edges and the images rather blurred.

"This is my great-grandmother Mabel." She handed the photo to Sebastian, and Harper leaned over her father to look at it.

"Wow," Harper mumbled.

"Right?" Betty gave an exaggerated wince. "She was not a kind-looking lady. In fact, around Shepherd, after her husband died, Mabel . . . well, all the Oppermans, didn't have the best of reputations. Thankfully, my grandpa and daddy changed that in the years that followed." Betty handed Sebastian a few more photographs of her grandfather and of the farm in the 1940s.

"Mabel Opperman wasn't cooperative in the investigation of Isabelle Addington's death?" Harper asked.

Norah was happy to let the Blaines interrogate their hosts. She took a tenuous bite of her cookie and listened.

Ron took over this part of the conversation. "From what we've been told, there was quite a kerfuffle about the entire situation. Mabel wanted nothing to do with it. Probably wise too."

"Why's that?" Sebastian raised a dark brow.

Ron leaned back in his chair and exchanged looks with Betty. "Because apparently the night in question—the night Isabelle Addington was murdered—two young women were witnesses to the murder."

"At least a portion of it," Betty corrected.

"Right. Betty's father told me the story was passed down that one of the women connected with a recent newcomer to town who claimed that Isabelle Addington was his wife. As the story goes, he and this young lady might've had something between them too."

"Not exactly the grieving widower," Betty concluded.

"Do you know the names?" Sebastian pulled out his phone to take notes.

Betty nodded. "The women who witnessed the murder were the daughters of the Jameses, the ones who owned the bank and who eventually came to own 322 Predicament Avenue. I believe Daddy said the one girl who caused the most scandal was named . . . um, Evie—"

"Effie," Ron corrected. "Her given name was Euphemia James." He pointed at Sebastian's phone. "You'll want to refer to her as that if you're searching the records."

"Yes, that's it." Betty drummed her fingers on the table as she recalled the details. "The stranger in town was an Englishman like you, Mr. Blaine. Not much was known about him, and I'm not sure what happened to him. Daddy didn't seem to know either."

"And they never found out who murdered Isabelle?" Harper dared a sip of her iced tea. Her eyebrows rose and she took another sip.

"No." Ron shook his head. "Leastways not that we know of."

"They never even found her *body!*" Betty clarified.

Norah thought of the grave marker in her backyard with Isabelle Addington's initials etched in the stone.

"How have you come by that information?" Sebastian must have been thinking the same thing.

Betty sighed. "I know there's a grave, but my daddy always said they just put that there 'cause Isabelle needed a gravesite to be remembered by. The only things linked to Isabelle's death were the bloodstains and a butcher knife. Of course, without DNA and all that science stuff, the knife was just a knife. There wasn't any way of telling for sure who killed the woman."

"What was the name of the Englishman who got together with the James woman?" Sebastian asked, typing something into his phone.

"Went by the name of Anderson. Not sure what his first name was."

"Anderson?" Norah stiffened. Her little outburst caused four sets of eyes to swing in her direction.

"It's a common name, Norah," Sebastian stated, "but do you recognize somethin'?"

"Maybe. I mean . . ." Norah tried to control the roll in her stomach. "One of the people questioned after Naomi's death was a LeRoy Anderson."

"That's right." Betty's fingers pressed against her lips.

"I'm sure there's no connection." Ron quickly tried to downplay it. "Probably coincidental is all."

"Yeah, Anderson is a very typical surname." Harper reached across the table as if to grasp Norah's hands.

Norah knew they were right. That nothing about Isabelle Addington's case had anything to do with Naomi's own murder decades later. But the similarities, the location, and now the name . . . it was bringing it all back.

She could no longer reason away the library card left on her dresser, nor the woman who had floated through the doorway.

The house at 322 Predicament Avenue held secrets, and they were screaming out to be revealed.

16

THEY STOPPED FOR COFFEE. Well, Sebastian and Harper did. Harper had sent Norah a covert text assuring her she'd get decaf. Norah sat in the car and waited. She wasn't a fan of coffee shops. They were always small and meant to feel cozy, but Norah felt claustrophobic, and the places were often packed. They were an extrovert's paradise and an introvert's duck-and-run hideaway. Yet for someone with as much social anxiety as Norah, they were the opening to the pit of hell.

Okay. That was an exaggeration.

Norah thumbed through her social media on her phone to distract herself. Ever since leaving Ron and Betty Daily's place, she'd been edgy again. She felt an oppressive weight on her chest, the kind that predicted a confrontation with everything Norah didn't want to confront.

Namely, Naomi's cold case.

She couldn't shake the significance of the name Anderson. Coincidence or not, now both murders were linked by name and by place. For different reasons, but still. Sometimes Norah wondered if God got frustrated by her avoidance of the truth and the grief and was now just going to thrust her into it without any room for her to argue.

"*You need to learn to live again,*" her mother had kept telling her. Her mother! The woman who should be as immobilized as Norah by the murder of her own daughter! And yet maybe Norah had been her distraction. Norah who had collapsed after Naomi's body had been found. Norah who hadn't fared well during the ensuing investigation. Norah who had all but blocked out the events of those months before the case was shelved as COLD. Yes, she had been her mother's distraction, but now? How could Mom and Dad go tour Europe as though Naomi's killer didn't still lurk in dark corners, laughing at their pain?

A hand came down to knock hard against Norah's window.

She screamed.

"Whoa!" the voice shouted from outside.

Norah dared to look out the window. Detective Dover. Way to make a fool of herself. She opened the door.

"Sorry to frighten you," Dover said with a grimace. He was dressed in a black suit and tie, his hair neatly combed back. Handsome. Older. "I saw you sitting there and thought I'd check on you."

"Thanks." Norah fiddled with the side button on her phone to shut it off.

"Have you heard anything from Mrs. Miller?"

"No." Norah shook her head. "My lawyer and I are preparing just in case, though."

"That's good." Dover crossed his arms and looked around before lowering his voice. "Just FYI, Mrs. Miller's son arrived in town. I hear he's an attorney."

"Great," Norah muttered.

"Doesn't necessarily mean anything. She probably doesn't want to travel home alone. Not to mention there's the arrangements that need to be made with Mr. Nielson to get Mr. Miller's remains home. But I thought you should know. I was hoping you'd connected with Rebecca."

He knew who her lawyer was? Small-town problems.

"Yes. I have. Sebastian Blaine is helping me put together what really happened with Isabelle Addington so we can have the full story and not have to deal with lawsuits against ghosts."

Dover laughed. "Yeah, that sounds so dumb, but you know how people can be these days. And I can hardly blame Mrs. Miller. I mean, if she saw what she thinks she saw—"

"She didn't," Norah interrupted, irritated by the detective's insinuation that maybe Mrs. Miller *had* seen a ghost after all.

"I'm not saying she did. I'm just . . . heck, sometimes I see things at night when I'm half awake. Pitfalls of being a hard sleeper."

"Have you ever seen a ghost?" Norah ventured, though she wasn't sure she wanted an answer.

"Me? Nah. My mom said she did once. But it was probably nothing, a reflection or something. One night, though, I woke up and swore my mom was standing over my bed with a towel wrapped around her head. You know, like a woman does when she gets out of the shower?"

Norah nodded.

Detective Dover continued, "Then I blinked and she was gone. But my mom was very much alive, so I knew it wasn't a ghost. Just my mind playing tricks on me."

Norah shivered.

Dover noticed. "Yeah, it was still freaky."

Norah didn't say anything more.

"Well then . . ." Dover slapped the roof of the SUV. "You have a good day, okay? And if you need anything—" he paused, and his eyes darkened for a moment—"I know looking into this old murder case can dredge up other memories. So if you need anything, let me know."

Norah narrowed her eyes. Why would he say such a thing? He certainly wasn't going to pull the files on Naomi's case and hand them over to her.

She watched him stride away. Maybe she should ask him if

he really meant what he said. Maybe Naomi's cold case files would look different to a pair of fresh eyes like Sebastian's. Maybe asking questions was a way to finish walking through her grief . . .

Not that she wanted to live again—not really. Not the kind of living that would make Naomi more of a memory. It wasn't fair to be asked to live this life without her sister. All the dreams they'd wanted to share together, she'd have to maneuver solo.

No. No cold case files for her.

Naomi's folder would stay closed. For no one's sake but Norah's.

Norah stared at him over the book she'd been reading. A book meant to help her escape from life, not reenter it with an announcement like that.

Sebastian's glasses emphasized the anticipation in his eyes, but there was caution in them too. Which didn't bode well. Norah steeled herself.

"I'd put a request in for the case files for Isabelle Addington before I arrived here."

"They have case files on a murder case from 1901?" Norah couldn't help but be a bit surprised that documents from so long ago still existed.

"A few." Sebastian raked his hand through his wavy hair. A dark lock bounced back against his forehead. He ducked his head, then lifted his eyes, looking very much like a guilty puppy. "I . . . uh, have a confession to make."

Here it came. Norah lowered her book, certain now that not even an Amish romance would be enough to steady her nerves.

Sebastian sniffed. "I might've gotten the files from your sister's case too."

"Might have?"

Sebastian scrunched his face with the worst sort of adorable and utterly horrid guilt Norah had ever seen. "Well, I did actually."

Norah dropped her book onto the floor of the porch with a thud. She pulled her knees up to her chest, resting her chin on them, and wrapped her arms around her legs. "You had no right to do that." She didn't know what else to say. Not really. She'd been on a roller coaster herself, and this was someone else making decisions for her. She didn't appreciate that, and yet it was ironic. Especially after Detective Dover had just offered to help her earlier today.

"I know I promised I wasn't goin' to cover your sister's death . . ." Sebastian leaned back in his chair with a frustrated growl. "An' I'm not, but there are certain things between the two cases that can't be denied." He winced in apology. "The similarities are uncanny."

She froze.

His eyes met hers, and there was a flicker of realization. "I don't want to make you feel like I'm tryin' to unbury the past and hurt you. I asked on impulse, and the case files were easy to acquire. But before I open them, I wanted to be honest with you about it."

Norah didn't know how to respond. She thought back to their dinner and how he'd agreed with her that leaving the past alone was sometimes the best way of dealing with it—him and his relationship with Harper, her with Naomi. Part of her appreciated his candor. Another part wanted to slap him for picking at a wound that had never scabbed over. He'd told her he was here to investigate Isabelle Addington, not Naomi, and now the fact that he had Naomi's case files—

Sebastian cleared his throat and pushed his glasses up his nose. "I'll not open them."

Norah lifted her eyes.

Sebastian didn't look away, and for a long moment something passed between them that Norah didn't quite understand. Apology. Concern. Kinship. Frustration. Fear. All of the above?

What would Naomi want?

Norah picked at loose threads that hung from a stylishly positioned hole in the knee of her jeans. She knew what Naomi would say.

Don't you dare walk away from me. You've been hiding for too long. Find out what happened, Norah. To me. To Isabelle Addington.

Norah allowed herself to drown for a long second in the depths of Sebastian's eyes. They were gentle. She could tell he cared, and his honest confession meant he wasn't trying to hide anything from her for the sake of his podcast or publicity. "Promise me you'll not talk about the details of my sister's case on your podcast unless you come to me first."

"I promise." He nodded earnestly.

"Where are the files?" Norah's stomach rolled. She didn't want to reopen Naomi's case, didn't want to revisit the details of her murder. To read about the investigation or see the list of suspects she already knew had been questioned and cleared.

Sebastian tipped his chin up. "They're in my room."

"Go get them." Norah's instruction came out as a choked whisper.

"Norah, I—"

"Get them before I change my mind."

She felt the eyes of the dead watching her as she chewed the skin near her fingernails. One cuticle was already raw and bleeding. Her anxiety was building. This was a bad idea. A very bad idea.

Harper plugged her laptop into a wall outlet. Her hair was pulled back in a messy bun. She wore her typical oversized hoodie. Norah wondered if Harper intended to wear the hoodie for as long as she could until it became impossible to hide her secret from her father.

Sebastian had several manila folders. Norah could see the

edges of photographs sticking out from one. She sank onto a chair.

Harper glanced up. "You okay?"

Norah nodded, gnawing at her finger.

Sebastian eyed her. "Do you want to look through Isabelle's case first? There's not much there, but it's somethin' to go on."

Norah debated for a quick moment, then shook her head. "No. Let's get it over with."

"Naomi's?" Harper verified.

Norah nodded.

Sebastian wasted no time. She wasn't sure if it was because he was afraid she'd change her mind, or if he wanted to get to it like someone yanking off a Band-Aid.

"There's nothing in there I haven't already seen at some point." Norah voiced her thoughts more to reassure herself than Sebastian or Harper.

"It's just copies of the reports. A summary of what happened. Suspect list. A few photographs." Harper began thumbing through the pages.

"I don't want to see her." Norah's eyes burned, and she tilted her head back to look at the ceiling.

"There are no photos of the body in here," Sebastian said. Whether the police didn't release them or whether he'd pulled them for her sake, Norah didn't know, and she didn't ask.

She lowered her head, eyeing the pages.

Harper closed one of the folders. "Before we look at these, why don't you tell us what you know—what you remember?" Her voice was soft and reassuring.

Norah nodded. It made sense. Why taint her memories with police reports? Her own testimony might help. Suddenly doubt wrapped its arms around her, tighter than she had wrapped her arms around herself. "I don't know if I can do this." She looked between father and daughter. "I mean, how necessary is it? Her case has nothing do with Isabelle Addington's and what

181

happened here in 1901. Mrs. Miller hasn't filed a lawsuit against me for Isabelle's ghost and Mr. Miller's death. Naomi's murder has nothing to do with your podcast, and . . ." Norah was rambling, the words spilling out faster and faster. She couldn't sift through her emotions, her thoughts. The entire situation was—

"Norah." Sebastian lowered himself into a crouch in front of where she sat. His calming voice urged her to meet his eyes. "Here's what we know. Two murders in Shepherd, both with ties to this place. Both with the name of Anderson somehow tied to the victims. An' now you had a guest pass away here an' people sayin' they saw Isabelle's ghost—who you think you saw a few nights ago. An' then your sister's library card showin' up out of nowhere. That's why, Norah. There's too much in and out and all around with these cases. You're not able to sleep. I can see it in your eyes. You're wastin' away, an' it's not healthy."

Harper came around on the other side and crouched beside her dad. "It's okay to be afraid, Norah." She gave her dad a sideways glance and then caught Norah's gaze. "I'm afraid sometimes."

Norah knew Harper wasn't trying to compare or compete with their different types of fear. One could argue fear of an unsolved murder outweighed fear of telling a parent you were pregnant. But then could one? Norah was well aware this was why a person didn't compete over whose trouble was worse. They were all trials. All of them encased in the sort of fear that couldn't just be washed away. There was no resolving her sister's death, even if the case were solved. There was no resolving a massive life change like an unplanned baby, even if it would be welcomed with open arms.

"My sister left for work in the morning," Norah started before she could convince herself not to.

Harper adjusted so she sat cross-legged on the floor. Sebastian eased up and onto a chair, but Norah noticed he kept his fingertips on her knee to reassure her.

"It was a normal day. Naomi just . . . didn't come home. She didn't respond to my texts. That wasn't unusual while she was at work—she worked at a pharmacy as an assistant. But Naomi always responded when she got off work after the pharmacy closed at ten."

"So it was nighttime when she got off work," Harper noted.

"Yes." Norah kept her eyes on Sebastian's hand as it lay gently on her knee. There was something profoundly comforting in the gesture. "When we didn't hear from her by midnight, Dad went out looking for her. That was when he found her car still in the pharmacy's parking lot. The doors were unlocked. The keys were in the ignition."

Norah swallowed hard against the bile rising in her throat. "Dad called the police immediately. They came and collected the info needed to file a report. By the afternoon of the next day, everyone seemed to be searching for Naomi. Aunt Eleanor, Otto, Ralph, Mom, me, people from church and in town. The cops. But she had simply disappeared."

"Who saw her last?" Sebastian asked.

Norah looked at him. "The pharmacist who was working that night. She said that Naomi was in good spirits when she left the pharmacy. She didn't notice that Naomi's car was still there when she left, but she had parked in the back of the building and Naomi had parked in the front. The police didn't find anything in the car to point us in a specific direction. Naomi's handbag was missing, along with her wallet."

"Which had her library card in it?" Harper deduced.

Norah drew in a steadying breath. "Naomi never went anywhere without a book. Her library card was as important to her as a credit card to a shopaholic."

The three shared nervous laughter.

"How long was it before she was found?" Harper's question was gentle, respectful.

Norah swallowed around the lump in her throat. "Three

months. A hunter found her in the woods. She had been . . ." Norah didn't want to elaborate.

"It's okay. We can read the report." Harper exchanged a nod with her father.

Norah shook her head and braved her way through. "Naomi had been strangled. They figured she had been killed shortly after her abduction. No more than two or three days."

Sebastian had opened a folder and pulled out a sheet of paper. He skimmed it. "No signs of a sexual motive."

"No." Norah had thanked God for that. "There was no evidence of assault, at least from what they could tell. She was . . . well, it'd been three months."

"You're right about LeRoy Anderson." Sebastian paged through one of the files. "He was a primary suspect."

"He claimed to be Naomi's boyfriend—which shocked all of us." Norah's admission dredged up the feelings of resentment she'd always harbored toward the man, who was now in his late thirties.

"Why is that?" Harper inquired.

"A few reasons. He was several years older than Naomi, and they had nothing in common. At all. He says they met at the bar of all places, but Naomi wasn't that careless—she wasn't even old enough to drink. But the biggest reason is, Naomi didn't keep secrets from me. So the fact she had a boyfriend was hard for us to reason through."

"Why was he named a suspect?" Harper's follow-up question brought an answer from Sebastian.

"According to the file, Naomi was seen talkin' to him on her break earlier in the evenin'. A witness said she looked upset. An' later, LeRoy didn't have a good answer for where he'd been that night."

"No alibi," Norah concluded for Harper's benefit. "He said he was at his apartment by himself, asleep. But there was no one to corroborate it."

"He must've had a motive for the cops to zero in on him."

Norah felt the color seep from her face. She couldn't look Harper in the eyes. She couldn't. It was too close to home. Too real. Too awful.

"That's gutting," Sebastian muttered, a stunned look in his eyes when he met Norah's.

"What?" Harper eased herself off the floor to draw closer to her father. "What is it?"

Sebastian turned the report toward Harper, and Norah looked away, blinking rapidly against the hot tears in her eyes.

"Oh . . ." Harper's acknowledgment brought Norah's face back around. "She was pregnant?" Harper whispered.

"Four months along," Sebastian said, looking at the report again.

Norah used her shirtsleeve to wipe the wetness from her face. She choked, coughed, and then sniffed back her emotion. "The theory is that LeRoy killed her when he found out Naomi was going to have a baby. But no one could prove it. Ever."

A low whistle escaped Sebastian, and both Harper and Norah froze at his words. "Nineteen and pregnant. Poor lass. I can see how it gutted all of ya."

Harper looked away quickly.

Norah dropped her gaze.

There were too many parallels coming up between the then and the now. Norah knew this was going to make it even more difficult for Harper to tell her dad about her baby. It was also going to make it tough for Norah not to feel as though she were reliving parts of Naomi's life all over again.

17

EFFIE

1901
Shepherd, Iowa

WHO WAS Isabelle Addington?

Effie eyed the lock on Polly's window. She noted the measures her father had taken around the manor to safeguard their home. Safeguard it against an unknown assailant whose fingerprints were only just now fading from Effie's throat.

She turned to her sister, who lay in her bed, silent and resting in the blessedness of sleep. Polly was sinking further and further away from her. And in these moments when that should be all Effie considered, all she agonized over, instead she feared that someone would once again try to cut short what little time they had together.

Time that had been stolen from Anderson when Polly had witnessed Isabelle's demise. A woman no one knew, only Anderson could give testimony of, and Polly had seen but couldn't speak about. It was a tornado of circumstances and assumptions that had brought them here, with only the strength of hands around Effie's throat to confirm it was not over.

Effie moved to Polly's bedside and eased slowly onto the mattress. She reached out and tenderly brushed away a strand of hair from her sister's face. Time was not her friend.

A soft knock on the bedroom door alerted Effie to the fact that she was no longer alone with her sister. The door opened with a welcoming creak of its hinges. "Miss?" It was the nurse. She entered the room with an expression of empathy and kindness on her plain face. "It's time for me to give your sister her medicine."

"Yes." Effie slipped off the bed from beside her still sister. "Yes, of course, Nurse Carlisle." She moved away as the nurse came closer to Polly. She balanced a tray in her hands and rested it on the table beside the bed.

With a glance over her shoulder, Nurse Carlisle offered Effie a smile. "You should take a break, Miss James."

Effie folded her arms over her chest, feeling the exhaustion, the weight of everything bearing down on them. She had not been a responsible older sister the night Polly's surge of adventure and energy had led them to try to make a memory together. A memory that had turned into horror and spiraled Polly toward her final breath. "I need to be near her." Effie's words were choked. Hampered by emotion and the uncertainty of tomorrow.

Was it wrong that she was beginning to dislike Isabelle Addington? Dislike the woman—Anderson's wife—who had left Anderson for whatever reason? Shown such disloyalty as to travel across the sea and then send her abandoned husband a letter with only a few self-centered lines about her need for forgiveness? And Anderson had come. Effie couldn't erase that noble act from her mind, which had become more impressed on Effie since Anderson's admission that he had not allowed himself to grieve for his wife. He had left his home to come retrieve Isabelle—a wayward woman for whatever reason and purpose—and he arrived only to be convinced of Isabelle's violent end. And now he remained? To find her? To lay her to rest? Effie couldn't comprehend the unanswered questions, pieces that made no sense. A man whose loyalty was remarkable but by his own admission had closed himself off from grieving.

Nurse Carlisle's movements jarred Effie from her musings. She watched the nurse mixing powders into a glass of water.

"What are you giving her?" Effie inquired. If it was for pain, Polly appeared to be resting peacefully at the moment. Did she really need the medicine?

The spoon clinked against the glass as Nurse Carlisle mixed the medicine. "It's for relief from pain."

"Must we give her more?" Effie asked. "It makes her even more distant from us than she already is." She wished for Polly to awaken again. She had only done so twice since the other day, yet both times she hadn't been coherent enough to converse with her family.

Polly had taken such a severe turn since that night at 322 Predicament Avenue. When she and Polly had returned home, Father was furious. Effie replayed the scene in her mind. Polly, still in shock, had mumbled something about the woman she'd seen attacked. About the man hovering over the woman and then plunging a knife downward. The screams. The unidentifiable features of the assailant. The woman's bloodied face as it had turned toward Polly and then . . . Effie recalled Polly's expression, her violent shaking. Nurse Carlisle hadn't been there that night. There'd been no reason to have her in the James manor around the clock yet. Polly hadn't been that bad. Not yet. She was sitting up doing her embroidery. She had been dreaming of what she wanted to do before she passed. She had been— Effie's memories hitched. She frowned as she observed Nurse

Carlisle spooning the medicine into Polly's mouth, dabbing at what dribbled down the side of her face.

Nurse Carlisle had arrived the following morning with new medicine. It was from Dr. Reginald, she'd said, to help calm Polly. To ease her discomfort from the shock of what she had witnessed the night before.

Polly hadn't been the same since.

Effie launched herself toward Nurse Carlisle, batting the glass from the woman's hand. The nurse cried out in stunned surprise and jumped backward.

"Get away from her!" Effie pushed herself between Nurse Carlisle and her sister.

"What is going on?" Effie's mother rushed into the room, her eyes wide.

"She's poisoning Polly!" Effie accused, pointing at Nurse Carlisle.

The nurse gasped, her mouth agape. "No! Absolutely not! I would never!"

Katherine James looked between her daughter and the nurse. "How? What makes you think this, Euphemia?"

Effie pointed at the jar of powders on the nurse's tray. "Since she's been giving those to Polly, Polly keeps getting worse." Effie stalked toward Nurse Carlisle, and the nurse shrank into the wall behind her. "Who told you to poison her?"

"I'm not poisoning your sister!" Nurse Carlisle was crying. Panic and fear warred in her expression. She turned to Katherine. "You have to believe me. It's for your daughter's pain."

"Did you let that man in the window the other night? To get to Polly?" Effie drew so close to Nurse Carlisle, there were mere inches between them. Fury surged through her. Whoever had attacked Isabelle Addington that night had hired Nurse Carlisle to keep Polly silent. "Who is paying you to do this?"

"Euphemia!" Her mother's stern voice broke into her accusations. "Stop this right now! You're exhausted. This has all been too much for you. Please, go and rest. I'll watch Polly. Nurse Carlisle is only trying to help."

"No!" Effie leveled a look on her mother. "Mother, she's silencing my sister!"

"I'm not . . ." Nurse Carlisle shook her head, weeping softly.

Katherine James moved to Polly's bedside. She caressed her ailing daughter's forehead and then looked to Effie.

Effie stared back at her mother. She must convince her mother what she knew deep in her gut. Nurse Carlisle was evil. Whoever had committed the crime at 322 Predicament Avenue had brought their malice to the James manor.

"Go, Euphemia," Katherine commanded. "You are not in your right mind—not since that evening. Not since your dalliances with that . . . that *man*."

"Mother, I—"

"I said go!"

Effie ran from the room, but not to flee from her mother. She ran to find someone who would believe her and help her to spare Polly these agonizing last days of her life.

Anderson.

Effie heard the footsteps on the sidewalk behind her before she turned. Oh my. She had not expected Patrick Charlemagne, let alone to be greeted with such warm friendliness. She continued her brisk hike in the direction of Anderson's small house.

"Hello, Mr. Charlemagne." Not too many weeks ago, she would have been beside herself with elation that he had singled her out to greet her. Now she wasn't of the mind to care in the slightest.

"I was on my way from Miss Bethany's home. We had a lovely picnic lunch."

Of course. Sweet Bethany. In her urgency, Effie was grateful that Bethany's life was continuing in the direction of the dreams they had shared as girls.

"Are you headed home? Would you like an escort?" Patrick offered.

Effie shook her head. "No, thank you."

Patrick tipped his hat. "Very well. Have a lovely day, Miss James."

Effie managed a polite smile but focused her attention on the walk before her. Patrick hesitated, and Effie noticed, slowing to question him with a look.

"Did you intend to walk past Predicament Avenue?" His question startled Effie. She hadn't realized in her hurry that her walk would take her past Predicament Avenue before she reached Anderson's house.

"I only ask because—" Patrick cleared his throat—"I know there have been dangers, for you and your family. I'm not certain you should be going there alone."

"You're probably right." Effie stopped to consider. It wouldn't be wise to put herself in jeopardy in an attempt to save Polly from it.

Patrick pointed. "The avenue is just up ahead. May I at least walk you beyond it until we're closer to your destination?"

"Of course." Effie acquiesced and followed Patrick's lead. Soon they approached Predicament Avenue, and Patrick pointed toward the house. Some people had strayed onto the porch. Effie recognized them and bit back a sigh. Folks were still touring the scene of the crime as if it were some sort of curiosity or sport.

"Did you know that Mrs. Branson came forward and stated she'd seen a woman at the house the day before you and your sister reported hearing the scuffle?"

Effie drew back in surprise. "No. No, I hadn't heard."

Patrick nodded. "She was quite insistent about it too. Said the woman was young with reddish-brown hair, dressed more decent than she would have expected a woman traveling alone to dress—that is, for someone drifting through an abandoned house looking for shelter."

Effie's breath caught. If it had been Isabelle, that would make sense. Mr. Anderson wore fine tailored clothing. He didn't seem to be lacking finances, so it would stand to reason there were still remnants of that in Isabelle's dress as well.

Her hand shot out to grasp Patrick's arm. "Where does Mrs. Branson live?"

"Just over the way." Patrick tipped his head to the side. "Why?"

"Will you take me there? I would like to speak with her."

"If you think that is wise . . ." Patrick was hesitant to comply. "It will only take a few minutes to walk there."

Effie convinced him. If she could speak to Mrs. Branson, perhaps she would learn something that would help Anderson uncover what had happened.

The little white house belonging to Mrs. Branson was perhaps half a mile from 322 Predicament Avenue. Patrick approached the door confidently and knocked, with Effie standing slightly behind him. The door opened to reveal a middle-aged woman in a crisp cotton shirtwaist and lace collar belted at the waist, with a dark green skirt draping to the floor. She wore spectacles, and her graying hair was pulled up properly.

"Mr. Charlemagne!" Her smile of welcome wavered as she spotted Effie. "Miss James. How may I help you?" Mrs. Branson inquired with a sweeping look from Effie to Patrick, then back to Effie again.

Patrick broke the awkwardness with a casual smile, hat clutched in his hands. "Miss James has a few questions for you."

"About?" Mrs. Branson's eyebrows rose.

Effie cleared her throat. "The woman."

"What woman?"

"The woman who came to an unfortunate end at 322 Predicament Avenue," Patrick said, assisting Effie.

"Ahh. Yes." Mrs. Branson nodded. "What about her?"

Effie swallowed. "Did you speak with her? Could you describe her for me? Can you tell me her name?"

Mrs. Branson frowned, adjusting her gold spectacles on her nose. "I've already told the police all of this. What business is it of yours? Are you one of those curiosity seekers who have been invading the neighborhood since you and that Englishman uncovered the crime scene?"

"No, I—"

"Mrs. Branson." Patrick offered a charming smile. "Miss James and her family have been directly affected by the situation. Any help you can provide would be greatly appreciated."

"Well then." Mrs. Branson sniffed and pursed her lips. "No, I did not get introduced to her. I am careful whom I spend my time with. People talk, and I'm a good Christian woman, so one must be cautious about entertaining women of questionable backgrounds." Another censuring look made Effie stiffen. She heard the underlying implications. Effie had been seen numerous times with the foreigner Mr. Anderson, who wasn't merely escorting her safely from one location to another like Patrick Charlemagne had. No. She had been seen in his carriage, with him at Predicament Avenue, not to mention at the house he was renting.

Mrs. Branson continued, "Not that I know the woman's history, but . . . well, it can't be good if she's no home, no husband, and is sleeping in an abandoned house with a child."

Effie jerked her head up. "A child?"

Mrs. Branson nodded. "A very young one. I doubt the child was more than a year old if that."

Effie exchanged looks with Patrick, who narrowed his eyes. "I wasn't aware there was a child involved in this awful situation."

Mrs. Branson's pinched expression grew tauter. "Well, I know what I saw. I can't speak for what happened to the child. God forbid it was slaughtered along with the poor woman—who should not have expected any other outcome considering she was alone. Women in those situations never fare well, and I suppose it was only bound to happen at some point."

"Are you certain there was a child?" Effie asked.

Mrs. Branson glowered at her. "Yes. There was a child."

"Was it hers?" Effie couldn't disguise her shock.

"How am I supposed to know?" Mrs. Branson said. "I would assume the child was hers if it was with her."

Horror flooded Effie as she backed down the steps, staring at Mrs. Branson as she did so.

"Miss James?" Patrick extended his hand, which she ignored.

"The child, we have to . . ." Effie couldn't complete the sentence. Her thoughts became jumbled. All she knew was that if Isabelle Addington was Anderson's wife, then the child was . . . Anderson's.

18

ANDERSON BARRELED OUT the front door the moment he saw Effie approaching his house, Patrick at her heels.

"Effie!" The dark thundercloud that stretched across Anderson's face was nothing in comparison to the turbulence in her heart.

He bolted down the stairs and the walkway. "Who are you!" he barked at Patrick.

Patrick grinned politely, extending his hand. "Patrick Charlemagne."

Anderson grunted and gave the proffered hand a reluctant shake. "Thank you for escorting Miss James."

Patrick looked between them and then frowned. "Are you . . . ?" He gave Effie a questioning look. "I mean, is your mother here perhaps? Or is she meeting you?"

Effie appreciated that he was concerned about her reputation, but at the moment she couldn't care less about that. A baby! Agitated, she shifted her weight to her other foot, wishing dear, good Patrick Charlemagne would take his leave.

"No. You may go now," Anderson instructed stiffly.

"Pardon?" Patrick reared back.

"I said *off with you.*"

"Miss James?" Patrick turned to her.

"Thank you, Mr. Charlemagne." Effie gave him a halfhearted smile.

Patrick pressed his lips together. Frowning, he nodded. "All right then." With that, he strode away.

Effie opened her mouth to call after him, to thank him. Without Patrick, she'd not know what Mrs. Branson had witnessed. Not know—

"Into the house," Anderson gritted through his teeth.

Effie lifted her chin. "Pardon me, but I will not be talked to as if I'm your . . . *belonging.*"

Anderson started to say something, then stopped. Effie could see he was trying to control his fury. Or was it concern, worry? Had he been worried about her?

Anderson lowered his voice. "My apologies, but I was quite concerned when your mother sent a carriage here to inquire after you. To get here, you had to walk past Predicament Avenue. What were you thinking? Then I see you strolling down the sidewalk with a strange man?"

"He's not strange to me. I know Mr. Charlemagne. We've been acquainted since we were children. He's respectable and—"

"Being unchaperoned with a man was your downfall to begin with!" Anderson pointed down the street toward Patrick's retreating form, now far in the distance.

Frustrated, Effie glared at him. She rarely lost her temper, but Anderson was testing her patience. "I don't care about that right now. What about *you*? What haven't you told me that I should know!"

Anderson's eyes widened. He motioned toward the house. "Let's go inside before this becomes so much worse."

She hurried up the steps and into the house. Gus was nowhere to be seen. Anderson shut the door firmly.

This was ridiculous. All of it. Every single moment of every single day had become a portion of a much bigger nightmare. And now? Effie turned to address Anderson. To confront him about the woman and the child.

Anderson spun toward her, and with the door at her back, Effie was quite trapped there. His expression had gentled, and she thought she even saw his chest rise and fall in what appeared to be relief.

"Patrick Charlemagne is trustworthy?" Anderson confirmed.

Effie nodded. "Yes. The Charlemagnes are honorable. He is courting my dearest friend, Bethany."

"And you are all right?" His eyes skimmed her from the top of her head to her toes. "Your mother is beside herself. She sent a message. Something about you accusing Polly's nurse—"

Effie reached out and clutched Anderson's forearm. "You must believe me. It makes sense. Ever since that night, they've been medicating Polly with powders. She's been unresponsive, suppressed. The day we went to Predicament Avenue, she had *life* in her still."

"Trauma can cause digression." Anderson stated it so matter-of-factly that Effie dropped her hold on his arm.

He still had her positioned between him and the door. His eyes softened as he looked into hers. His English accent grew thicker for some reason, his voice huskier. "I believe you."

Those words meant the world to her. Effie expelled a pent-up breath. One she had been holding in, it seemed, since she'd left the manor in a rush. Now she looked up at Anderson and searched his face. He was withdrawn still, as she was growing accustomed to, and yet something in his demeanor tugged her toward him.

But first . . . "Do you have a child?"

His body went rigid. "What did you ask?"

"Do you have a child? You and Isabelle?"

Anderson took a step toward her.

Effie backed away, hitting the door.

"Tell me what you know," Anderson insisted.

Effie tilted her nose upward. He could interrogate her. Intimidate her. Show her kindness. Even smile at her—what would that be like?—but he could not hide from her. Not any longer. She deserved to know the whole truth. "Mr. Charlemagne told me that Mrs. Branson had seen a woman at Predicament Avenue the day before Polly and I were there. The woman had a child with her—no more than a year old, Mrs. Branson said."

Anderson gripped Effie's arms in the first sign of urgency she'd seen in him. He wasn't hurting her, he was intent. Even hopeful. "Was the child all right?"

"I-I don't know." Effie shook her head. "Mrs. Branson said no one has seen the child since. But I—"

Anderson dropped his hands from Effie and turned his back to her, driving his fingers through his hair with force. He let out a long groan, and then in a rare show his arm swept out and sent a glass vase from the side table flying across the entryway. It shattered against the wall into a million little pieces.

Effie cried out, stunned.

Anderson gripped the sides of his head and dropped to his knees.

"Mr. Anderson!" Gus pushed into the room past Effie. He took in the sight of the broken vase, the concern on Effie's face, and Anderson on his knees holding his head. Gus hurried to the man's side. "Mr. Anderson, are you all right?"

Anderson's response was low, pained. "The child was spotted, Gus."

Gus gasped. "Are you for certain, sir?"

Anderson twisted to look at Effie. "Are you certain? This woman said she saw the child with Isabelle?"

Effie nodded and then bit her lip. "Well, she didn't mention Isabelle's name. She just said there was a woman and a child."

"It's her," Anderson said to Gus. "Isabelle had her as recently as a few weeks ago."

"Most likely, yes." Gus's expression was eager, yet his voice was shrouded in caution. "But where is the child now?"

"Whose child is it?" Effie already knew. But if indeed there was a child, it changed *everything*. This was no longer a mystery of murder. This was about finding a child.

Anderson was in his bedroom, but Effie didn't bother to question etiquette—that was of no consequence now. He paced back and forth at the foot of the bed, his hands clasped behind his back. "Leave." His plea shattered the silence.

Effie remained in the doorway. The man was half doubled over. She tried to understand. "Please tell me. Let me help you."

Anderson stopped and dropped his hands to his sides. The look he gave her was incredulous, lost, despairing. "What do you think you can do?" he groaned, accusation in his tone. "It has been ten *months*! Even if we find her—"

"The baby, she's your daughter?"

Anderson stared at her, his chest heaving in agony.

Effie took a tentative step toward him. "Did Isabelle take your daughter? Did your wife—?"

"Isabelle Addington is *not* my wife!" Anderson spat the words with vehemence. The veins in his neck bulged, his face contorted with everything that he had hidden deep in his soul. "She's not my wife!" he repeated. Tears sprang to his eyes, and he wildly swiped them away and reached for the bed's footboard.

"I don't understand, you told me . . ." Confused, Effie's breath hitched.

Anderson strode to a trunk across the room beneath a window. He lifted the lid with a force that was far more than needed. Snatching a framed picture from within, he marched over to Effie and shoved the photograph into her hands.

She took it hesitantly.

"*That* is my wife!" He jabbed his finger at the picture.

She looked down at the photograph of a pretty woman with a kind smile, delicate features, and light-colored hair. Somehow the black-and-white tones had captured the silken beauty of the woman's blond hair.

This was not the woman with the reddish-brown hair whom Mrs. Branson claimed to have seen with the child. This was not Isabelle Addington. Or was it? Bewildered, Effie lifted questioning eyes to Anderson.

He stared back, his mouth twisting, his face creasing in a desperate attempt to regain control, to steel himself. Anderson blew out a breath and sank onto the edge of his bed, burying his head in his hands.

Effie waited for a few long seconds before daring to approach him. She stood looking down at his bent form. He was silent, his shoulders hunched, his face hidden from her.

Finally, Effie said, "She is . . . beautiful." She studied the photograph of Anderson's wife once more. A twinge of jealousy—she didn't know why—touched her inside, and then Effie immediately squelched it. That Anderson loved this woman—the child—was more apparent now than it had ever been.

"Where is she?" Effie breathed, hesitating before moving around him and giving herself permission to sink onto the edge of the bed beside him. "Where is your wife?"

"I told you. She's dead." Anderson's admission was familiar, but this time it was said so solemnly, muffled by his hands, that Effie knew they were no longer speaking about the woman at 322 Predicament Avenue. The pools of blood, the splatter on the mirror—those belonged to someone else. Someone who had written a letter, referring to a "songbird" and leading Anderson on a chase across the sea—not for her, but for his child.

Footsteps shuffled in the hallway, and Effie looked up to see

Gus standing in the doorway. The old man looked as beaten down and defeated as Anderson now did.

Gus stepped into the room, his eyes filled with sadness. He ran a hand over his mustache, then cleared his throat. "Her name was Laura. She passed away eleven months ago—in childbirth. The child was their daughter, Cora."

"And who's Isabelle?"

Anderson raised his head from his hands, glaring down at the floorboards. "The woman who took my daughter from me."

The weight of his declaration settled on Effie's chest, stealing her breath. She met Gus's eyes, beseeching him to confirm that all of this was the truth. His nod brought another moment of speechlessness.

Gus went on to explain. "We've called Isabelle his wife so it wouldn't create suspicion. Or any trouble."

"Trouble?" Effie questioned.

Anderson rubbed the back of his neck. "Two men following a woman? Who would you side with and try to protect? But a man asking questions and searching for his wife is far less threatening. And I've no idea who has my daughter or what they will do to her if I'm vocal about her. If I tell the police—*anyone*—whoever murdered Isabelle may do the same to my daughter." He let out a groan. "If they haven't already."

The air in the room was suffocating. Effie, stunned by the revelation of Anderson's daughter, scrambled to piece it all together, to identify the missing pieces. "So . . ."

"I'm not married. Not anymore." Anderson locked eyes with her, and the pain Effie saw there pulled her in. She recollected his admission beneath the willow tree.

He was terrified of grief. Fearful of its repercussions. Yes, she could understand now. Anderson couldn't afford to grieve. He couldn't waste time or effort to face that his wife had died almost a year before and his baby girl had been taken from him. The child wouldn't even recognize him were he to find her!

Effie noticed his hands, which were on his knees now. His fingers kneaded his trousers with a nervous type of energy as he worked to control his breathing and calm himself. Before he could disappear inside of his soul, convincing himself to shut out the world around him, Effie reached over and placed her hand over his.

Anderson stilled. He stared down at her hand, her palm pressing into the back of his hand. She ached to say something that would bring comfort, both to him and to Gus, who stood by in silent witness. But there were no words to be had when the reality of life's horrors was splayed out for all to share in.

Effie's terror of losing Polly was equaled only by the fact that Anderson had already gone before and walked that road with his wife, Laura. Perhaps one day, when and if this was all over, they could face the grief together. But for now, for today, they just needed to be together. For the sake of Polly, at the risk of whoever and whatever was hunting at Predicament Avenue. And for the sake of baby Cora, who wouldn't know her father but whose existence was what gave Anderson his determination, and whose life hung in the balance and in the void of the unknown.

She had been wrong, Effie decided, even as Anderson continued to stare at their hands stacked together. Death wasn't the worst monster. Not knowing was. Not knowing when Polly would die. Not knowing if Polly was even safe. Not knowing who and what had created such a heinous scene at 322 Predicament Avenue. And not knowing if Anderson's baby girl was even still alive to save.

Her

DOES GOD REPLAY your sins for you after you die? These are the sort of thoughts I ponder as I stare down at the gravestones. The moon is absent tonight, the earth silent. "Silent as the grave," they say. I shall soon find out.

I remember my sins. I remember many of the small ones, most of the bad ones, and all of the terrible ones. Sometimes I question why—why did I choose that path instead of a safer path?

But I am still good. I am not evil or wicked. The most important of the commandments I have kept, and sacredly.

God will take that into account once I am dead, won't He?

I bend down to brush sticks from a stone. The name stares up at me with a hollow void. I try to imagine what this person was like in life. Their smiles, their joys, their dreams. So empty now. They took none of them with them into the afterlife. When a soul leaves its body, the corpse is left behind to decay. Loved ones sift through belongings and determine what to keep or discard. Property, if owned, is sold or handed down. Photographs may stay on display for a time, but in one, two, most certainly three generations, they will be tucked into a trunk. No one will recognize the person's name anymore. The family tree will have expanded, their name unmatched to their image.

What does a person take with them when they die? Nothing. They go before God with a naked soul.

That is what I am perhaps afraid of the most. What brought me comfort here in this life will stay here in this life. What I hoped to acquire will be the death of me, and what I hoped to avoid such as death will come whether I wish it to or not.

In the end, I am powerless. I am barren. I own nothing, I hold nothing, I take nothing. It is me. God. My sins.

I rise from the grave, although my eyes continue to stare at the unfamiliar name of the unfamiliar person who lived an unfamiliar life.

One day my name will be carved into stone.

But where will my spirit be?

19

NORAH

Present Day
Shepherd, Iowa

THERE WAS SOMETHING about an old farmhouse in the night that was creepy, even if you'd grown up there. Norah padded down the hallway, lit only by a small night-light plugged into an outlet. She was thirsty and had forgotten to take a bottle of water with her to set next to her bed. Today had been grueling. She needed something stronger than water, but that was a recipe for disaster.

Unless it was coffee.

Norah glanced into the dining room, pausing in the doorway. The case files were spread across the table, pieces of her past scattered like dirty laundry. Then there was the folder with bits of Isabelle Addington's past. A newspaper clipping. A copy of a handwritten note explaining what had been found in this very house over a hundred years ago.

A creak behind her made Norah look quickly over her shoulder.

Nothing there.

She was creeping herself out. No one in their right mind looked at cold case murder files at two in the morning. Especially ones that she was specifically related to or involved in.

Another creak, like a floorboard protesting the weight of someone's presence. Norah turned, squinting down the hallway. No one was there. The stairs leading up to the second floor rose like a dark tunnel, but there was a night-light at the top landing where the stairs turned to continue their journey up. No one there either.

Norah shook her head, trying to clear her thoughts—and her ears—from imagining things. It helped that she was wide awake this time. At least she wouldn't see spirits moving around her bedroom.

She turned her back to the dining room and went into the kitchen.

Sebastian had made coffee earlier that evening, and the light on the heating component was still on. Which meant it was still hot. Granted, Norah was sure he hadn't done so on purpose, but it served her well now. Forget water. She was going all in tonight.

Pouring black coffee into a mug with a yellow sunflower on the side, Norah stared out the back window as she sipped the brew. The moon was out tonight, just a fingernail of light that glowed just enough to make the tops of some of the old gravestones visible.

The glowing gravestone.

Norah smiled to herself. As kids, she and Naomi had told all their friends that if you visited their aunt Eleanor's graveyard at night, sometimes a stone would glow. It was the spirit of a dead soul hovering over their resting place.

It was, in fact, the moon reflecting off a glossy marble surface. But for a ten-year-old, the sight was the creepiest thing ever.

Aunt Eleanor had chased many kids from her backyard in the wee hours of the morning because of Norah and Naomi's tales. She'd always scolded them, but she'd always smiled while she scolded too.

Norah remembered her aunt as a sweet lady who'd been old for as long as she could remember. It seemed Aunt Eleanor had always had white hair, always had horn-rimmed glasses, that she'd always spoken in a voice with the vibrato of age in its notes. She'd been feisty and fun, ever patient, devoted, and wise. She'd told the story of Isabelle Addington's ghost as if it were as entertaining a tale as the headless horseman and Ichabod Crane.

A murder. At 322 Predicament Avenue.

"*The blood. Ohhhh, the blood.*" Aunt Eleanor always dragged out the word *oh* to bring more terror to the story.

Spattered on a mirror, hidden under a dresser. Blood everywhere once folks saw fit to finally move the furniture around. Whoever had murdered poor Isabelle had done a stand-up job of making sure she was dead. No one could survive losing all that blood. It was found behind paintings hung over the spatter on the walls. Found beneath the bed. Found dried and crusty along the wainscoting behind the dresser. "*Blood. Ohhhh, the blood.*"

At twelve, Naomi had sat perched on the edge of her chair, eyes wide with intrigue. Norah had resisted the urge to dive under the table and cover her ears. Yet Aunt Eleanor was the old lady who watched every episode of the TV show *Unsolved Mysteries* and then watched them all again. If Aunt Eleanor were alive today, she'd be in front of her old computer with its dot matrix printer, printing out sheets of "What Happened to Naomi?" and stapling them to the telephone poles around town.

Aunt Eleanor had been *crushed* when Naomi was killed. Her smile had disappeared right along with Norah's. They never spoke of Naomi again. Eleanor existed. Norah hid away. Eleanor died. Norah refused to leave the house for her funeral. Eleanor willed 322 Predicament Avenue to Norah . . . and the nightmare continued.

Another sip of now-lukewarm coffee brought Norah back to the present. Sleep was elusive as usual. But standing there looking out into the abyss of the backyard's graveyard was going to accomplish nothing. Neither was drinking Sebastian's highly caffeinated coffee. She moved to leave her spot at the window when something caught her eye.

Norah stilled, cupping the half-full mug, and craned her neck to peer out the window. The kitchen was mostly dark behind her save the light she had on over the stove. She went and shut it off to avoid the reflection on the window and, if she was being honest, to prevent anyone from being able to see her silhouette.

Staring out the window, Norah felt a bit like an old lady spying on her neighbors. Only this was her house, her yard, and frankly, her cemetery. The tree line behind the graves rose tall and dark against the dark sky. Norah could make out the outlines of the headstones, the shrubbery on the west side of the lawn, and the blue-black of the one evergreen that stood stark and alone behind one of the graves. A remembrance tree planted decades before by a mourning loved one.

There was no further movement.

The night was quiet and still.

Norah, feeling especially brave now that nothing was there, moved to the door and went to check the lock.

She frowned. The dead bolt was unlocked.

Norah tried to recall whether she'd forgotten to lock it before going to bed. She tugged the door open and put her palm on the screen door to push it outward.

The night song of crickets met her ears. The rustling of the breeze as it made tree leaves dance.

A stick cracked.

Norah's breath caught. She took a short step onto the back

porch just far enough to see around the screen door, but not far enough to completely leave the house.

A shape shifted near the far end of the graveyard, closest to the woods beyond. Norah froze, her eyes fixed on the dark figure as it bent and ran its hand along the stones as if memorizing the names.

It was a woman, though her face was hidden from view. She had long hair, blowing freely in the breeze, and wore a shapeless gown. Norah opened her mouth to call out, to scream, to say *something*! But the words got stuck in her throat.

The screen door creaked as Norah's body tensed and put weight against it. The sound of the hinges ripped through the quiet. The figure in the cemetery straightened. Norah shot a panicked look at the door as if she could somehow shush it. She looked back at the woman.

She had disappeared.

"On *Ghost Tales* the documentary, someone captured video of kitchen drawers opening on their own." This from Otto, who had let himself in that morning, along with Ralph. As the two older brothers ate breakfast with Norah and her houseguests, Norah had shared what she'd seen last night in the graveyard.

"All you need is fishin' line," Sebastian stated, moving his coffee mug away from the papers so as not to spill on them. "You pull the line when the camera's on, an' it looks like a ghost."

"Trickery." Otto nodded in agreement, slurping his coffee as though the act of bringing air along with the liquid into his mouth simultaneously would cool it faster.

"And then the woman just vanished?" Harper directed her question to Norah, who was wishing now she'd just kept her mouth shut. Two sightings of Isabelle Addington in one week?

"Yes," Norah replied. "When I looked up a second later, she was gone."

"She could've run into the woods," Sebastian suggested.

Otto frowned. "Or evaporated. Spirits do that, ya know? When I saw that woman's face in the attic window years ago, I swore she turned into mist and just floated away!"

"If she ran into the woods," Harper added, "then one might argue she was real, not a ghost."

"It's more believable." Sebastian nodded.

Norah fiddled with the edge of a manila folder. "What reason would anyone have to be in a graveyard at two in the morning?"

"This." Ralph's voice cut through the room. He tottered over, his shoulders hunched, the straps of his bib overalls so loose that they sagged in the front. His jowls matched and were covered in a week's worth of white whiskers. His rheumy brown eyes were yellow around the irises. Aging was a friend to no one, Norah realized. But it was what he held aloft like a trophy that grabbed her attention. He shook it in the air. "This is what someone does at two in the morning in a cemetery. They leave mementos at a grave!"

Norah couldn't tear her eyes from the object in Ralph's hand.

"What is it?" Otto squinted as if his glasses prescription wasn't strong enough and he couldn't see clearly.

Ralph dropped it onto the table with a thud.

A Coach wallet.

Sebastian shot a look at Norah before eyeing Ralph. "That was in the graveyard?"

Ralph snorted and looked peeved. Grumpy. "Goin' to beat up that ghost lady myself if she doesn't leave our Norah be. What kind of poppycock is this?" He gestured at the wallet. "Leavin' a wallet on Naomi's grave!"

"Didn't you say . . . ?" Harper's question hung in the air as she looked at Norah.

Norah sank onto her chair. Otto shuffled toward her, and she felt his comforting grip on her shoulder. She quelled the nausea churning in her stomach. "It's exactly like Naomi's wallet."

"Is it hers?" Harper asked quietly.

Sebastian glanced at Norah, then at Ralph.

Ralph held his hands up, palms out. "I didn't open it. Just found it and brought it in the house."

Sebastian pressed his lips together as he reached for it. The checkbook wallet was brown and tan with the standard Coach logo and symbol. It was worn at the corners but otherwise looked in good condition. As he opened it slowly, Norah steeled herself for a shock. It came seconds later.

"Naomi Elizabeth Richman." Sebastian read the driver's license inside the wallet. His nostrils flared as he looked to Norah. "I'm sorry, Norah. It's your sister's wallet."

"What kind of sick prank is this?" Otto's hand dropped from Norah's shoulder. His words equaled the rising angst in Norah that she didn't even know how to express. "Where again did you find it?" he snapped at his brother.

Ralph mirrored Otto's anger. "Some tomfool left it on Naomi's grave." He swept his hand over the case files spread across the table. "You're here digging up the past while someone out there is mocking you with it? Ain't right. Ain't right at all!"

Norah shoved back her chair. "I can't. I can't . . ." And she couldn't. She couldn't stomach seeing Naomi's case files, her library card, and now her wallet? She fled the room because that was what emotionally mature people did when they were confronted with something they didn't want to see. She charged from the house into the backyard. Her feet pounded across the lawn as she marched into the cemetery, weaving around the gravestones until she got to Naomi's resting place. Isabelle Addington's grave—or what was believed to be hers—was in line with Naomi's, set back near the woods. A simple I. A.

"What do you want from me?" Norah screamed to the trees, the words ripping from her throat.

Let the spirits hear her. Let the ghosts rise from their graves and haul her down into hell. There was nothing to live for, and just when she thought she might see a tiny pinprick of hope, might conjure the smallest amount of tenacity to reopen the questions around Naomi's death, this happened.

The woods were silent, the brisk wind blowing Norah's dark hair around her face. She wrapped her arms around herself, her short-sleeved shirt doing little to provide warmth against the cool spring morning.

"I can't do this . . ." Norah's cry turned into a whimper as she dropped to her knees by Isabelle's grave. It was more of a declaration to God than to anyone else. Then she felt a sweater settle around her shoulders, and knowing God hadn't miraculously shown up in person, Norah waited until Sebastian knelt beside her at the graveside.

He studied her for a long minute before clearing his throat. "I won't even ask you if you're all right."

"I'm not all right. I'm a mess, and I'm . . . not helping anyone. Not you with your podcast, not Rebecca with the information she needs in case of a lawsuit, not Naomi—"

"Don't be bothered about anythin' to do with my podcast. It's not important now."

"Sebastian . . ." Norah lifted her eyes to his. There was comfort in his expression, tenderness. And right now she could use that warm teddy bear type of guy.

Somehow he knew, for in a moment Sebastian reached out and pulled her into his chest and half in his lap, considering they were both on the ground. Norah breathed him in, soaking up the warmth and strength of the arms that embraced her. Platonic or not, there was something magnetic about him. But it wasn't romance, it wasn't attraction—it was need. It was the human need to be held, to be told everything was going to be okay even when Norah knew it would never be okay. Not really.

After a few silent minutes, Norah shifted, pulling back from him. Embarrassment flushed her cheeks. She hadn't been weeping. She'd just been . . . well, snuggling with the man and siphoning comfort from him like a hungry, lost animal.

"I'm sorry," Norah sniffed.

"Don' be." Sebastian's smile was soft, even though the rugged lines of his face made him appear a bit weathered. He adjusted his glasses. "Fact is, this is no small thing. The wallet. Someone was here last night. You can't convince me it was a ghost. No. Not Isabelle Addington. But why put the wallet here. What're they tryin' to say?"

"Should we call Detective Dover?" Norah wiped her nose with the back of her hand, tugging the sweater Sebastian had brought her closer around herself.

"Yes. The wallet might get 'em to reopen Naomi's case. Wouldn't that be somethin', I mean to find that someone out there is maybe tryin' to come forward with new information? Evidence?"

"You think they're trying to help?" Norah hadn't thought of that. She'd interpreted it as taunting, as mockery.

Sebastian shrugged. "I don't know. But it is no ghost. An' if it does have somethin' to do with this old graveyard and Naomi, and even Isabelle Addington, then it's time to dig deeper. Who was she really? Does the Anderson name have somethin' to do with it all? An' are you safe here?"

"What?" Norah stared at Sebastian, perplexed.

"Are you safe here?" Sebastian posed the question again. "There's been two killin's over time, an' now someone has your sister's things that would've been with her the night she was killed. Norah, that means the person who left the wallet here, and who probably left Naomi's library card in your bedroom, was with Naomi the night she died. All these years they've either been hidin' the killer or"—he screwed up his face in a wince—"they're Naomi's killer. Either way, lass, you aren't safe. An' I don't intend to leave you be now."

20

Now that Sebastian had planted the thought in her head, Norah's fear of life took on an entirely different level of intensity. Was she potentially in danger? If someone was leaving Naomi's old things at 322 Predicament Avenue, was it to taunt and tease, to help solve the case, or was it some sort of desperate plea? Did they want to come forward and confess and just didn't know how?

Still, that didn't answer the other question swirling around in Norah's mind. Isabelle Addington and her ghost. The murder from 1901. Otto had seen a woman's face in the attic window. *She* had seen a woman that night in her own bedroom, then again last night in the cemetery. Could the female form in the graveyard have been human? Possibly. Yes, probably. But the one in her bedroom?

In her mind's eye, Naomi could still see the woman's figure floating through the open door. She hadn't been transparent, but she hadn't looked real either. Not flesh and blood. But then sleep was a strange twister of reality. She wasn't sure which she preferred, a spirit that could be anything from wandering soul to poltergeist to demon, or a human being that could be anything from some weirdo wandering off the street to a murderous stalker who had stood over her while she slept, staring down at her, considering how to kill her.

Now she followed an extremely determined Harper and Sebastian Blaine to the local county historical society. They'd already been to the police station. Dover had questioned them. He'd examined Naomi's wallet, her library card, and the look he'd leveled on Norah was one of sympathy and even pity. Yes. They'd investigate, he promised. But the tone in his voice made it sound as though they could run in circles searching for ages and still get no closer to solving anything.

The historical society was both a distraction and a necessity. Once inside, the historian, Brandon Hill, led them to a room with large volumes already open on a table. "It's so great to meet you, Mr. Blaine." Brandon fawned over Sebastian, viewing him as a celebrity. "I listen to your podcast regularly, and I can't tell you how excited I am to help with this case." He glanced at Norah. "I know you're the owner of 322 Predicament Avenue, and who in Shepherd doesn't know that story?"

Norah hadn't the stomach to ask which story he meant, Isabelle's or Naomi's.

Brandon kept on chattering. He was balding but had to be barely in his thirties. He looked as though the proverbial history nerd, complete with sweater vest and khaki pants. "So, when you emailed about wanting to find out more about who Isabelle Addington was, I thought a good place to start would be to show you some documents that were written in the local paper around that time, which survived the devastating tornado back in the thirties." Brandon pulled on white cotton gloves and ran his finger along the newsprint inside a logbook. "This is a report on the investigation the day after the James daughters, Euphemia and Polly, stated they heard a woman's screams."

Sebastian held the page as Brandon read aloud, "'No evidence of a crime was found at the site. Multiple members of the community toured the home and repeated having seen nothing out of the ordinary.'"

"Wait." Harper scrunched her face up in confusion. "They let just anyone go into the house and look around?"

Brandon smiled, his mustached upper lip stretching thin. "Yeah. That's how it was back then. No CSI to cordon off the place. It was open season for crime solving. Entire communities would often show up when there was an act of violence."

"An American coliseum," Sebastian muttered.

"Sort of." Brandon nodded. "Now, flip over a couple of days and there's a new report. A Mr. Lewis Anderson of London, England, and none other than Euphemia James, who originally reported hearing a woman screaming and informed the authorities they'd found evidence of a crime. I'll read it for you."

Norah noticed Brandon didn't wait to see if they wanted to hear it.

"'After revisiting 322 Predicament Avenue, the police have confirmed that evidence of a violent crime has indeed been found. Mr. Anderson and Miss James took it upon themselves to relocate furniture within the home under the assumption it may have been repositioned in order to hide the crime. The startling discovery was made that the old house was splashed with blood from the floor to the backs of furniture. A bloodied butcher knife was also recovered. It is presumed to be the work of tramps, but Mr. Anderson believes the victim to be his wife, Isabelle Addington. No body, however, has been recovered, and so the tragedy at Predicament Avenue remains a mystery.'"

"And that was all?" Harper asked before Sebastian or Norah could respond.

Norah found a chair along the wall and eased onto it. Sebastian noticed and offered her an encouraging smile.

Brandon was oblivious to the weakness in her knees. "No. Another page here states—and this is a mere few days after— that Mr. Lewis Anderson was again seen in the company of

Miss Euphemia James. It's quite insinuating, a woman and man together, unchaperoned in that era?" Brandon chuckled. "It's newspaper meets gossip rag."

"But this Mr. Anderson was claiming the supposed victim, Isabelle, to be his wife," Harper argued.

"Right." Brandon held up his index finger as if they were close to unveiling a mystery. "Here's where it gets really interesting." He turned more pages in the logbook. Instead of a newspaper article, he revealed a photograph of a woman posed in a chair, wearing a high-necked silk dress. Her eyes were open but appeared glazed over. Even from where she sat, Norah could tell the woman was dead.

"*This* is Isabelle Addington." Brandon poked the woman in the picture with his gloved finger, smiling as if they all understood.

Sebastian tucked his chin into his chest and eyed the historian, rolling his lips together expectantly. When Brandon still didn't say anything, Sebastian urged him on. "Soooo?"

"She's dead," Brandon said. "In the photograph, I mean."

"That's . . . um, obvious." Sebastian sounded wary as he eyed the photograph.

Brandon's brow furrowed. "Oh. Well," he hurried to explain. "The story goes that her body was never found. It's even a question as to whether anyone is even buried in the grave on your property." Brandon looked to Norah, who stared back at him. "What the story *doesn't* mention is the logical conclusion that Isabelle Addington *was* found dead. Her body was cleaned and dressed. As was the practice at the time, a postmortem photograph was taken and then, yes, she was buried on the property at Predicament Avenue."

Harper leaned closer to the photograph. "She doesn't look murdered."

"Stab wounds would be hidden by clothing," Brandon explained. He pointed at the corpse's throat. "A high collar like that would hide any slashes to the neck."

"And *how* do you know this is Isabelle Addington?" Norah inserted incredulously.

Brandon smiled. "Because her name was penned in ink on the back of the photograph. See?" He turned it over to reveal spidery handwriting.

"So we can't know for *sure* it's her. Just that someone claimed this was her dead body," Norah concluded.

"An' why isn't this part of the story—that Isabelle's body was found and photographed?" Sebastian asked.

Brandon tapped the photograph again. "People didn't want that part of it to be known. The Opperman family of Shepherd owned a lot of property, along with the Charlemagne family. The Charlemagnes were wealthier and more respected, while the Oppermans were reclusive and mysterious and unfriendly. They also had a son. Well, two of them, but the one in question was named—"

"Floyd?" Norah perked up.

Brandon nodded. "Yes. See?"

No. Norah didn't see at all.

"Okay." Brandon was trying to connect the dots. "The Oppermans owned 322 Predicament Avenue, where supposedly Mr. Anderson's wife, Isabelle, was murdered. Years later this photograph, with the name Isabelle Addington written on the back, was found by an Opperman descendant. It was stuffed in a trunk with most of Floyd's belongings. Floyd had been sent to an institution. After he died, his belongings were returned to the Opperman family. No one wants that information out in the open. Institutions back then are not something we're proud of in American history. Anyway, once Floyd's trunk was opened, it was the first time anyone had ever seen this photograph. People left that part out—perhaps out of respect for Floyd."

"Why would Floyd Opperman have a photograph of Isabelle Addington?" Harper mused aloud.

"Why didn't Ron and Betty Daily tell us about the photo-graph?" Norah's suspicion spiked.

Brandon waved her off. "Oh, they probably don't know about it. I believe that Aaron Opperman, Floyd's brother, would likely have kept most of it on the down-low. At the time, cases of people with intellectual disabilities weren't handled well. So, Floyd's trunk was placed in a family attic, then later Chuck—Betty Daily's father and Aaron Opperman's son—donated it to us here at the historical society. Back in the sixties, people started reporting the atrocities being committed in such institutions, and I think Chuck wanted his uncle Floyd to be remembered, not shamed. It was meant to be noble—donating Floyd's belongings to the historical society."

"Who found the picture of Isabelle Addington?" Sebastian asked, and Norah could tell his mind was spinning trying to keep up.

Brandon nodded as if he'd figured that out too. "The Op-perman family donated the belongings of Floyd Opperman—who'd been institutionalized not long after Isabelle Addington's death—to the historical society. They were picked through and then stored. When I moved to Shepherd and came on staff a year ago, one of my jobs was to go through articles that still needed to be preserved. I came across Floyd Opperman's trunk and discovered Isabelle Addington's postmortem photograph."

"So, you're the only person in Shepherd who knows this pic-ture exists?" Harper seemed skeptical, and Norah couldn't blame her.

Brandon gave an embarrassed little shrug. "Well, I've men-tioned it to several people. We've logged the photograph in our inventory. It's not been kept secret, but we haven't made a big thing of it either. I don't have an answer for you as to how Floyd Opperman acquired a photograph of a murder victim. I also can't tell you if anyone ever found out that Floyd *had* seen Isa-belle Addington after she died. But the picture doesn't lie."

"Unless that's some random lady's photograph an' someone scribbled Isabelle Addington's name on it as a lark," Sebastian said.

"But why do that?" Brandon challenged. "What would Floyd Opperman gain from doing so if he was in a hospital for the remainder of his life?"

Sebastian shook his head. "The bigger questions are: Wouldn't a photo like this have been taken almost immediately before decomposition began? Who took the photo? Where was the body in between the time the photo was taken an' when she was buried in the cemetery behind the house, if indeed she was buried there? Wouldn't people have noticed a fresh grave? Not to mention, who was Isabelle Addington—if anyone—to Floyd Opperman?" Sebastian met Norah's troubled gaze. "An' why would Lewis Anderson from England be searchin' for his wife, but then so readily seem to attach himself to another just days after his wife's murder?"

Brandon looked blindsided by the list of questions Sebastian had thrown at him. He coughed. Cleared his throat. Then he nodded, a form of apology perhaps. "I wish I could answer all that for you." He carefully closed the book of scrap papers. "This story has always had me intrigued. The fact you're making a podcast of it and trying to solve it once and for all? It has me in a tizzy!"

"I see that." Sebastian's expression was grim.

Brandon didn't seem to notice. "Oh! One more thing. I did some tracing along the way about Lewis Anderson from England. I'm not sure if I've done an accurate evaluation of his family tree, but if I'm right, Lewis Anderson was of the gentry."

"The gentry?" Harper interrupted. "Like lords and ladies and such?"

"Mm-hmm." Brandon nodded. "His title and full name was Lord Lewis Anderson Archibald Mooring. Lord Mooring, to be exact. Upon arriving to the United States, he changed his name to simply Anderson. In fact, you can ask the Andersons more about it. They might know."

"The Andersons?" Norah gripped the arms of her chair.

Brandon, a proud smile on his face, responded, "Yeah. LeRoy Anderson here in town—he's Lewis Anderson's grandson three times removed."

Norah sagged in the chair. Not even a hacksaw could unravel this confusing mess of loose ends and tangled threads.

"I'm not leavin' you here alone with all that's goin' on." Sebastian was being overprotective.

"No one is going to try anything in the daytime." Norah bit her fingernail, sounding far more confident than she felt. "Besides, no one's tried to hurt me. We don't even know if—"

"It's human, lass. You can't convince me it's Isabelle's ghost."

"I'd rather be dealing with a ghost." Her voice sounded small even to her own ears.

"I know." Sebastian held her gaze for a moment, then added, "You can wait in the car if you want. I'm not expectin' you to meet up with the man you think hurt your sister. I just want to talk to him about his ancestor, not Naomi."

"But Naomi will come up. You know she will. *I'll* come up. You can't separate Isabelle Addington and Naomi. Even if LeRoy talked to you, it'd be all lies." The phone rang, and Norah snatched the receiver off the wall, the vintage phone cord slapping her leg. After a few minutes, she'd taken down information for a new guest to check in the following month. Good. That would help business. Get things back to normal.

She noticed that Sebastian hadn't moved. He'd patiently waited through the entire call, arms crossed over his broad chest, glasses poised perfectly on his nice nose. Wavy hair flopping over his forehead, his craggy face not so much handsome as it was warm and inviting. His dark eyes watched her.

"What?" Norah was feeling snappy. Very snappy.

"How can we fix anythin' if we do nothin'?"

"Fine." Norah waved him off. "We'll go. Meet my sister's murderer face-to-face."

About an hour later, they were parking outside LeRoy Anderson's green ranch-style house. It was as unimpressive as Norah remembered LeRoy being. The bushes out front were untrimmed. Of course, not everyone was blessed with people like Otto and Ralph, who helped maintain the greenery, but still. The lawn was unmown and already had dandelions spiking up through the crabgrass and going to seed in puffs.

Norah gripped the seat belt. "I can't do this."

Sebastian turned to her. She wasn't able to hide the trembling in her hands no matter how tightly she gripped the seat belt. "You don't need to come inside, Norah. He knows I'm comin' an' he knows why, but I never told him I was bringin' you."

The front door opened before Norah could respond. The world rewound itself to thirteen years prior as she stared out the window at the man. He hadn't changed much, and yet there was a weariness in his face. Evidence that he'd once been good-looking had since been marred by time and maybe too much alcohol. Life had been hard on all of them the last thirteen years. Even so, Norah felt little sympathy for LeRoy.

As his eyes met hers, his expression shifted from wary to shocked. He ran a hand over his brown goatee in a nervous gesture while his other hand lifted in a halfhearted wave to Sebastian, who'd exited the vehicle.

Why did LeRoy agree to meet with Sebastian? Was he so naive as to think Sebastian would only want to ask him about his ancestor's connection to Isabelle Addington? Had he been enjoying his game of cat and mouse, and now, thirteen years later, he saw an opportunity to play it all over again? To flaunt his freedom while Naomi lay in the grave?

Norah unbuckled the seat belt, flinging the door open and

jumping out of the SUV. She charged past a surprised Sebastian, infused with gumption.

"Norah, I—"

"Why are you doing this?" Norah stopped just shy of slapping LeRoy across his smug face. Only he didn't really look smug. Sheepish was more like it, though Norah wanted to believe otherwise.

"Doing what?" LeRoy held up his hands. He cast a nervous look toward Sebastian, who had approached as well. "What am I doing? You called me!"

"Norah." Sebastian's hand rested on her shoulder.

She shrugged it off, glaring at LeRoy. "Do you think it's funny? Taunting me like this? Her wallet! Her library card!"

"What are you talking about?" LeRoy looked genuinely perplexed. Enough so that Norah took a step back and allowed Sebastian to ease in front of her to create some space.

"I thought you wanted to talk to me about some sort of ancestry or something?" LeRoy's shock was wearing off and turning into offense. "Cornering me with Naomi Richman's sister? Not cool, man." LeRoy's accusatory glower settled on Sebastian.

"I'm sorry, mate. Let's all take a moment an'—"

"Why'd you kill her?" Norah spat out the question that had been eating her alive for the last thirteen years. "Was it the baby? You didn't want to be a father?"

"Okay!" LeRoy reared back, his face twisted into an affronted scowl. "That's it. I don't need to take this. For thirteen years I've had to carry the label of your sister's murderer when I didn't do *anything* to Naomi. That was my kid too, you know!" He swore and spun to retreat into his house. The door slammed in their faces. Sebastian and Norah stood shoulder to shoulder staring at its chipped white paint.

"That went well." Sebastian sounded none too happy.

Norah worked her mouth back and forth, afraid to cry. Afraid to feel. She hadn't intended to fly off the handle like that. Hadn't intended to even get out of the car. "I'm sorry," she gulped.

Sebastian spun on his heel, obviously irritated by her lack of self-control. "You know, he might've helped us. Guilty or not, there are things he prob'ly could tell us that would send us in a proper direction. Now you've gone an' ticked the man off. Lot o' good that'll do us now."

Norah hurried after Sebastian, eager to defend her actions. "He killed my sister!"

"You don't know that!" Sebastian shot over his shoulder.

"I *do*! Who else would've done it?"

Sebastian stopped abruptly, and Norah almost ran into him. He twisted to look at her. "You don't know he did it, Norah. There's not enough evidence. You read the case files. Just 'cause he doesn't have an alibi an' she was pregnant with his baby doesn't mean he went an' killed Naomi. Besides, you wrecked my chance at gettin' in thick with him. This is what I do, Norah. When I find out what happened to people, I have to get close to fellas I may not like. May not be doin' what I like, but I do it anyway."

His accent had grown thicker with his frustration.

Norah had nothing to say. She'd ruined Sebastian's attempts to not only help her but also continue with his livelihood, which was his historical crime-solving podcast.

"I have a life too, you know. If you care at all, let me have it."

Norah wrapped her arms around herself like a shield. "You have a life?" She stared at him. Every part of her had to refrain from spilling Harper's secret. Sebastian's *life* wasn't going to be his much longer if he had any fatherly responsibility left in him. He was so keen on her splaying out her past and moving forward and trying to heal, but did he? He stayed behind his casual façade, his easygoing lifestyle, and he included Harper in everything but in his deepest self. She'd not seen Sebastian show his daughter any affection.

"Your life stopped being yours when you had Harper." Norah let the words slip out as they stood by the car, one on each side, staring each other down.

Sebastian's look was one of confusion. "What does that have to do with anythin'?"

Norah deflected her anger on to him. "You're so keen on your podcast. So quick to come to my aid even. But what about your daughter?"

"What about her?"

"When are you going to be her father? Really her father?"

"That's got nothin' to do with LeRoy Anderson and your sister's cold case. I shared my past with you 'cause I wanted to be your friend, not have you throw my own daughter in my face. I have an ex who can do that, thank you very much." Sebastian got into the car and slammed the door. He waited, leaned forward, and looked out the window at her. "You comin' or do you want me to leave you in LeRoy's front yard?"

Norah bit her tongue and climbed into the car. She wanted to cry. She wanted to rant and kick. Life wasn't fair. Not for any of them. And *that* was what hurt the most.

21

EFFIE

May 1901
Shepherd, Iowa

EFFIE CURLED UP on the window seat, her back pressed comfortably against a pillow. Polly was still asleep, her mother was furious, her father indignant, and Nurse Carlisle avoided Effie as if she were a monster.

She allowed her tears to trail down her face. How could she assist in the urgency and desperation to help Anderson find his child and yet never leave Polly's side, making sure she was safe? In times past, she would have reveled in being here. In this nostalgic position, soaking in the memories and wishing they would never end.

She pressed her forehead against the window, staring emptily into the flowers and trees at the edge of the lawn. Life would never be the same again. This room would always be marred by the last days of Polly's life, shrouded in violence and suspicion.

In a moment like this, she could almost pretend things were normal. Polly was merely taking a nap, not slowly dying.

She stiffened. Movement near the bushes captured Effie's attention. It was midafternoon—no reason to be concerned about another intruder. But there also was no reason for anyone to be trespassing in their yard. The man did nothing to disguise himself either. He bent and picked up a leaf, then let it float back to the ground. His hat hid his face. He wore blue trousers and a buttoned-up shirt, but no jacket, no tie, no cuff links or jewelry of any sort that Effie could see.

The man ducked behind a tree, and Effie straightened. Alert. She glanced over at Polly. This wouldn't do. She would never sleep tonight if she knew there was a stranger traipsing about their property. It might be common for 322 Predicament Avenue, but the only time someone had come unwelcome onto the lawn of the James manor, they had climbed the trellis and entered Polly's room.

Effie hurried from Polly's room, ducking into both brothers' bedrooms. Neither Ezekiel nor Charles was there. Her mother was at a ladies' event. Effie steeled herself. Father was away at work. Nurse Carlisle had gone home for a spell while Effie kept watch over Polly. The last thing Effie wanted to do was confront a trespasser, but she had to do something about his skulking in the bushes.

She wound her way down the stairs and through the back hall to the door that led to the driveway and back entrance. She moved onto the porch with hesitant steps. There. He wasn't even hiding or skulking. The man merely seemed to be surveying the gardens at the edge of the property. She observed him for a minute and noticed he had a limp.

Effie pressed against the banister, grabbing ahold of it. She'd seen the man before. There was something familiar about him.

He lifted his face, and Effie knew instantly.

Floyd Opperman. Mabel Opperman's son.

Everyone in Shepherd knew *of* Floyd, but most rarely saw him. Mabel was protective of him. Everyone in town had heard how Floyd had been kicked by a cow as a young boy and had never been the same since. People avoided him. They avoided Mabel too. No one spoke to either of them unless it was necessary. No one questioned the Oppermans because no one knew the Oppermans.

Effie felt a small shudder pass through her. The recollection of Mrs. Opperman's cold eyes staring at her as she and Anderson had left her house lived deep in her memory. Something was not right about the Oppermans. Not with Mabel Opperman, and not with her property on Predicament Avenue. And Floyd?

He started ambling across the yard toward Effie. There was a strange look on his face she couldn't interpret. As he drew closer, her heart thudded against her chest. His shirt had dark rust-colored stains on it, reminding her of the blood she'd seen at Predicament Avenue.

"What do you want, Floyd?" Effie asked, deciding to be direct. He had to be in his early forties. Folks said he was harmless, but no one was completely sure.

Floyd narrowed his eyes. He didn't smile. He didn't speak. The longer the silence went on, the more Effie trembled.

"Floyd?" she said, taking little solace in the barricade of the porch railing she stood behind. "Can I help you with something?"

He took another few steps closer, and Effie realized how large the man was, his bulky frame solid and sturdy-looking. He took another step.

Effie forced herself not to retreat into the house. There was no good reason to be frightened of him. His shirt wasn't the only piece of clothing with the rust-colored stains. His pants had splotches on the thighs and knees that hadn't been as noticeable before he'd drawn closer.

"Are you all right?" she asked.

He was definitely limping. Yet she didn't see any injury that would have created what appeared to be bloodstains on his clothes.

"Floyd, I—"

"You got to run, miss." His voice was deep. His words held no emotion, neither urgency nor concern.

"Pardon me?" Effie dug her nails into the railing.

"Run." He looked over his shoulder for a quick moment, and when he turned back to her, the ominous look in his eyes matched the one Effie had seen in his mother's. There was a glint of malevolence. Of darkness. "Do you know how to run?" His question sliced through her like the blade of a killer silencing his victim. "If you do, then run."

Frozen, Effie stared as Floyd turned and lumbered away, calmly bending over to pluck a dandelion and then stuff it in his pocket. As he did, the yellow blossom popped off its stem and landed in the grass, its face staring at Effie as though the blossom knew it was dead even before it hit the earth.

Floyd Opperman.

Yes. He would probably be a frequent visitor of his mother's property on 322 Predicament Avenue. If Floyd had an attachment to it, then of course Mabel Opperman would be protective over the place.

His warning to run? He had seen Polly—maybe Effie too—the night of the woman screaming. The night Effie's world tilted off its already precarious axis and threatened to plunge into the unknown. He had probably been the one to attack her in Polly's room!

The bloodstains—if that was what they truly were—on his clothes? They could be Isabelle's. He would know where he'd taken her body. He would know what had happened to—

"Baby Cora!" Effie breathed.

"What's that?" Her brother Charles came from behind her, causing Effie to yelp and twirl in fright.

Collecting herself, Effie reached for Charles and pulled him into a quick uncustomary hug.

Charles's eyes widened, and he drew away from her. "What is wrong with you?"

"Charles, I need you to watch Polly."

"Where're you going?" Charles called after Effie as she raced down the steps, trying not to trip over her dress that tangled about her feet. She was wearing house slippers, and she didn't even care.

"I'll be back!" She waved her hand over her shoulder as she ran in the direction where Floyd had disappeared.

This was what Anderson would do were he here, she was sure of it. And there was no time to try to find help or to reason through the dangers involved. If the baby was still alive, Floyd Opperman might lead her right to Cora. Images of returning the baby girl to her father flashed through Effie's mind.

Effie ducked under branches as she pushed her way into the woods. Floyd hadn't taken the main walk or gone by way of the cobblestone street. Instead, he had gone into the woods, and now Effie struggled to find his path. She knew the direction he was headed. Knew it was at least a mile away through the woods if he was going to Predicament Avenue. Her feet sank into a mud puddle hidden by dead leaves still wet from the spring rains. The mud seeped into her shoes, and she could feel the moisture hit her toes. Branches clawed at her hair, pulling it from its simple yet tidy roll and leaving it to trail down her back and tangle.

She was out of breath and filthy by the time she caught sight of Predicament Avenue through the trees. She hadn't seen Floyd once, and as she pushed her way through the brambles, she debated the wisdom of her actions in chasing after him. But every question was answered by the recollection of the man who had broken into Polly's room, and by the knowledge that, somewhere, Anderson's baby girl was without her father and now most likely without the woman who, for better or worse, had been her caregiver.

Effie stumbled against a tree, palming its bark as she caught sight of the gravestones through the trees. The old cemetery. Though it was mostly forgotten now, the place remained a bold statement, reminding Effie of death's shroud, one that was moment by moment lowering over her.

Isabelle Addington, Anderson's wife, Laura, Polly, now maybe baby Cora too?

Effie pushed forward. She stretched out her arm to hold back a branch covered in thorns and green buds promising to be wild roses—a bush that should exemplify beauty, but instead infected the woods around them, an invader that was uncontrollable.

Not unlike death.

When Effie reached the clearing, she ducked down behind a tall grave marker that tapered into a cross at its top. It was covered in moss, the side facing her boasting the name of a child no more than two years old who had died during the war. The year 1863 was not so long ago. Less than fifty years. This child would have been the age of her own mother. Life had not been a friend to this young one.

She turned her attention to the house that loomed ahead. The sky was growing gray, and Effie's heart increased its rapid beating as she heard distant thunder. Only an hour before she had been perched in the sun in Polly's room, listening to her sister's labored breathing, pretending today was normal, pleasant. Now she was covered in dirt, her feet wet from trudging through the woods, and crouching at the headstone of a dead child while praying desperately to save another.

Movement on the back porch of 322 Predicament snagged Effie's peripheral vision and she crouched lower behind the marker, knowing full well if someone was looking toward her, she was not fully hidden. But Floyd didn't look in her direction.

Instead, he crossed the porch and reached up to the lion's head door knocker, the one Polly had kissed the first night Effie had stepped foot on the property.

He lifted it and knocked three times as though there was someone inside to answer. No one did. Effie studied the windows in the farmhouse that sagged as if exhausted after years of abuse and neglect. From the burden of watching people with no family or home come and go through its doors, peer out its windows, and then disappear. Carrying on with their travels? The people of Shepherd always assumed so. But what if they hadn't? What if Isabelle Addington wasn't the first to have met her demise here? What if the stains of blood were from more than one victim?

Effie watched as Floyd sank onto the top step of the porch, a smile stretching across his face. A wicked smile.

He looked in her direction then, and his fingers lifted in greeting. "Hello, Effie," he called.

Effie scrambled to her feet.

Before she could do anything, the air was cut off in her throat as hands from behind gripped her neck. Fingers dug into the hollow of her throat, squeezing. Effie clawed at the fingers. A woman's hands. It was a woman's form she fell back against, and a woman's laugh she heard as she faded into oblivion. Her eyes tried to focus, growing blurry. She stared toward the attic window of 322 Predicament Avenue. As she lost consciousness, she thought she saw a woman's face in the attic window, hand pounding against the glass, silent in its aggression. Ghostly. As she slipped into the darkness of her mind, Effie knew she was the only one who saw the face of dead Isabelle Addington, screaming from the grave.

And now Effie would join her.

22

NORAH

I'M A MESS," Norah said and sank onto Otto's porch step. The elderly man lumbered out of his house and eased himself onto the step beside her. She never came to Otto's place, nor Ralph's one-level house across the street. The boys had always come to her at Aunt Eleanor's place. But today she needed to get away from 322 Predicament Avenue. From the case files spread across her dining room table. From Sebastian's intense study of the crime and the rumbling of his voice as he made verbal notes into his phone for his podcast. She even needed to get away from Harper—poor girl—who she'd heard throwing up in the bathroom. Harper's pregnancy was going to come out soon, and Sebastian was going to have to deal with the reality that life was more than unsolved historical murders. Sometimes it was in-your-face trauma.

She'd faced her share, and she wished it on no one.

"What brings you over?" Otto's breathing was a bit raspy, and Norah looked sideways at him to make sure he was all right. He noticed and added, "Oh, I'm fine. I was just working in my tool-shed out back. Getting too old to be moving around heavy stuff."

Otto and his toolshed. It was where he'd kept all his tools to garden with and tend to the bed-and-breakfast's lawn for decades. The man was a bit of a tool hoarder, Aunt Eleanor had always stated with fondness. Otto claimed to have three different riding lawn mowers in the metal shed that he never used. Said he preferred to walk behind his self-propelled mower. He also wouldn't let his brother Ralph or even Norah convince him to let them help him get rid of stuff that might be in his way—like the three unused riding mowers. He refused, saying he might need them someday.

"I saw him today, Otto." Norah picked at the hole in the knee of her jeans. Frayed edges were better to pick at with her anxious energy than her cuticles, which were sore from her bad habit. "LeRoy Anderson."

"Awww, kid, why'd you go an' do that?" Otto's sigh was bigger than any Norah had managed to expel. He stared across the street at Ralph's place. "You spent all these years trying to avoid that man."

"I don't know." Norah shook her head. "Sebastian didn't want me home alone—Harper had gone shopping—and so I went with him. I ruined it too. I laid into LeRoy like it was yesterday that he killed Naomi."

Otto nodded vehemently. "As you should. I woulda sucker punched the man. Passed LeRoy once in the department store, and it took every ounce of me not to kick over his cart and pummel him for what he did to our girl."

Norah smiled sadly at the image. "Otto, you'd get arrested if you did that."

"I know. It's why I didn't do it," Otto groused. "The *only* reason why I didn't."

"It just makes me sick," Norah admitted. "All these years I've known—*you've* known, Mom and Dad have known—that it was LeRoy. Heck, even the cops have known.'

"Just not enough evidence," Otto said. "I know, kiddo." He patted Norah's knee. "Unfair, isn't it?"

"Horribly. And now? I don't know how to process Naomi's things just turning up out of the blue. And who was in the graveyard, Otto?"

His brows drew together, and he tapped his stubby fingers on his knees. "Don't know. Sure is bothersome, though."

Norah brushed away an errant tear. "I called the police, and they said they'd 'pass it on' and to 'keep them posted.' *Keep them posted?* What does that even mean?"

"Means they don't know what to do with it either," Otto supplied. "Can't really do much with old things you find in your house and out back in the yard. Cops will say it just took you thirteen years to notice Naomi never had them on her to begin with."

"And I just happened not to see her library card on my dresser for *thirteen years*?" Norah spat.

Otto shrugged. "Didn't say the police would make a lick of sense. Just said they don't know what to do with stuff like that. Not like the case can get reopened just 'cause you ran across your sister's wallet in the graveyard."

"Well, it didn't just land there all by itself!" Norah's sarcasm overwhelmed her, her nerves spiking so high that she could see black shutters at the corners of her eyes. She needed to calm herself. Needed to think rationally. Needed to draw strength from someone other than herself because she sure as heck didn't have any. "Otto?"

"What is it, kiddo?" He turned his head to give her a grandfatherly understanding scrunch of his face.

"Do you think if I called Dover again, he'd do something?"

"Mike?" Otto nodded slowly. "Might not be a bad idea."

"I mean, he did offer to help if I wanted to see Naomi's case files." Norah ran her fingers through her hair. "Maybe if I follow up again, push a little . . . wouldn't they want to check the library card for prints or the wallet for any trace evidence? If they found something they could tie back to LeRoy, that might be enough to reopen the case—"

"Now, don't go gettin' your hopes up," Otto interrupted. "Watchin' all those TV crime shows is going to send you in circles with ideas that won't get us nowhere."

"I don't watch those shows." How could she? It would be like putting Naomi's story on replay over and over again.

Otto grunted. "Probably a good thing ya don't."

Yes. It was a good thing she didn't watch those shows. Because half the time, the murders went unsolved anyway, and there was just a lonely 800 number on the screen at the end to call should anyone have anything to contribute to the cold case. As far as Naomi knew, no one ever did, and that phone never rang.

Most bad things happened in the dead of night. This time was no different, and it was a shout from Harper that instigated Norah into a full-on run. She catapulted up the stairs, almost tripping in her too-long flannel pants, in time to see Sebastian holding his daughter around the waist as she struggled to free herself from him. Harper strained toward the window, her hands outstretched as though she were grasping after someone.

"Call 911!" Sebastian shouted at the sight of Norah.

Without questioning, she retraced her steps and snatched her phone from the nightstand by her bed. Moments later, phone in hand and dispatch on the line, Norah was back upstairs as Sebastian picked up Harper's limp form and laid her on his bed. The covers were tousled, and Harper's dark hair fanned across Sebastian's pillow.

"Is she breathing?" Norah repeated on behalf of the 911 dispatcher.

"Yes." Sebastian had his fingers to Harper's pulse at her wrist. "Her heartbeat is fast but steady."

Norah recited the information to dispatch, then informed Sebastian, "Help is on the way."

Sebastian's nod was short as he hovered over Harper. His hand had a gentle hold of her chin. "Harper. Sweetheart, are you all right?"

A small moan escaped Harper's throat.

"What happened?" Norah asked for herself and for the dispatcher.

Sebastian caressed Harper's forehead, stroking back her hair. "I dunno. I woke an' she was shoutin'. Somethin' about bein' quiet. Tellin' someone to be quiet. When I got to her, she was delirious. Reachin' out like there was someone standin' there, only there wasn't. None at all."

Norah heard the sirens and informed the dispatcher. She ran down the stairs again to unlock the door, then hurried back to be by Sebastian's side. Within minutes, the EMTs hurried into the bedroom, asking similar questions. Taking Harper's vitals.

"Has she taken any medication recently?" they asked Sebastian.

"Not that I know of." Sebastian's hands were planted on the sides of his head, elbows sticking out. His tortured and worried expression dug into Norah's soul. She moved to his side to try to offer him comfort and was stunned when Sebastian's arms came down to draw her in close. She hugged his middle awkwardly and felt the trembling in his arms.

"Any past history with heart issues or losing consciousness?"

"No."

"Are there any conditions we should be aware of?" The male EMT shot questions at Sebastian as the female worked at reviving Harper.

Harper moaned again, her eyelids fluttering.

"No." Sebastian shook his head while holding on to Norah as if she were a lifeline. "No, she's in perfect health."

"All right." The EMT nodded.

"She's pregnant." The moment the words were out of Norah's mouth, she both regretted them and she didn't. It was vital information that needed to be communicated, but the way Sebastian stiffened sent guilt pummeling through her. She'd betrayed Harper's confidence.

"That's good to know." The EMT turned to his partner.

Harper's eyes opened, then closed. "She's coming to," they informed them.

Sebastian's arms dropped, and he pulled away from Norah, staring down at her incredulously. "Whaddya mean Harper is pregnant?"

"I'm sorry. She was scared to tell you, but—" But the EMTs needed to know.

Harper was lucid now. An EMT was pumping the blood pressure cuff. "Daddy?" Harper's weak voice filled the room, and Sebastian hurried to her side.

"Lass, what—?"

"Sir, we're going to take her to the hospital. We need to have her examined more thoroughly. When was her last prenatal appointment?"

"I don't know!" Sebastian's face darkened. "I didn't know she was pregnant!"

The EMTs exchanged looks.

"I'm sorry, Daddy." Harper's watery voice was weak.

"Don't worry about it. We'll figure it out." His words of understanding conflicted with the storm in his eyes as he looked at Norah. "I'll have Norah fill me in."

The EMTs prepared to transport Harper to the hospital. Sebastian bent over her. "What were you seein'?"

Harper's brow furrowed. "There was someone in my room. Then I got all dizzy and felt like I was going to throw up."

"No one was there," Sebastian countered.

"But there was!" Harper protested. "A woman. She was at the window. And then when I stood up, I started to black out. That's when I shouted."

"Where did she go?" Norah inserted, then bit her tongue at Sebastian's dark look.

"I don't know." Harper's face was wet with tears. Her lips were pale, and all the color was gone from her cheeks. "The music box. She was playing the music box."

"Music box?" Norah straightened, ignoring Sebastian. "What music box?" There had never been a music box in that guest room. The only one she was aware of was downstairs in her bedroom. The one her own female intruder, or vision, or whatever she'd been, had replayed with the bird chortling its song.

"Sir, I'm sorry," an EMT interrupted, "but we need to get your daughter to the hospital now."

"I'm comin' with," Sebastian stated.

"Of course."

The next several minutes was a flurry of activity. Norah stood as close to the wall as possible to be out of the way and out of Sebastian's glower. She noticed a police car outside in the driveway, and when she followed the EMTs out, an officer was positioned at the bottom of the stairs.

"Would you mind giving a report of what happened?" he asked Norah.

"Yeah. She knows more'n I do, it seems." Sebastian's look sent a wave of hurt through Norah. He brushed past her and the officer, refusing to look in her direction again.

It wasn't her fault that Harper had told her about the pregnancy and not him. And Sebastian's reaction right now was evidence as to why his daughter probably hadn't told her father. His pained expression was mixed with resentment.

"You've made me mad, Norah Richman. You knew an' yet you said nothin'. Did nothin'. Now look at Harper. It weren't no ghost neither." He turned to the officer. "You'd be smart to dust for prints. This isn't the first time a lass has been seen in the house when she's not welcome. An' Norah here, she ain't doin' nothin' about it."

It was a dig, and it hurt. Sebastian had no idea what it was like to live in the ongoing shadow of her sister's murder. To cohabit in a house with a century-old ghost. To be afraid of the slightest movement. To know that no one would believe her if she tried to tell them what happened. If the police couldn't catch Naomi's murderer, they sure couldn't catch a ghost.

23

NORAH TOLD THE OFFICER all she knew as the ambulance pulled away from the house. He followed her into Harper's room to see what, if anything, had been disturbed. Norah scanned the room. It all looked normal to her. The bed was unmade, the covers tossed to the side. Harper's sweatshirt hung over the back of a chair. The shelf on the wall with antique knickknacks was in place, along with the painting of a girl and her cat. Norah observed the window. She frowned, pointing. "There. The window is open a few inches."

The officer hiked over to the window. He eyed it, then looked over his shoulder at her. "Is there a chance Harper opened it?"

"Maybe."

The officer peered outside. "Second floor. There isn't a trellis or any easy way to climb up, is there?"

"No." Norah crossed her arms over her chest. She wanted the officer to leave. At the same time, she was afraid for him to go. She glanced at an antique table in the corner of the room. On the middle of the table sat a music box identical to the one in Norah's room. After she explained quickly to the officer, he approached the music box and, with a glove on, flicked the button on the front of it. The lid popped open, and the same feathery bird began to sing.

"Is your music box in your room downstairs?" he asked Norah.

Norah opened her mouth to respond with a yes and then snapped it shut. She was at a loss. She assumed it was still in her room.

Footsteps at the doorway alerted her and the officer. It was Detective Dover. He wore blue jeans and a sweatshirt, looking far different from his typical suit and tie. "I heard on the scanner. Thought I'd come over and make sure you were all right."

Norah gave him a weak smile, and the officer gave Dover a rundown of the situation. Dover's frown didn't encourage Norah.

"Let's go check out your room." He extended a hand toward the stairs, and Norah followed him. "I've got it from here," Dover told the officer. The two men exchanged some words and instructions before Dover and Norah moved on.

Once in Norah's room, she went directly to the dresser where the music box had lived for years. The space where it sat was empty. She gave Dover a perplexed look. "It's not here," she stated.

Dover took her words into consideration. "Do you remember moving it to Harper's room?"

"No, and I wouldn't have," Norah said firmly.

Dover's eyebrow rose. "Why's that?"

"Because it was Naomi's. It was given to her as a gift a few months before she died."

"Do you know who gave it to her?"

"No." Norah stared at the spot where the music box should have been. "It was an antique. Naomi liked old things. I assumed some old lady at church gave it to her."

"And the one upstairs is identical?" Dover inquired.

"I'd say it's the same one," Norah said. "But who would move it?"

"Harper?"

"She's never been in my room. This part of the house is off-limits to guests." Although that was a rather flimsy argument considering the kitchen was also off-limits and yet Sebastian and Harper seemed so at home there, no one thought twice of their using it. Just as Otto and Ralph routinely used the kitchen without permission. Still, no one ever came to the back bedroom. There was no reason to.

Dover nodded. "And are your doors kept locked?"

"Yeah, they—" Norah bit off her words. The other night when she'd seen the woman in the graveyard, the back door hadn't been locked. She strained to recall if she'd locked it last night.

Dover read her face and sighed. "Let's go check, shall we?"

In seconds, Norah knew that her sense of security had been shattered. The back door was again unlocked. Anyone could have come and gone without being noticed. "I don't understand. How did it get unlocked?" She sank onto a kitchen chair.

Dover raked his hand through his hair, oblivious to how he gave Sebastian's rugged good looks a run for his money. He lowered himself onto a chair near her. "Not sure, but I'm going to have an officer patrol the property for the next few nights."

"You don't believe it's—" She stopped. Norah would sound outright silly if she said what was on her mind.

"The legendary ghost of 322 Predicament Avenue?" Dover finished, giving her a thin smile. "Doubtful. Not if actual objects are being moved. Only far-advanced ghosts have that ability—or so I've heard."

"Isabelle Addington has had a century to become *advanced*." Norah's observation was laced with irony.

Dover chuckled. "Well, be that as it may, the whole thing is suspicious. I mean, you reported the library card and the wallet, both of them Naomi's. Now this? It's all concerning. I don't know it's enough to reopen Naomi's case, but—"

"But there's a chance?" Norah leaned forward, hope shooting through her.

"A chance? Sure." Dover seemed resistant to the idea. He narrowed his eyes. "I just don't see it as likely. There's no evidence those items were with Naomi the night she was killed."

Norah wanted to argue. Dover hadn't been on the force thirteen years ago. How would he know what Naomi was supposed to have on her person that hadn't been found? Unless he'd read the cold case files. She relaxed a bit. That was it. He'd read the same files she had right now spread out on her dining room table.

He changed the subject back to the old ghost story. "Maybe Isabelle Addington is just trying to help."

Norah studied his face and the casual way he lounged in the chair as if he'd been there many times before. Only he hadn't. "Maybe," she said. At this point, she wasn't sure she trusted anyone anymore. Dead people or living ones.

"Are you coming back here?" Norah dared to ask. She would understand if Sebastian didn't want to. Keeping Norah safe had been his side gig, but Harper? She should be Sebastian's priority.

"For now" was his brief, unsatisfactory answer.

The phone call had ended abruptly. Harper was all right. Sebastian didn't want to talk further. Norah held Naomi's music box. Dover hadn't bothered to take it as evidence. He said there was no sign of a crime, and an object getting moved didn't justify their dusting for fingerprints. Norah saw things differently, but she couldn't tell Dover how to do his job.

She stood in the entryway, the front door open, the screen door the only barrier between her and the porch. She hesitated. Should she take the music box back to her dresser, or should she put it in another room? What was the deal with the music box and this woman—apparition or real?

"Where'd you get that?" The voice came from just outside the screen door.

Norah jumped, almost losing her hold on the box. She performed a juggling act and came up the winner, clutching it to her chest. She blanched when she saw LeRoy Anderson standing there on the porch. "What are you doing here?" Norah demanded.

"Where did you get that?" LeRoy demanded back.

"That's none of your business." Norah had the sudden irrational wish that she'd never recovered enough to move here to 322 Predicament Avenue. She wished her years of therapy hadn't been so helpful and that she was still paralyzed with enough fear that she needed to live with her parents. It was worse being here. Being alone. Being expected to face her fears every day and having life continue to throw them at her with unmerciful vengeance.

"It is too my business." Without asking, LeRoy opened the screen door.

"Stay back!" Norah shouted, holding the gold-plated box before her like a shield.

LeRoy's eyes grew wide. "Don't worry, I'm not going to attack you!"

Norah gave a nervous shout of laughter.

"Let me see that." LeRoy reached for the music box.

In an act of desperation and self-preservation, Norah shoved it into his hands and took several steps backward. She felt along the wall behind her. The telephone hung there, its yellow cord dangling to the floor. He could strangle her with that! Norah stayed in front of it, feeling behind her for an umbrella in the stand she knew was beside the phone.

LeRoy wasn't paying any attention to her. He seemed to know exactly what he was doing with the box. He popped the lid open, and once again the eerie chortling of the bird filled the entryway. LeRoy gave her a look empty of threat but not at all trustworthy.

"I gave this to her," he said.

"What?" Norah's fingers wrapped around an umbrella handle behind her back.

LeRoy lifted the music box. "This. I gave it to Naomi."

The thought brought little comfort to her. "Another thing you haven't confessed to until now?"

LeRoy's eyes darkened. "There wasn't anything to confess about this box. It was never part of the questioning."

"But Naomi was. Your relationship with my sister was. Why wouldn't you have mentioned it?" Norah was ready to beat him over the head with the umbrella if she had to. And if she did, she wouldn't stop until he was dead. For Naomi. It was the first time she had ever felt such rage in her soul. The kind that would almost find satisfaction in pulverizing the man in front of her.

LeRoy set the box on the console table near the door. He didn't come closer. "I stopped by because . . ." He cleared his throat uncomfortably. "Your visit wasn't expected. But I just wanted to tell you once and for all, from me to you, that I had nothing to do with Naomi's death."

Norah shook her head. "I don't believe you."

"I know," LeRoy said. "She didn't want you all knowing about us. About the baby. Said y'all wouldn't approve."

"We would have accepted her and the baby." Norah's protest was met with a small snort from LeRoy.

"Sure, but you wouldn't have accepted me."

Norah clenched her jaw. He was right. They wouldn't have. "Norah deserved better."

"Better'n what?" LeRoy crossed his arms over his chest. Norah could see the dark hairs on his hard-muscled arms. The navy-blue T-shirt he wore boasted a beer logo and was frayed around the neck.

"You." She laughed in disbelief that he couldn't see it. "You met her in a bar, for heaven's sake. She was underage."

"She didn't drink," LeRoy stated.

Norah pressed her lips together. "She wasn't even twenty yet."

"Yeah, but she had life in her." LeRoy nodded, a look of nostalgia sweeping across his worn features.

"Until you took it from her," Norah accused.

"I didn't kill Naomi!" LeRoy insisted.

"What's goin' on here!" Ralph tottered in from the kitchen and took a quick glance at Norah to make sure she was all right. He jabbed his finger in LeRoy's direction. "You get, boy, ya hear? You aren't welcome here."

LeRoy gave a curt nod. "Fine." He tapped the box as he turned to leave. "Used to belong to my great-grandmother." LeRoy's eyes drilled into Norah's. "You think I'd give a priceless heirloom to a girl I'd want to murder? Mother of my kid? I loved your sister. But believe what you want, Norah. You always did anyway."

"What is that supposed to mean?" Norah demanded.

LeRoy sniffed. "Naomi said you were afraid of a shadow. Of a speck of dust. Of anything that moved that you couldn't explain. Wouldn't let her out of your sight for fear something would happen to her. Why else do you think she didn't tell you about us? It wasn't your parents she was afraid of—it was you."

Cold, Dead, But Never Buried
Hosted by Sebastian Blaine

*I*LL BE HONEST. *As your podcast host here at* Cold, Dead, But Never Buried, *I've never had the dead reach out from the grave before. But today I feel it. I feel it like never before. It's hard to tell which direction is up and which is down.*

As the story goes, 322 Predicament Avenue is a place of nightmares. It always has been, and now, in my experience, it always will be. It's hard to find the good between the front door and the back door of that place. Whether you believe in ghosts or not, they play with your mind and conscience. And if you didn't believe before, you pretty much do once you walk out the door of that house for the last time.

Is it my last time at 322 Predicament Avenue? I don't know. What I can tell you is that I'm no closer to understanding what happened to Isabelle Addington than the day I first arrived. Suddenly I'm not sure I care to either. Maybe it's better to leave old ghosts locked away.

As for the present ones? The ones who linger and are current enough maybe to still be resolved, but are too sensitive to talk about here on the air? I have to ask myself, What are we afraid of when we look at cold cases of the last few decades? My answer is simple. We're afraid of them becoming like Isabelle Addington's story. No longer trauma and heartbreak, but instead intrigue and entertainment.

The fact is all crimes are laced with fear. And fear is a beast to war against. So, whether you listen to my podcast to be entertained, or you fancy yourself an amateur crime-solver like I've always fancied myself, just know this: Real people still exist who have been touched by these crimes. Some of them are so afraid to find the answers, they become afraid to live too. And then there are people like me. People who are afraid to live in the present, so instead we keep exploring the mysteries of yesterday. It's safer in the past. For all of us. Because the past has already been lived in, already been broken, already been ruined. Tomorrow? Tomorrow is one giant question mark, and none of us are sure we want to go there. Not just yet.

But we have to. Tomorrow doesn't wait for us to be ready.

Tomorrow doesn't wait for us to stop being afraid.

24

EFFIE

May 1901
Shepherd, Iowa

I F FEAR HAD A TASTE, it would taste of blood. The tangy iron of it would seep through every pore in a person's body. But instead of tasting it filtered through her nerves, tightening her muscles until they cramped and creating a haze as she tried to open her eyes, it was voices that were the hollow echo in Effie's ears. She tried to remember what had happened, but all she could identify was the desperate fear that paralyzed her where she lay.

"Effie?"

The voice was distant. Unfamiliar.

"Effie?"

A hand touched her forehead. She cried out, slapping the hand away. Effie could remember now. The bony fingers around Effie's throat. The way the fingernails dug into her neck . . .

"Shhhh!" Whoever it was stayed out of focus.

Effie whimpered, trying to push herself off what felt to be a soft mattress.

"Did you send someone to fetch the doctor?" A woman's voice.

The rumble of a man's voice. Floyd. It had to be Floyd Opperman.

Effie twisted on the bed, the blanket trapping her as it tangled with her legs.

"Please. Effie, stop fighting." The woman's voice was vaguely familiar. Younger, like Effie.

Effie blinked wildly, trying to clear her vision. Her throat hurt when she swallowed. Worse than the night at the James manor when she'd been assaulted by the man in Polly's room. She squeezed her eyes shut one more time and then opened them. The form of a young woman took shape. She hovered over Effie, her blond hair arranged beautifully around an equally pretty face. The walls were papered with tiny yellow flowers. Effie could hear rain pattering against the windowpanes, thunder rumbling across the sky in a gentle spring storm.

"Effie, do you know who I am?" The young woman eased onto a chair by the bed, concern and hope flooding her features.

Effie recognized her finally, and the tension—the fear—began to ebb. "Bethany," she croaked. It was Bethany.

A man cleared his throat, and Effie looked beyond Bethany. Patrick Charlemagne stood in the doorway of the room. He appeared quite concerned as well, conscientious of propriety.

"I've summoned a doctor, Effie, as well as sent a messenger to the James manor." Patrick's words brought a wave of relief over Effie. "And Bethany insisted I send one to Mr. Anderson's." Strangely, she was more relieved to hear Anderson had been called for than she was her own mother.

Her eyes swept back to Bethany's, and Effie knew there was question in them, but her throat hurt too badly to speak.

Bethany reached for Effie's hand. "Patrick found you. You

were lying on the side of the road in the rain. Not far from Mrs. Branson's house."

"Do you remember what happened?" Patrick asked, still standing at a cautionary distance from the bed.

Effie remembered the terror. She scrambled to collect the memories and put them in some kind of order. Floyd Opperman. At the manor. The stains on his shirt!

"Floyd," Effie rasped out.

"Floyd Opperman did this to you?" Patrick stiffened, outrage filtering across his face.

Effie shook her head. No. No, she had followed Floyd, but it had been a woman. Definitely a woman. She could remember the feel of the woman's hands gripping her throat, the form of the woman as she'd pulled Effie back against her.

"H-how?" Effie managed to ask.

Bethany tugged the blanket up over Effie's shivering body. "My home is not far from where Patrick found you. He wanted to get you in from the cold."

"I'd no intention of taking you to Mrs. Branson's," Patrick supplied.

Effie gave a nod of gratitude.

Footsteps sounded in the hallway outside the room. Within seconds, Anderson was in the doorway, his face set but his pallor white. Patrick stepped aside as Anderson pushed his way into the room.

"Effie!" Anderson wasted no time in crossing the room.

Bethany stood and moved out of his way, but Anderson ignored the empty chair and bent over the bed.

Effie felt his eyes skimming the length of her and then coming back up to settle on her neck. He touched her throat, his eyes alight with a fury she'd not witnessed in him before. Always intensity, but never fury.

He whirled, his angular face made more defined by the set of his jaw. "Who did this to her?"

Patrick held up his hands in a subtle gesture to bring calm to the situation. "We don't know. I found Miss James on the side of the road."

"The road?" Anderson bellowed.

The doctor chose that moment to arrive, and the next several minutes felt like chaos to Effie. Anderson was urged from the room by Patrick, who shot Effie a searching and rather indistinguishable look as he led Anderson away. Bethany remained off to the side as the doctor examined Effie.

He clicked his tongue many times, especially when he examined her throat. Pushing her wet hair from her forehead, he checked her hairline for cuts or abrasions. Finally he eased back, his green eyes stern, his white mustache draping on either side of his chin. "You are a lucky young woman." He nodded to Bethany, including her in the conversation. "You will need to rest your voice and your body for a few days. You've experienced trauma, but miraculously you've no further injuries besides those to your throat."

Bethany's "oh, good" was spoken for Effie as well.

The doctor turned to Bethany. "I shall commune with the men who await word as to Miss James's condition. I assume the police have been notified of the attack?"

Bethany nodded.

"Good, good. Now, which gentleman should I speak to regarding Miss James's care?"

Bethany shot Effie a rather hesitant look. "Mr. Anderson, I believe."

Effie gave a small nod.

The doctor, with his fingers to his forehead in salute, retreated from the room.

Bethany hurried forward. "I'm so sorry. I wasn't sure if you wished for Mr. Anderson to be apprised of your condition or if you preferred we wait for your father."

Effie offered a wordless smile.

Bethany chewed her bottom lip, making it rosier than it already was. "Effie, are you . . . becoming fond of Mr. Anderson?"

Effie struggled to speak, to reassure Bethany.

Bethany shook her head. "Forgive me. I only wish the best for you. And if Mr. Anderson is the best, it is not for me to say. Only that we will continue to pray that God protects you. Something terrible seems to be following you, and . . . and I worry for you, Effie." Bethany moved toward the door. "I'll go see if your parents have arrived yet. And I'll see to Mr. Anderson and to Patrick—Mr. Charlemagne."

Effie noticed Bethany's stumble over Patrick's name and the quick blush that came and went. Bethany swept from the room in a fluster. Effie closed her eyes. There were too many questions in her mind and in her heart. Too many unknowns. The biggest one, which made absolutely no sense to her, was that she wished Anderson would return to be near her. When he was near, she felt safe. When he wasn't, she simply didn't know whom she could trust.

Through their growing-up years, Effie and Polly had shared many nights together. As they entered young womanhood, however, that all stopped. Yet their parents had not seen fit to argue last night.

Polly's eyes opened, and the sisters soaked in the vulnerability of the moment. At last, Polly whispered, "Are you all right, Effie." Her eyes gleamed with tears.

Effie's voice was hoarse. "I tried to be brave like you."

Polly's laugh was weak but still touched with a mischievous note. "Oh, Effie. I'm not brave. I'm merely . . . adventurous."

Effie reached out and pushed a lock of Polly's hair behind her ear. "That's why I love you so."

Polly pursed her lips, which had lost their pink tint of health. "Who hurt you, Effie?"

"I don't know." Effie shook her head, her cheek rubbing the pillowcase as she lay on her side. "It was a woman, though."

"A woman?" Polly raised her voice, and Effie shushed her so she wouldn't draw their mother's attention. Effie wanted to prolong this time alone with Polly. How many more moments would they have together? Like this, snuggling, as if they were little girls sharing their secrets and dreams. "The woman should be imprisoned forever."

"Polly!" Effie exclaimed in a hushed whisper.

"Well, she should. You can't see the bruises on your neck. It's obvious we have a nefarious couple at large." Polly's outrage mounted even in her weakness, and Effie saw a spark of life in her sister's eyes. Always. Polly always wanted to solve mysteries, to sneak around in the dead of night, to be daring. Yet here they were. Polly confined to her bed, and Effie, who'd always wanted nothing more than to be a wife and a mother, now traipsing through the woods to creepy houses like 322 Predicament Avenue and getting attacked not once, but *twice*!

"A couple?" Polly's words finally made their way into Effie's thoughts. "What do you mean?"

"Isn't it obvious?" Polly whispered. She paused to catch her breath and for a few seconds wheezed as she tried to breathe. Then, "Charles told me yesterday that a man was in my room—and now a woman has taken it upon herself to literally try to squeeze the life out of you?"

Effie hadn't put the two together, and yet now it made sense. She pondered for a moment and then offered her own suspicions. "I followed Floyd Opperman to Predicament Avenue." She regaled Polly with her short and cryptic conversation with Floyd that led her to follow him. She told Polly of the stains on his clothing.

Polly took in the story, not interrupting, especially as Effie struggled as her voice grew sore. When she was finished, Polly didn't say anything. Instead, she reached for Effie's hand beneath the covers, squeezing it. "I'm sorry," she whispered.

"Sorry?" Effie countered.

Polly's face fell with a weight Effie had never seen. She waited for Polly to explain. "You wouldn't be in this position if I had not instigated it." A tear slipped down Polly's cheek. "I didn't intend this. Not this."

Effie reached out to dab the tears on Polly's face with the bedsheet. "You couldn't have known. Neither of us could have known."

Polly smiled sadly. "No. But God saved us from my foolishness anyway. Life isn't a game anymore, Effie." Her eyes became downcast, and yet there was a small bit of hope in them. "Life is so precious. So beautiful. It is a gift. I want you to live it, sweet Effie. I want you to live it not for me, but for all that God will do for you. All He has planned for you."

Effie's throat ached now for the tears that were stuck there. "I don't want to live without you."

Polly's chin quivered even as she smiled weakly. "You won't. I'll always be a part of you. And as you live your adventure of life here, I will continue mine in eternity."

"You truly believe that?" Effie whispered.

Polly's smile was gentle. "A promise has never been broken by our Creator. I may be foolhardy, but my belief is as strong as my will, dear Effie. He will not break His promise to me now. Many grand adventures await me. Of that I am certain."

25

EFFIE HAD WATCHED their cook can tomatoes once, and right now she related to the jars that were lowered into the pressure cooker. Too much more and she might explode like a Mason jar, sending spatter all over the room. At the thought, she felt herself blanch.

"This must be put to an end." Her father paced the parlor floor.

Constable Talbot was in attendance at the impromptu gathering to address Effie's attack. Gerald Ambrose, the town councilman, was there also, with a furrowed brow and an outraged expression that was far more intimidating than any action Mr. Ambrose could supply. He was all bluster, and Effie resented that he had inserted himself into the recent events.

Anderson stood by her chair, his hand resting on its back, laying silent claim to Effie in a way she hadn't expected and didn't quite know what to do with.

Effie understood she was only here because of her testimony and nothing more. In normal circumstances, the men would have completely excluded her, but up until this point, in the last twenty-four hours since her attack, they had only speculated on the details of what had happened.

"You said Floyd Opperman was covered in blood?" Mr. Ambrose leveled a look on Effie that caused her to shrink back in her chair.

"His clothes were stained," she answered.

"With blood?" Mr. Ambrose pressed.

"I don't know for sure if it was blood, but it was rust in color, and I—"

Mr. Ambrose turned from her to Constable Talbot. "There. That's evidence of a crime. He should be arrested and charged with the murder of this Isabelle Addington, as well as Miss James's recent assault."

Constable Talbot held up his hand. "Wait just a minute. We have no body and therefore it's difficult to prove murder. We can presume there has been a death, we can even suspect Floyd Opperman, but he can't be charged with anything criminal when all we have is supposition."

"And my daughter's attack! Twice! Once in our own home."

"Which you don't know was carried out by Floyd, any more than Miss James here knows it was Floyd."

"It was a woman yesterday," Effie inserted, though she hesitated in doing so. She had no desire to relieve Floyd Opperman of responsibility for crimes of violence he might have committed. But she also knew without a doubt that he had been on the porch at 322 Predicament Avenue, and it had been a woman who attempted to strangle her.

"So we have the potential of Floyd Opperman and an unknown woman as suspects," Anderson concluded, still not mentioning the massive concern that his daughter was also missing. It was a crucial piece of information that would have increased the urgency tenfold. Yet Effie could understand his continued reticence to bring his daughter into the conversation. Whoever had baby Cora had already enacted violence against Isabelle Addington. Their trustworthiness to not do something to the child was slim, and if the town became aware, the subsequent witch-hunt of sorts could result in the perpetrator disposing of baby Cora as a means to wash their hands of kidnapping on top of murder.

"Mabel Opperman." Carlton James snapped his fingers. His eyes were sharp as he swept them across his daughter's bruised neck. He pointed. "She could very well be in cahoots with her son Floyd—or better yet, attempting to cover up his tendency toward violence in order to protect him. She may have attacked Effie merely because Effie had seen the stains on Floyd's clothing and followed him to their property."

"And the man who broke into your home?" Gerald Ambrose was following Carlton's theory with wide, interested eyes.

"Floyd himself. Why not? Polly was on the porch when he was in the throes of murder. He believes she saw him. The newspapers did nothing to assist in lessening the sensationalism of"—Carlton shot a look between Anderson and Effie—"the entire situation. It merely put a name to the face of the person Floyd believes saw him committing a crime. He's not a smart fellow, so he breaks into my home to silence Polly and instead is crossed by Effie here."

"And then," Ambrose added, fully invested now, "he comes by to warn you, Miss James. He tells you to run because he's threatening you and your sister. He intends to harm you."

"Precisely." Carlton nodded.

"So it's Floyd and Mabel Opperman. It has been all along." Ambrose clucked his tongue. "It doesn't surprise me in the slightest. That family is standoffish and has allowed riffraff to come and go at Predicament Avenue for far too long. And Floyd's the untrustworthy kind."

"Are you suggesting the Oppermans have paid the nurse to poison Polly?" Effie broke into the conversation, squeezing the words painfully from her sore throat.

The constable's head jerked up in surprise.

Her father closed his eyes as though to control his reaction.

"What makes you say that?" Constable Talbot directed his question to Effie but looked to her father.

Carlton James ran a hand over his beard. "Effie believes that Polly has been silenced by our nurse."

"She has! I had a conversation with her just this morning, and that's because we asked the nurse to take leave since I've been staying with Polly!" Effie's words caught in her throat from the strain of speaking. She felt Anderson's hand on her shoulder, calming her.

"Do you believe this to be true?" Constable Talbot asked her father.

Carlton shook his head. "I don't know. At this point . . . is it out of the question? No." He met Effie's eyes, and she knew that her father was listening now. Finally and truly listening.

Anderson pulled her aside into an alcove by the carriage house. She had agreed to take a stroll with him. Her parents believed it was to help strengthen her, to give her fresh air. She knew differently. Now Anderson looked down at her, wordless, and studied her face.

"Why keep Cora a secret?" Effie insisted. He owed her that information, didn't he? She had followed Floyd for baby Cora alone. She had been subjected to violence because she was hoping to rescue Anderson's daughter.

"I can't risk further harm coming to her," he stated frankly.

"But doing nothing will potentially bring her further harm also."

Anderson drew in a steadying breath and let it out slowly. He glanced around them. They were out of view of the main house, and he seemed to take comfort in the privacy afforded them. "You must understand, Effie, there are implications—reasons far beyond that affect the entire situation. I must tread delicately."

Effie nodded.

"I must go now. The men inside will begin hunting for the Oppermans by noon, which will only exacerbate things."

"If they can apprehend Floyd and his mother—"

"Do you truly believe it is them, Effie?" Anderson's question made her pause.

She frowned. "What do you mean?"

"Think of it." Anderson pointed to the side of his head. "What motive would they have to kill Isabelle? To take my child?" He leaned closer to her, his eyes glistening with a shrewdness he'd not revealed when he observed the meeting with her father, the constable, and Gerald Ambrose. "The last few times I saw Isabelle Addington, she had been in thick with someone, and that someone is what brought her here."

Effie knew confusion was stretched across her face.

Anderson continued, "Perhaps the story of Predicament Avenue and the events since make sense as a viable theory from Shepherd's point of view, but that doesn't hold a candle to being legitimate from mine. At best, Floyd is a bystander who is causing his own sort of trouble."

"Who is Isabelle Addington to you?" Effie struggled to understand. She deserved to know the truth.

Anderson's expression darkened, and he looked away.

Effie dared to reach out and touch his arm lightly. It drew his attention back to her, and all the little parts inside of Effie that made her nervous around him evaporated. She could see his pain. Not only pain, but a sort of lostness that came with the absence of loved ones and the uncertainty of their return.

"If she is not your wife—has never been your wife—then who is Isabelle Addington?"

Anderson shook his head. "I've come too far to risk—"

"What risk is there?" Effie interrupted. "I'm a woman from a small town who has spent her life reading books and wishing to one day have her own home, a husband and children." She blushed as his eyes came up to meet hers. "I'm not an exciting woman, and when I'm not motivated to protect my family, I'm rather dull to be honest. How would I be a risk to you and your purposes of getting baby Cora home to you?"

Anderson's jaw worked back and forth. He moved suddenly, taking her hand and leading her from the alcove of the carriage house into the building. It was quiet and stale. It smelled of wheel grease and straw. It was evident he wanted to command their privacy as he closed the carriage house doors.

He turned as he dropped the latch on the inside of the doors. His head was tipped to the side, his tie in place and his shirt crisp—Gus's doing no doubt. He struck an interesting pose, one that in another time and place Effie might have given more thought to. Not handsome exactly, but striking. Not imposing, but forceful. Not aggressive, but confident. Not untrustworthy, but full of secrets.

"My full name and title is Lord Lewis Anderson Archibald Mooring of Tiffany Ridge." Anderson paused, allowing it to sink in.

When it did, Effie lifted her fingers to her mouth to cover her silent *ohhh*.

"My family goes back many generations in England. My wife, Laura, was also from an established family. Isabelle Addington was brought on to our staff as a nursemaid when we discovered that Laura was expecting our first child. Isabelle was a blessing to Laura—we both appreciated and liked her."

He stopped, stretching his neck as though the very act of conversation was exhausting every part of him.

"What happened?" Effie breathed.

"I'm not entirely certain what soured Isabelle toward Laura and me. Shortly after Cora's birth, Laura passed into the hands of God, and I was left with an infant. Cora was three weeks old when I awoke one morning to find Isabelle gone, and she had taken Cora with her."

Effie leaned against a wooden post for strength. The very horror of Anderson awakening to find his motherless infant daughter missing was awful.

He continued, his voice without emotion as if reciting a long, memorized, but never given explanation. "There was evidence left behind that Isabelle had been having an affair with an American man. I believe a plan came together for Isabelle to steal my daughter from me and meet this man here in America, wherein they would together proceed to blackmail me for a ransom for my daughter's return." Anderson cleared his throat. "At least that is my assumption. But somehow between London and Shepherd, Isabelle had a change of heart. She mailed me the letter. I believe she was found out, and that is why she is dead. It is also why no ransom for Cora has been delivered."

Anderson took a deep breath and went on sharing what he knew, Effie hanging on his every word as the truth became clearer with each moment that passed. "With my position back home, too much can be used against me in recovering her. Gus is in regular communication with my brother in London. No ransom notes have arrived there either." His eyes became stormy, volatile. "I curse the man who coerced Isabelle into such a heinous act. If she needed more money, I would have given it to her. But to take my child? To dishonor my dead wife in such a way?"

Effie didn't know that it would help him, but it was the only thing she could think of to lessen the burden Anderson bore alone. "But she still brought you here. With her letter. It speaks of some goodness in her. I'm sorry you've felt obligated to try to protect me while you've been searching for your daughter. Please don't feel such . . ." Effie winced as she swallowed. "Please go find your daughter."

Anderson crossed the distance between them, gripped her upper arms, and while lightly holding her, he said, "You are *not* an obligation. You have given far more in Cora's behalf—in my behalf—than you should have been asked to do. You are innocent in all of this, and I will not allow you to be harmed again."

Effie didn't know how to reply. The possessiveness in his tone didn't balance with the time they had spent together or the missing pieces of themselves they'd yet to share. She couldn't expect romance or fairy tales from this preposterous kinship she felt with the Englishman. An English *lord*! But she couldn't deny the invisible thread that pulled them together. It seemed unbreakable as much as it was inexplicable.

"I'll be fine," she whispered. Not really believing it herself, and not truly wanting Anderson to set her free—though she couldn't have explained why if she'd been asked. Not reasonably or logically anyway.

The lines in Anderson's face gentled. His eyes narrowed as his hand came up, knuckles brushing the length of her cheek. "Yes. Because I will destroy anyone who attempts to hurt you again. Anyone who hurts Cora. That is the way of it. That will be their consequence."

26

NORAH

Present Day

HOW DARE LEROY SUGGEST Naomi hadn't told the family about him—about her pregnancy—because of Norah!

"Don't listen to him," Ralph groused as he shut the door firmly on LeRoy as the man headed back to his car parked on the street. Ralph turned to glower through saggy eyelids at Naomi. "You weren't that bad."

Naomi blinked at Ralph's choice of words. "*That* bad?"

Ralph had the decency to flush through his stubby white whiskers. He waved her off as he lumbered into the kitchen and away from her. His left overall strap threatened to slide off his sagging shoulder.

"Ralph." Norah raised her voice in warning. "Ralph, you come back here!"

The old man ignored her and exited like an ashamed puppy dog. The screen door slammed shut behind him.

"Oh no, you don't," Norah grumbled, slipping her feet into a pair of sandals and hurrying after him. She shoved open the screen door and chased Ralph into the cemetery, where he was picking up a rake that was lying next to a grave dated 1894. "What do you mean I wasn't 'that bad,' Ralph?" Norah stood, hands on her hips, demanding he answer her.

Ralph was the quieter one of the two brothers, while Otto was the more expressive and affectionate one. If Norah needed comfort, she went to Otto. But she could always trust Ralph for his blunt honesty, his crotchety defense of her and Aunt Eleanor, and his loyalty. Always loyal. Norah had never questioned why the brothers didn't live in the same house. They were alike in so many ways and yet different enough that they likely would have imploded. Ralph wanted his privacy, and Otto wanted his toolshed. They needed some distance from each other, their own space.

But now? Now Norah wanted Ralph's honesty. Well, truthfully, she didn't *want* it, but she felt she needed to hear it anyway.

Ralph laid the rake over a wheelbarrow, then squatted to pick up a stick that was tarnishing the grave of Katherine Humperdink, who'd died in 1873. What a name, *Humperdink*.

"Ralph?" Norah pressed.

"Fine." He tossed the stick into the wheelbarrow and faced her. "You've always been a worrier, a fretter. So much so that you can't leave people alone sometimes."

That didn't fit with Norah's view of herself. In fact, she avoided people. Had for years. It seemed Ralph saw through her.

"Oh, sure." He waved her off. "You don't hound folks now, but back in the day when it was you two girls runnin' around here, you just didn't know when to let up when you were worried about somethin' or you didn't understand. It was like you couldn't find any peace until you had control, and you couldn't have control unless you pestered the heck out of people for explanations to help you stop frettin'."

Norah felt that gnawing in the pit of her stomach that came with hearing the truth, but not wanting to admit it was the truth. She challenged Ralph further. "Give me an example."

Ralph grabbed the rake, planted it, and leaned against the wooden handle. "How 'bout that time Eleanor wanted to send you to church camp, paid for it and everything, but you ended up not going 'cause she couldn't tell you all the details. Which cabin you'd be stayin' in, who your counselor would be, if they'd make you eat eggs for breakfast or if they had a cold cereal option."

"Okay, well, I was only eleven. A new place? New people? Any young girl would have questions."

"Mm-hmm." Ralph adjusted his grip on the rake. "All them times you tried to follow Otto home to his place?" Ralph adjusted his voice to sound high and like a child's. "'What if your tools aren't hung up right, an' they fall on ya an' cut off your head?' Or 'You know there's such a thing as killer bees, an' if they make a nest in your shed, we'd best get them out.'"

"Both are rational concerns." Norah pursed her lips.

Ralph gave her a cockeyed look. "How's it rational that a teenage gal can hang tools better'n someone like Otto, who's been doin' it for years?"

"Maybe it wasn't worry so much as curiosity. Maybe I just wanted to have a look inside the man's shed." Norah crossed her arms over her chest.

"We all got a right to a little privacy. It's why I ain't never bugged my brother about his shed, and he ain't never bugged me about my bathroom."

"Your bathroom?" Norah quirked an eyebrow.

"Never you mind." Ralph shook his finger at her. "Fact is, you had a way of not only frettin' but also not givin' up trying to find reasons so you didn't have be afraid. Even if it meant steppin' on others' toes, or hurtin' their feelings, or just being dad-blamed nosy."

Norah let her shoulders droop. They were probably sagging lower than Ralph's now. He noticed and gentled his tone.

"I'm not sayin' Naomi was right not to tell you about LeRoy back then. I'm no fan of that boy anyway. I'm just sayin' I understand a bit why Naomi didn't say anything. She wanted something for herself and didn't want to answer twenty questions and give fifty reasons to justify her decisions were good ones."

Norah nodded. She had to consider what he was saying. Ralph wouldn't exaggerate the truth, and he wouldn't candy-coat it either.

"What else did Naomi not tell me?" Her question was rhetorical, but it spawned another she truly wanted answered. "Do you think Naomi didn't tell me some things because she was worried I'd be *more* afraid?"

"You mean did she keep secrets to protect you?" Ralph clarified. Norah nodded.

"You bet I think she did." Ralph's face wrestled with various expressions as he fought back emotion. "That girl loved people as much as you feared for people. Both are good and bad, you know? You fear for people, but then you're mighty protective of them too. Naomi, she loved people hard, but then they could use her and spit her out 'cause she'd let them."

"Yeah." Norah remembered, and with the memory came a revelation. Ralph was silent, letting her think. After a moment, Norah sucked in a determined breath and reached out to give Ralph's forearm a squeeze. "Thank you, Ralph. For being honest."

He smiled.

She smiled in return and then headed back toward the house, sidestepping a grave so she didn't walk over it. It was time she looked at the cold case files again. This time by herself. And let Naomi speak to her from beyond the grave, and maybe shed new light on what Norah's fear had always blocked her from seeing.

She fingered the folder of Isabelle Addington. Sebastian had been right. There wasn't much in it of substance as to who she was, nor was there much regarding the story surrounding her murder. A few handwritten notes by a Constable Talbot stated that the initial crime scene had been hidden, then later discovered by Euphemia James and Lewis Anderson. Apparently, Lewis Anderson had identified the alleged victim in all probability to be Isabelle Addington. Constable Talbot's note stated that Mr. Anderson had followed Miss Addington to Shepherd, having had firsthand knowledge that she was staying at 322 Predicament Avenue. However, no body had been found.

Two names were scratched in pencil and underlined. Norah stared at them for a long moment, recalling the visit to the Oppermans' descendant Betty and her husband, Ron. There on the copy of the old pencil scratching were the names Floyd Opperman and Mabel Opperman—along with a question: *But if she's dead, where's the body of Isabelle Addington?*

Aside from that, Norah could see why the case file would have disappointed Sebastian. There was nothing to expand on the tale. Not that would be worth episodic retelling on his podcast anyway. And his wasn't a podcast of ghost stories and the paranormal, and spouting off the so-called sightings of Isabelle Addington through the years wouldn't add much either.

Frankly, there wasn't much basis for Mrs. Miller to sue the bed-and-breakfast as though responsible for her husband's heart attack should she decide to take legal action. But then enough time had passed that Norah was fairly certain the Miller family had accepted that their loved one's death was the result of natural causes and not the fault of Norah and her business.

As to the question this Constable Talbot had written concerning the mystery of Isabelle Addington's missing body, Norah wondered if that wouldn't be enough to show beyond doubt that the house wasn't haunted by Isabelle after all. Her body had never been found—unless she was to believe the postmortem photograph of that woman truly *was* Isabelle Addington. And if so, it was never proven that she'd been murdered on the premises of Predicament Avenue. It put to rest the notion that her ghost snuck through the house, scaring people and causing heart attacks.

Yes. She'd call Rebecca, her lawyer, and feed her that idea. Just in case.

Norah closed the folder. Isabelle Addington wasn't her primary focus now. She bit the inside of her lip as she stared at the great number of photocopies and notes and folders that had to do with Naomi's disappearance.

She pulled out a spiral notebook and made a timeline to remind herself of the events. Naomi's disappearance and the subsequent search for her. The hunter who found her remains three months later in the woods—a place with no connection or reason anyone could think of other than it being remote. Norah pulled out paperwork outlining the questioning of suspects. Her parents had been cleared, she had been cleared, coworkers, Aunt Eleanor . . .

Norah winced as she read the names of a few suspects with no alibis but no motives either.

Ralph Middleford.

Otto Middleford.

Mike Dover.

Norah's breath hitched. *Mike Dover?* Detective Dover had been a suspect? She'd never known that, or if she had, it hadn't registered for some reason. Norah thumbed through the pages, reviewing notes.

Mike had been employed by the same combination retail store and pharmacy as Naomi was at the time—him working in the store, her in the pharmacy. The two had been seen flirting a few times, but coworkers later stated it was congenial and there had never been an issue between them. Mike had been at the store that night when it closed. He'd been the third person in the store besides Naomi and the pharmacist, who had an alibi. Mike Dover did not. According to his statement, he'd locked up, driven home, and fallen asleep in his apartment where he lived alone.

Norah sank onto a chair. Dover had been inserting himself into her life here and there, especially since Mr. Miller's heart attack, and had reawakened not only the stories about the first murder victim of Shepherd, Iowa—Isabelle Addington—but also the questions that seemed to pop up again about Naomi's unsolved murder.

She focused on a printout of LeRoy Anderson's information—height, weight, other physical attributes. He'd also not had an alibi, but according to the notes, he'd had a motive. The baby.

Norah wrote in her notebook.

Mike.

LeRoy.

The only other names on the list with no one to account for their whereabouts on the night of Naomi's abduction were Ralph and Otto. That would be like accusing Santa Claus of murdering Rudolph. Norah could have told the cops that had she known they'd even considered the two brothers as suspects.

Norah lifted the page that reported the condition of Naomi's body when it was found. She steeled herself as the heaviness of anxiety began to seep into her.

"You can do this," she breathed aloud to herself. A prayer would probably help too, so she tried that. What was it about being afraid that pushed a person away from God instead of toward Him?

Deciding to explore that conundrum later, Norah let her eyes examine the report.

Norah had been found in the woods just twenty yards from a gravel road. She had been fully dressed. No signs of sexual assault. In spite of the condition of the body having been lying there for three months, the investigators were able to identify her based on the graduation ring she wore that was inscribed with her name.

Norah drew in a shaky breath. Yes. She remembered helping Mom give the police a list of articles Naomi would have had on her. The ring, her cellphone, her Coach wallet . . .

She stilled. Norah stared at the next line.

Her hands were bound behind her back with a pink bandanna.

Pink.

Norah began to tremble. It traveled from her head down her neck and shoulders, then through her torso and down her legs until she had to grip the edge of the table.

A pink bandanna.

She knew Naomi had been found with her hands tied together with a bandanna. The cops had mentioned it several times. A few had commented on a bandanna being a flimsy way to control a prisoner.

But she'd never heard the color before.

That pink bandanna had been Naomi's! The person who bound her had taken the bandanna from Naomi's belongings. Naomi never went anywhere without her pink bandanna, which was given to her by one of the most important people in her life.

"Always have a bandanna on ya. Can use it as a nose wipe, a rag, wet it down to keep ya cool in the summer, and can even make a tourniquet out of it. People underestimate the power of a bandanna."

Those words had come from Otto—and Ralph too—but Otto had spoken them for the brothers. Norah heard them as clearly as the Christmas when they'd both opened their gifts with the bandanna of their favorite color. Naomi's was pink. Norah's had been green. Norah had lost hers rather quickly, not fully believing in the so-called power of a bandanna. Naomi, though, was fiercely protective of hers. Because she was fiercely protective of the brothers.

The room began to whirl as Norah struggled to retain her equilibrium. Now was *not* the time for the panic attack to return. How dare someone use something so precious to Naomi as her pink bandanna to bind her for her death! If Otto and Ralph were to find out, it would break them. Norah stared at the names and then reached for a pencil and crossed out Otto's and Ralph's. She would *never* tell the boys that Naomi had been restrained by the very gift they'd meant to be sweet and special.

Norah shifted her attention to the remaining two names.

LeRoy.

Mike.

Strangely, she might be led to believe that either of them could have done it. But now just a little bit more of her was less suspicious of LeRoy and more concerned that Dover wasn't who he said he was. If Dover had been Naomi's coworker, he would've had ample opportunity to see her with her pink bandanna. He would've known that Naomi was carrying in her bag the very restraint that would eventually be the tool used in the taking of her life.

27

S HE HADN'T REALIZED how long she'd been sitting there, staring at the document in front of her.

The front door opened and shut, causing Norah to startle. She looked up and out the front window to see the world was shrouded in darkness already. All afternoon she had scoured through the files.

She was losing her mind over this case. She was losing her mind over everything.

Norah looked toward the door, expecting to see Sebastian there. Only he wasn't. The entryway was dark. She really *had* lost track of time in her frantic searching of the files.

She took a moment to push back the hair from her face and tugged her T-shirt down over her hips. She stepped into the hall and glanced at the grandfather clock. It was past ten. Sebastian had to have snuck in and slipped past her without saying hello or good night. She squelched the hurt his distance had created. Right now she'd like nothing more than to run all this by him.

Norah padded her way across the entry, not bothering to flick on lights. She didn't want to risk waking Harper whom Sebastian had helped home from the hospital just that morning.

They'd stayed distant from Norah, for whatever reason. But even without interaction, Norah knew the poor girl needed to sleep. Norah knew that sometimes the lights from downstairs could seep through the cast-iron floor vents and shed light into the bedrooms above.

A thump in the kitchen caused Norah to stop. She strained to hear. "Sebastian?" she called softly.

There was no answer, just the rhythmic ticking of the clock.

She needed a glass of water. Or maybe she'd make herself a cup of orange-spice tea.

The kitchen was dark save for the small light above the stove. She must have left it on earlier in the afternoon when she'd made a sandwich for lunch. Norah made quick time of filling a mug with water and popping it into the microwave. She punched the appropriate buttons and then stood in front of it, staring through the glass door as the mug rotated slowly.

She pondered everything she'd read in the past few hours.

Isabelle Addington. A moot point, and not much else needed there considering the Millers hadn't bothered to file their frivolous lawsuit against her. She'd send a sympathy card and flowers to Mrs. Miller if Rebecca thought it'd be well received and not seem antagonistic.

Naomi. Everything she'd read had only brought back memories of what she already knew, except for the suspect list that included the two brothers, LeRoy, and Mike Dover.

Dover . . . She had refrained from calling him for obvious reasons. What if—?

Another thud made Norah jerk her head to the right and toward the door. Was something outside on the porch? A raccoon or possum? Wouldn't be the first time. Still, Norah was unnerved as she reached up and jammed the end button on the microwave.

Click.

What the heck was that?

Norah spun around and peered into the dark corners of the room. If Isabelle Addington came rushing at her on all fours, her head twisting around and her black hair dangling beside her face, Norah would scream so loud that the entire house would crash down.

But there was no ghoulish form of a possessed dead woman. Nothing.

Then she heard a creak. It seemed to come from the front of the house. Floorboards in the entryway? Norah tiptoed in that direction, the light from the dining room casting a much friendlier glow than the darker kitchen to her back. She peered to the right and down the hall toward her bedroom.

Nothing.

Halfway up the stairs to the second floor.

Nothing.

Norah held her breath, trying to listen for more sounds of disturbance. Sounds that were foreign to what was typical of 322 Predicament Avenue at night.

All was silent.

She let out her breath.

Good. Teatime.

Norah turned to go back into the kitchen.

A woman stood behind her, eyes wide and horrified, her hair stringy and short, hanging down on either side of her face. She was breathing through her mouth, short gasping breaths. She held up her hands, the tips of her fingers bloody, the nails half ripped off.

Norah opened her mouth to scream, but the sound that squeezed through was strangled. She desperately tried to suck in air and failed. Norah gaped in terror at the ghoulish woman in front of her. And when the woman spoke, her words came out in a puff of breath that smelled musty and swept across Norah's face.

"Help me."

28

EFFIE

May 1901

HER VOICE WAS COMING BACK stronger now. Another night's rest had lessened the strain on her vocal cords and eased the soreness in her throat. She'd sat with Polly this morning, but she had been antsy and preoccupied. She knew today was the day the men had planned to confront the Oppermans. Effie's claims about the nurse had also been reinforced when the nurse failed to return to the James Manor and had disappeared. A witness had seen her boarding a train, Constable Talbot stated. The fact Polly was reviving even further reinforced Effie's assertions. They had gently questioned Polly again about the night in question. But Polly's answers were unchanged from her original, stilted ones the night they'd been to Predicament Avenue. There had been a man attacking a woman, but she hadn't seen enough to identify him.

Today, the plan was to question the Oppermans and try to get one of them—either Floyd or Mabel—to fess up to the murder or, at a minimum, Effie's attack. Yet Effie couldn't get Anderson's story from her mind. She knew he was doing his own investigating alone, without consulting anyone and keeping to himself. He had given her strict instructions to stay at the James manor and not venture out without him or a male chaperone like her father. This time it had nothing to do with etiquette but rather safety. And no, Anderson had added, her younger brothers were not considered proper escorts.

Effie worried over the fact that Floyd Opperman was being assertively confronted. He had told her to run, and they had interpreted it as a threat. But what if he'd meant it to warn her? What if he was warning her away from Predicament Avenue and away from the woman who had attacked her?

Her mind spun for most of the morning. Now she was glad for the diversion of Bethany Todd and, to her surprise, Patrick Charlemagne's visit. Effie sat across from them in the parlor, struggling to maintain a calm, polite exterior while her insides churned.

"We're so thankful you're all right." Bethany smiled with her eyes.

"Thank you."

"We've brought you a gift," Bethany said, extending a pretty box tied with ribbon. "To help bring you healing and happiness."

"A small token," Patrick added with a nod.

Effie took the box, untying the ribbon. She lifted the lid and let out a small gasp. "Oh my!" She reached inside and lifted a gold-plated box. Effie appreciated the beautiful scrollwork that embellished its edges.

"Flick the lever, if you will." Patrick pointed to a small latch, and Effie pushed it. The lid popped open, and she jumped. She couldn't help the grin that stretched across her face at the sight of a small bird that began to move, its chirps filling the room with cheery notes.

"It's beautiful!" Effie lifted questioning eyes to Bethany and then to Patrick. "But it's too much. I can't accept."

"Oh, please do accept it, Effie!" Bethany insisted. "You deserve to be comforted."

"It gives us pleasure to bring encouragement where it's needed." Patrick's mustache emphasized his smile.

Effie blushed as she looked down at the bird. Tears sprang to her eyes, and she struggled to find her voice. "I-I . . . thank you." She nodded. "Such an act of friendship is . . . unexpected and a blessing." Her eyes met Bethany's, and her friend's bright smile flooded Effie's soul with sunlight. She needed it. The pall that had hung over her these last couple of weeks had been enough to make her feel as if every day were an impending thunderstorm.

"I hope you will continue to get well," Patrick said.

Bethany and Patrick rose to take their leave. Effie left the music box on a table in the parlor and followed them to the front entrance.

Effie opened the door for them, and as she moved to bid them goodbye, she glanced at the cobblestone street at the end of the walk. A man shuffled along the bushes, almost as if he believed he were hidden from view when in reality it was quite obvious who it was. Floyd Opperman.

She heard Bethany and Patrick speaking to her, but their voices faded as she concentrated on Floyd. He was here again—at the manor. Only he wasn't in their yard; he was simply passing by. In the daylight again. But why would—?

A child's whimper cut through the air.

Effie pushed between Bethany and Patrick and rushed onto the veranda to try to keep sight of Floyd. Did he have a child with him? Hidden in the folds of his coat? It was impossible to tell. It was probably her misplaced hope that somehow it was Anderson's child.

"Effie, are you all right?" Bethany's concern snagged Effie's attention.

She spun. "That's Floyd Opperman."

Patrick stiffened. His chin went up as he, too, strained to identify the retreating back of the brawny man. "Why would he be in this part of town?"

"I need to go." Without thinking, Effie cast them both an apologetic look. If he had a child with him, a baby, and if it was Cora . . . She hurried down the steps.

"Effie, wait!" Bethany cried.

Effie turned, unwilling to waste a moment. "Stay with Polly, please!" she called to Bethany over her shoulder.

Patrick bounded down the steps behind her. "Let me come with you. So you will be safe."

Effie didn't argue but only nodded. If Patrick wanted to help her, she would welcome his assistance. Without another word, Effie hitched up her skirts and rushed for the street. Toward Floyd. Toward the hope, however misplaced, that the child she'd heard was Cora.

"That way," Patrick stated.

"Did you see him turn there?" Effie half jogged beside Patrick, annoyed that she was wearing shoes with heels and that her skirts inhibited her. No wonder Polly always wore their brother's trousers when going on an adventure.

Patrick nodded. "Yes, and it's in the direction of Predicament Avenue."

It made sense. Too much sense. Her nerves tingled, her breath coming in short gasps, not because of the physical exertion but because she remembered the hands wrapping around her throat. The ghostly image of Isabelle Addington in the attic window that she knew had to have been caused by lack of oxygen but still was clear in her memory. She looked at Patrick, whose focus was intent on the horizon ahead of them. Searching for Floyd.

He was turning out to be a good friend, and as expected, he

had obvious intentions with regard to Bethany. Effie was glad about that. He was a good man. Patrick had come to her aid without even asking to know why she was so frantic in her chasing after Floyd. She took comfort knowing Bethany would naturally wait at the James manor, so that when Mother returned home or if Polly needed someone, Bethany would be available to provide help where needed.

"Over here." Patrick urged Effie around another corner.

She took heart that he had seen where Floyd had gone. And now, as 322 Predicament Avenue came into view, her stomach curdled, and she stumbled.

Patrick paused, reaching for her elbow to steady her, concern in his brown eyes. "Are you all right?"

"I'm fine," she assured him, even though Effie didn't sense that assurance in herself.

Patrick leaned closer and pointed toward the house. "Let's circle around to the back. We'll sneak along the tree line. If we can manage not to be seen, then we may get an opportunity to confront Floyd."

Effie nodded, following Patrick's lead and ducking low as they entered the woods to the west of the house. The trees hid them from both the road and the house. Effie breathed a prayer of gratefulness that Patrick was with her to help her confront Floyd. He'd even said so aloud. Somehow he must have been privy to the fact that Floyd was a suspect in the recent violence. But Effie knew Patrick would have no idea about Anderson's baby.

They snuck into the graveyard, moving between and around the headstones. Patrick held his finger to his lips for Effie to be silent. So far, Floyd had not seen them. But then, Effie noted, she hadn't seen Floyd either.

Patrick eased up the stairs of the back porch. The middle of the porch sagged. He motioned to a broken board in the floor and mouthed *Be careful* to Effie. She nodded and tiptoed around it.

Both anticipation and uncertainty washed through Effie as Patrick reached for the doorknob. The door opened slowly with his silent shove inward. They waited at the threshold. Patrick's hand was raised to stop Effie from moving forward. Finally, he stepped inside, the hardwood floor creaking beneath his weight. He motioned for Effie to follow. Once fully inside, Patrick closed the door softly behind them.

They moved through the kitchen with stealth. Evidence that someone had been there was in the corner by way of a mound of dirty blankets and an open can of moldy food. Effie wrinkled her nose, following Patrick into the entryway.

"I don't see anyone." His whisper sounded loud. "Let's check upstairs."

Effie didn't question him, only followed as they crept up the stairs. What they would do if they found Floyd on the second floor, she wasn't sure. The cry of the child had been the impetus to move her into action so quickly, but now with Floyd no longer in view and unsure as to where he was—or if indeed he had baby Cora—Effie wondered if it would be wiser to return home and send for Anderson. She could tell him what she'd seen and suspected. He could find and confront Floyd and then—

Patrick lifted his hand at the top of the stairs, stopping so abruptly that Effie almost collided into him. He gestured toward the back bedroom, and she shrugged. He nodded and started forward again. They took a few steps more until they reached the bedroom door. It was closed, unlike the other rooms on the second floor.

Floyd had to be inside.

Effie's breath quickened. Her heart thudded rapidly, jarring her nerves even further. She held her breath as Patrick reached for the doorknob, twisted it, and flung the door open. She let out her pent-up breath with a whoosh.

"It's empty." Effie couldn't hide her disbelief. The house at 322 Predicament Avenue was empty. "Floyd's not here."

"Unfortunately." Patrick strode across the room and peered out the window that overlooked the front yard and the street. He reached for the shutters and closed them, blocking out the daylight.

Effie protested. "Must we close the shutters?"

Patrick gave her a gentle smile. "If they're open, then anyone can see inside the house."

She was all right with that. There was an element of security not to be boxed into the house like it was the dead of night, and the house a prison.

Patrick skirted around her to the door and, to Effie's dismay, closed that as well.

"Mr. Charlemagne?"

He engaged the lock.

"Patrick," Effie said more sternly, although the quaver in her voice belied her confidence.

The man turned, his well-polished air still in place, his gentle smile still fixed on his face. His eyes were almost tender, sorrowful. "Oh, Miss James." He blew out a huge sigh. "I wish you hadn't been such a problem."

Her

MAYBE ONE DAY I'll haunt the earth. I've always wondered if spirits walk among us. Some have told me that to be absent from the body is to be present with the Lord. But I don't know that the Lord will want me to be present with Him. At least not until I've served some sort of penance. Which brings me back to these graves, that house, and myself.

Will I linger after I am dead?

Will I try to reach from the beyond and touch the living?

Will they even hear me or see me if I try?

All I know for certain is that if I tell it truthfully, I am not ready to die. I am not ready to uncover what lies beyond. I am not ready to wander the halls of an empty house, waiting for the moment I am freed from the prison of penance, kept from the bowels of hell, and allowed to enter the sanctuary God has ready for those who make it there.

But I am going to die.

I know this now.

I can feel it. A premonition. An awareness. A reality that is unavoidable.

I have dug the pit of my own grave and am simply waiting to be placed inside of it.

It will happen soon.

When night falls on Predicament Avenue.

29

Norah

Present Day

NORAH FLUNG HERSELF BACKWARD, pressing against the wall as the woman stepped closer.

"Please. Help me."

Norah couldn't speak. Words twisted in her throat, clutching at air and stealing her ability to breathe deeply.

"Please?"

Still Norah couldn't reply. She struggled to suck in air, to scream, to do something—anything—but the fear that encircled her was paralyzing.

The woman stumbled, tripping on her own feet, and then swayed. Instinctively, Norah reached for her. But the woman jerked backward and bumped into a kitchen chair, sending it crashing against the table.

In a flurry, the woman sprinted for the back door, which was half open. She rammed her palms against the screen door, and Norah saw spots of blood staining the wood, left behind by the intruder's injured hands.

"Wait!" Without thinking, Norah raced after the woman. The cool night air hit her lungs, and she gratefully sucked it in as she spotted the woman dodging between the gravestones.

Norah ran after her. The woman's expression was imprinted in Norah's mind, and as the surprise and terror fell away, Norah interpreted the fear in her eyes. Fear, not threat. Desperation, not intention to cause harm.

Sticks snapped under Norah's feet, and she heard the underbrush along the tree line rustling as the stranger plunged through the woods.

"Wait!" Norah cried again, but she was answered only by the sound of crashing into the leaves as the woman tripped and fell. She saw the petite form dive across a fallen log, then shove to her feet. She looked over her shoulder, and in the moonlight, Norah made out the whites of her eyes.

"Please! Let me help you!" Norah called.

The woman didn't stop, but instead increased her pace. She skirted the backyards of a few more houses on Predicament Avenue. Norah chased after her, glancing toward the neighbors' homes. She debated whether she should run to one of them for assistance, but none had their lights on. If she did, she'd lose sight of the woman, whose bloody hands and horrified expression now haunted Norah.

She couldn't help but feel the weight pressing on her chest as she ran, branches scraping her face and clawing at her clothes. Was this what Naomi had looked like the night she'd been attacked and murdered? Her hands bound? The reports stated she was found facedown on the earth. Someone had shoved her face into the dirt, suffocation mingling with strangulation.

Tears scored their way down Norah's face. She wouldn't let it happen again. She had no clue who this woman was. But now it was clearer than ever to Norah that the woman was like Naomi. A victim. A victim of something—of someone—and she needed saving.

The woman cut across a back lawn, and Norah followed. It seemed the woman knew she was there, knew she was chasing her, but she refused to stop running. Norah increased her pace despite the pain in her side. She'd never been athletic and was definitely out of shape, yet the woman ahead of her wasn't remarkably fast either. Perhaps malnourishment had weakened her.

A shed's silhouette loomed in the distance, and the woman aimed for it. She glanced over her shoulder at Norah and then continued. Norah opened her mouth to plead with her to stop, but her breath came out in a gasp. Her chest felt as if it was going to explode for lack of air.

Running around to the back of the shed, the woman kicked at the wall. A board popped out, and she squeezed through the gap. Seconds later, Norah approached the shed's back wall and, disregarding the warning thrumming through every nerve of her body, tried to follow where the woman had gone through. But because she was larger, she didn't fit through the opening. She grabbed at the board next to it and pulled hard. It gave way, and Norah was able now to slip through the wider gap.

She stood in the shed, breathing heavily. All was still inside. Dark. Norah could barely make out the shapes before her. A clanging sounded, the collision of metal on metal. A tool falling on something?

"Hello?" Norah called out.

She saw movement, then heard what sounded like a wood board striking a plastic bucket.

Norah edged forward in the darkness, her hands moving from side to side to feel her way. There were no windows in the shed to allow the moonlight in. Even with her eyes adjusted, Norah could see only the forms of items in her way. Her shin collided with the dull metal edge of something. She winced, grabbing at her leg.

Just ahead, Norah thought she saw a trapdoor. It was propped open. She stepped around it, the square hole in the floor nothing but a black outline. Norah crouched down and peered into the opening. A rickety metal ladder became visible the longer she stared.

Norah hesitated, afraid to go down there. She'd run headlong after a strange woman, lost her bearings in the darkness as to where in the neighborhood they were after running most of the way through the woods. And now she was alone in a stranger's shed with a cavernous hole in the floor—

"Help me." The woman's white face jumped out at Norah from the ladder below as she rose from the depths, like rising from the grave.

Norah screamed, falling backward. She fell onto the deck of a riding lawn mower. Her arms flailed wildly, pushing over a barrel that held long-handled rakes and shovels. The tools crashed to the floor, bouncing off the lawn mower and onto another one before clattering into a pile atop one another.

She struggled to pull herself up by gripping the edge of the lawn mower's seat. Her feet braced against the second lawn mower, and in front of her she noted a third.

Three unused riding lawn mowers.

A toolshed.

Tools.

No windows.

Dread filled her. The image of the pink bandanna flashed through her memory. Naomi. Otto.

This was Otto's shed.

The bleeding woman had led Norah to her prison in Otto's shed.

EFFIE

May 1901

"Mr. Charlemagne!" Effie's hand flew to her throat as the man before her leaned against the locked bedroom door. His words and his actions made no sense to her. He was an upstanding citizen in Shepherd. His family were pillars of the community. He was a good Christian man!

"Miss James," he said, his tone apologetic, "you were never part of the equation, nor was your sister. I was disappointed when I saw your sister through the window. Reading the accounts in the papers verified it was your sister Polly who'd been on the porch that night. What a dreadful thing for her to witness."

He continued speaking as he straightened his vest from their harried run toward Predicament Avenue. He was nonchalant, seemingly unaware of the discomfort Effie felt.

"I truly believed the suspicion would be cast on Floyd and his mother—as it has been. But you and your *Mr.* Anderson are an unfortunate twist of fate." Patrick tipped his head to the side, studying her. "Truly. I expected him to a degree, but you? And Polly?"

"Mr. Charlemagne," Effie managed. "What have you done?"

"Done?" He stared at her incredulously. "Effie, what are you implying?"

Effie gathered her wits and started toward the door that he blocked. "Please. Let me through."

"No, no." He wagged his finger at her. "Let's chat a bit more. You see, I enjoy a good debacle, and this is most definitely one of them. The best laid plans must always have a contingency included because they never go as they're supposed to. Don't you agree?"

Effie didn't answer. She took a step backward from the man. "Did you . . . kill Isabelle Addington?" It was a bold question, but it slipped out regardless of her anxiety.

A flash in Patrick Charlemagne's eyes confirmed her suspicions in spite of his answer. "Me? Kill Isabelle? That's a harsh accusation." He smiled grimly and gave a small shrug. "Your sister knows what happened. I'm sure you've already discussed it. Oh, that's right. She's been heavily medicated. Although"—he gave a wayward toss of his head—"it's unfortunate your nurse fled Shepherd. She was working out quite well for me."

"It was *you* in Polly's room that night!" Awareness flooded Effie. She toyed nervously with the buttons on the cuff of her blouse.

Patrick smoothed his mustache and frowned. "I don't like to admit to something so awful, Miss James, as it's quite the blot on a man's reputation."

Effie stared at him with disbelief. "You could have killed me."

"Actually, your sister was the primary reason for the intrusion."

Effie tasted bile in her throat. A fierce defensiveness of Polly rose within her breast, pushing aside her reticence to confront him. "You would have murdered a dying woman?"

"Dying?" Patrick reared back. "I'm so sorry. I had no idea!" His sympathy was disingenuous. "But if your sister had not gone onto the porch—like you who chose to keep a proper distance— and if she had not peered through the windows, she wouldn't have been traumatized by Isabelle's untimely end."

"Where is Isabelle?" Effie asked. Then she dared to inquire about what was truly haunting her. "Where is baby Cora?"

Patrick's expression turned cynical. Touched with annoyance. He pushed away from the bedroom door and approached Effie. She backed away until she hit the wall behind her.

"Baby Cora. You know of her?" he sneered and released a short bark of laughter. "The reason for it all. The mess and the delight and the labor of a plan long in the making. You know, Isabelle was very helpful—until she wasn't."

"It was you who took Cora?" Effie struggled to put the pieces together. The jigsaw puzzle of it all was overwhelming and perplexing.

"No!" Patrick waved her off. "Of course not! That was Isabelle." He pondered something for a moment and then stepped even closer to Effie, his body threatening to push against hers, squeezing her between him and the wall. "That music box Bethany and I gifted you this afternoon?" He didn't wait for Effie to acknowledge. "It was Isabelle's. I met her while I was in England." He nodded at Effie's look of surprise. "Yes, I was in England last year. My father sent me abroad, and it was my time to make something of myself. My family might be known here in Shepherd, but I've debts. Monetary debts. Wooing an employee of an English lord? There were several ideas in the making. Isabelle called little Cora 'the songbird,' and she found the music box to be sentimental. In fact, I was quite pleased to get it back recently." He chuckled. "It made a fine gift for Bethany, who in turn was so *kind* as to pass it along to you. What irony!"

"Isabelle cared for Cora?" Effie eyed the door behind Patrick. But reaching it would be almost impossible with him standing so close to her.

"Of course she did. Cora was like her own. She was more than compliant when I recommended that she leave with the baby. That the child needed her more, and that together we could be a family here in the States."

"But you had no intention of that." Effie was beginning to understand. To see the deviousness of his plan. Good Christian man? It was all a horrible façade.

"Of course not. I already had my sights on Bethany Todd. She is the most eligible young woman in Shepherd, and I've long admired her. However, that would never happen—not with the debts I've acquired. I need money, and I'm not going to my father for it. Lord Mooring has plenty of money, however, and I was certain he would part with it in exchange for his daughter."

"He's never received a ransom request." Effie glared as meanly as she could.

Patrick nodded. "Ah, I know. You see, it's difficult to demand ransom for a child when you don't actually have possession of it." He gritted his teeth, and Effie felt the dotting of his saliva on her cheek as he spat out his next words. "Isabelle and her conscience. She was here in the house for a day when I met her here. Then she admitted she'd written weeks before to the child's father. Lord Mooring was coming? Here? It was such a sad mess."

"Where is Cora?" Effie blinked back angry tears. They would only give Patrick Charlemagne more satisfaction with his power over her.

"The better question is, where is Floyd?"

"What do you mean?"

"There were more than just you and Polly here that night." Patrick reached out and ran his finger down Effie's cheek, digging into her skin so she felt his fingernail leaving a mark. "And 322 Predicament Avenue is a place no one visits. So why? Why that night? The one night I'm here to meet Isabelle, to rid myself of *that* bit of traitorous baggage, the two of you showed up on the back porch, and Floyd Opperman came out of nowhere."

"Floyd stopped you?" Effie pulled back in stunned surprise.

Patrick snarled. "No. Isabelle is dead. You yourself found the evidence of that."

"And Cora?"

Patrick glowered, curling his upper lip in disdain. "This is what I would like to know. It would solve so many problems."

30

NORAH

Present Day

THE WOMAN CRAWLED from the hole in the floor and scurried to Norah's side. "Shhhh!" She looked frantically over her shoulder. "He'll hear you!"

Norah's throat and eyes burned with the realization. It couldn't be Otto's shed. The place no one ever went. His "man cave." Why would he have a woman here? Why—?

"How long have you been here?" Norah whispered.

The woman shook her head. "I don't know. Months maybe. I didn't want to hurt Otto—don't tell anyone." Her frantic words made no sense. If Otto had held her here, why would she want to protect him and at the same time beg for help to get away? "Please don't get Otto in trouble. He's just an old man."

Norah tentatively touched the woman's shoulder. She couldn't be older than Harper or older than Naomi had been. "It's okay,"

303

she tried to reassure through the shakiness of her voice. "Let's just get out of here. We'll figure it out."

The woman nodded.

"What's your name?" Naomi whispered.

"Lyla," she answered.

A door slammed open, and the two women huddled together against the lawn mower as a beam of light swept over them.

"Norah?" Otto's exclamation of disbelief broke through the night. He cursed. "What'n the heck are you doin' in my shed?"

He stepped closer. Norah held up her hand to shield her eyes from the flashlight's beam he aimed in their faces.

Lyla pressed into Norah's side, and Norah wrapped her arm around the teenager. "Otto, turn off the light. You're blinding me!"

Otto flicked it off, but there was bite to his question, "Why're you here?"

Fury began to fill Norah. Astonishment too. "I'm here because your *friend* came to me for help."

"How'd you—?" He bit off his words, switching the flashlight back on and sweeping it around his shed. Otto noted the boards missing in the back wall. He cursed again.

"Otto, tell me what's going on!" Norah demanded. She had never doubted him, never questioned his innocence in Naomi's case. But now? More questions flooded her mind, accusations she wanted to make. Naomi. Had he . . . had it truly been *Otto*?

Otto waved the flashlight beam as he flexed his wrist. His voice sounded weary when he answered. "Norah, let's go inside my place, and we'll talk."

"No! I'm taking Lyla, and we're going back to *my* place. And then I'm calling the cops."

"Don't . . ." Otto's elderly voice was wobbly but firm. "No, we've been family for a long time. We can get through this."

Norah almost believed him because she'd always believed

him before. The part of her that craved a logical explanation spilled out into words. "Otto, tell me the truth. What's going on?"

Lyla shifted against Norah, reminding her of the frightened girl who had terrified her less than an hour ago.

Otto shifted his feet. "I'm old, and I'm tired. We need some coffee, an' then we'll figure this thing out."

"Does Ralph know?" Norah spat.

"Kiddo, you could rob my brother and clean out his house an' he wouldn't notice a dad-blamed thing. 'Course he don't know." Otto gestured toward Lyla. "Poor kid like that needing some TLC? Ralph ain't good at that. You know I'm the sensitive one!" He gave a little laugh, one that sounded not a little shocked that Norah would think less of him.

Norah turned to Lyla and asked, "Were you here of your own free will?"

Lyla hesitated. She looked at Otto, whose features remained kind and soft.

"Tell her, girl," he urged Lyla. "Tell her I ain't done nothin' to ya!"

Lyla glanced at the trapdoor in the shed's floor.

Norah followed her gaze. "Then why don't you have her in the house?" she challenged as she moved to stand up. "Why not bring her to me so I could help if she's in need? Why the secrets, Otto? Why?"

"You sure ask a lot of questions. Why this? Why that? You've always pestered and not just been willin' to trust people."

"I trust people!" Norah argued.

"Do ya now?"

Norah's mind began spinning as she tried to make sense of the chaos, to see the truth amidst what her heart refused to believe. And then . . . "Did you take Naomi from me?" Her words sent the toolshed into sudden silence. "Did you kill Naomi?"

EFFIE

The room had grown chilly, whether from the temperature or from the threat of Patrick Charlemagne's presence, Effie didn't know. She was thankful Patrick had stepped away from her for the time being. She moved her fingers to her neck to rub it, recalling the way the hands had squeezed her throat. A woman's hands.

"Who was the woman here the other day?" she asked.

Patrick was pacing by the door. He halted and stared at her. "What woman?"

"When I was attacked. It wasn't you. It was a woman!"

"Hmm." Patrick rubbed his chin. "Mabel Opperman, probably. She would do anything for Floyd, her half-wit son."

"Stop it!" Effie snapped.

"Stop what?" Patrick stiffened. "Telling the truth? The man's as dumb as an ox."

"He's suffered!" Effie argued, though she wasn't quite sure she should be defending Floyd.

"We all have, Miss James. We all have. In one way or another, suffering comes to us all. Most people, though, who get kicked in the head by a cow *die*. Unfortunately, he didn't. Maybe the cow didn't kick him hard enough. But whatever the reason"—he waved his hand haphazardly—"it would have served me greatly had Floyd Opperman died as a lad and stayed out of my way."

"You're awful." It was all Effie could think to say.

Patrick smiled. "No, I'm smart. Unlike Floyd."

"Are you smart, though?" Effie took a few small steps toward the door. "I'm not sure that you are. It doesn't appear that any of your plans have worked out."

Patrick's expression darkened.

Effie continued, taking another step. "In fact, as it stands, you're a murderer, your partner Isabelle is dead, you have no child to hold for ransom, and you're still very much in debt. What will Bethany's father say when he finds out?"

Patrick scowled at her.

Effie lifted her chin, feeling empowered to speak the truth. Her fear began to ebb, replaced by confidence, courage even. "You, Mr. Charlemagne, are a beast. More so than Floyd Opperman *or* the cow that kicked him."

"I will kill you," Patrick said with an air of certainty.

Effie swallowed a surge of fright. "I'm sure you would. And you'd gain nothing from it. You'd be found out, and evil will have failed once again."

"Evil!" His shout of laughter startled Effie. "I am not the devil, Miss James."

"But *I* am." The bedroom door was kicked in as the words bellowed through the doorway. Anderson barreled into the room, charging Patrick. The men collided in loud grunts, falling to the floor. Anderson leveled a solid fist into Patrick's face, but Patrick was quick to weasel from Anderson's grip and swing back.

Effie ran for the door. The men crashed into the wall, and she heard another grunt, followed by the sound of fists hitting flesh. She catapulted down the stairs and had almost made it to the bottom when her foot caught on the hem of her dress. She flung forward, tumbling down the remaining steps. Effie felt the rush of blood from her nose and the throbbing pain in her shin where it had scraped against the stairs. She grabbed hold of the banister and hauled herself off the floor.

She could still hear the ensuing fight above as she raced for the front door. Flinging it open, Effie hurried into the street. Gus was running toward her as fast as the older man could run.

"We need to get help!" Effie cried. "Go! Get help, Gus!" Gus whirled around back toward the carriage. He made it there before Effie could, her leg giving out beneath her. She waved at him from the walkway. "Go, Gus! Please, go!"

Gus slapped the reins across the horse's back, and the carriage lurched forward.

Glass shattered from the second story window. Effie saw Anderson and Patrick brawling, Anderson's arm half through the shattered window.

Effie pushed herself off the ground, ignoring the pain in her body from her tumble. She wiped away the blood that dripped from her nose into her mouth.

Trying to gather her bearings, Effie limped toward the main road. If she remembered right, Mrs. Branson's house wasn't far away. Perhaps she would find help there.

The world began to spin, and Effie fought against the feeling of losing control. Anderson needed her. Patrick would kill him if he could.

NORAH

"You did, didn't you?" Norah choked through tears. Sensing Lyla behind her, Norah held out her arm in a protective gesture.

Otto shuffled over to the wall and flicked a switch. Light flooded the toolshed, and Norah and Lyla blinked rapidly against the sudden change.

"Don't worry none. I'm not runnin'." Otto shook his head. His expression was sad—no, it was hurt. Norah had hurt him by asking her question. By her accusation that he would have ever done anything to harm Naomi. Yet she couldn't discount the young woman behind her. Couldn't ignore the trapdoor in the shed, the ladder leading down into the earth.

"What's down there?" Norah pointed.

Otto grimaced and looked away.

Lyla answered, "That's where I live."

"Where you *live*?" Norah's anger was barely contained. She bit her lip hard and turned her face from Otto. "I can't even look at you."

"She's comfortable!" Otto protested.

Norah swung her head back to glare at him. "Comfortable? In the *ground*?"

Norah turned to Lyla. It was apparent even now that Lyla was suffering from some form of Stockholm syndrome or something. Her begging for help was countered by her weak defense of Otto. Norah leaned closer to her. "You need to go now. Run back to my house. Wake up the man upstairs. Get yourself some help."

"Lyla, you stay here," Otto ordered.

Lyla looked between them, torn. Norah faced her and gripped her shoulders. "Listen to me. You're the one who's been in my house, aren't you? You played my music box?"

"I like the bird," Lyla said.

"Yes, the bird. Okay." Norah could hardly believe she was having this conversation, let alone with Otto standing yards away, who was not the man she'd always believed him to be. She directed her attention to Lyla. "And you probably brought me Naomi's library card too, didn't you?"

Lyla nodded. She pointed at the hole in the floor. "It was down there in the wallet. Got her license in there too, so I knew where it belonged. I returned it."

"Yes, Lyla, you did." Norah seethed almost as much as she wanted to collapse into weeping for the betrayal she was unveiling. "Thank you. Now go back, all right? Find my friend Sebastian. Wake him up—don't bother the girl," Norah added. "Wake up the man." She felt as if she were talking to a child. It was becoming obvious that Lyla had been in Otto's toolshed far longer than a few months. Her loyalty to her abductor played with Lyla's senses. The healthy side of her mind had known she needed to escape, but the abused portion of herself had created a faithful devotion to the man who held her captive. Which was what had brought her back time and again. Otto's age had made him sloppy. How many more girls had he—? Norah gagged and swallowed quickly so she didn't vomit. She coughed, doubling over, and then gave Lyla a push. "Go, Lyla."

This time Lyla did as she was told.

Norah saw her slip through the opening in the back wall of the shed. She startled when Otto's hand rested gently on her shoulder. There was a kindness in his aged eyes she couldn't understand. An affection and a devotion in his expression that tried to convince Norah she was wrong to be appalled by him. He had done nothing abhorrent. All he had ever done was care for Lyla. Love her . . .

"Norah, girl." Otto squeezed her shoulder and gave her the wounded look of a man who wasn't sorry, but who was hurt by her actions against him. "I only ever helped them. Naomi? She needed me. Her baby? I only ever helped."

31

EFFIE

May 1901
Shepherd, Iowa

SHE HAD NEVER BEEN so grateful to see her father in
all her life. She'd been limping as fast as she could toward
help. Carlton James leaped from his carriage as it rumbled
to a halt beside her. Two more carriages, including Gus's, raced
by. She thought she caught a glimpse of Constable Talbot in one
next to Gerald Ambrose's.

As it was, she collapsed into her father's arms. The heel of
her shoe had been broken. Her hair stuck to her cheek where
blood had dried from her nosebleed. Her legs were quivering.

"Euphemia!" Her father hoisted her up, guiding her to the
carriage. "I'm taking you home right away."

"No! Anderson! He's in trouble. It's Patrick, Father—Patrick
Charlemagne!"

"Charlemagne?" Carlton drew back in shock. "I don't understand."

"Please, Papa." Effie reverted to her childhood endearment out of instinct, but it must have moved something in him.

"Yes. Yes!" Carlton helped her into the carriage and vaulted up beside her. With a slap of the reins, they barreled toward 322 Predicament Avenue.

Effie had never been so thankful as the moment they pulled to a lurching halt in front of the dilapidated house. Anderson sat on the front porch steps. His face was swollen, his eye already turning shades of purple. His shirt was half ripped off his shoulder, revealing part of his lean chest.

Gerald Ambrose had Patrick pinned to the ground in the yard as Constable Talbot secured him.

"Anderson!" Effie climbed down from the carriage before her father could help her out.

Anderson's head shot up, and he struggled to stand. Effie didn't think, didn't bother to consider, she just threw herself into his chest. He stumbled back, and she released him instantly.

"I'm so sorry!"

The first hint of a smile she'd ever seen on him touched his face. Anderson winced and held his ribs.

"Did I break them?" Effie cried, knowing how ridiculous she sounded when the question popped out.

Anderson laughed, then winced again. "No. I'm afraid that honor goes to the rat over there." He glared at Patrick, who had steeled his features and maintained a stony silence.

Ambrose hauled him to his feet, and Constable Talbot shoved Patrick forward. Patrick looked as bruised and beaten as Anderson did. Effie looked down at Anderson's left hand. It was wrapped in cloth that was already showing red.

"Your hand!" she said.

"Apparently, glass and flesh don't get along well." Anderson's statement reminded Effie of the smashed window.

Anderson lifted his good hand and pushed hair from her face.
"I think Floyd has baby Cora!" Effie declared.

"What?" Anderson bit out.

"What baby?" Carlton James approached them.

Gerald Ambrose stilled. "Baby?"

Effie ignored them and focused on Anderson. "Mr. Charlemagne alluded to Floyd somehow being involved in Isabelle's death. But I think he tried to *save* her. And I think maybe his mother has tried to protect this place and him and baby Cora. That's why she attacked me. They thought I was here to hurt the baby!"

Understanding seeped into Anderson's face. "Good heavens," he muttered.

"What baby?" Effie's father demanded.

Effie turned to explain. "Anderson's daughter. She was taken from their home in England. He's been chasing Isabelle Addington to get baby Cora back."

Carlton's shocked expression mirrored the constable's and Gerald Ambrose's.

"Did you find Floyd?" Anderson gritted out against the pain from his beating.

"No." Carlton shook his head. His hand went protectively to Effie's elbow. "We thought he was here actually—it's why we came."

Effie frowned, then eyed Anderson. "How did *you* know I was here—with Mr. Charlemagne?"

Anderson gave her a pained expression as he adjusted his position on the stairs. "I came by the manor. Miss Todd was there and your mother. When they invited me in, I saw the music box on the table. It had belonged to Isabelle. She used to play it for Cora. The pieces fell together then. Miss Todd affirmed that Mr. Charlemagne had indeed visited England last year. The timeline made sense."

"And Miss Todd told you Mr. Charlemagne and I had seen Floyd?" Effie verified.

Anderson gave a short nod. "Yes. So I came here. It was the natural conclusion, although you would think Charlemagne would avoid this place." He grunted against the pain he was feeling.

"Come on, man." Gerald Ambrose reached out. "We need to get you to the doctor. And you, Miss James."

"No," Anderson snapped. "I am going to find my daughter."

"Then we need to find Floyd," Carlton added. "And his mother."

NORAH

"Why?"

It was the burning question. The one Norah had always dreamed of asking Naomi's killer. She just hadn't imagined it would have been directed at Otto. That Otto would be some sick sociopath who kept girls locked under his toolshed.

Lyla's comments that Naomi's belongings had been down in the bunker came back to Norah. Had Otto kept Naomi there? For how long? She'd been missing for three months. Her remains had reflected that approximate amount of time.

"Why?" Norah asked again.

Otto rested on one of his lawn mowers. The atmosphere felt as though they were having a chat just like the good old times. But it wasn't the good old times. Those times didn't exist anymore.

He sniffed and wiped his nose on his sleeve. "Well, there's not a great answer to that, I suppose." Otto was so calm, so resigned. Maybe it was his age. Maybe if he hadn't been in his late seventies, he'd have reacted with intent to kill Norah. To protect his dirty secret. As it was, Norah wasn't even afraid of him.

He was a feeble old man, stooped-shouldered and just . . . pathetic.

"See, Naomi always liked helpin' me, and I was the first one she told about that baby of hers." Otto seemed almost proud of himself.

Norah tried not to be sick.

He went on, "Fact is, I've helped a couple young women in past years. You know, they don't got anyone to help them through—some of 'em at least."

Norah stared at him in disbelief. Wordless.

"There's only been two 'sides Lyla. Lyla was homeless a few towns over from Shepherd. I met her one day about six months ago."

"Two other women?" Norah repeated, ignoring Otto's explanation of how he'd met Lyla.

"Yup, two. First one goes back a ways—a bit before you were born actually. Tried to get her help 'cause her brother was always knockin' her around. So I had her come over one day, and I showed her the bunker. She decided to stay."

Norah had a strong feeling it hadn't been that compliant of a situation.

"Then she up and passed on one night. I brought her breakfast, and she'd used a sheet to—" he shook his head and gave Norah a sad look—"well, after that I learned not to put sheets on the bed for those girls. Didn't want another gal hangin' herself."

Norah's throat burned, and she swallowed back the need to vomit once again. "What about my sister?"

"Naomi?"

"Don't use her name." Hearing Otto say her sister's name so casually—so normally—filled Norah with a ferocity she could scarcely comprehend. She looked around. There were plenty of tools. If she wanted to, she could take him out. Didn't Naomi deserve that?

Otto didn't seem to pick up on the violence that was swirling in Norah's mind. The vengeance. The desire for justice. "Well, Naomi came over to help me, and I told her that the best thing to do is to get away and have her baby in peace. LeRoy Anderson was nothin' but a loathsome bar-hopper, and he wouldn't've made a good daddy."

"She had *us*," Norah pointed out, glaring at him.

"Sure. An' you'd have fussed and fretted until you made Naomi run away from all the suffocatin' worry. And your parents? Churchgoin' folk that they are, they'd have been praying for some sort of confession. An' your aunt Eleanor would've only smothered Naomi. No, she was better off with me here. Where I could take care of her." He dropped his gaze. "Only . . ."

"Only what?" Norah demanded.

"Well, you know your sister!" Otto scowled. "She's so strong-willed an' all. Kept trying to get away, until one night I told her I'd drive her home. We got in the car, and I realized then that she wasn't ever goin' to be happy. There was just no way. So I drove out to the woods and . . . well, I made her happy."

"You made her happy," Norah repeated, her voice devoid of emotion.

"Yeah. I mean, eternal life and all that. Most of us are much better off dead."

Norah's scream of outrage turned into a bloodcurdling growl. She flew at Otto and slammed her palms into his chest.

The elderly man flipped over off the lawn mower and landed with a thud on the floor of the shed. He looked up at Norah in consternation and not a little fear.

She stood over him. "How dare you! That's not how it works! You don't get to play God and decide when someone goes! Naomi had her whole life to live! And we would have loved that baby no matter whose it was or how it was conceived. You twisted, narrow-minded—" Norah drew back her foot to kick Otto as hard as she could.

"Norah!" Sebastian's voice broke through the shed, and Norah stopped. Her body shook violently. She lifted her eyes to see through the open shed door that Otto had left behind him. Sebastian rushed toward them. Ralph was close behind him, moving much slower and wobbling from side to side.

The trauma began to take over. The shock. Norah's knees gave out, and she collapsed to the ground next to Otto. She felt Sebastian's arms come up beneath hers, hauling her away from Otto, holding her against his strong chest. She saw Ralph as he approached his brother, Otto still sprawled on the floor of his shed.

Then, in the shock of the moment, Norah heard Ralph's voice, a distant echo in her fading consciousness. "Yeah. I need to report a crime . . . Predicament Avenue . . . yeah. My brother. Otto Middleford."

32

EFFIE

May 1901
Shepherd, Iowa

THEY DIDN'T KNOW where to look for Floyd. The men had already been to the Opperman farm only to find it deserted and Mabel nowhere to be found. Effie could feel the tension growing in Anderson. He paced the manor's sitting room, the doctor throwing his hands up in exasperation.

"I'll come back in an hour," he said to Mother, who gave the doctor a thin smile and nod that expressed she understood his impatience with the Englishman.

Anderson had allowed his ribs to be wrapped, and that was all. The cuts on his hand were still encircled by the bloody cloth. His face needed care, his right eye swelling shut. He was in no mood to sit and be tended to when he knew a group of men were out searching for his child.

"I should be there," Anderson growled, then strode past Mother and the doctor toward the door.

Effie popped up from her chair. "I'll come with you."

"Euphemia James!" Mother gasped and hurried toward her. "No! The doctor only just tended your leg and your nose. You look as if you've been squeezed through a meat grinder, not to mention you've consistently put yourself in danger. You're giving me fits of worry."

Effie couldn't help the smile that stretched across her face. She gave her mother's cheek a quick kiss. "That is the *nicest* thing you've ever said to me, Mama."

Her mother appeared stunned as Effie hurried after Anderson.

The next few moments passed in a flurry, yet Effie was distracted by Anderson's move to take her hand in his as they hurried down the steps of the veranda.

His hand was large, his knuckles raw and bruised from his altercation with Patrick Charlemagne. Still, he gripped her smaller hand with such gentle firmness, it was a contradiction of everything she had known of this aloof and reserved man. This man who had dared to break before her and then act as if he never had. This man whom she knew so little about and yet was developing such a fierce loyalty toward. This man whose bland and composed exterior belied a fiery protectiveness for his own—even for his late wife, Laura, whom Effie knew deep in her soul would always be a part of him.

A knocking on glass snagged her attention. Effie pulled back on Anderson, and he paused, giving her a questioning look.

"I heard something." Effie pointed to the side of the manor. She tugged on Anderson's hand, unwilling to remove hers from his grip. He followed with caution, a frown on his face.

They rounded the manor, the grass beneath Effie's feet soft. She looked up to the windows on this side of her home. On the second story, Polly's form was in the window seat. The window was open halfway.

"Polly!" Effie stared up at her sister, who had managed to crawl from her bed to the window seat on her own. Her face was pale, but her expression was earnest.

"I saw him!" Polly's voice was weak and high-pitched. She coughed, and Effie and Anderson waited patiently. Polly pointed to the back of the manor, toward the yard, the carriage house, and the woods. "Floyd Opperman."

Anderson instantly jerked his gaze in the direction Polly was pointing. He released Effie's hand and headed for the back of the manor. Polly waved for Effie to follow him, then blew a kiss to her sister below.

The two strode onto the manor's back lawn. All was silent in the yard. The carriage-house doors were closed and barred from the outside, indicating no one had gone in.

Anderson cleared his throat, calling out in his English accent and breaking the stillness. "Floyd! I will not hurt you. Do come out."

Effie held her breath and, without much thought toward impressions, held Anderson's arm.

"If you have my daughter, please, Floyd. I beg of you!" Anderson's voice cracked.

"Anderson!" Effie whispered. She motioned toward the edge of the woods. A flash of blue—the same color of jacket Floyd had been wearing earlier when Effie had seen him on the road in front of the James manor.

Anderson, alerted to the spot of color, took a few steps toward it. Cautious so as not to frighten Floyd if that indeed was the underlying reason for Floyd's subterfuge.

Effie released Anderson's arm. She looked up at him. "Let me," she said. She remembered Floyd's stained shirt, his warning for her to run. She had interpreted it as a threat, as though he planned to hunt her—to hunt Polly. That Floyd, the big man with the sad, misunderstood past, had been the one to take Isabelle Addington's life. To abduct Anderson's child. To then cover the heinous crime by moving furniture and covertly hiding all that remained of the shocking scene. It was savvy, it was calculated . . . and while Effie meant no insult to Floyd, that level of scheming seemed far beyond what his mind was able to conjure. And now that she knew the truth about Patrick Charlemagne, his presence in England, and the beautiful yet awful music box, Effie felt deep in her soul that Floyd Opperman posed no danger.

In fact, he was a savior.

"Floyd?" Effie took tentative steps toward the woods. The spot of blue hadn't moved. She focused on it, realizing Anderson was letting her go. Trusting her. "It's okay now, Floyd. Mr. Charlemagne is in custody. He can't hurt anyone anymore."

The spot of blue shifted.

Effie glanced over her shoulder at Anderson. He gave her an encouraging nod.

"Floyd, thank you for telling me to run. I know you were trying to protect me." Although it didn't explain the woman—his mother, Mabel?—who had tried to strangle her. Effie would address that fright at a later time. "Floyd," she continued, taking more slow steps. "If you have the baby . . . please, Floyd. Her father is here. That is Anderson—Lord Mooring." The name was unfamiliar on her tongue, but it sounded important. Weighty. Authentic and purposeful. "He has come all the way from England to reunite with his baby girl. Cora."

The sound of a small whimper met her ears.

Effie whirled to look at Anderson, to see if he'd heard it also.

He had. His eyes were wide. His body tensed. It was obvious it was taking everything in him not to race to the woods and reclaim his child.

Effie turned back. "Floyd, why did you bring her to the James manor?" An idea began to form. "Did you realize I was . . . attached to the baby's father? Is that also why you came here this morning, only to see Mr. Charlemagne and then turn to run away? You knew he was dangerous to the baby, but you knew I would help you, didn't you?"

Another whimper, as if someone were clutching a child tightly and it wrestled to protest.

"It was your mother, wasn't it?" Effie tried again, drawing closer to where the woods met the lawn. "She attacked me, but . . ." Effie hesitated. Dare she voice her theory out loud? Not one she preferred to believe, but one that made the most sense as she dwelled on it. "Your mother thought I was dangerous, didn't she, Floyd? That I meant to harm the babe, just like the other woman and Mr. Charlemagne meant to? She didn't know that you'd just warned me to stay away from Mr. Charlemagne. She's been protecting Predicament Avenue for you, hasn't she? It's *your* place that you go to in order to be alone."

No response.

Effie's footsteps were silent in the grass. "You were there the night Mr. Charlemagne met Isabelle Addington, weren't you? You saw him kill her and so you took the baby so she wouldn't be hurt—is that right?"

A flash of blue and then Floyd stood from his crouch in the undergrowth. His arms were empty. There was no baby Cora. Effie scanned the woods. Nothing. No whimpers either.

"He killed her," Floyd said. His voice had the same gravelly tone as the day he'd warned her to run. "He made a mess of her. She screamed and screamed and then . . . ain't nothing left. Just quiet. But then the baby started cryin'." Floyd stared at her with wide, earnest eyes. There was gray at his temples. His burly form seemed far less intimidating now. "I grabbed that baby and run. Run to my mama's. An' she took care of her when I went back. That poor lady was all bloody. I took her body, and Ma and I—we did right by her. Proper cleanin' and dressin', a nice and proper photograph—Ma's cousin's got a camera, and he don't ask no questions. Then I got her buried proper-like in back of that house. Put sod and leaves over it so no one knowed."

"That was good of you." Effie hoped her words were reassuring to Floyd. She glanced behind her. Anderson was still standing there, poised to spring forward at the first sign of his daughter. She turned back to Floyd. "And then what happened?" she urged.

Floyd lifted his shoulders to his ears in a shrug. "After I took that dead lady to Ma's with the baby, I went back, and that man had moved stuff. Cleaned up. So I figured there wharn't nothin' else to do but go home and make sure he didn't come after the baby girl."

"He'd seen you, hadn't he?" Effie surmised.

"Ohhhh yeah." Floyd's affirmation was laced with a vibrato to emphasis how right Effie was. "He's not a nice man. Said he'd kill me and the baby both. He'd kill you and your sister too. I ran. I ran hard. I've been runnin' ever since. Ma an' I keep taking the baby to different places so he can't find her. Ain't safe. Ma don't trust you. She don't trust *him*." Floyd tipped his head. "Ma, she don't trust nobody. I'm right sorry she tried to hurt you. She—" Floyd hesitated and winced—"she thinks I need carin' for, but she ain't always thinkin' right herself."

"It's safe now, Floyd," Effie said. "That man behind me? That's the baby's father. Please. The baby needs her papa."

A glimmer of doubt flashed in Floyd's eyes as he looked past Effie toward Anderson. "I'm not stupid." He returned his frank gaze to Effie.

"No, you're not. You're a *very* smart man." Tears sprang to Effie's eyes at the truth of it. "You saved that baby—you did. Now let's finish rescuing her and get her back to her papa."

Floyd didn't respond. He looked between Effie and Anderson, then ducked back into the woods.

Anderson launched toward baby Cora, only to pull up short as he realized the child had shrunk into Floyd, the only familiar person in her life. Effie's breath hitched. Of course Cora wouldn't know her father! The heartbreak of the moment almost equaled the joy.

Floyd worked at loosening Cora's fingers, which gripped the fabric of his shirt. "That's your daddy," he explained to her, even though the infant didn't understand him.

Anderson approached slowly. Effie could see the tightness in his body as he restrained himself from taking hold of his child.

"Hello, Cora." His voice was strained with emotion. "I am your papa."

The little girl stared at him, her long lashes and delicate features giving her the appearance of a porcelain doll. She hung on Floyd, her protector, and then suddenly Cora leaned forward toward Anderson, letting go and holding her arms toward him.

Anderson grabbed hold of her and clung, drawing the babe into his embrace. Cora held back, unsure, but her hand extended to touch his face. His nose. Curiosity and an expression of confidence not unlike her father's reflected in her eyes.

"I cannot thank you enough," Anderson choked out, addressing Floyd. "I'm more grateful to you than you will ever know."

Floyd ducked his head. "Wharn't nothin'."

Effie held her tongue, not wishing to interrupt. But she wanted badly to refute Floyd's remark.

Nothing? No. He was so wrong. So in error.

It was everything.

Everything.

Cold, Dead, But Never Buried
Hosted by Sebastian Blaine

I'VE LEARNED THAT REGARDLESS of resources like the internet, historical documentation, websites of ancestries and the like, some mysteries are left to the people who lived them. Maybe they know. Maybe they understand.

I can't help but think, based on what little actual evidence I've been able to uncover, that there was more to Isabelle Addington than just simply being a transient passing through Shepherd who was brutally murdered. Did the Opperman family who owned the property at the time have anything to do with it? Perhaps. But in searching the newspaper archives, the story seems to fade away. Unsolved. Questions never answered. Yet maybe that's the way of it at 322 Predicament Avenue. Maybe the us of today aren't supposed to understand the them of yesterday. The people who came and went through 322 Predicament Avenue. The folks in town who, after the sensation of discovering a crime scene, remained remarkably silent.

Perhaps they were protecting someone. Perhaps each other. Or maybe it was just that Shepherd, Iowa, isn't unlike any other small town in America—or the rest of the world, for that matter. We love our thrilling stories, that is, until the truth is revealed and our darker sides are exposed. The sides we'd rather were kept secret, hidden away forever.

In my career of solving historical cold cases, I've come to the conclusion that the story of murder—the heinous taking of a life—is like dominoes falling. One person may be left holding the knife, but many played a part in the process of getting there. Maybe societal pressures.

Maybe parental misguidance. Perhaps mental illness or greed. And when I find what I can about Isabelle Addington, I'm led to wonder if she was just a person in the wrong place at the wrong time, or if she was part of something larger. Something that got away from her, and in the end, the consequences were far more than she'd expected to pay.

Whatever the ending to the story of 322 Predicament Avenue, I'll say this: Evil never goes away. Once it stains a place, the mark remains for generations. Its horror is repeated. It rises from the grave to haunt.

So, what do we do with that?

Are you afraid to grieve the loss of a loved one?

Are you afraid to lose a loved one?

Are you afraid to go on living without a loved one?

Or perhaps, in all of this, you're more like me. You realize you're missing time with your loved one because you're afraid you will fail them.

This is evil at its core.

Fear.

Fear is a lack of hope and a belief in the murder of our dreams, our lives, and even our salvation.

But if I've learned anything during my stay at 322 Predicament Avenue, it's that to live—to truly live—is to hope that there's a deeper purpose for our lives. That a person's life, no matter how short or how long, how peaceful or how turbulent, how adventurous or how tragic, is not wasted. Not when you have hope. It might be a tiny pinprick of light in a world of darkness, but it's there all the same. It was planted there by God, and the more you pursue hope, the brighter it becomes, and the more we discover that fear is not of Him. Hope is. We need only to surrender to it.

Most of us resist this surrendering to hope, and yet we surrender to fear every day, easily and without much of a fight.

Today, listener, I challenge you. Surrender to hope instead.

33

NORAH

Present Day

FOR NORAH, 322 Predicament Avenue would never be the same. It wouldn't hold the nostalgia it had before, and yet it was enveloped in something entirely unexpected.

She sat beside Ralph, both of them on the back steps of the porch overlooking the cemetery. The old graveyard with all the people no one remembered anymore, and with Isabelle Addington and Naomi Richman. Someday no one would be left to remember them either. To remember any of them really. But Norah had today. Today was still alive, still a part of her. In spite of the grief and the agony of betrayal, Norah sensed a new beginning on the horizon.

"It will be hard," she stated.

Ralph knew what she was talking about without her having to explain. There were more new lines in his aged face, a deeper stoop to his shoulders. There was a guilt he should have known, should have suspected.

"Yes, it'll be hard for a while," he agreed. Then, after a pause, he added, "Maybe for the rest of my life."

"Do you think . . . ?" Norah couldn't say it aloud. Couldn't express herself in a way she felt would make sense.

"What?" Ralph gave her a sideways look. The familiar overall strap dropped over his shoulder, and Norah fought the urge to straighten it.

"Do you think any of us could've stopped it? Could've done something for Otto, for Naomi, even for LeRoy that would've maybe shaped their lives into taking a different path?"

Ralph snorted. "Doubtful. Don't mean to sound bitter, but my brother's got a messed-up head, and it looks like he hid the fact his whole life. We can't prepare for that. No way."

"But I mean—"

"Can you change what's comin' in life?" Ralph looked at her directly, stating her thoughts more bluntly than she felt she should.

Norah simply nodded.

Ralph shook his head and pointed at the graves before them. "Those folks lived life and then died—who knows what they saw and had to suffer through? We can't be afraid to live just 'cause we're afraid of dyin'. Seems to me we'd be better off seekin' out the truth of it."

Norah frowned. "The truth of what?"

"The truth of what comes after," Ralph said with a shrug. "People say Isabelle Addington haunts this place, but I ain't never seen her. You ain't never seen her. Every time we thought we saw her, it was that gal Lyla. Poor kid. So alone in the world, ain't no one cared she went missin'. So you see, people *see* things, but do they really? My momma once said that if you have hope in the hereafter, then the *now* ain't scary no more."

"But how do we have that hope?" Norah felt like she was being blasphemous even asking such a thing. There were so many beliefs these days, so many theories and philosophies, yet if she dared not ask if God was real and why He allowed evil to exist in the world, then how could she ever know the truth? How could she stop being afraid when truth had no standard and no foundation, but instead was whatever a person made up to make themselves feel better?

Ralph wiped his nose on his sleeve, sniffing, whether because of emotion or a runny nose, Norah wasn't sure. He eyed her for a moment before offering a reply to her question. "Sometimes, Norah, it's as simple as believin' what was said and what's never been proven to be wrong."

"What's that?" Norah whispered.

Ralph gave her a pat on the knee. "That we're all a bunch of screwups. God ain't."

"He let Naomi die," Norah challenged without regret.

Ralph nodded. "Yup. He did. But He left you to live. So live, Norah. Believe there haven't been mistakes, only a busted-up old world in need of hope." He shoved off his knees and stood, hefting a sigh and nodding toward the graveyard. "I got work to do."

Norah watched him shuffle away. There were no easy answers and yet, in a way, the answers had been there all along. Live. Hope. Believe. Surrender. They were difficult words. Impossible most of the time.

But hope was something 322 Predicament Avenue hadn't had living in it for years. Maybe it was time to let hope move in.

Harper grinned at Norah and rolled her eyes. "I had one bad night, and you all think I'm made of glass."

"No," Sebastian retorted from the doorway. "I'm just realizin' that my little lass needs some TLC."

"I'm nineteen, Dad," Harper laughed.

Norah could sense the shift between father and daughter.

There hadn't been any miraculous come-to-Jesus moments or mind-blowing emotional reunions. It just seemed that night Lyla had terrified Harper in her room and Sebastian had been faced not only with the fragility of his daughter but also his future grandchild . . . *grandchild?*—Norah reined in her thoughts—well, it seemed Sebastian had experienced some sort of revelation that it was time he be an *involved* father. That wasted time was a form of death he didn't want to face and really didn't need to face. Death of a relationship, at least in this case with Harper, was avoidable.

"Fine," Harper said, "I'll stay in bed the rest of the evening and night, but tomorrow I'm up. Okay? The doctor didn't order bed rest for nine months. He only advised rest for a day or two. And it's been four." She leveled a stern glare on her dad.

Norah bit back a smile.

"Good," Sebastian conceded, then raised a finger. "But you aren't goin' anywhere unless you check with me."

"Okay, okay," Harper said, rolling her eyes again.

Sebastian gave Norah a look she couldn't quite interpret. "I'll be out back." He left, leaving Norah and Harper to stare at each other, holding their breaths and then laughing the moment they were sure he was out of earshot.

"Oh my gosh!" Harper's eyes were wide. "I always wanted Dad to be more involved, but I might regret this."

"You won't." Norah smiled and adjusted a blanket for something to do, then motioned to the music box on Harper's nightstand. "I'm not sure if you want that or not. I know it was creepy when you first heard it, but—"

"But it was Naomi's," Harper finished. She reached out and touched Norah's hand. "I'm honored you want me to have it. I'm honored LeRoy Anderson is letting you keep one of his family heirlooms."

Norah swallowed a lump in her throat. "Yeah. I've a lot to make up for with LeRoy. He's lived for thirteen years unable to grieve 'cause we all blamed him. He still wouldn't be my choice for Naomi"—she eyed the music box—"but I can't help but feel he came from a good family. Whoever that man Anderson was, and however he was tied to Isabelle Addington."

"Dad said he can't find a thing in the papers with any more clues as to what happened," Harper said. "So maybe they did all get destroyed in natural disasters like the papers concluded. Or else Dad can only assume they never found out."

Norah nodded. "It's sad."

"But!" Harper's eyes lit up. "Dad did find an article about Floyd Opperman! Seems Betty and Ron Daily were wrong. He wasn't sent to an institution. After his mother died, he was too much for his brother to care for, but apparently he ended up getting a permanent position as a worker in the carriage house on the manor's property."

"The James manor?" Norah drew back, surprised. "That place is the epicenter of historical homes and tours in Shepherd."

"I know. It was a small blip in an article, stating that Floyd Opperman had been celebrating his tenth year on staff at the manor and had become a beloved member of the family."

Norah smiled. "Good. Something about a man like that being institutionalized bothered me to no end."

Harper grinned back, a perky glint in her eyes. "See, Norah? Sometimes God brings us a happy ending—they're just small and so we need to look harder for them."

Sebastian held sentry at his station where the coffeemaker brewed. He looked up sheepishly. "I know. It's past five, but I'm needin' some, so don't be judgin' me."

"No judgment." Norah held up her hands. She was tired. She wasn't sure where she stood with Sebastian. He seemed . . . normal. At least he was back to his casual self instead of brooding and acting as if she'd ruined everything. But he hadn't said anything about it to her either, and Norah was afraid he never would. It seemed to be his way. Just move on. But that didn't always work. Look at Harper and the years she'd ached for more of his attention—that being heart-to-heart talks and the presence of an engaged father in her life.

"Want some?" He lifted the full coffeepot.

Norah shook her head. She watched him pour coffee into a mug and then replace the pot on its hot pad. He turned toward her, his dark eyes piercing into hers as he held the mug like a shield in front of him.

"So I'm a fool, Norah Richman."

She blinked in surprise.

He sipped the coffee, then nudged his glasses up his nose. He had a nice nose. He had a nice face. She'd noticed, but she'd avoided dwelling on it. Dwelling on the fact that anytime Sebastian Blaine walked into the room, her insides threatened to melt like a lit wax candle.

"I've been speakin' in my head all the things I want to say to you. I don't know as I've made any progress."

"Like what?" Norah maneuvered a chair out from the table so she could sit down.

But Sebastian was quicker. He set down his mug of coffee and was beside her before she could sit. His presence was magnetic enough that she stayed standing, only she swayed a bit, and Sebastian reached out to steady her.

His eyes were pools of liquid, warm and inviting like coffee, and . . . dangerous in a way.

"You've been important to Harper. An' I want to thank you for bein' there when I wasn't."

"I—"

"Don't say it was nothin' 'cause it wasn't. She was afraid to come to me, an' I can't say as I blame her. I've been in an' out of her life all her life. She needs a home. An' I was scared to let that be me."

Norah mustered a small smile. Part of her was jealous of Harper. Oh, heck, all of her was jealous of Harper. She'd like her home to include Sebastian too. Somehow. Someway. She wasn't ready for her houseguest and his daughter to check out of 322 Predicament Avenue, yet she wasn't foolish enough to think they'd progressed to the stage in their relationship where she'd feel comfortable asking them to stay.

"I'd like to stay—for a while anyway. I'd like to have some time with Harper, an' . . ." Sebastian's words were such a close echo to Norah's thoughts, she stared at him, horrified she'd actually spoken them aloud. He hurried to continue. "I'll pay the room an' board for Harper an' I. But I think it'd be good for us to stay here. Fresh start an' all." He paused, then seemed to realize Norah was drowning in his coffee-colored eyes, and his grin turned slightly cocky and lopsided. "An' I think it'd be good for you too."

"Me?" Norah tilted her head.

"Aye. Think about it. Have you ever realized you've no one here who can brew a good pot of coffee?"

"Oh." She felt dumb.

Sebastian tilted her chin up with his thumb. "An' have you imagined what your days would be like without me around?"

She had. Norah looked away, embarrassed.

Sebastian moved with her, commanding her gaze. He winked. "An' just think about it, lass. If I'm here, I can chase away all your ghosts."

She didn't mean to miss the comedy in his words, but the phrase caught at her soul and at her innermost fears, and she couldn't help but ask seriously, "All my ghosts?"

He leaned in and dragged his mouth across her cheek to her ear and whispered, "All your ghosts. All your specters. All your ghouls. Until only I'm left to haunt you."

His mouth trailed back along her jaw, and Norah let him. She closed her eyes as he kissed her. A breathy kiss, the kind that made her want more and wonder what a deeper one would feel like.

"Whaddya say?" Sebastian asked, pulling back.

"Haunt me then." Norah mimicked his accent.

"Aye, lass." He pulled her closer.

Norah realized then that hope, true hope, came in many different forms. She was just fine with this one.

34

EFFIE

June 1901

THE TOWN OF SHEPHERD had changed.

Effie sat beside Polly on the veranda and stared out over the town before them. The cobblestone street, the trees lush with leaves, the flower gardens in bloom. Polly was a shell of herself, but today she'd asked to be carried outside. The soft perfume of the lilac bushes carried across the breeze.

But Shepherd itself was different. The town seemed softer than it had been before. Its people had somehow been humbled from the pride of lofty ambition and vain appearance when one of their own had fallen into the pit of wickedness. It was a surprise that even the newspaper failed to write about Patrick Charlemagne. Of course, it was also an odd happenstance that the Charlemagnes had purchased the paper for a rather large sum around the same time as Patrick's being captured.

No one wanted to remember what had happened at 322

Predicament Avenue. No one wanted to know who Isabelle Addington was or where her body was buried. No one pestered Mabel Opperman about the vacant property or her son, Floyd. The James family didn't even pursue charges against Mabel Opperman for her part in attacking Effie. Effie had asked her father not to. For Floyd's sake.

It was as if all the changes to Shepherd took place internally, yet no one spoke about them. As if by not speaking, the bad would disappear in time, and the sun would shine once again and they could all continue, albeit a little bit less prideful, a little bit more cautious, and a little bit less likely to draw conclusions about those who weren't like them.

But as secrets went, Polly's life was drawing to a close. The weight on Effie's heart threatened to break it into tiny little pieces. The James family no longer attempted to pretend or keep up appearances that all inside the manor was well. The flowers had come and now adorned Polly's bedroom, there to encourage and uplift. Yet Effie knew that soon they would be used instead to perfume the parlor for when the neighbors visited to pay Polly their last respects.

"Death is a calming thing." Polly's whispered words broke into Effie's thoughts.

"What?" Effie shouldn't have been surprised. While Effie had grown more courageous, Polly had become more introspective. Perhaps that was the difference when one chose to live life fully and the other chose to embrace death completely.

"It's calming," Polly said with a soft smile on her lips. "That moment you know what is coming. There are no more questions. Just rest. And peace. And hope."

"How do you find such peace, Polly? The adventures you wished to have had? The life you'd planned?"

Polly turned to Effie, blanket pulled high on her lap, hair hanging in a loose braid, handkerchief clenched in her thin fingers. "I have so many adventures coming, sweet Effie." Polly smiled. "Who said they stop when a soul goes to heaven?"

"But heaven is perfect," Effie argued. "There won't be any mysteries to solve."

"God is a mystery." Polly's laugh was weak. "It will take an eternity to understand Him."

Silence stretched between them. A warm blanket of sisterhood. A love that was guaranteed to continue long after Polly left the world.

Effie mustered the words, and Polly seemed to know just how hard Effie was *mustering*. She reached across the space between them, and Effie took Polly's hand. She looked deeply into Polly's tired eyes.

"I will try, Polly, to be brave," Effie promised.

"Don't be brave." Polly shook her head. "Be hopeful. Tears of missing someone aren't tears that lack courage. Instead, you have the courage to feel the empty spaces, but hope for when they'll be filled again." Polly sighed softly, and Effie could see the physical effort it took for Polly to draw enough breath to do so. "Don't be afraid to live, Effie. I'm not afraid to die. Fear steals our joy and is the agony of those with no hope. It will not define us. Fear is the enemy we will defeat."

"You're returning to England?" Effie managed to ask. She didn't want to admit how empty she felt at the thought. As traumatic as the last few weeks had been, there was a comfort, a steadiness that Anderson had brought into her life.

Anderson nodded. "That is the plan, yes." Cora struggled against his hold, and he reluctantly released her, setting her on a blanket on the floor, which she immediately abandoned, crawling to the window and pulling herself up by the sill. He watched his daughter for a long moment. "She needs to go home.

To family. To everything England can give her. She needs to grow up near her mother's grave and know of Laura's legacy."

Effie nodded, swallowing back tears she knew were selfish. Tears that betrayed the fondness she'd allowed to grow within her for the man before her. "I would like to thank you," she said. "For everything you did to help protect Polly . . . and I as well."

Anderson's jaw worked back and forth, and he gave a polite smile. "Of course. It was the least I could do. And now in retrospect, I feel I owe you so much more."

They looked at each other for a long, uncomfortable moment.

At last, Effie cleared her throat. "When do you leave?"

"Next Tuesday," Anderson answered. He chuckled. "Then you shall be free of that horrid Englishman who has put you at risk of a sullied reputation. I do believe the town of Shepherd will move beyond it in time."

Effie's laugh was watery, and she hoped Anderson didn't notice. She had once hoped for that. More than that, she ached for what she saw before her now. A man, a child, a family, a quiet future as a wife and a mother. God bless her sister, but Effie would be happy never to be independent or adventurous ever again. It had nearly gotten her killed, for pity's sake, and for a woman who preferred *Ben-Hur* over that sort of fear in real life . . . well, perhaps Anderson was right. Maybe in the months to come, a young man would come out of the woodwork of Shepherd and steal her heart once and for all.

The very thought disappointed her.

Effie stood quickly, and Anderson jumped to his feet.

"I should be going." She reached for her purse.

"Ah, yes." Anderson gave a nod. He called for Gus and instructed the man to watch Cora and that he himself would see Effie to the door.

They moved silently together onto the porch of the little cottage.

"I suppose this is farewell then," Effie said.

Anderson nodded. "Yes."

"Thank you. It's been quite the adventure." Effie managed a smile.

Anderson returned it.

She waited just one more second in case this English lord wanted to change his mind and say something more personal. But no. He didn't. He was still a man grieving the loss of his wife. A man overcome with needing to invest in his daughter so he could make up for lost time.

There was no need for Euphemia James in the life of Lord Lewis Anderson Archibald Mooring of Tiffany Ridge.

She made it to the front gate and pushed it open, hearing the front door close quietly behind her. It closed on her past, and yet it felt as if the door closed on her future too.

EFFIE

Two Months Later

She sat under the willow tree, blanket beneath her. The August heat was eased by a refreshing breeze. Effie felt the most contented she had been since Polly had passed away two months before. The James manor had become a place shrouded for weeks, and though they all managed their grief in their own ways, Effie found solace here beneath the willow. Where color bloomed and sunshine made sure the earth was warm, and she could hear the echoes of Polly's laughter floating through the clouds.

Her father had hired Floyd to help out occasionally. Word had it that Mabel Opperman was failing. Effie had never had the heart to have the old woman held responsible for Effie's attack. She had merely been trying to protect Floyd and baby Cora, and

Effie could not blame her for that. Still, she'd no desire to see the old woman. But Floyd? He was different. Even now, as he lumbered by with a wheelbarrow, she took comfort in the good that had emerged from the bad.

"Effie?"

A long shadow cast across her open book in her lap. Startled and scarcely believing, she looked up at the man who towered over her.

"Anderson!" she exclaimed.

Effie struggled to stand, her book falling to the ground. "What are you . . . why are you . . . *how*?" He was supposed to be in England. There was no way for him to have sailed home and returned already.

His face remained in his familiar expressionless way. But his eyes stormed and rolled like thunderclouds. She could see emotion in him again. Emotions he'd quenched and squashed deep below the surface.

"How is it you are here?" she asked again.

"I made it as far as New York." His admission sent a delicious shiver through her.

Effie nodded only because she didn't know what else to do, and not because she understood.

Anderson swiped his hat from his head as a belated after-thought.

"And Cora?" Effie asked politely.

"Cora is fine," he said equally as polite.

"Gus?"

"Also well." He mustered a thin smile and then abruptly flung his hat to the ground. He raked his hand through his hair. "Dash it all, Effie! I am not ready."

Her eyes wide, she waited. Unsure. Unsteady really. She braced her hand against the trunk of the willow tree as Anderson stepped closer.

"I'm not ready for this."

"For what?" she asked breathlessly.

"For you."

"Me?"

"Us."

"Us?"

"This."

"What?" Effie was utterly and completely lost, if not afraid to hope.

"Dash it all," he said again and grabbed her around the waist, hauling her against him. "I wanted to do this for far too long, but I am not ready." And yet he was. Because he kissed her then. Under the willow tree. With no promise, no plans, just hope. And absolutely zero fear.

Effie pulled back, staring up into his eyes, searching and finding no answers. "But if you're not ready—"

"I'm not ready for you." A smile broke through his countenance, and it took Effie's breath away. "At least I kept telling myself that. But then it drove me mad until Gus insisted I return. So here we are. Again."

"But England? Your lordship. What about . . . ?"

"This is why I'm not ready." Anderson managed a little chuckle. "I have no clear answers, but I do know this." He tipped his head closer to hers. "I know I am not afraid to live again. I'm not afraid to grieve what I have lost, but also embrace what I've been given."

"What have you been given?" Effie whispered, daring to place her palm on the side of his face.

"You," he stated. "I do believe I have been given you."

And he had. And she had been given him, and Cora. Though Polly was no longer here, and Anderson's wife, Laura, had also passed away, Effie knew that together she and Anderson could journey the crevices of grief. Because in the dying, new life sprang forth. It was the bittersweet reality that for some purpose God allowed to exist—until He made all things new.

HER (ISABELLE)

I KNEW I FLIRTED WITH DEATH. Isn't that how poor choices end? Eventually? I knew that it would meet me the moment I made the choices that I did. I am not proud of them. Now, as I stare out this attic window, I know that he is coming. I know that he will be angry. I have made a grievous error, and this little songbird beside me suffers for it. A father suffers for it. And somehow I know I will suffer for it, until I am perhaps not even a memory that lingers long after my spirit has departed this earth to face God and answer for my sins.

Does a house like this hold the memories and the emotions in its walls? Can generations hear the echoes of them and be reminded of what should have been? What *could* have been?

No one likes to speak of sin, or death, or fear. But maybe that is what our memories are meant to remind the future of. So that new beginnings forged from truth and hope can be made, and old legacies of wickedness can be laid to rest.

I don't know, but I believe I will always be a memory here at 322 Predicament Avenue. And when the night falls, those who sleep can choose to fear or hope, turn away or believe, rebel or reconcile. Because in the end, that's what life really is. The moments before we are face-to-face with God, and He enacts justice or grace. I fear the first, but truly, in spite of my sins, I believe He offers the second, even if I am almost too late in asking. For that is what I know to be true. It always has been. It always will be.

Author's Note

Predicament Avenue became a predicament for me to be sure. A story that was originally so clear in my mind soon became a journey through the different facets of grief. A journey shrouded in the fear of death, the fear of grief in its aftermath, and the fear of choosing to live again. As the story evolved, each character drew from one element or another of this grief.

Effie feared death.

Anderson feared grief.

Norah feared living.

But Sebastian? What did he fear? He feared himself. The inadequacies of who he felt himself to be as a father, instead cheating himself of the greatest gifts God can bestow.

And then there's Isabelle, or "Her" as we knew her through most of the story. A sinner. An evildoer. A woman easily manipulated, broken by the struggle between right and wrong.

Is grace given recklessly? No, it is not. It's given through sacrifice, rooted in the preciousness of love and life. It's given by surrendering to the One who laid down His life. It is a recognition that without the hope offered by the Savior who so willingly gives, who overcomes evil, we will live in fear. In the clutches of fear that suffocates and drains us.

No. Grace is costly. But it is ours. And in receiving it, we find our weakness infused with His strength. His hope. His future.

Live it.

Acknowledgments

Thank you to the One who brings me hope. If life has taught me anything in the past three years, it is that hope rooted in truth can blossom even in the darkest of nights.

So while there are many who influenced this story, who touched the words on these pages, who journeyed with me until the moment of its publication, this story really just belongs to You.

Because it is "in peace I will lie down and sleep, for you alone, Lord, make me dwell in safety" (Psalm 4:8 NIV).

Reading Group Discussion Guide

1. Do you have an abandoned building or house near you, and if so, what stories have you imagined taking place inside its walls?

2. The story of Predicament Avenue was inspired by an actual newspaper article the author found that was written at the turn of the last century. It included the story of an old house with a very bloody crime scene, the discovery of such, and the question of who had been murdered there. What old newspaper articles have you uncovered that have piqued your curiosity further?

3. Both Effie and Norah are facing grief. While different, they also parallel each other as they must find hope

within their sorrow. How has hope affected your own personal journey with grief, and how has it changed your perspective on the loss of a loved one?

4. If you were faced with protecting your family by inserting yourself into an active crime investigation or had the option to leave it to authorities with offered police protection, which would you choose and why?

5. This novel touches on the wildly popular true-crime documentaries, podcasts, books, and the like. What are your thoughts on the matter? Do you believe true crime has been sensationalized, or do you think these types of outlets can assist with cold case investigations?

6. If you were going to cast the characters of this story for a movie, who would you cast to play the various roles?

Read on
for a *sneak peek* at
the next book from Jaime Jo Wright

SPECTERS

IN THE

GLASS HOUSE

Available in the fall of 2024

Keep up to date with all of Jaime's releases
at JaimeWrightBooks.com
and on Facebook, Instagram, and X.

MARIAN ARNOLD

Müllerian Manor
Near Milwaukee, Wisconsin–October 1921

DEATH HAD ALWAYS BEEN fashionable. Women celebrated it by donning black silks and feathers, shawls, and lace. Men acknowledged it with a band on their hat or a mourning ring on their finger. Of course, that was more to announce their re-eligibility than anything else. For what man could flourish in life without a wife to manage his household and rear the children?

But what did a daughter do when in mourning? An adult daughter whose marriageable prospects had withered to next to nothing, and who was just dull enough not to be able to lean on their personality to charm a man?

The motorcar rumbled across the country road with the tenacity of a horse that was nearly dead but determined to make it one last time around the racetrack. The vehicle wasn't the sleek and shiny kind that Marian Arnold was accustomed to. Rather, it was dusty and brilliantly held together by pieces of metal welded to its joints and hinges. Marian didn't understand automobiles any more than she'd ever cared to understand her liquor baron father's brewery business. Neither mattered anyway. They were both dead: Father, now in his grave, and Arnold Breweries belly-up in the bankruptcy that Prohibition had ushered in.

"I will *not* become a soda manufacturer, and I've no interest in *cheese!*" Marian could still hear her father's irate words ringing through the hallways of their marble-floored mansion in the elite corner of Milwaukee. That had been two years ago, along with the threat of the federal government listening to all the "pearl-clutching mothers" who thought "liquor was the devil's brew." Father had created monikers for everyone he disagreed with, and neither the government nor the female population was spared his derision.

Marian bit back a yelp as the motorcar hit a pothole and sent her off the seat for a moment. She reached for something to hold on to, but her gloved hand only found the edge of the seat.

Father had followed Mother into the otherworld after his fury had culminated in a stroke. Could she blame him? Marian couldn't. Their livelihood was dependent on Milwaukee, its breweries and its influence. Their social patterns drew them to the beer gardens, where they enjoyed the magnificent homes that lined the shores of Lake Michigan and reveled in Germanic roots declaring Milwaukee a new "Little Germany." That Father wasn't German didn't matter because Mother was richly German, distantly related to the Pabst family. A rival brewery to be sure, but a relation Father monopolized on nonetheless.

"We're almost there, miss!"

The shout from her chauffeur brought Marian's attention back to the present, to the summer home she was being shuffled to. The one that Father had built for Mother over thirty years ago. The only remaining portion of his estate that her lawyers had been able to retain on her behalf.

Milwaukee was no longer her home; Müllerian Manor was. A lofty name, Marian concluded as it came into view, considering it was a summer house. She'd spent summers here growing up, and as she surveyed the sprawling brick three-story home with its gables, chimneys, and lawns featuring maple trees, Marian knew she could have done far worse.

The motorcar backfired, and this time Marian couldn't squelch her cry. A cloud of dust, a flurry of blackbirds clearing the way, and the rust-colored foliage waving in greeting all welcomed her to her now-permanent home.

Marian's muscles relaxed as she caught sight of Frederich, who had managed Müllerian Manor since before she'd been born. This time he was alone with no footman at his side. Father had attempted to maintain his English roots by employing a household staff that would mimic an English estate. Apparently, that too had been affected by the recent fall of the Arnold Empire.

The car door was wrenched open with a protesting groan. Marian palmed the hand of her chauffeur and crawled from the innards like a butterfly from its cocoon. A rush of fresh air filled her nostrils, the crispness ripe with the scent of dying leaves and the out-of-doors. Her shoes connected with the brick drive, and she held onto her turban-wrapped hair as the wind picked up and threatened to undo her.

"Miss Arnold." The warmth in Frederich's voice was accompanied by the shaky vibrato of age. His smile was oh so familiar, and Marian hurtled herself into the older man's arms.

Frederich stiffened, unaccustomed to such displays by Marian or anyone of the upper class, but he returned her embrace regardless with a grandfatherly embrace of his own.

Marian pulled away, her hands holding either side of Frederich's shoulders. "I'm so thankful you're still here!"

"Of course." He gave a nod. "Where else would I go?"

"Can we afford you?" Marian looked to her side as though the lawyer who had attended to her for the last six weeks would still be there.

"Don't fret about that." Frederich waved her off. "All has been taken care of."

"Who is left?" Marian inquired of the household staff as her chauffeur took on the task of depositing her trunk at the door since no one else had come to assist him.

Frederich's wince wasn't disguised, but he smiled anyway. "Felix is home from the front, missing a leg and I'm afraid a large part of his soul. War took a toll on the boy."

Marian offered an appropriate nod. Felix had worked in the gardens with his father as a boy and grown up alongside Marian. He'd gone to France no more than three years ago. She'd never inquired as to his welfare. "And his mother?"

"Still here, thank the good Lord, or we'd all be starving." Frederich chuckled and offered Marian his arm. Together, they took the rounded stone stairs up to the veranda.

"I do love Mrs. Dale's cooking."

"Mm." Frederich nodded, but a strange look crossed his face, and Marian was quick to notice it.

"Frederich?"

He patted her hand even as she extricated it from his elbow as Frederich stood to the side to allow Marian passage into the manor. "Don't worry, Miss Arnold. I was only thinking how little Mrs. Dale and Felix are appreciated these days. I'm glad to be here in the countryside."

Marian cringed internally. Mrs. Dale's German roots in spite of her married English name. The war had done awful things to many people and had created a sentiment toward the German population in Wisconsin that was unwelcome and yet more real than imagined.

"Thankfully the war is over," she reassured Frederich. "Feelings will fade away in time, and then all will go back to the way it was." Well, as normal as it could, she supposed.

Marian noticed a maid glide through a doorway at the back of the hall.

"Who was that?" Marian turned questioning eyes to Frederich. She'd not seen the servant before, and it seemed odd they would be hiring new staff after releasing others due to lack of funds.

"Who was who, miss?" Frederich asked.

"That maid." Marian pointed to the hall, now empty.

"There's no maid," Frederich said, and Marian frowned before shaking her head.

"Never mind then. I was sure I saw . . ." She bit her tongue. It had happened before, the *seeing*. It happened more frequently of late, though she preferred not to dwell on it. None of the faces she ever saw were ones she recognized, and although no one else ever seemed to see them, Marian knew they were there.

"You've always been a sharp child," her mother used to observe. *"You see and read people in a way no one else can."*

Marian followed Frederich toward the broad flight of stairs that led to the upper floor and the wing of bedrooms. The carpet snuffed out the sound of her footsteps, yet she heard footsteps regardless. Those of the maid who had disappeared, but who Marian was certain followed her now.

"Please," she implored in a whisper to the unseeable soul beside her on the stairs, "leave me alone."

"What's that, miss?" Frederich said over his shoulder as he ascended before her.

"Nothing, Frederich." Marian smiled in spite of herself. "All is well."

Though it probably wouldn't stay that way. It never did. Not in a house that had become a sanctuary for the ghosts invited to hide away here. Ghosts who had no care of Prohibition, or Germany, or financial instability. Ghosts who attempted to find a place to continue long after their lives had been snuffed out by death.

Yes, death was fashionable. But admitting to others that she saw death regularly? That was not.

REMY CRENSHAW

Müllerian Manor
Near Milwaukee–Present Day

A DEAD MONARCH BUTTERFLY lay flattened on the stone step at the front door. Its wing was tilted precariously from its body, its orange-and-black body having dried into a crisp corpse. Remy stared down at it. She had been staying at Müllerian Manor for a week now. She craned her neck to peer through the study window. It was like looking at a manor house in the Black Forest, only she wasn't in Germany. Müllerian Manor wasn't particularly inviting either—not with its ignored gardens, collapsing outbuildings, and worse, its eccentric occupant.

Elton Floyd. The infamous biographer of famous persons from history such as Martin Luther King Jr., General George Custer, and Pope John XII. His more obscure biographies highlighted the controversial lives of the lesser known: Kimball Brey, the serial killer of San Antonio in 1867; Lisa Cummings, the female spy during the 1962 Cuban Missile Crisis. And now Marian Arnold, the Milwaukee socialite and daughter of a brewery baron, including her interludes with the Butterfly Butcher of Pickeral County during the Prohibition era. A story of a killer, a disturbed heiress, and the eventual disintegration into history, leaving behind many unanswered questions.

Who wouldn't want to be Elton's research assistant? Apparently, everyone. Everyone except Remy. She preferred the familiarity of the Twin Cities. She could get lost there, whether in one of the downtown areas or in the parks that encircled Minneapolis and St. Paul. But here in the southeastern corner of Wisconsin, in the woods, without the luxury of being able to merge with the masses and become a nameless face? She missed the sounds of an indie band playing at the park, children squealing and laughing at a splash pad, bicycles zipping by with no heed to her. Being anonymous was important to Remy because she had always been *seen*. From the moment her mother had abandoned her, and her dad had overdosed, she'd been seen. Social services saw her for what she didn't have, foster parents saw her for what she could bring to them by means of government aid, and schoolteachers saw her for all the trouble she *might* make—the stereotype slapped on to every kid in foster care.

Remy had been none of that, focusing instead on flying under the radar. Which was far easier to do when one could get lost in the city. But here at Müllerian Manor? Not so much.

Elton was his own sort of eagle-eyed host. Then there was Aimee Prentiss, Elton's nurse, Flora Flemming the housekeeper, and Charleton Boggart, an apocalyptic version of Kermit the Frog. If Kermit turned into a zombie, that would be Charleton. So, Remy had learned to avoid the gangly old groundskeeper. That left her with the other three for company of which Elton was the most normal. *Normal* being a term frowned upon these days for classifying people as better, which wasn't Remy's intent. She just didn't have any other word for it.

She pushed open the arched wooden door that gave way with a groan, just like a haunted house should—only she'd not seen an apparition yet, even though Elton had promised she would.

"There you are." The voice of Flora cut through the stillness in the front hall with its dark-stained beams that spanned the ceiling and a chandelier of antlers that lit the hardwood floor below. A staircase, open on one side with a thick balustrade, was bordered on the other by tall bookshelves. There was one window, and from it a beam of daylight cast its path down the stairs, and dust particles danced in it.

"Remy." It was a jolt back to reality, a command from the pinched-face housekeeper who appeared as though she'd never been allowed to leave Müllerian Manor. Only she did. Every night at seven, once the remains of dinner had been cleaned up and the cook was ready to depart. "I am speaking to you."

Remy finally locked gazes with the older woman. She didn't answer.

"Mr. Floyd has been calling for you for the past twenty minutes. Aimee is on her break, and I don't have time to entertain his whims. Go, do what you're supposed to be doing, and *aid* him." With a flick of her bony wrist, Flora pointed toward the stairs, her black eyes skewering Remy. "I don't know what you were doing outside anyway."

Remy tossed a polite smile and edged past the woman, taking the stairs with soft footsteps. She ran her fingertips along the book spines as the stairs curved and then, on reaching the top, Remy hesitated. Once again, Müllerian Manor was a confusion of illogical halls and doors. In fact, there was a door directly ahead of her, but Remy had already opened it on her arrival at the manor only to find it went nowhere. There were four feet of empty space and then a wall. It wasn't large enough to be a closet, but it was tall enough to look like a hallway that had begun in construction but had ended in error. To fix it, they'd attached a door and forgotten about it.

"Take the second door on the left. Staircase up to the attic level. At the top of the stairs, open the first door on the left. Not the right—the right is Mr. Floyd's living quarters, and he's not to be disturbed."

Remy heard Aimee the nurse giving instructions in her head as her body followed them. She ducked through a doorway and moved to the narrow stairs leading to the attic. There was an elevator, but that went to Mr. Floyd's quarters and was reserved only for the rare times he left the attic. Otherwise it wasn't to be used by anyone, ever.

Finally, Remy reached the doors—one on the left to Elton's study, and one on the right to his mysterious living quarters.

"Remy!" The quaver was evident in the old man's voice, but his volume didn't suffer.

She twisted the copper doorknob that had the etchings of a snake curving around it and pushed inward. Musty air mixed with ancient books and ink met Remy's senses.

Elton Floyd squinted up at her through gold wire-framed glasses. His wispy white hair was sparse and feathered from either side of his balding head dotted with age spots—patches of melanoma that Elton refused to treat with the prescribed chemotherapy cream.

"Well?" His tone was warm but laced with expectation. He twiddled his thumbs that were misshapen due to arthritis.

"Well what?" Remy could only seem to find her voice and her sass around Elton. Which was odd, considering anyone in their right mind would find the intellectual elderly man intimidating if for no other reason than his analytical stare.

"Did you find it?"

"The butterfly house?" Remy asked.

"What else? The garden rake?" Elton's eyes twinkled then—he was teasing her.

Remy offered him a thin smile, one that told the man he wasn't going to one-up her, and she could match wits with him.

"Actually, I did find a garden rake. Quite old. The handle appears to date back to the turn of the century," she quipped.

"Ah, yes." A gnarled finger tapped the arm of his wheelchair. "I believe it was circa 2001, from Home Depot."

"Menards," Remy corrected. "Somehow the store's sticker on the handle has never worn off."

Elton snapped his fingers. "You got me!" A crooked grin revealed aged teeth that were one hundred percent his own. "Now"—Elton tapped his finger on the thick journal lying open on his lap—"you have work to do."

Remy leaned forward, propping her elbows on her knees. She knew she didn't look the part of research assistant, and even now wondered if that was a hint of doubt she saw flicker in Elton's eyes. Still, he'd given her a quick once-over like older men were wont to do, overlooking the nose ring in her left nostril and the little tattooed cross at the corner of her left eye.

"Marian Arnold." Elton's finger thudded on the journal again. "I like to imagine she was a bit like you."

"Me?" Remy raised her eyebrows. She could never just raise one—she wasn't that talented.

"Of course." Elton closed one eye and assessed her with the other. "It's why I decided you were the best candidate to assist me with this project. You're awkward and not run-of-the-mill."

"Thanks, I guess." Remy's response was flat, even to her own ears.

"Now don't get miffed." Elton waved his gnarly fingers, callused where his pens rubbed against the knuckle. "Nothing was as it seemed at Müllerian Manor back in the twenties. Everything was made to look normal, proper, to imitate the golden age from which America had just exited. Instead, it was a cacophony of ideologies and culture and war and individualism that sent keen young minds into rebellious independence—Marian Arnold notwithstanding."

"And the butterfly house?" Remy provided rhetorically. Her

recent jaunt outside had brought her only to its outskirts. The skeletal remains of a building shrouded in the spirit of Marian.

Elton gave a short nod and drew his bushy brows together as he closed his eyes and templed his fingers beneath a clean-shaven chin. "Yes, the butterfly house. Marian Arnold was never the same after what happened there. The darkness, the interpretation . . . the hauntings."

"The butcher," Remy added.

Elton's blue eyes snapped open, colliding with Remy's. "Ah, the butcher . . ." He stared at her, unblinking.

Remy felt herself shrink back into her chair.

Elton leaned toward her. "The Butterfly Butcher is as much a mystery as Marian Arnold. As Müllerian Manor. As the Great War that came to land on this very property, this very house."

Remy couldn't respond. She didn't like the way her throat constricted at Elton's words, or the way her skin rose in tiny bumps. Her intrigue awakened, but also her trepidation.

Elton brought his palm down on the book in his lap with a sudden slap that shocked Remy. She jumped, her foot kicking out and striking the leg of the coffee table between them.

A grin stretched Elton's mouth, and a gargled chuckle collected in his throat. He laughed and coughed simultaneously, then said, "You're here because of her, Remy Crenshaw. She said you would come, and you did."

Remy frowned. "Who said I would come?"

Elton sagged backward, his shoulders slumping, yet his gaze remained sharp as it rested on Remy. "Marian Arnold, of course. She's as alive in this place as she was a century ago." The old biographer's eyes narrowed then. "You need only listen, and you will hear her whispering."

Jaime Jo Wright is the author of ten novels, including Christy Award- and Daphne du Maurier Award-winner *The House on Foster Hill*, and Carol Award-winner *The Reckoning at Gossamer Pond*. She's also a two-time Christy Award finalist, as well as the ECPA bestselling author of *The Vanishing at Castle Moreau*, *The Lost Boys of Barlowe Theater*, and two *Publishers Weekly* bestselling novellas. Jaime lives in Wisconsin with her family and felines. Learn more at JaimeWrightBooks.com.

Sign Up for Jaime's Newsletter

Keep up to date with Jaime's latest news on book releases and events by signing up for her email list at the link below.

JaimeWrightBooks.com

FOLLOW JAIME ON SOCIAL MEDIA

Jaime Jo Wright – Author   @JaimeJoWright   @JaimeJoWright

More from Jaime Jo Wright

When Greta Mercy's brothers disappear from the Barlowe Theater in 1915, she will do anything to uncover what threat lurks beneath the stage. Decades later, revealing what happened to the boys falls on Kit Boyd, who must determine whether she's willing to pay the price to end the pattern of evil that has marked their hometown for a century.

The Lost Boys of Barlowe Theater

In 1865, orphaned Daisy Francois takes a housemaid position and finds that the eccentric Gothic authoress inside hides a story more harrowing than those in her novels. Centuries later, Cleo Clemmons uncovers an age-old mystery, and the dust of the old castle's curse threatens to rise again, this time leaving no one alive to tell its sordid tale.

The Vanishing at Castle Moreau

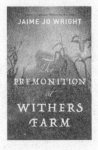

In 1910, rural healer Perliett Van Hilton is targeted by a superstitious killer and must rely on the local doctor and an intriguing newcomer for help. Over a century later, Molly Wasziak is pulled into a web of deception surrounding an old farmhouse. Will these women's voices be heard, or will time silence their truths forever?

The Premonition at Withers Farm